DEATH'S COLLECTOR: SWORD HAND

BILL MCCURRY

BOOKS BY BILL MCCURRY

DEATH-CURSED WIZARD SERIES
Novels
Death's Collector

Death's Baby Sister

Death's Collector: Sorcerers Dark and Light

Death's Collector: Void Walker

Death's Collector: Sword Hand

Death's Collector: Dark Lands (forthcoming)

Novellas
Wee Piggies of Radiant Might

© 2021 Bill McCurry

Death's Collector: Sword Hand

First edition, June 2021

Infinite Monkeys Publishing

Carrollton, TX

Bill-McCurry.com

Editing by Shayla Raquel, ShaylaRaquel.com

Cover Design by Books Covered

Interior Formatting by Vellum

ISBN (e-book): 978-1-7356487-3-6

ISBN (paperback): 978-1-7356487-4-3

❀ Created with Vellum

For Kathleen:

Without you, none of this would have happened.
(The good parts, I mean.)

ONE

I keep count of the people I've murdered to remind me how much I have stolen from the world. I try to kill only people who deserve death, because they're cruel, or they threaten me, or because I think they should be dead. I enjoy killing them, which is of course a thing to be detested afterward.

That part about my victims deserving death is crap, of course. I yearn to take their lives, and that is the fact. A better person than me would laugh at my sophisticated excuses. That's fine. My sophistry may be the only thing keeping that better person alive.

I considered all that one morning on my way to assassinate somebody. The irony unsettled me, and the assassination did too. I had committed to this killing, but I still hadn't been told the target's name or even his description.

Reaching my unknown victim meant crossing the northern frontier, which was as hot as perdition even in the early morning. The heat was one reason only poor people lived there. They were grim folks, and I felt glum riding across their land. I was inclined to bitch and kick things.

I nearly failed to spot the small village squatting out in the middle of nothing. Far behind me, my young companions certainly

1

had not yet seen the little place. Earlier that morning, they had required me to ride ahead, far ahead of them, as they had wearied of all the bitching and kicking.

Stan, who was my older, degenerate companion, shaded his eyes against the glare. Then he whispered curses for a few seconds, which made him look like a disgruntled chicken. He said in an offended whine, "Look at them crumbly, awful piles of mud bricks. Same mealy yellow as everything else for the past thousand rat-gagging miles."

That was an awful exaggeration, but I didn't want to point it out. Stan complained hard enough to make a statue's ears bleed. I said, "I don't disagree with your sentiment, but we'd be foolish to pass them by."

Stan pushed back his hat. I still wasn't accustomed to seeing him without a helmet, but when he gave up soldiering to join us, he had bought a wide-brimmed purple hat with a crown like a beehive. "Hunkered down over there all untidy . . . that nasty fart of a place looks like a parcel of turds dropped by some great, shitting plains monster." He swallowed, and his skinny neck looked like somebody was shoving their fist through a sock.

I didn't react to Stan's groaning and vulgar gestures. I had heard and seen them often. "Stan, maybe they have something to trade. Food, or supplies." I nodded toward a big field of millet this side of town. Farther away, a sizable pen held brown goats.

"I hate goat. It's greasy as a whore's . . ." Stan glanced toward our young friends, Pil and Desh, still a quarter mile behind us. Lately, Stan had begun holding back some of his saltiest comments, even though none of us cared if he swore hard enough to shatter marble.

"If not goat, then what about beer?" I asked.

"Probably sour." He raised a hand. "I know, sour beer's better than no beer, and it's dead sure better than water, which would kill us."

I asked, "Are Pil and Desh following along?"

Stan turned in the saddle. "Yeah, they're coming, but they're making an ass-smacking holiday of it. Listen, Lord Bib, if you would stop acting like a red-rimmed horse's ass, maybe we wouldn't desert you."

"Stop calling me that. Do you mean you're leaving too?"

Stan kept looking away toward Pil and Desh, but I saw his neck blushing.

I could have spent ten minutes making Stan stutter and sweat by glorifying the depth of his undeclared love for Pil. However, that sort of behavior was why my companions had told me to eat mud while they struck off without me tomorrow. Instead, I scrutinized the village as we rode toward it. The millet field looked odd. It had a crop but no farmers. "Stan, do you know of any farmer in the history of the world who didn't start work before the sun was up?"

Stan squinted at the furrows and grunted a curse. Then he loosened his sword in the scabbard as he scanned around us. "What awful kick in the nuts is waiting for us now?"

Due to my contrary nature, the more frustrated Stan got, the happier I felt. "Maybe these people are having a holiday and they'll give us presents!"

"Shut up, Lord Bib."

We crossed the field and dismounted at the closest brick house. I led my horse down a deserted lane with Stan following, and we soon reached a big, open area. I wouldn't have called it a proper town square as much as an irregular dirty space where they forgot to build anything.

The area was full of people who were busy. Well, six of the people were busy robbing the rest. Everybody, including the bandits, wore undyed, woolen clothes smudged with yellow dirt, and the criminals each held a sword or a club. Two of them were mounted on puny nags, I guess to supervise the robbery, while the others shoved through the sullen crowd. One robber, a skinny young fellow, was stuffing live chickens into a sack. A short bandit tripped and let some loaves of bread roll out of his bag. He jumped up and recaptured them.

Stan had walked up beside me. "This is a crappy celebration," he muttered. "No presents for us, I guess."

A couple of victims saw us and edged away, silent but with eyes stretched wide. They all appeared thin and hollow-cheeked, especially the kids. That told me who was wicked and needed to be killed in this situation. I started breathing faster, but I felt light and loose.

"Stay back and let me do this," I told Stan, who grunted. If it came to a fight, I didn't want Stan killing any of the ones I might want to kill myself.

To be accurate, I both wanted and needed to kill them. I had years before bargained with the God of Death for something precious. In return, I owed him a certain number of murders before he released me, and only he knew what that number was. Once my killings had reached two hundred, I assumed that the final number was too big to ever reach in a lifetime, but the God of Death wouldn't let me stop.

That was another reason to keep count of my killings, although I didn't talk about it. If somebody pressed me hard on whether I kept count, I often added them to the count. In other cases, I might say that I did the killing but let Death do the bookkeeping. That was just smart-ass talk about murder. It was a good way not to think about the sad people from whom I had stolen my victims.

I drew my sword to slaughter these wicked, thieving bastards, but I hesitated. The robbers deserved death for making children go hungry, or even starve. They likely had done other cruel things every day for years. But I didn't see any villagers with knives sticking out of their chests, so I clenched my teeth and forced a deep breath. With my sword hand shaking, I strolled into the square and waved.

Everybody quieted down except for the chickens in the sack. One of the mounted robbers, a long-haired fellow, said, "Who are you, old man?"

I smiled. "I'll excuse that comment on my age, since I do look older than my years. I am Baron Barger, of the Yellow Valley Bargers."

Behind me, Stan howled, "Beware the Bargers!" like somebody's idea of a ghost.

"I don't need a chorus," I muttered toward Stan, who shrugged and spit on the yellow dirt. I pointed around the square and yelled,

"We Bargers have owned these lands going back for a hundred years, and now I'm out surveying our holdings. You, with the swords and clubs, if you're robbing this place, just go away and I'll forget I saw you doing it." I pointed my sword toward the ground and started sketching figure eights in the air with it.

The two horsemen whispered together for a bit. The second one, a bald man, shouted, "Just what exactly are you saying?"

I almost ran out and started killing men, but I gritted my teeth instead. I could give them another chance before the slaughter commenced. Stepping farther into the square, I bellowed in a seagoing voice, "Go home! Leave! This place belongs to me! Go get your own shitty little town! And drop that food before you go!"

Before I finished yelling, almost every person in the clearing was running in different directions. I saw three men bash into one another, fall, and get stepped on.

The horsemen and their thugs didn't run. That surprised me. They couldn't know how dangerous I might be, and their only gain from killing me would be chickens, bread, and whatever else these poor people owned. It seemed an unwise risk. However, both horsemen raised their weapons. The nearest one urged his nag toward me at a trot, although the mounted man behind him hesitated. The four thieves on the ground were hidden in the mass of trampling feet and jerking bodies.

These thieves had chosen to attack me, so I felt extra justified in killing them. The shaggy man's gaunt pony picked up speed. He had long arms and a longer sword, giving him an immense reach. When he swung at my head, I guided the blade aside, stepped in, grabbed his wrist, and dragged him close enough to pierce his neck with my sword.

I could almost taste his death, as sweet as an apricot. I felt a little sick about it.

The other horseman was middle-aged and bald. He stared at his friend's spraying neck and dragged on the reins, making his horse whinny and sidestep. Then he raised his sword and kicked his horse, trying to kill me and run away at the same time. I later wished I had let him run, but that seemed contrary to the situation at the time.

The bald man swung at me from too far off. I leaned away from the blow and thrust back into his chest. He was a persistent fellow, because he swung at me again. This time, I severed his arm above the elbow. He opened his mouth to scream, but only a squeak came out, probably because of the chest wound. Then he seemed to forget all about me as he peered around at the dirt, trying to locate his sword, or maybe his arm, from horseback.

He would be easy to finish, but I turned away. It wouldn't be any harder to kill him in a minute or two, and he had allies someplace in the square.

At least thirty people still charged around in the open space, some of them shouting nonsense. I spotted three of the bandits out there, so I strode toward the two closest villains.

These were young, good-looking men with strong chins, alike enough to be brothers. Well, if they wanted long lives, their family business should have been tailoring or baking instead of banditry. Both waved stout, knobby clubs at me as they stood side by side.

I raised the sword that Desh had enchanted for me, lunged, and thrust it into Tall Chin's throat with a snap. It happened before he could move.

As Tall Chin staggered, I darted aside to put him between Short Chin and me. Short Chin checked his swing, and I snaked around to hamstring him. On the return stroke, I cut halfway through the back of his neck. Short Chin dropped like a bucket of rocks. Tall Chin gurgled and fell on top of him.

I caught a breath. This was a pitiful little fight, but my heart was tapping fast.

The third bandit in the square was the skinny man still carrying a sack of live chickens. He had been charging to help the Chin brothers, but now he spun and sprinted to the closest hovel. He started kicking the wooden door while shouting to be let in.

I paced toward him, holding my bloody sword to the side. When Desh had enchanted that sword, he told me it wanted things to be dead. I wanted that too. But before I reached Skinny, the hovel door opened. He fell inside, and the door slammed shut. I heard a bar drop on the other side.

My shoulders fell as if somebody had taken away my beer before I was done. Whoever lived in that house had perplexed me. People don't often give sanctuary to folks who rob them.

I sighed, and my pulse faded as I scanned the square. The one-armed bald man had slid out of the saddle and landed on his side. The shaggy man lay underneath his old horse. The Chins lay dead together. No living person except me stood in that clearing.

I peered at the wooden door, wondering if somebody might throw Skinny back outside, but that didn't happen. I never expect thanks from anybody I help, but most of the time someone speaks to me at least.

The one-armed man had rolled onto his back by the time I reached him. I had planned to kill him after I dealt with the others, and I still wanted to. But now he was no more dangerous than a puppy. I judged that without serious magical help, he would die, and my judgment about death was pretty damn good, so maybe I should end his pain.

He died while I was dithering over the question.

I glanced around and saw my young companions on their horses at the edge of the square. Desh shouted, "No!" with his eyes wide above his round cheeks.

Pil jumped down from the saddle and drew her sword, flipping her black braid behind her shoulder. She ran to Desh and touched his calf with one hand while she scanned the area. "What? Is it that man? Is it Bib? What?"

Desh didn't answer or move.

I said, "Hell, Desh, did you want to kill him? It's unlike you, so I didn't know. You can kill the next one."

Desh dismounted, stumbled to one knee, and jumped up running toward me. He came at me so fast I stepped aside, but he skidded to kneel beside the body. Grabbing the dead man by the shoulder, he gazed up at me, his face blank. "Where's his arm?"

I blinked at that question but pointed. "Back there a bit. I imagine that blood trail leads to it."

Pil walked up behind Desh and lay a hand on his shoulder.

"Desh, what in snake snot is going on? You're being weird, and it's making me nervous."

Desh shrugged off her hand, shook his head, and knelt there as stiff as a brick. "This is my father!"

"What?" I shouted. I knew that Desh hailed from the frontier, but I had never thought about it beyond that. I examined the corpse's face. He and Desh favored one another, right down to the pudgy cheeks and balding skull. I dropped to my knees and pressed my palm against the old man's forehead, hoping to find he hadn't fully gone. However, I had killed him thoroughly.

With my hand still on the dead man, I said, "I'm sorry, Desh. I didn't know he was your pa. I'd bring him back if I could."

Pil had run down the blood trail for the severed limb and now gave it to Desh as she knelt beside him. "That's right. Bib didn't know, how could he know it was your father?"

Desh examined his father's arm as if it were a new thing, and I guess it was since he had never seen it separated from his pa. "No, you couldn't know, but . . ." He swallowed and shouted at me, "You know what? Other people besides Pa deserve to live too! Not everybody has to be killed!"

His words didn't quite make sense to me, but I put that aside. "I'm sorry, Desh." I almost said it again before I realized it was impossible to apologize a sufficient number of times for murdering somebody's father.

Desh confirmed that by yelling, "I don't care if you're sorry, you pinch-butt bastard!"

After waiting to be sure he was done, I said, "I don't mean offense by asking this, but why was your father robbing those poor, struggling farmers? It seems harsh."

Desh gazed at the cloudless sky. "You don't know a single damn thing about the frontier, do you? It's a dry summer. Towns survive by raiding other places that may have a little more. He wouldn't have hurt anybody who lived here, not in a thousand years."

I considered that for a moment. "Why were they armed, shaking swords like they were trying to scare away bad spirits?"

"The raiders have to be armed to preserve the dignity of those they rob. Who could yield their food to an unarmed man and keep any self-respect?"

Of all the traditions I had encountered, this was far from the most ridiculous. I wouldn't have predicted it, though.

Desh continued, "This little town will probably raid some other place before long."

I stepped back. "Huh. It seems a chancy system to me."

"No, it's not." Desh sat on his butt beside his father, holding the old man's arm. "The food gets shared, no one is hurt, and the system balances itself." He placed the arm beside his father's stump and then cocked his head at it. He picked up the arm again and laid it on his pa's chest. Then he shook his head and lifted the arm again, hesitating. "I don't know what to do."

Desh was a mighty sorcerer, maybe the most powerful in the world, but he seemed mystified. He shook his head and lay his father's severed sword arm alongside the unwounded arm, but he didn't let go of it. He stared and chewed his lip.

Pil put her arm around Desh's shoulders. "I'll help you out. There's an answer, and we'll find it."

I raised my eyebrows at Stan, but he looked away.

Pil scowled at me. "So, I guess you just had to kill someone today, didn't you?"

From what I had been able to see, I was protecting those people, and I had given the robbers plenty of chances to run. Even though I killed Desh's pa, I couldn't think of a thing I had done wrong.

Stan spoke up, "It's a day, so why wouldn't Bib wipe somebody out?"

I considered the matter for a few seconds and then felt sick. "I guess that's right. I could have thrashed those sad fellows without hurting them too much, but I was looking for an excuse to kill them."

I crossed my arms to keep my hands from shaking. That was foolish, since my companions were already familiar with my regular, post-murder regrets. I rubbed my face hard and then stared at the man I had stolen from Desh.

TWO

The world gave Desh ninety seconds to accustom himself to losing his father. That sounds mighty brief, but I guess it's luxurious compared to what many people are allowed.

Desh was still sitting beside his father's body when a deep voice from behind me yelled, "Desh! What are you doing with that monster? The devil that killed your daddy?"

The skinny chicken-bagger stood in the middle of the square, with several dozen villagers around him. The robber who had dropped the bread stood beside him, a short, middle-aged fellow with a sprightly mustache. Another young man with a pinched red face stepped up to stand with Skinny. I assumed he lived in this village.

Desh sighed and clambered to his feet as if he were climbing out of a thornbush. But when he met the skinny man's eyes, he stood taller and made his jaw hard, or as hard as his round jaw could get. He called out, "I wish we had met in better circumstances, Doss. Bib here didn't know what he was doing. He's practically an idiot. We shouldn't let him loose with a sharp stick."

"Who cares? He killed my daddy, and your daddy, and Balt, and Colter. Now we're going to kill him."

"Don't!" Desh shouted. "He's stupid as sand, but he's dangerous. Let's take him home and judge him there."

"Bullshit!" I muttered. "Anybody who tries to judge me should prepare to be dead."

Desh held up a hand to me.

"That's no good," Doss said. "Pittle will loan us a horse, so that's three." Red Face nodded. Doss pointed his sword at me. "We need that murdering demon bastard's horse to make four, then we can get all our people home."

"No. He's coming home with me." Desh looked over his shoulder. "Pil, Stan, would you please carry my pa out of here? Take him just outside the village." He shouted to Doss, "We're taking Pa and going. That leaves you with three horses for the other three men, which is plenty."

"Don't do it! If you run, we'll follow you to hell!" Doss shouted.

"I don't feel like running. It's too hot." Desh rubbed his eyes. "Come to hell with me if you want to. I won't make you run very hard."

Doss paused with his mouth open and then whispered to Mustache.

Pil and Stan were already hauling the body away. Desh collected their horses and followed. He turned away from me as he passed, but I saw his face crumble. Desh had made a bargain with the gods to never know happiness, but the gods must have felt fine about him knowing sadness.

That left me standing like a fool in the rear. My pride wouldn't let me back up and slink away like the littlest dog on the road, so I stepped out where I could be better seen, then smiled and raised a hand. "I'm sorry, everybody! I didn't understand your ways, and I believed I was saving you from being robbed, or worse."

A woman in the crowd called out, "What about the hand?"

Like a toddler, I looked at my hand. An instant later, I realized she was talking about Desh's pa's arm.

The people stirred themselves in just seconds, shouting about hands, and magic, and hell. They hurled anger at me like a wave smacking the beach. An old man shuffled right up and spit on my boot. He ran back to the crowd, waving over his head.

The villagers sounded like they thought spitting on my boot was a significant development. Their shouts grew twice as loud, and for poorly educated people, they abused me creatively. I was damned and cursed quite a bit. Somebody bellowed, "Witch!" and that soon proved popular.

I turned and led my horse around. "To hell with helping these folks," I muttered, not stopping to consider that I hadn't helped them one little bit.

A rock popped me on the neck, and one hit my hip. They stung but didn't hurt. Then a stone smacked my horse in some tender spot. She shied away and turned, bashing into me. Her massive shoulder sent me stumbling toward the crowd before I slipped and fell to my hands and knees.

The villagers roared as if I were free food. Stones pelted me, maybe a dozen or more. One of them banged against my skull, and my vision wavered.

I had few good options. I could curl up in a ball to protect myself from rocks and thus end up kicked to death. I could run, be dragged down, and get kicked to death. I could call up some magic to convince horses to trample people. While the horses were being convinced and getting back here, I would be kicked to death. I could wait for my friends to come back and help me. They'd probably be too late and might get kicked to death along with me.

Or I could draw my sword and kill or terrify every person between me and safety. I wanted that one. My veins throbbed with the idea of it. But these people didn't really deserve death, never mind that they were trying to kill me. I had sort of provoked them.

I chose a half measure. I shoved myself to my feet, knocking down the villagers closest to me. I struggled ten feet toward the edge of town while a dozen stones smacked into me. One smashed my lips, and I felt teeth crack. I threw down two more people, but folks were pushing in on me by then. I only made it six feet. At least the bunching made it harder for people to fling stones at me. Just as I thought that, a stone smacked me on the back of the head, and another whistled into my groin.

I drew my sword, slicing the man ahead of me across the chest, just a shallow cut. I hated to do it, but at the same time, I was thrilled to do it. I twisted and almost cut the throat of somebody who was pushing at me. I bashed his forehead with my sword's crosspiece instead. It was Doss, who fell back with glazed eyes.

I didn't stop fighting, but I cursed to Krak and Effla. I hoped that Desh didn't care too much about these people. I also hoped that Desh didn't have a brother or a nephew in this crowd. I feared that the gods would make sure I killed some more of Desh's relations.

Three more running cuts brought me to the edge of town. I had held back to avoid killing the villagers, and none was wounded badly. My mercy allowed a woman to whack me on the left elbow with a hoe and another to slam a mud brick into my cheek from three feet away. But those wounds didn't hinder me so much as aggravate me.

Now the villagers gave me plenty of distance. They also doubled their volleys of stones. One crunched against the side of my knee, and my running became limping. I turned the corner around the last mud brick house and stopped. The urge to go back and kill every single one of those people hit me, but it was weak, and I pushed it down.

I dragged my ass out of town, finding Pil and Stan, who were riding to rescue me. They were prepared to cover my escape, but from the sound of things, the witch killers had already declared victory and were making up songs about their valor.

"Damn you, Desh Younger!" I spat, rubbing at the broad scrape on my cheek. "May your asshole be eaten by spiny lizards!" I didn't say it with much fire, though.

I wondered whether Desh had left me behind on purpose, hoping I'd be hurt or killed. Or maybe he hadn't meant to do it. He just hadn't exerted himself to save me. Hell, maybe it wouldn't have been wrong of him to leave me behind.

I spat out bits of tooth and glanced at Pil. "Desh?"

Pil pointed away from the village. "He's over there, waiting . . . in case you ran that direction."

I snorted. The chance of my running that far out was slim.

With big eyes, Pil said, "Stoning agrees with you, Bib. I've seen you looking a lot worse than this."

My tongue was already worrying at the stubs of my broken teeth —two of them just to the right of my top front teeth. "Did you catch my horse?"

Pil shook her head. "Desh was closer, so maybe he caught it, but if it doesn't come back, I'll buy you a stubby-legged mule."

I hissed and sheathed my sword. "Let's go find out."

Pil gave me a hand up, and we rode toward Desh, with me hanging on behind her. Desh's pa's body lay across his mount, and Desh was gazing out at the empty plains. He didn't look up when we dismounted.

None of us said anything for an uncomfortable time. Then Pil sighed. "Boys, I wish I didn't have to bring this up now, but I'd be dumb not to. Desh, do you realize that you enchanted the sword that killed your own father?"

Desh jerked as if she had hit him. "I guess I did."

"Sure, you did," I said, "just like we were in some sort of tragic play. When we find ourselves in situations like this, the gods generally have nudged us into them." I swallowed against the revulsion that came from speaking about the gods.

Desh said, "Why did . . . never mind." He bent over, trying to brush his father's blood off his trousers.

Pil said, "The main question is this: Do the gods want this sword to kill somebody else now?"

Desh glared at her. "That's wrong. The question is whether the gods want this sword to kill one of *us* now."

Pil stepped closer and stared at Desh. "Well, I think the man who made the sword to be so magical can help us make sense of this. Desh, what can you tell us about the nature of that sword, and does it have hidden properties, and do you plan to kill me with it?" She smiled but just for a moment.

"It's powerful," Desh said, glancing at his father's body. "But it's no subtler than a kick to the gut. It's amazingly good at only one thing."

I nodded. "You said that it really, really wants things to be dead."

"That's right," Desh said.

Pil put up a hand. "No, that's wrong. You didn't say that."

Desh leaned away from her. "I said it. I should know."

"Although you were as drunk as a mule in mash," I added.

"No!" Desh insisted. "I said it really, really wants things to be dead."

Pil put a hand on Desh's arm. "You didn't. You said it wants things to be really, really dead. Trust me."

I stared at her. Desh glanced at his father before staring at her too. Pil's memory was perfect. I had never known her to misremember anything. "Desh, what the hell does that mean?"

"I don't know! I thought I said the other thing!"

Pil said, "Well, what do you think it means? Speculation, you know, can't hurt at this point."

Desh sighed and looked at me like I was a tall patch of weeds. "Give me the sword."

I stepped back. "This is fine. You can look at it from over there."

"You can trust me," Desh said. "I enchanted it. If I wanted to hurt you, I could make it blow up in your hand."

Before I could dig up a snide reply, a fast-moving figure arrived from what seemed like nowhere. A beautiful, blue-skinned, unclothed woman smacked into Desh and squeezed him tight enough to make him flush.

This was Limnad, a river spirit and Desh's lover. She kissed him and whispered something, leaning away to touch Desh's chest with her palm. Desh whispered back and gestured toward his father's body on the horse. Limnad whispered some more, kissed Desh's forehead, and stroked his hair. The rest of us waited, examining the god-blighted frontier bushes, checking the horse's saddles, or just watching all the nothing out on the plains.

After more than a minute of this, Limnad released Desh and turned to me. "Bib! I'm so happy that you're not dead yet!"

"And it's fine to see you looking so healthy." I got on well with Limnad, having once done her a favor. It pleased me to see her, especially if she comforted Desh.

Limnad ran past me with shocking grace and started playing with Pil's hair. "You're still so beautiful. I thought you might be shriveled with sadness like Bib."

"I am not shriveled nor sad either!" I frowned.

Limnad laughed at me and sniffed Pil's hair. Pil leaned so Limnad could better admire her. "Be proud of your hair," Limnad said. "I met a young man with hair like yours. It was so fine I had to keep it for myself."

We didn't comment on that. The silence got uncomfortable.

"Don't be shocked!" Limnad said. "I didn't tear the hair off his skull! I kept him prisoner so I could enjoy his hair whenever I wanted. I even released him before he died. I set him free when his hair fell out."

We all made vague noises.

Limnad reached out and grabbed my wrist. I told myself not to pull away, since she was strong enough to rip me apart with her hands. "Bib, I expect you to care for Desh since he's so sad and you're his friend. Promise me you will."

"I promise to make a special effort, Limnad."

Limnad flowed back to Desh and slipped both arms around him. "I should go away before long. It's that prissy Spirit of the Salty Fork of the Great Bend in the Northwest Copper River again. She's behaving like a dripping, chalk-fed slut. She acts like she's the Spirit of the Entire Ocean."

Desh had told me that Limnad could be impatient and even spiteful. He was to be admired for surviving so long.

"I needn't go yet, though." Still clinging to Desh, Limnad showed her teeth as she shrugged, letting her hair float above her shoulders. More embracing and whispering followed.

Stan muttered loud enough to hear thirty feet away, "I guess it ain't polite to stare, since you said so, Bib. Especially not to stare at magical things that could smash us to lumpy bits, but when they're naked as a jaybird . . ." He sighed and walked away.

"Bib!" Desh said. "I'm taking my pa home. Will you come with me?"

"Sure, I never got to bury my own pa." I stiffened. That had just jumped out of my mouth without thought. I had been planning to go with Desh anyway because I felt bad about his father. "Desh, I'll come. You'll have to fight me to keep me away."

"That's good. We won't try to judge you or punish you—nothing like that." Desh smiled. I guess he meant to look encouraging, but the smile sat poorly on his pained face, like a strand of pearls on a rotten stump. "Except you won't be riding, Bib. You'll be walking, because Pa will be on your horse."

"Like hell I will. I've got a busted knee. Stan won't mind walking, will you?"

Stan grinned, showing the few horrible teeth he had left. "Of course, I could walk if I wanted, but would it be right? Seeing as I don't travel about stabbing people's fathers in their heart. It don't seem fair to make me walk, considering that, does it?"

"That makes Stan morally superior," Pil said. "I never thought I'd say that."

"All right, fine, I'll come!" I scowled to make sure Desh knew I wasn't happy about it.

Limnad lifted her head for a moment and then squeaked. She didn't sound so much like a mysterious creature of enchantment as she did a terrified duckling.

"What's wrong?" Desh asked.

Limnad answered by running away with astonishing speed. Within a few seconds, she was a dot on the horizon.

Desh drew his sword, and the rest of us did the same a second later.

A low, slow man's voice came from behind me. "This is so disappointing."

"Krak! Where'd that tubby ganker come from?" Stan said.

Before I even turned, I knew who I'd find. A fat, almost spherical man in a bright red robe stood pursing his lips at me. This man, Dimore, didn't look like a mighty being that wandered between the world of man and whatever other realms might exist, but that's what he was.

I had learned that Void Walkers like him were elusive and unpredictable, but I knew hardly a damn thing more. Their powers were vague, although Dimore had always delivered on any promise or threat. He had once locked up Limnad in a stone tower, so I understood why she'd be shy of him. He also had blinded Desh and cut off his hands, so by not running, Desh was showing an uncommon amount of grit.

"You're disappointed, Dimore?" I said, pushing my hat up off my forehead. "It grieves me to hear about such disappointment. Would you cheer up if I sing you a fisherman's love ballad?"

I glanced to the side and saw Desh approaching, his sword still in his hand. Pil stood with her hands relaxed. She was probably holding her sharp enchanted knife in one of them, unseen. Stan shifted and craned his neck.

Dimore sniffed. "Tell me that you have not forgotten that you promised to murder someone for me. I haven't forgotten. I recall it with intense clarity. I do not remember that you promised to carry around dead farmers."

"Hell no, I haven't forgotten! You want somebody killed out that direction . . ." I pointed vaguely northeast. "And I am partial to killing. Why would I go anyplace else?"

"I suspect you intend to deviate."

"I do not intend to deviate in any significant way." I glanced at Desh.

"Home is to the northwest." Desh gave a tight shrug.

I smiled at Dimore. "We're headed straight toward your killing ground except for a small detour. Tiny. A merciful act that will require almost no time. I don't claim to know how Void Walkers perceive time, but it's possible you won't even notice me pause."

Dimore sighed. "I see that you cannot be reasoned with." He walked past me toward Desh's horse. "I suppose that this beast is exceptional in its own loathsome way." He shrugged.

The gelding crumpled. A burlap sack spilling peaches lay where it had been standing. At the same time, Desh dissolved into balls of dandelion fluff that began floating away.

"Oops." Dimore faced me, chewing the inside of his lip. "Now, which way do you intend to travel?"

"Just wait a minute—"

Dimore glanced at Pil. When he glanced away, Pil had become a well-stacked tower of wine bottles. The ones I could see looked full. He pointed at Stan, who squeezed his eyes shut and stiffened. "So, tell me again what direction you are traveling."

When Dimore pointed his chubby finger of obliteration at Stan, I understood that I had been too nice. I am almost never accused of being too nice, but with Dimore, I had been reasonable and even affable.

Now the Void Walker felt free to employ threats and murder to compel my obedience. Sure, he was more powerful than me by unknown orders of magnitude and could kill me the way I'd pluck lint. But I had spent years aggravating gods and calling them bad names. This Void Walker couldn't be more terrible than a god.

I crossed my arms and squinted at Dimore, who was still pointing at Stan. "Put your finger away, you sunburned, oozing bag of filth. If you harm even one more person, I will never kill a soul for you. Not a person, a bug, or a bottle of whiskey."

Dimore smiled with otherworldly condescension. "I'll just turn you into a stack of dead turtles. Then I'll destroy everyone you have ever liked, or even tolerated. No, I will annihilate every person who has ever seen you, just to be certain. You are fairly old for a man, but the total couldn't be more than ten thousand."

I smiled back at him. "Then whoever you want killed will just have to go on being alive."

"I will find some other murderer to do it." Dimore turned and gazed down his pointing finger at Stan. The ex-soldier scrunched his eyes tighter and swallowed.

Chuckling, I said, "You went to some trouble finding me for this task. Do you want to go to that trouble again, you woolly-headed memory of your mother's greatest regret? Or do Void Walkers even have mothers? If you don't, pretend I called you a rank asshole."

Dimore didn't drop his hand, but he did stifle a yawn with his other palm while looking back at me. "Are you trying to make me destroy you? Do you want to die? You aren't capable of making me angry."

I shook my head. "You have no reason to kill me even a little. I agreed to do this murder for you, so don't be such a pathetic whiner about it. Don't say shit like, 'I suspect you intend to deviate,' and 'You can't be reasoned with,' and other such wobble-spined nonsense. A few days can't be that critical to a mystical, realm-spanning being like yourself." When Dimore didn't answer right away, I waved like I was swatting a fly. "I swear, the gods are the most self-involved, impatient, bitchy individuals in existence—or at least I thought they were until a minute ago."

Dimore's jaw clenched.

I pointed at his face. "Hah! Lower your finger. I'll kill whoever this is that you dislike so much. But I won't be herded toward the spot like the stupidest sheep in the pasture!"

The Void Walker stopped pointing and wiped his palm against his belly. "You are even more irksome than I was told. I find this unacceptable on many levels."

"Name seven," I said.

He ignored my comment. "Go if you wish—for now. But prepare yourself to abandon whatever you're doing at any moment to resume your task for me."

I pointed at the bottles and the dispersing fluff. "Bring them back."

Dimore glanced at what was left of Pil, Desh, and Desh's horse. "It won't be cheap."

"You're right. It'll be free."

Dimore shook his head.

"Don't flop your head around at me! If we're both to be reasonable, whoever you hate will be dead pretty soon, and I'll take this man's noble father home to be buried, or maybe burned. I'm not sure what rituals they follow in these parts. Anyway, I can't very well help Desh get his father home if Desh is a bunch of fluff scattered over the whole plains." I raised my eyebrows.

Dimore didn't move or even blink, but Pil, Desh, and his horse reappeared. The horse neighed and bolted. Desh turned to watch, tripped over his own feet, and cursed as he fell. Pil backed away from Dimore fast, her jaw tight.

"Thank you, that was honorable and even pleasant," I said.

Without acknowledging that I had spoken, Dimore began blowing away as if he were a sand statue. Within a few seconds, he was gone.

An enormous sigh exploded out of Stan, and he sagged against his horse. "I ain't a coward. I wouldn't mind so much getting killed if it could be clean—hell, everybody does it—but getting turned into fruit or booze is unnatural. Thanks for saving me from that horror, Bib. I don't know how—"

"Buy me a drink sometime," I said.

"Right!" Stan nodded as if everybody knew his life was worth exactly one glass of beer.

THREE

For a sorcerer, not doing things can be as perilous as doing things. I learned that while shoveling horseshit.

The sorcery masters kicked me out of training early for being willful and insulting. A rancher took me on, and whenever possible, I visited the nearby villagers to fatten their sheep, cure their children, and so on.

Two soldiers came for me one day. It seemed that I had not given the villagers fat enough sheep, and I had allowed their children to be homely and stupid. People had tired of my negligence and intended to judge me.

I told the taller soldier that the people had gone crazy, and he agreed. I didn't want to be judged by crazy people, and he agreed with that too, right before he grabbed my arm.

I knocked the tall soldier down and ran, but his short friend grabbed me and pulled his dagger. I cut his throat with my pathetic little knife. The tall soldier started yelling, which wouldn't have helped my escape, so I jammed the dagger into his heart.

Half a mile down the road, I started puking. Once my stomach had emptied, I felt steadier. I ran on, considered what had happened, and concluded that I had done the proper and logical thing. My empty stomach disagreed by heaving some more, and I ran on toward the harbor, confused but grateful.

That was the first time I killed somebody on purpose.

Ten minutes into Desh's journey home, I regretted coming along. I doubly regretted agreeing to walk. We had strapped Desh's father onto my horse, and I limped along leading her. I made sure everybody knew that I was damning them and everything else I saw. In truth, my knee didn't hurt that much, but it gave me something to complain about.

I could have pitched the corpse off my horse and ridden away, but I didn't because I felt bad about killing Desh's pa. Also, I had promised Limnad I would take care of him, and I didn't care to tell her I had abandoned somebody she loved.

But mainly I joined Desh out of foolish sentiment. He had come to me as an eager young fellow in love with every secret of sorcery that he imagined could exist. I helped him become a potent sorcerer who loved magic no more than he loved his shoes. I felt a little bad about that.

"Desh, what was your daddy's name?" Stan asked from horse-back. "I'll make up a song for him."

I almost grinned but stopped myself. Most of the songs Stan knew were randy. It would be interesting to see him rhyme a body part or unclean act with Desh's pa's name.

"His name was Desh Elder."

After a little silence, Pil said, "I never once thought to ask you why you're called Desh Younger, but now it makes sense. I'm sorry I never knew your father."

Desh nodded and said in a tight voice, "Almost everybody liked him."

I heard Stan muttering, "Belled her . . . geld her . . . swelled her . . . that's a good one . . ."

I heard what might have been far-off thunder.

Stan jerked his head toward the empty plains. "Damn, it's going to storm. I wish I was inside someplace. This trip is a shitty idea, eh? Well, I don't mean to crap on the notion of taking your daddy home, Desh, I just hate riding around in a rainstorm."

Stan's babbling wasn't holding my attention. Sorcery gave me a superior weather sense. "We won't be getting wet. We may get buried in sand, though."

Desh swore. Pil swore and even slapped her leg with her hat. Stan's head drooped, and he stared ahead between his horse's ears.

A week earlier, a sandstorm had caught us, but a big village had been close by. We raced to it for shelter, and the villagers had taken us right in. It seemed that all suspicions and feuds were dropped during such a storm. Afterward, our saviors described the terrors of frontier sandstorms in finer and finer detail until we offered some coins in gratitude. We owned horses for riding, which in their minds made us rich. Compared to their poverty, they were right.

"How long do we have?" Desh asked.

I squinted. "Half an hour, maybe."

Desh scanned the horizon. The plains looked the same to me in every direction. Desh must have seen something I was too ignorant to notice. "There's a village this way that will shelter us."

Pil helped me up to ride behind her, and we galloped away north following Desh.

The wind had risen by the time we reached the village. Pil followed Desh between two little houses, and they both halted.

"What is it?" I peered over Pil's shoulder.

Pil whispered, "Lutigan and Krak burn it."

I slid to the ground, strode around Pil's horse, and stopped. I could see ten dead villagers tumbled and stretched along the lane, both men and women. Somebody had killed them with precise thrusts to the chest, neck, or head, and the blood still looked wet in the afternoon sunlight.

Drawing my sword, I stalked down the lane ahead of Desh. If people needed to be killed for this, I wanted to do it in an expeditious fashion and then get inside a house. I found no murderers on the next lane, though, nor on the two after that. I did discover about forty of their victims. Some were children and even babies.

We hurried to search houses for survivors, but all we found were more poor slaughtered farmers. By then, the wind was hurling dust and dirt at us hard enough to sting. We gave up the search to take shelter.

The little town had no stables, but we had found two bigger houses, maybe owned by the richest families in town, that each could shelter a couple of horses. Desh led his horse and mine, with his father's body, into one, trailed by Stan. I walked into the next house and kicked some miserable furniture out of the way before Pil brought in the other horses.

The wind had already been battering us, but soon it shrieked through every chink in the walls. The horses stamped and shifted, so we whispered and petted them, lest they go mad and kick us to death inside the house.

A few minutes after the storm began screaming, Pil shouted, "Somebody's out there!"

"That seems damned unlikely."

"They are! I saw them run past the door."

I leaned around the doorframe and saw a man's outline hurrying down the street and into one of the other houses. A few seconds later, another man hustled out from between two houses down the way and followed the first man. He didn't even glance my direction.

I nodded at Pil. "You're right! I don't think they're survivors, but who the hell are they? The killers, I guess."

While my head was turned, a short, broad man ran inside our house and scrunched to a stop. He stared at us with eyes bigger than his fists, and even through my surprise, I acknowledged he had one of the biggest chins I had ever seen. He wore thick, yellow traveling clothes with black boots, and he carried a spear on his back alongside a small shield. Without doubt, he was a Hill Man.

My sword was sheathed, so I reached to grab him. He twisted like a trout, faster than I had ever been, and leaped back outside. I didn't follow, but I watched him sprint to the house down the street. He rushed inside, and a moment later, he was likely inviting his friends to come kill us and set our horses free.

"Was that a Hill Person?" Pil yelled.

I nodded. "And not the only one!"

"Shit!" Pil closed her eyes and tossed her head as if she'd learned somebody were coming to yank out all her teeth.

I watched the other house, and Pil joined me. Less than a minute later, a Hill Person appeared in the doorway of that house and gazed at me. I stared back, not moving. For a situation that might explode into bloodshed, it was a pensive moment.

The Hill Person pointed at another house, one across the lane.

"He wants to meet," Pil yelled.

"Or maybe he's saying that's where he plans to kill me," I shouted. Then I muttered, "I can't believe I rode away from some-body who loved me to have this kind of fun."

I hadn't thought Pil could hear me, but she said, "Ella left you before you rode away."

Before I could say something mean to her, she cut me off. "We can argue about it later. Tomorrow you'll be just as wrong as you are now."

I examined the house across the lane. It looked deserted, which meant not a damn thing since I couldn't see through walls. But I'd be foolish not to go. The Hill People were devastating fighters, and if the fellow down the lane had more than a couple of companions, they might destroy us. But if I could face them in smaller groups instead of one ferocious, whirling bunch, we might survive.

"How many did you see run past?" I yelled to Pil.

"Two plus the one that came inside here. Don't go out there, Bib, you can't gain a single thing by doing it!"

"You're almost certainly correct, so don't follow me."

"Don't go! You just let him stand out there by himself and get beaten to pieces!" Pil yelled in my ear. "What will you get from talking to him? Nothing!"

"What about when the storm ends? What if there are twenty of them? I'd prefer they not run over here and kill us all."

Pil grabbed my sleeve, but I shook her off. I drew my sword and ran across the lane to the house that the Hill Man had pointed at, hoping to hell that it wasn't already waist-deep in deadly spearmen.

Despite the brutal wind and dirt, I stopped outside and eased into the house. Inside it was one big room, empty apart from a sad scattering of bedrolls, chairs, a firepit, and one ancient wooden chest. I trotted to the middle of the room and faced the door, still holding my sword.

The Hill Person who issued the invitation turned out to be a woman. In the past, I had seen women fighters among the Hill People as often as men, so this didn't surprise me. She entered the house with careful steps, holding a spear of unusual design, and she slowly lifted her spear over her head. When I didn't move, she raised her eyebrows at me.

As smooth as honey, I sheathed my sword, and she stowed her spear at the same time. I didn't mind going unarmed. My size might give me an edge if we fought with our hands and feet. The woman took a small step toward me and pulled the scarf down from her face.

The Hill Woman stood a bit over five feet tall, which I understood to be on the tall side for a grown Hill Person. Her face was dark brown and pretty in a serious way, and I put her at about thirty years old.

"I am Bib," I shouted, introducing myself first according to Hill People custom.

"I think you must be a thief." Although she was loud, her words were calm and controlled.

"Not since I was a boy! Why do you think that?"

"The sword you carry was made by the Hill People."

My foolishness stunned me for a moment. My sword had once belonged to a king's champion. Nobody knew where he had gotten it, and he couldn't say after he was killed. I had never seen a weapon so beautiful, economical, and poised to kill. It made sense that the Hill People had made it, since they crafted superior weapons. Hell, they made superb tools, clothing, and even spoons.

I said, "Well, I didn't steal it, and I killed the thief who did. You're welcome."

The woman smiled for a moment, which stunned me.

I shook my head. "I apologize, but I have never known a Hill Person to smile."

"They probably did not think you were funny. People say I have a strange sense of humor. You must give me the sword." She sounded like a constable demanding that I give over a stolen loaf of bread.

"I fear I can't. This sword has been enchanted for me. If any other person lifts the sword, it might rot off their arm."

"Or it might not," the woman said. "I will take that chance."

"If I give away the sword, I'll anger the gods."

"Which ones?" she asked.

"A bunch of them. Definitely Fingit and Harik, and probably Krak as well. And Lutigan will get mad at me for being an ungrateful squat, so no."

The woman squinted at me and then smiled again. "I am Semanté."

I recalled hearing that name more than a year before. "I've heard of you," I yelled.

She nodded. "You are a thief and a liar too."

"I admit there may be two people named Semanté, though it seems unlikely. I knew a young man a thousand miles from here who shouted your name before he got into a fight. Pretty damn romantic."

Semanté paused for several seconds. "His name is Bratt. Is he dead?"

"I am afraid he is."

She didn't change expression. "Did you kill him?"

I was glad I needn't lie about that. She might not have some sort of truth sight, but she looked at me as if she did. "No, I didn't kill him. We were allies. An imp, a demon from the Gods' Realm, murdered him. Bratt was a good boy—brave but unlucky."

Semanté examined me for a moment. I felt like a raw soldier being inspected by his sergeant. Then she gave a wan smile. "Yes, he was all those things. What about Larripet?"

"Him too. He died saving my life."

She nodded. "This news is not happy, but thank you for telling me." She spit out some sand. "It is an unlikely event to find you here, telling me these things, far away from your home and mine. Do you think the gods wanted us to meet?"

"Hell, I hope not!"

Semanté laughed until she wiped her eyes. "If I kill you, that would be like saying my uncle Larripet was stupid to give his life for you. So, I will not kill you when I kill everyone else."

I stared at Semanté for a few seconds. "The wind is loud. I didn't hear that."

"While I am killing everyone else, you may go home and live." She looked into my eyes, and I didn't see any sign of humor, strange or otherwise.

"Do you mean there are people in this town you haven't killed yet? Besides my friends and me? And our horses?"

Semanté squinted one eye at me. "I guess I can let your friends live too. I have finished with the others here."

I didn't want to say something stupid just now. "That is interesting. Are there other places we shouldn't go? So that we don't get in your way?"

"Ah." She stared at the sooty ceiling. "Do not go to the places where the Soulless Who Shit on the Land and the Ocean live."

I considered that. The Hill Lands lay at least five hundred miles southeast of us. Semanté's clothes were the exact color of this dirt on the northern frontier, so she had planned to come here. "I'm afraid I don't know any people by that name. Do they have another name?"

Semanté nodded. "In their own language, they call themselves the Empire. Stay away, because we will kill them all."

I swallowed twice. The Empire was the most powerful nation in the world. It spanned a thousand miles. Millions of people lived there. Killing them all sounded ridiculous, but it had been said that a thousand Hill People could conquer anything. I didn't know how many Hill People there were in all the world, but there had to be more than a thousand of them.

I smiled. "It sounds like a worthy endeavor. I do wonder something. These frontier people aren't part of the Emp— of those Soulless Shitters. Why kill them?"

"You would not ask that if you were a military person. We cannot leave people alive behind us to attack our supply lines."

"So . . . you have already killed everybody on the frontier south of here?" I closed my eyes. That had to be thirty thousand or more mostly defenseless people.

"Yes." Semanté sighed. "I regret it," she said as if she was sorry to have slaughtered some sick hogs. "At least they have not been hard to kill. Bib, go home. That will be safest. We will not come to your home to kill everybody this year." She winked. "We are too busy."

FOUR

aybe I should have leaped at Semanté and strangled her or smashed her skull against the brick wall, but I couldn't imagine that it would've saved a single person. If she died, would the entire force of Hill People decide they didn't know how to fight anymore and go home? Hell, they might not even notice she was gone.

I waved at Semanté. "Good luck with your war then."

"Go home." She pointed and said it as if I were her dog.

I smiled, stepped around her, and ran across to join Pil. The sandstorm's violence hadn't faded even a smidge.

"What happened?" Pil shouted.

I paused to consider it. "The Hill People are killing everybody on the frontier. Then they'll get around to wiping out the whole Empire. After that?" I shrugged.

Pil squinted at me and then wiped sand out of her eyes. "Is that true or just another tale?"

"I'm serious, Pil. They will allow us to run for safety because of our mutual acquaintances."

"What . . . no, I don't want to hear the story you're about to tell."

"I'll say it plain then. We're lucky as hell. If we ride back the way we came, we can circle north and take a ship all the way down to Cliffmeet. From there, Dimore can point me to this fellow he hates so much. I'm getting to hate the fellow too now. He's putting us to a mountain of trouble."

"Did you say ride back the way we came?" Pil smiled. "Let's go as soon as the storm blows out. I don't have anything to take care of first. This detour shouldn't add more than a few months to the trip, and I don't care much anyway since I'm not the one who agreed to assassinate whoever I'm told to. Bib, think about it. You might end up killing your brother!"

"You've said that same thing every day for three weeks. Think of something else to say."

Pil paused. "Bib, what if the Hill People have already killed everybody in Desh's village?"

"Then we'll bury the old man and gallop straight out of this war."

The Hill People departed a couple of hours later when the storm had eased. I would have still considered it unbearable, which told me they were as tough as pine knots. They weren't perfect, though. They bumped into a couple of walls, and one felt his way along. Thirteen of them disappeared into the dust.

Sunset had passed when the storm dwindled to a stiff breeze. We all met in the street, where Pil and I explained about the Hill People.

Stan walked away.

"Where are you going?" Pil called after him.

As he walked into an unexplored house, Stan said over his shoulder, "To find a shovel, or a sharp stick. We can bury Desh's pap here and then run!"

I had seen Stan face a lot of dangers with a sort of aggravated courage, but Hill People had nearly killed him once.

Desh said, "We shouldn't bury my father here. These aren't his people."

"They're deader than dog shit and ain't nobody's people now!"

Stan yelled from inside the house. "Your pap can make new friends."

"Stan!" Pil spoke out, scowling.

Stan walked out with his shoulders sagging. "I'm sorry, Desh, that wasn't nice. Please don't turn me into something bad."

Desh said, "That's all right," but his jaw stayed clenched. "It's not far."

Pil nodded at Desh. "Well, we're mounted and can outrun the Hill People, or I hope we can with Bib's butt perched on my horse. If they do catch us, at least it'll be less painful than listening to Bib sing and moan."

I softened my voice. "Desh, we have to ask. What if your people have already been killed?"

"What if they haven't?" Desh raised his chin. "They'll need somebody to help them."

Stan started to say something but looked down instead.

Pil glanced back and forth between us, her eyes narrowed. "We can bury your father, but I don't see how we can save a whole town."

Desh said, "We're three sorcerers, and we haven't even begun to think about the problem. Let's not quit before we start."

"No, I believe Stan is wise on this," I said. "We'd be foolish to prance along to your home and assume that a hundred Hill People aren't already there."

Desh paced thirty feet away and faced me. I watched him, a little puzzled. He called out, "What would you say if it was your daughter who needed to be buried?"

Before I stopped myself, I had drawn my sword and bounded four steps toward him. Pil was shouting at me, and Desh was backing away fast, his face pale.

I sighed as I sheathed my sword. "You rank, baby-slapping son of a pig's ass. What right do you have to talk about my little girls?"

"None," Desh said, rubbing his cheek.

"You're damn right none!"

Desh didn't speak, move, or back down. For all I knew, he was hiding some magical doodad in his hand that could cut me into forty-three pieces, so backing down might have been unnecessary for him.

I walked up to face him at arm's length, and he held his place. "Desh, I guess you want this a lot. I'll go along to bury your pa. As for the town, I'm sometimes a fool, but I won't die trying to save people who can't be saved."

"Thank you, Bib," Desh said. "Sincerely."

When Desh walked away to gather horses, Pil leaned close to me. "What are you going to say when we get there and he begs you to help him save all his friends and neighbors?"

"I'll tell him no. It's easy to say and hard to mistake for something else."

Pil gave me a wry look and went to help Desh.

I appreciated the nearly full moon that night. Some groups of Hill People might be ahead of us. The moonlight would help us avoid riding into the middle of them.

Desh set a hard pace northwest, leading my horse with his pa strapped across it, while I rode with Pil. It was an awful journey. The weather was hot even after sunset. My butt still hurt. I dropped my kerchief, watched it flutter away behind us, and had to wipe sweat with my sleeve. Our pace made conversation impractical, even with Pil, which denied me the pleasure of goading my companions.

Well before midnight, I began to regret coming along with Desh. Then I began lamenting this entire journey for Dimore. Sulking is beneath a sorcerer's dignity, but I moped extra hard and tossed in some quiet blasphemy.

In the middle of the night, I saw movement ahead of us. We halted, and I said, "Somebody's up there. It looks like eleven people."

"Mounted or afoot?" Stan asked.

"Not a horse in sight," I said. "Good chance they're Hill People."

Stan cursed under his breath.

I said, "I'm a silver-plated idiot. Semanté said I could go home, and instead I'm riding away from home." I watched for another minute. "I believe they're moving away from us."

"Toward my village," Desh said.

Pil asked, "How far is that? Can we ride around and beat them there?"

Desh said, "I doubt it. Even if we do, they'll arrive close behind us. We might not be able to bury my father before that."

I said, "What if the Hill People get there when the hole is half-dug? That would be awkward. They'd have the advantage of scouting us before they attack, and Desh's people would be right there in a good spot to get killed. No, if we're not going to run, let's fall on them from behind, right now. Surprise and distance will give us the advantage."

We flung a plan together in a minute. We would ride to within three hundred paces of the Hill People and dismount. Desh and Pil would attack from a distance. If the Hill People rushed us, I would take the lead as we fought them with hand weapons. If the Hill People ran, we would fire until they were out of range, mount up, and follow until we were in range again.

We closed with the Hill People and dismounted. Pil and Desh fired at the ones on the ends. Both targets tumbled and didn't move.

Before Desh and Pil could reload, the Hill People turned to run toward us.

"That's the discipline of the Hill People," I said. "They didn't hesitate to charge this way, as if they didn't need to be ordered."

Desh and Pil fired again. This time, no Hill People fell. They didn't even bobble.

"Damn, damn it to my mam's beard!" Stan yelled. "Did you both miss?"

"I don't think so," Desh said. They fired again, and the Hill People were close enough now for me to see better. I peered and felt stupid. "They're using shields. Fire for their legs. Or head."

The man Desh fired at stumbled and staggered aside. Whoever Pil fired at didn't fall.

"Mother slap it!" Pil shouted.

Desh hurled a stone and struck a Hill Woman's head. She fell aside and lay still.

I called out, "Shoot for their legs, Pil!"

"I am!" Pil said before she fired again. Her arrow arrived at the man's chest, and he blocked it.

The Hill People had almost reached us, but I laughed.

"What? What's funny?" Pil yelled.

"You'd better practice more. You'd have missed every time without a magic bow. Even with magic, you didn't have the skill to hit their legs instead of their chests!"

"Damn!" Pil snarled, drawing her sword. "They shouldn't have been able to do that with their shields."

I stayed quiet. Pil didn't need to hear me say that the Hill People were superlative fighters. They would demonstrate that for her in a few seconds.

When the seven Hill People were fifty feet away, Desh shouted, "Close your eyes!" Two seconds later, a light flashed, bright enough to show through my eyelids. "Open them!"

Five Hill People staggered toward us, leaving behind two red glowing corpses on the ground. Desh drew his sword and charged the dazed Hill People right behind me.

I faced a man and a woman. My friends each faced a man. I ignored my allies at first because I was busy doing stupid and reckless things with a sword. I knew better. I blamed it on the weapon, which seemed to make recklessness look like brilliance.

I lunged to disable the man in front of Stan, ignoring the two attacking me. The wounded man turned toward me, but even stumbling and half-blind, he nearly killed me with a spear thrust. I dodged and sliced open his throat, then threw myself aside inches ahead of the others' spears.

Rolling to my feet, I knew exactly where my enemies were, almost like seeing a picture. I whipped the point of my blade in and out of a Hill Woman's throat. She staggered back with her long, black hair flying. I felt a wave of satisfaction.

The dying woman's friend, a muscular, deep brown fellow, thrust at my face. I dodged, and he thrust low. Then I saw it play out in my head. He could attack me three ways, and all were strong attacks. Ignoring everything else, I made a blinding, off-balance thrust through the man's right eye. He stiffened for a moment and then collapsed.

Glancing left and right, I saw Desh retreating from one woman. On the other side, a man turned and sprinted away from Pil and Stan.

"Chase him!" Pil yelled to me. "We'll help Desh!"

It made sense for me to pursue. Pil and Stan were younger and faster than me, and they might catch the man if they ran hard. And when they caught him, he'd stab them to death.

For fifteen seconds, I outpaced the Hill Man, and I might have caught him. As soon as I thought I might haul him down, he spun. Hardly missing a step, he threw his spear and kept running. I wasn't sure anybody I had ever known could make such a throw. I sure as hell couldn't. I only saved myself by diving straight onto my face amid the dirt, rocks, and nasty grass.

My wind was failing. By that point, I could have run for the rest of my life and never caught that Hill Man. I walked back to the others, dabbing the bloody scrapes on my face.

Desh stood over the woman he had been fighting. She now lay dead, wrapped up and strangled by a rope of woven cloth. I stared for a moment and said, "Desh, I don't imagine she expected that."

He shrugged. "I wasn't sure it would do that."

When the Hill Woman was overcome, she had somehow thrown her spear and struck Desh's horse in the neck. Pil and I knelt by the animal, and she soothed it while I removed the spear.

Pil watched me pull a green band of magical power. "I didn't know that you'd be willing to spend power to save a horse. In fact, I was pretty sure you wouldn't, since I can't remember you ever healing an animal, not even once."

I said, "If bunches of Hill People are crossing these lands, horses will be worth more than gold. Hill People don't travel mounted, so speed will be our only sure advantage."

Pil frowned. "We'll need it. That man you let escape will run right back and report to his boss. That was careless of you."

I picked up one of the Hill People's spears, which wasn't like any I had seen before. "Everybody, come look at this."

When the others had gathered, I held out the spear in the weak light.

Desh took it from me without asking. "This is new. Look, the point is sharp steel for punching through armor, but the rest of the spearhead is unusually broad and rough. A less accurate throw, but it tears flesh all to pieces." He tried to flex the spear shaft, but it resisted like iron. "The shaft is longer than you'd expect, but strong —made of Pepporin wood."

I reached out for the spear. "What kind of wood?"

"It grows in the Hill Lands and is tough. It's not magical, but hard to break or cut. And valuable."

"How much can we get for it?" Stan asked, pushing past me to look at the weapon.

"Hard to estimate," Desh said. "It's believed to be uncommon in the Hill Lands, and you hardly ever see it here in the west." He stared into the sky. "The right buyer might trade six or seven good horses for it."

Stan whistled. "Let's gather 'em all up!" He ran off to find spears in the spotty grass by moonlight.

"He'll be rich, if they don't overwhelm him a hundred miles down the road," Pil said.

"That's not important," I said. "We know that the Hill People came here to fight armored men and mounted men from close enough to spit on them."

Desh shook his head. "That's not even the most important thing. This war is crucial for them. They don't mind arming their people with a stunning fortune's worth of weapons for this adventure."

"I know you're both clever, and maybe I'm not sure what the heck the most important thing is," Pil said, "but it looks like the Hill People have taken months or maybe years to prepare for this war, so whenever we have a good idea about something, we ought to assume that the Hill People already thought about it. Their dang grandparents may have thought about it."

FIVE

The morning was young enough to throw near-endless shadows when Desh's home appeared off to our left. Even when we rode closer to the village, I couldn't tell much difference between it and the cluster of hovels we had sheltered in the day before. The exception was a large pond, maybe fifty feet across, in the middle of the town.

As we slowed to a trot, I called out, "Desh, I expect you to show us all the exciting diversions your home has to offer. I can spare five minutes."

"Bib!" Pil snapped from behind me. "He's coming home to bury his father."

"That won't take more than an hour. We'll have plenty of time to see the five-legged goat." It was mean to needle him, but I had lost some opportunities to prod him throughout the night.

I wanted to kill Desh. It wasn't because of any misbehavior on his part. I wanted to kill Stan and Pil too. I could feel their deaths and practically taste them. I was not going to kill them. I don't mean that I would try not to take their lives. I absolutely would not do it, and I was prepared to die before I killed one of them.

But since I wasn't killing them, I just had to tease them, and sometimes I teased them hard enough to hurt. I believed that all of them would rather be baited than murdered, but the entire situation was difficult to explain to a person I wanted to kill.

We had come close enough to the village to distinguish men from women when Desh dragged on the reins to stop. I thought maybe I had upset him, but he ignored me.

"Is something wrong?" Pil asked. "What do you need us to do? Or do you want us to make it worse?" She flashed an uncertain smile.

Desh ignored her too. After ten seconds, he slapped the reins and his horse trotted onward.

Forty or fifty people were crowding at the edge of town, including farmers running in from the fields. They stared at us, and a few pointed, but otherwise they didn't do much. When we reached them, Desh dismounted before any of them spoke. Pil slid out of the saddle to the ground, but I enjoyed a better view from horseback, so I stayed there.

A short, lean woman stepped out. If the gods had beaten a hickory root into the shape of a woman, this would be her. Her mouth sagged, and tears ran as she moaned while running toward Desh. She smacked into him with a hug. He didn't hug her, but he didn't pull away.

Two years before, in Desh's first deal with the gods, he had given up all memories of his mother. If this hard woman was Desh's ma, things were about to get awkward.

Everybody watched the reunion without comment. At last, the woman pushed Desh to arm's length and bellowed like a calf, "Why? Where? You aren't dead! How?" She hugged him again, but just for a second before pushing him away.

Now the woman showed her teeth, and her brows drew in. "You must have had fun. You stayed gone long enough. I guess you're full of yourself, aren't you? Creep out of here in the night like a bald-ass rat, don't say a damn word to anybody! You look awfully pretty in your town clothes. Did you steal them from some prostitute?" She pointed at the horizon, I supposed toward where she thought the prostitutes lived.

Calm-faced and relaxed, Desh said, "No, I have a lover."

"Well, that's nice as hell for you!" The woman leaned toward Desh, both fists clenched. "Why did you come back then, you weepy little twat? Get! If you don't like it here, go on, drag your ass across the thorny bushes back to wherever they can stand a whiny twerp like you!"

Without moving, Desh said, "I assume that you are my mother."

I now realized that by losing his memories of his mother, Desh may have made the best deal in the annals of sorcery.

The woman stomped back to Desh but didn't touch him. Glaring up at his face, she yelled, "Don't be stupid! As if any other woman could stand to have you inside her. Yes, I'm your mother, you stupid turd! And then you thank me by abandoning your family, turning your shitty ass to us, and running off to have whatever prissy fun people have out in the goddamn towns. You ungrateful tadpole. You should never have been born. I should have taken a stick and gouged you out of me."

Desh nodded toward his father's body, still on the horse.

His mother turned, saw the body, and blanched as if she'd been burned. She ran to her husband and grabbed his corpse before shoving her face into his neck. She wailed, and her shoulders shook. The woman's grief sounded so pure and hopeless it made me uncomfortable.

The crowd of farmers began talking and shuffling about. I finally dismounted.

Desh's ma backed away, red-faced, and pointed at her dead husband. She shouted, "You ignorant, reckless, tweezy, no-dick bastard! Why didn't you stay home? I begged you to stay home! No, you wanted to run around acting brave, you nasty weakling! Why didn't you listen? You never listen! You wouldn't listen if your dick was on fire and I told you to jump in the pool!" She drew a breath, sobbed for a second, and then kept yelling, "Well, I won't miss you —not a knock-kneed, old fat man who's too stupid to do what he's told!"

Desh's mother swiveled her head like an owl searching for a mouse. She locked onto me, her tears still running. "And we don't want any fancy cowards like you around here. Couldn't do a day's work if your life depended on it, I can tell just by looking at you with your nasty-ass beard. Go on, get out of here! We don't have any little girls for you to grope, nor boys either, so turn your ass around and go!"

I stepped forward and punched her in the nose, not too hard. She squawked and staggered back. "Ma'am, I have urgent tasks to undertake elsewhere. If I didn't, I'd stay whether you liked it or not."

I glanced at Desh to see whether he was upset that I struck his ma. I didn't expect he would be. I also didn't expect to see him stride toward his sputtering mother, shove her to the ground, and pull out his knife.

He said, "I don't remember you. But I must have wanted to do this." He raised the blade but hesitated. Pil trotted toward the farmers and glared away any who might interfere. They didn't seem inclined to get involved in Desh's killing anyway. He took several deep breaths, staring down at the weeping, bleeding, mean old woman. Then he sheathed his knife and walked back to begin unlashing his father's corpse.

I leaned toward Stan. "More entertaining than a five-legged goat, eh?"

Before he answered, I felt something seize my spirit and pull it straight up through the top of my head, stretching me as it went. Nausea slammed me, but just for a second.

I arrived at the trading place. It lay in the Gods' Realm, where the gods traded magical power to sorcerers who were willing to do horrible things in exchange. Or have horrible things done to them. It was a bit more involved than that, but not much.

Gods preferred to bargain with ignorant sorcerers. So, they had charmed the trading place to mask all the senses, except for the words that gods wanted heard. I had never appreciated what a bargaining advantage that was until I was given a sword that let me see as the gods see. As long as they hadn't realized I possessed that sight, I had the advantage.

I had then proven that even with an advantage, I cannot

outtrade the gods. They like deals to go a certain way, and being gods, they get what they want.

Krak, Father of the Gods, had recently taken that sword away from me and given it to Pil, so I had lost my advantage for a while. Then I began seeing and hearing in the trading place even without the sword. I didn't know why, and my smartest acquaintances didn't know, either. But I intended not to let the gods find out. Maybe I wouldn't piss away that advantage this time.

Since I was pretending to be blind, I couldn't gape around like a chick just out of the shell. Even so, I appreciated quite a bit. The air was cool and dewy, and the smell of flowers and fruit almost made me sneeze. The dirt under my feet was brown and coarse, which the gods said was appropriate for a sorcerer's loathsome feet.

The yellow sunlight was rich enough to pour. When it touched me, I could imagine that I hadn't done twenty years' worth of stupid, wicked, harmful things. It almost drove me to my knees, but I managed to straighten up instead.

Harik, God of Death, sat wiggling his toes on the lowest level of the magnificent, white marble gazebo. It caused him to look less than completely divine, and I considered that good evidence that he didn't know I was watching. He also ruined the impact of his ideally beautiful face and muscular form by fiddling with the sleeve of his black robe.

Harik was sinfully proud of his black robe, since it was the counterpoint to Father Krak's white robe. However, Krak's robe was known to be the whitest thing in existence, while Harik's robe was merely the fourth blackest thing in existence.

Fingit, Smith of the Gods, explained it to me one day when we were swapping dirty stories. Among all the gods, Fingit was the softest touch.

The third blackest thing in the universe was the ebony diamond worn by the Unnamed Mother of All Existence, given to her by Krak at some point in the hazy past. Since she was Harik's mother, he usually acknowledged the diamond's third place standing, but with pettiness that endured throughout the millennia.

The second blackest thing in existence was the Void itself. Harik denied that and argued that the Void couldn't have any color since by definition it is the absence of everything. A few gods countered that since black is the absence of color, the Void is as black as it gets. Whenever Harik started bitching about this, most of the gods pretended that he didn't exist for a few days while they enjoyed parties, races, orgies, and ritual combat, along with every possible combination of those pastimes.

Without argument, the blackest thing in existence was the heart of Cheg-Cheg, the Dark Annihilator of the Void and Vicinity. The gods had made periodic war on Cheg-Cheg for tens of thousands of years. They always achieved victory over the creature, driving him back into the Void, although he destroyed most of the gods' works and servants before he fled.

Lutigan, God of War, once speared Cheg-Cheg in the heart. That made Cheg-Cheg quite irritated, and he destroyed two cities and a mountain that afternoon. But a bit of his black heart clung to Lutigan's spear, and it leeched the color from everything within a mile. The spear became transparent, and Lutigan couldn't find it for days. Several gods became transparent too, although they restored themselves straightaway.

Cheg-Cheg's heart sucked the color out of things. Everybody but Harik agreed: a thing that destroys color must be blacker than the mere absence of color.

"Hello, Murderer." Harik's voice was deep, rich, and a bit short.

I made a show of looking around at nothing. "Mighty Harik! Make it fast, I was busy beating the shit out of an old woman."

"Weak humor." Harik paused. "That was humor, correct? I can wait if you want to end her life."

"No, she won't be able to outrun me. Say your piece, you sagging udder of malice."

"Very well. This is simplicity beyond reason. I offer one-fourth of a square of power if you will turn around and go back to where you began this pointless journey."

"Huh." It was an odd proposal. Harik was offering me a modest slice of power if I would simply go some place I had already been.

Harik added, "You might encounter interesting people."

It was too obvious a trap. Then again, why did the gods need subtlety when they could both create and smite? I almost looked at Harik but caught myself and gazed beside him instead. "Go back? Krak's knobs, why?"

"If you do not, you will be overtaken by a mass of ferocious, stubby people. You cannot survive, even with your chilling new sword. By the way, I did not think the Nub possessed such skill."

"I'll tell Desh that you're tickled."

I paused and let my eyes wander. A month ago, the gods let it slip that they wanted me dead but didn't want to slay me themselves. With that in mind, what did Harik's offer mean? Did he really want me to go back? Or did he just say that, knowing I would do the opposite? Or did he want me to ride any direction except the way I came from?

Maybe pain and slaughter waited in every direction, and he was just screwing with me.

Harik said, "If such a simple offer strains your intellect, perhaps you should kill some more old women in the hours before the stubby people slaughter you." He smiled. "If you return to the beginning of your journey, you may find that the blonde woman you lust for will have returned as well."

I managed not to curse. Even if Ella had forgiven me, Harik would never send me someplace where happiness was waiting. He would send me to where a lot of people were waiting to kill me.

I said, "No, I'm afraid that won't work, Mighty Harik. I won't take your piddly quarter square, and I'll go wherever the hell I want."

"Well . . ." Harik drawled. "If your life means so little to you, it means even less to me." He hurled me back into my body, and I staggered.

Pil raised her eyebrows at me, but I walked toward Desh.

"Desh, Harik says he admires your work and asked if you would make some forks for him."

Desh stared into my eyes. "I won't just ride off and let these people die. I'm moving them. Will you help me?"

I rolled my eyes. "Desh, be realistic. You couldn't get them moving in less than a week. Once they got going, a crippled skunk could overtake them."

"The Hill People are coming, and they'll kill everybody here."

"I don't know what the Hill People will do, and you don't either," I said. "Semanté may have lied to me. They may dig a tunnel to the ocean for all we know!"

"They're coming." Desh gave a little shrug.

Pil said slowly, "Did somebody tell you that?"

Desh scowled at her for a moment and then relaxed. "Just assume that I know. Bib, do what you want. You always do anyway." He turned and walked toward a tall man with a fringe of white hair who was arguing with five other men.

I turned to Pil. "Well?"

"I wish I could help these people, and Desh is a fine idiot for trying." She shook her head. "If I want to die a pointless death, I'll sit naked in a hot bath and eat pie until I choke."

"Well . . . I can see Desh's point," I said. "These are his people."

Pil grimaced. "Then you go help him. Anyway, I thought you owed Dimore a killing."

"Hm." I spit on the ground. "Where will you go?"

"I think this trip is cursed. Maybe I'll just turn around and go back to Castle Glass."

"Me too." Stan nodded as his purple hat flopped.

Riding away seemed like the only sane plan, regardless of what Harik told me and what Dimore wanted.

"I can't help Desh, that's a certain thing," I said.

Pil nodded. "He's a better sorcerer than you and a tougher individual as well."

"Right. All we could do is stand beside him while we get spears shoved into us."

Pil raised her voice. "You don't need to convince me. I'm leaving."

"Desh was a squishy, ignorant boy when I met him." I couldn't think of anything else to say at that moment.

Pil stared at me, blank-faced. "He's likable too."

"Shit! Can you think of anybody less suited for evacuating a village than me?"

"My horse, maybe," Pil said. "Although you can distract Desh's mother, keep her company and so forth. You know, she's a widow now." She winked at me.

I swallowed and imagined fleeing across the plains with Desh's ma to Castle Glass. I shivered. Going with her to go get crowned king someplace would make me shiver just as much.

I swallowed. "I'll be ready to go in ten minutes."

SIX

Desh buried his father right after his mother got done abusing us. She directed the work and criticized the digging for the first two minutes, until Desh whacked her on the elbow with the shovel. She kept on criticizing but did it from fifty feet away.

After the man was buried, Stan and I stood beside the big pool, watching Desh stride from one villager to the next. He was trying to convince them to run away from everything they had ever known to escape a threat they couldn't see. He had not yet succeeded, nor made any visible progress, but I hadn't concluded he would fail. I had learned not to dismiss Desh when he promised to do some impossible thing. For example, if this evacuation fell apart, as I expected it might, I felt confident that Desh could escape the Hill People by himself.

Desh faced a severe challenge in convincing his people to flee, but he had two advantages. First, he was a clever man, so he understood that logic would be useless with them. Second, he had grown up there. He knew what frightened them.

Mopping sweat off his red face, Desh stomped over to us. He

pointed at the tall, white-haired man and murmured, "That old fellow is Yoadie, the town elder."

Pil was squatting beside the pool, collecting water for our journey. "So, you have to convince the elder? Do you want me to flirt with him before I go? Or put him in an arm lock?" Pil smiled, even though a spate of Hill People might flow in and kill us all soon if we tarried.

"That wouldn't help." Desh wiped his sparsely bristled chin. "See those six men shouting at each other? They're the rest of the elders. They help Yoadie make decisions."

I said, "All right, you go convince them all. I'll give you five minutes to do it before I leave. Do your people drink beer?"

"Convincing them is no good," Desh said. "If people don't like their decisions, nobody pays attention."

"How does anything get done?" Pil asked.

"Mostly, it doesn't."

Pil stood, hefting a water sack. "It sounds like your task is hopeless, Desh."

I nodded. "It sure does. Let's just buy some beer and ride out of this place."

Desh glared toward the elders. "No, nothing's hopeless. The sure way to get action out of everybody is to scare them." He paused.

"Well?" Pil said. "What kind of things are they afraid of? Lightning? Demon goats?"

Desh bit his lip. "I think they're afraid of my mother."

I stared at the young man. "Is she a witch? Or a hexer? Krak's eyeballs, is she a sorcerer?"

"No, or at least I don't think so. I don't remember her, but I remember everybody else. They fear somebody who's mean enough to make a washtub cry. That has to be her."

"Good!" Pil said. "You just need to get her on your side, and then she'll scare everybody else into running away." She pointed at Desh's mother, who was limping down the lane, leaning on a long stick. "I guess you hurt her leg when you knocked her down, Desh."

"Do you really need the old husk?" I asked. "If you kill her, won't they be afraid of you then?"

"It might work . . ." Desh said.

"Don't talk that way, Desh." Stan had walked up behind us. "I know you went and forgot your mam, so she ain't no more than a drunk on the street to you now. But you might remember her some-time. She's as nasty a kick in the nuts as I ever saw, but she's still your mam. You only got one, and you ain't got her forever."

Desh examined Stan's face as if he were a new kind of animal. The ex-soldier gave him a single, emphatic nod. Desh sighed. "All right, let's try to talk her into saving her people." He nudged me.

"No. I don't think she likes me," I said.

"Well, I know she hates me," Desh said.

"A pair of whining infants! I'll do this, and then I'm leaving." Pil stepped out in the lane and then turned back. "What's her name? I can't walk up and say, 'Hi there, Desh's mama,' can I?"

Desh frowned. "I don't know what it is."

Pil glanced at the hard, blue sky. "Lutigan's fourteen swords! All right, I'll find out for you." She strode over and caught up with the old woman just before she reached a small, mud brick house.

The old woman and Pil spoke too quietly for me to hear, but the conversation appeared cordial. Then with no warning, the woman slammed the end of her stick down on Pil's left foot. Pil yelped and jumped back as the woman scurried into the house. Pil stared at the door and then hobbled back to us.

"Her name is Tira, and she's not interested in helping us. She wants to see us dead, and she suggested two ways I could kill myself." Pil flexed her foot inside her boot.

"I guess you have to kill her now, Desh," I said. "Or you could forget all this sandy, whining nonsense and leave with us. Somebody is still out there waiting for me to murder them."

Desh eased around to face me and said in an even voice, "Is there nothing left of you but killing? You grew up in a nasty, poor town like this, didn't you? Have you even looked at these people? Or are they only important if you can kill them?"

I couldn't have been more shocked if Desh had pulled a dead

beaver from behind his back and whacked me with it. I opened my mouth, but that was all.

"Desh, Bib can't help it," Pil said. "If he could, do you think he'd be this way?"

"I don't understand," Stan added. "Desh, you gave him the sword that wants to kill every damn thing that walks on the earth. Why are you cracking his walnuts now about wanting to kill?"

Desh didn't look at them. "Those aren't important questions!"

I cleared my throat. "I'm not a farmer. I was a fisherman."

Desh shoved his face in mine. "You hush! Just stand there and watch these people. They're more than objects on which to dirty up your sword. Stand there and watch until I come back!" Desh stomped away toward the town elders. Pil grinned at me and swaggered over to begin loading her horse.

I felt as if I had fallen through the dirt into a big, dark hole. I looked at Stan, and I'm sure my eyes were enormous. "This isn't like Desh."

"It's sure as hell like him today, isn't it?" Stan said around the bit of dried meat he was chewing. "Poor Desh watched you kill his pap one day and the next day finds out his mam is crueler than a king's torturer. When I think on it, I believe he's treating you pretty damn gentle. Lord Bib."

"What do you think I should do?" I was so stupefied I was asking Stan for advice.

"Don't ask what I think! I'm just a broke traveler, not much above digging in the gutter for a bent coin." He rubbed his hands together. "But since you do ask, if I was you, I'd go right back to watching these skinny turds like Desh told you." He jogged over to join Pil.

I didn't concentrate on the villagers, but I sort of allowed myself to notice them. No matter what Desh said, I had no more in common with them than I had with a flounder. They'd be killed, and that was sad, but really these people were already dead, never mind that they still walked around, ate their meager food, and gossiped like fiends.

Desh came back in a few minutes, and I concentrated. I didn't wish to aggravate him further. He murmured, "Maybe they'll all die."

"No maybe, it's certain."

"What do you think about that?"

"Well, I think it's a shame, but we can't prevent it. They'll be wiped out like thousands of other frontier people."

"So, you don't care." It sounded like a fact when he said it.

Although I wanted to lie, I said, "Not too much, I guess."

Desh smiled. "Then why, not an hour ago, did Pil have such a hard time convincing you to leave? She just about hit you on the head and tied you up. Hell, she threatened you with my mother!"

I shouldn't have been surprised about anything Desh knew. "That's not true!"

Desh stared at me.

"Even if it were true, I don't care!"

He looked at me as if I had said something a four-year-old would find stupid. "Do you think these people are pathetic?"

"That would be rude to say out loud."

"More pathetic than you in that pitch-dark hole, squatting with no hands for a year?"

I glared at him. "You're trying to manipulate me again, like you did with my daughter."

"That doesn't mean I'm wrong, does it?"

I stepped back so I'd have plenty of room to tell him to kiss his mother's ass.

Desh cut me off. "So, you're staying with me then." He smiled and slapped my shoulder. "Good! You may die, but you'll feel better about things."

"I didn't say that!"

Desh leaned toward me and murmured, "Bib, why are you so eager to run? Is helping these people so foolish?"

"Of course it is!" That sounded more confident in my head than it did when spoken.

"Bib, I have seen you do a dozen things more foolish than this, and none was intended to save a single person. Why won't you try to save some now?"

I clenched my teeth. "It doesn't sound like something I'd do."

Desh laughed as if I had told a joke. "It does now! Thank you, Bib, I'm happy you're staying. Now you're in charge." He sprinted toward his horse.

"Wait!" I shouted.

Desh mounted and galloped away. I watched him like a confused, elderly donkey. I had forgotten that Desh was the only sorcerer who had ever bargained the gods into a reasonable deal.

Stan trotted over to join me. "Damn, what did you say to make Desh desert so fast? At least now there's no call to stay here to get cut up and tortured to death, eh?"

Pil squinted at me. "Is Desh all right? Are you all right? Are you ready to leave?"

"I'm staying to help." I felt embarrassed to admit that to her. For a second, I wondered whether Desh had used sorcery to make me stay. I shook my head at Pil. "Not everybody has to get killed."

Her jaw clamped shut.

"Desh put me in charge," I said, as if that meant something.

Pil stared as if the next time I opened my mouth a snake would fly out.

"I can't just let them die. I guess."

Pil turned without speaking and walked toward her horse. Stan followed her.

I called out, "I invite you both to stay and share in our complete lack of glory!"

Pil mounted and cantered her horse away without looking back. Stan glanced over his shoulder once to wave.

I wondered where Desh had gone and why. Within a minute, part of me began to fear he had left me behind to face the Hill People without him. That sort of harsh behavior wouldn't be typical of him, but only one day had passed since I killed his father.

Whether Desh was returning or not, I had sort of agreed to move these people along. That meant dealing with Desh's ma right off.

I examined Tira's crumbly mud brick house. If I treated the bitter old viper politely, maybe she could be persuaded to assist me, or at least not oppose me. Or maybe she would smack my foot too. I swaggered up to her hut and called, "Hello!"

"Who the gritty hell is that?" Tira blared.

"It's the lazy man with the raggedy-ass beard. Can I come in?"

"You can if your damn legs work."

I bit my tongue against a mean reply and walked inside. As soon as I passed the doorway, somebody strong punched me in the jaw. I bit off the tip of my tongue and staggered to my left. Somebody else punched me in the ribs from that side. I threw myself backward, but a third man grabbed my shirt front and dragged me deeper into the dim building.

A glance showed me three young men, all bigger than me. Tira stood in the corner with her stick and a big smile.

A table-high stack of mud bricks stood to my right along with two stools made of sticks and goat hide. Some sort of pallet lay in the corner on the dirt floor. Those were all the furnishings I had time to appreciate, since the man who was dragging me shifted his grip from my shirt to my head, probably aiming to slam my skull against the brick table.

I spun around to shake him loose and shoved my shoulder into his ribs. Then I thrust my arm straight underneath one of his and threw him backward over my leg. I hoped he'd fly headfirst into the wall, but he hit the dirt like a sack of meal instead.

The other two fellows each grabbed one of my wrists. They were stout boys, and they pulled my arms tight. Really, they were pulling against each other like heaving on opposite ends of a rope, although I doubted they knew that.

I twisted, letting the left-hand brute's strength pull the other man off-balance. That man leaned back to catch himself. I writhed like a fish the other way, letting him pull the first man off-balance too.

Then neither of those strong, cruel farm boys was standing firm, and they had no hope. I twisted free and crushed one's windpipe with my fist. I kicked the other one on the shin, hauled him over, and broke his neck on the corner of the brick table. The third fellow had just reached his feet, and Tira leaped between us, her leg entirely uncrippled.

The boy with the crushed throat was wheezing and flopping on the ground. Ten seconds earlier, he hadn't expected to be dead soon. They had tried to murder me and had probably slain others, so killing them seemed right. Desh might not say so since they were his neighbors. Well, he didn't have three muscular farmers beating on him.

Tira shouted, "Stop, you dripping bastard! Don't you touch this one!" She swung her stick at my head, but I dodged it. The surviving thug pressed himself against the wall behind her, slack-faced and staring at the boy whose neck I'd broken.

I almost cursed Tira with such profound hatred it would give her nightmares until she died. But when I opened my mouth, blood dribbled out. My first word was no more articulate than a magpie's, and my tongue hurt like hell. I pointed at her and shouted, "Say here! Bih!"

I stomped outside, looking around for Desh. Instead, I saw that Pil and Stan had returned. I hollered, "Pil!" Fine droplets of blood shot out of my mouth.

Pil and Stan ran to me. "Krak's bile, what happened?" Pil asked, wincing. She reached out toward my face but hesitated.

"Ambush. Bih my 'ongue." I pointed at my mouth.

"Really?" Stan sniggered but pushed it down. "You sure you didn't chew on a wine glass, or try to eat a weasel?" He turned away, chuckling.

I grabbed Stan's arm and pulled him around. Nodding toward the house, I said, "Keep her ih here." I drew my sword. Stan glanced at it, nodded, and drew his sword too. Then he watched the door as if wolves might run out.

Pil walked with me back toward the horses. "He only laughed because it's funny."

"'Oesn't feew fuhey. Why 'id you come back here?"

Pil gazed around the frantic village. "Oh, I decided we may not die—we may just be horribly crippled instead."

"Wha'?"

She leaned toward me. "Mainly, I concluded it would be useful for you to owe me a favor."

That worried me. I trusted Pil as much as I trusted any sorcerer, which was not much—unless I could see them and what they were doing. Besides, Pil had betrayed me in the past, although under duress.

Spitting blood on the dirt, I said, "Why not 'esh? He shoul' owe you a favor."

"I don't want a favor from Desh. I want it from you." She gave me an honest, even gaze that made me suspicious as hell.

"I 'on't jus' 'row favors around 'ike f'ower pe'als," I said. She looked confused, so I made motions like I was tossing flower petals in all directions.

Pil nodded. "Fine, when I call in the favor, if you think it's too much, you can just not do it."

It was the most reasonable thing I had heard in weeks, which meant I must be missing some important hazard. Still, I wanted Pil to stand with us in this dumber-than-dog-shit rescue. If she helped me survive, she deserved a favor. If we all died, it wouldn't matter.

I nodded.

"Good!" Pil lowered her voice. "You know this is crazy."

I nodded.

"But you want to do it."

I nodded again.

"Are you crazy?"

I might have laughed, but her face was dead serious. "I 'on't 'ink so." I shrugged.

Pil sighed. "Well, you'd better take care of your mouth, unless you think you'll enjoy us laughing every time you say something."

I opened my mouth to be mean to her, but a little more blood trickled out. I closed it and hung my head.

Somebody shrieked from deeper in the village. Within a couple of seconds, at least six more people began screaming and yelling. Pil and I ran toward the sounds, but we stopped partway there.

Blood was oozing up out of the dry earth, welling out of cracks in the ground. We stared at it for a few seconds as howls rose from all over the village.

I couldn't pronounce any of the oaths I wanted to say, so I whistled in amazement.

"This should terrify the holy pee out of them," Pil said. "I feel a little shaky about it myself."

In three places near us, blood began spurting out of the ground like gory little fountains.

"'Esh?" I asked.

Pil nodded. "I sure hope it's Desh doing this."

SEVEN

A geyser of blood shot five feet out of the ground in front of Pil, splashing her from the waist down before she jumped back. Screams still clashed all over the village. Some people scrambled to hide while the rest charged around in the lanes. A young woman running with two small girls nearly bounced off me. She gaped at my bloody face, stared at the gory ground, and ran straight back the way she came.

"Wait," Pil said.

"For what? For it 'oo get worse?" I wiggled my tongue, but the bit-off part still hurt like fire.

"Something's wrong." She squatted.

"Really?" I raised my eyebrows at the blood gushing around us. "Happens every Sa'ur'ay where I come from."

Pil sniffed drops of blood on her hand. She touched her tongue to one, screwed up her face, and spit on the ground. "It's not blood, although it looks like blood, but it smells wrong and tastes like sucking on a rusty nail dipped in vinegar and grease."

I didn't understand how I could have mistaken anything else for blood, but I had. Once Pil pointed it out, the difference in smell was obvious. "I guess it's magic."

Pil raised an eyebrow and shook her head like I was the dumbest guppy in the pond.

"Let 'em believe it's blood so 'ey will run away!" I rubbed my mouth.

Pil stared at me for a second. "Let them believe it's blood so they'll run?"

I nodded.

"Fine, I'll grab Stan. We'll ride around the village gathering them up and moving them north."

Pil and I ran to Tira's house. There Stan said, "I had to knock 'em down and boot 'em back inside a couple of times, but they're in there."

Poking my head through the door, I saw Tira and the trembling thug sitting on the two stools. She sneered. "You look like a fool with blood all over your chin."

"Come with me."

I left the hut, but Tira didn't follow me. She shouted, "We're coming out, you touchy, gap-tooth twat! Don't hit us again!"

Stan shouted, "Come ahead then, you nasty old rat!"

Tira followed me outside and squinted at the ground.

"Everybody's f'eeing," I said. "I mean, leaving."

"I wonder why?" Tira sneered, but her hands were shaking.

"Help me ga'er up everybo'y an' run, or you'll all 'ie."

"Liar." She curled her lip. "Choke on sand, you mealy twit. You called some demon to do this to our poor village."

I looked down for a second. "'amn right it's a 'emon! How 'o you 'ink 'is kind of shit happe's? But I'll save your vi'age because you're so sweet."

The woman ignored my insincere compliment. Her eyes flicked side to side.

Yoadie, the elder, trotted up to us with a heavy sword over his shoulder. He was well splashed with false blood, and his fringe of white hair dripped red as he glared at Tira. "We can't sit around in all this gore. We're running past the fields, Tira, so stop farting around."

"Go ahead, run and piss yourself on the way!" Tira shouted.

Yoadie bellowed, "You want to stay? You can stay—I'll just take your head with me!"

"Oh, is that what happened to your wife? Maybe we'll find her if we dig a few holes." Tira raised her chin.

"E'ough!" I barked. "Anybo'y who isn' coming will be sacrificed 'oo 'e blood 'emon."

They both stared at me. Yoadie asked, "Sacrificed to the blood demon?"

I pointed at Tira and then Yoadie. "Move your people 'at way!" I nodded to the north.

Yoadie glanced that direction, pulled back his shoulders, and trotted off. Tira bustled over to some indecisive farmers and commenced giving terse, profane orders loudly enough to make any scarred-up old sergeant smile.

I walked back to the edge of the village to keep watch for Hill People. I saw none, but soon Desh rode back from the scrub plain at a fantastic gallop. He gazed around at the red mess and grinned. "Better than I hoped. What did you do to your chin?"

I waved that away. I pointed north, past the center of town. "We're moving everybo'y 'at way."

"What did you say?"

I opened my mouth to say it again, saw his smirk, and gave him three foul gestures instead.

"I'll ride up and check the status of this goat migration you're leading," Desh said. "I'd be surprised if they don't bring along every goat in the village."

"Goo'. I'll wait here for 'e Hill People."

"Bib . . . don't fight them by yourself."

I laughed at him. "I'll come war' you whe' I see 'em." I patted my horse on the neck.

Desh nodded and rode to gather up his people on the north side of town.

I healed my tongue and teeth. If Desh really wanted me to lead, I expected to tell the farmers some unpleasant things soon, and I wanted them to understand exactly how bad it would be.

I examined the southern horizon but saw nobody coming to kill us. I watered my horse and tied her up where she'd be handy beside one of the houses. Then I climbed atop that house for a better vantage and settled in to keep watch for Hill People.

After a few moments' consideration, I pulled a white band of power and whipped it around a good part of the village. If I fed a bit of power into it now and then, I could keep it simmering. I might need help in a hurry, so shaking up the village ahead of time seemed wise.

Just as I was coming to appreciate how hard and hot those sun-cooked bricks were, Dimore's voice came from behind me. "You choose to do this rather than kill for me? I have endured profound boredom, even stunning boredom, but I have never sat on an uncomfortable place to watch nothing. Come, mount your animal and take up my task once more."

I didn't turn to look at him. "Shh. I'm thinking philosophy. You wouldn't understand."

"Why not?" He didn't sound as if he cared much.

"You're immortal. Philosophy only makes sense to people who are going to die."

"That's a narrow view. Never mind, I'm done with you."

I stood and looked down at him from the rooftop. "So, I can forget about this murder?"

He raised an eyebrow. "You had best not. You must keep your word, on pain of mass slaughter. I just find you too annoying to deal with."

I chuckled. "I know several dozen women who would agree with you."

"Oh, stop attempting to be humorous. I am not one of your young sorcerer hangers-on who will laugh at your ribald humor."

"I'm not being humorous," I said with a straight face. "One of those women stabbed me."

Dimore frowned. "You are one of the most tiresome creatures I have ever met, and I've existed for many thousands of years. I have decided to give you to someone else. Someone who has nothing important to do." Dimore made a vague gesture to his right.

A three-foot-wide hole opened in the earth, and a man crawled out of it. He was a tall, rangy fellow. His face showed the narrowness and hooked nose of a hawk, and his shoulder-length hair was black to the point of appearing blue. He wore a superb green silk coat and black trousers, carried a walking stick, and could have been anywhere between thirty and fifty years old.

Of course, since he was a Void Walker, his physical appearance meant nothing. He could just as well have shown up as a baboon, or a talking nail.

I clucked my tongue. "That was downright inelegant. Dimore, it's entertaining when you arrive or blow away like dirt, but even a damn frog can crawl out of a hole."

The new Void Walker didn't smile, but his eyes twinkled as he gave me a small nod.

"Dimore has a toady, eh?" I said. "Hell, I need to think up some blistering new insults for you."

The creature's eyes kept twinkling.

Dimore turned to him and said, "Gek, this is the one I told you about. You might not want to destroy him right away, but you must use your own judgment. In any event, I don't want to hear anything more about him." Dimore began blowing away like sand, and soon he was gone.

I said, "Krak! I'm glad he finally left. Do you want to throw dice? I guess you have everything you could possibly want and could cheat me besides. But if you roll fair, I may end up owning whatever realm you knock around in."

"Bib, I won't claim that you cannot anger me. Certainly, you can, so let us set aside threats and jibes." Gek spoke in a deep, deliberate voice, as if he thought about every word before he said it. "You will perform one killing for me, and I do not wish you to delay. However, I know that living is a wickedly complex thing to endure. Possibly you have obligations other than murder. I can exercise patience up to a point."

"Why, Gek, you seem to have philosophical pretentions."

Gek tapped the end of his walking stick on the dirt. "Oh, no. I revile philosophy. It is for beings who pretend to know things. Philosophy shrivels in the face of true knowledge."

"Spoken like a pissant fourteen-year-old who thinks he's discovered the truths of the world."

This time, Gek smiled before turning to limp away. I was surprised that his walking stick wasn't just a stylish affectation. "If you wish, I could also say that you cannot step in the same river twice. Or that reality is a collision of miracles. Or that everything happens for a reason."

"Harik's squeaking ass! If you keep that up, I may murder myself."

Gek didn't look back. "Watch out."

I stared at the Void Walker for a second before spinning around to look south. Five Hill People were running toward me, close enough for me to see their faces. One had already thrown a spear at me. I scrambled backward, and the spearhead gouged the side of my calf.

Falling flat on the roof, I rolled off the edge toward my horse. I landed on my feet and was on horseback within a few seconds. As I galloped north past Gek, I yelled, "What's the reason for this happening?"

Gek called after me, "You let people talk you into things."

EIGHT

When I fight more than one person at a time, the first thing I do is hope they are poorly trained, or at least drunk. Then they'll have no idea what their friends might do next. In fact, they're more likely to be surprised by their comrades' antics than by mine, since they're watching me pretty damn hard. Their friends may wound or kill them before I get around to it.

All that is true up to a certain number of enemies. At some point, they will drag you down and break all your bones, even if they're just raw boys. Being outnumbered is always perilous.

A Hill Person is deadlier than an untrained drunkard in the same way a panther is deadlier than a grumpy chipmunk. And five of the bastards were chasing me as I galloped my horse through the village. I believed I could kill almost any Hill Person in single combat, but my belief would not actually kill a single one of them. If I fought them often enough, some quick Hill Person would eventually kill me and carry my head home to his or her sweetheart.

I had no call to believe that Hill People really did bring their enemies' heads home to their loved ones. It would seem an unwieldy practice. But my entire body of reliable Hill People lore could be written on two sides of a sheet of parchment. The sheet needn't be too big, either.

As I wove through the mud brick hovels, I lost sight of the pursuit, but the scouts couldn't be more than a minute behind. When I reached the edge of the village, I jumped down and slapped my horse on the rump. The creature obliged me by running north as if chased by starving, bitter wolves. I hoped to retrieve her later, should I be in any condition to ride.

I pulled another white band to cover the village and the chunk of plains beside it while I drew my sword with the other hand. Then I concealed myself by pressing my back against the wall of the closest building so that I gazed out at the plains and my running horse.

The Hill People ran with soft steps, but even so, I heard them before they rushed out from between the houses. I intended to assault them from behind when they chased my horse right past me. With the help of such surprise, I might kill one or even two before they knew I was there.

I pulled another band, threw it out in a big circle, and squeezed.

The scouts loped out from between the houses, two on my left and three to my right. I fell in behind the fighters to my left, closed with one, and thrust.

Maybe she heard me or saw my shadow, because she twitched, writhed, and spun around inside her skin. People may say that is impossible, but I swear that's how she ended up with a mere gash across her ribs instead of a transfixed liver.

When this Hill Woman spun, she also kicked me in the stomach. She likely would have stabbed me too if her spear hadn't been pointing the wrong way. I jumped back to absorb the blow. On the way, I tripped over a scraggly bush so gray and wilted it might have been damned by every god, and I fell on my butt.

I thought, *Sure, I'm a killer. Behold me and tremble.* I ignored those words and squeezed the bands of magical energy again.

All five scouts exclaimed and ran toward me. I didn't understand their words, but their smiles made their feelings clear. Before the closest one could pin me to the ground like I was a bit of parchment blowing away, their happy chatter switched to surprise. Then they cried out and hooted while every nearby creature that possessed a stinger arrived and stung them.

Jumping to my feet, I smiled at the Hill Woman who had kicked me. I considered a sarcastic comment, but that was just inviting her to find a tricky way to kill me. I stabbed her right in the heart. The man near her was on his knees grabbing at his throat, so I sliced through the back of his neck. He collapsed like a pile of rotten plums.

The remaining three men did not run off as I had hoped they would. Their shouts were pained but also infuriated. I could see bugs crawling on them, stinging as they went. Although the three men were suffering, they charged me.

I ran toward the house so they couldn't surround me. I guess they expected that because one of them, stocky but fast, sprinted to cut me off. The other two distracted me with their spears. I almost retreated to avoid being trapped, and that would have been smart. Instead of being smart, I guided a jabbing spear past me, so close it grazed my cheek, while I lunged and thrust toward its owner's chest.

The Hill Man dodged and nearly escaped my attack, almost too fast to believe he was human. I pierced him, but he wasn't dead and maybe wasn't even dying. He did hesitate for an instant to steady himself.

I turned my back on both him and the fellow beside him to run toward the chunky man near the wall. My swing broke his spear and went on to cut him deeply through the thigh. He fell, and I kicked him in the face while at the same time glancing behind me to parry a spear.

I realized I had descended into ridiculous, even desperate maneuvers. I didn't feel desperate. I felt as calm as if I were shaving, not ramming steel through strangers.

The two standing Hill Men retreated a step. One of them, a man with apelike arms, guarded his wounded friend. I should have taken a moment to plan. Instead, I feinted toward the injured man, then twisted and sliced his friend, Ape Arms, from shoulder to elbow. Ape Arms staggered while his hurt friend swung his spear in a near-perfect arc. If fairness meant anything in this world, he would have killed me. I leaned back so far that I nearly fell again. The spearhead whipped past my nose. I recovered and stabbed the man with more precision this time, and he fell backward.

Ape Arms shifted his spear and swung at me with a one-handed grip. I knelt almost into a ball to duck it. An untrained boy wouldn't have behaved so foolishly. But as I raised my head, I thrust my blade up through the man's jaw into his skull. Ape Arms dropped and lay twitching. His friend was crawling away from me, leaving a wide trail of real blood on the reddish-yellow dirt.

Over many years and many fights, I had come to cherish making smart choices in combat. In the past minute, I had made five foolish choices that would have been fatal had I hesitated an instant.

This shit could not be allowed to continue.

I had one more scout to deal with, the thick man who had flanked me. He tried to stand on his wounded leg, almost collapsed, and leaned back against the brick wall. Looking around, he spotted the sharp end of his broken spear far out of reach. He sucked air and gritted his teeth. Then he waited, glaring at me past a hornet stinging his eyebrow.

As I walked toward the Hill Man to thrust my blade into his heart, he pulled a big iron ladle off his belt and tossed it at my feet. I glanced at the ladle and then the man. He nodded once as if he had done something of great importance.

I lifted my foot to jump past the iron utensil, but I hesitated. It might be a magical ladle, although I had never heard of such a thing. It might turn into a serpent or grow into a giant bush with steel thorns. Maybe it would just lay there and rust until the end of the world, but I knew more about tea parties than about Hill People sorcery.

A scorpion crawled onto the man's trousers, and he swatted it off. His face was already pocked with welts, and tears were running down his cheeks. He said something in his language and shooed at me with one hand. Or maybe he was shooing the insects, or maybe the ladle.

The stocky fellow leaned to stand on one leg, still without a weapon. He shouted at me, then at the ladle, then at me again, his deep brown face getting darker every second. He must have hated both me and the ladle a lot.

The scout's leg collapsed, and he fell. Sighing, he reached into a pouch for a nice slip of parchment and a sleek pencil. He wrote for ten seconds, looked around, and stared at me as he pointed at a fist-size rock out of reach. The man patted the ground and lay his fist on top of his flat hand.

I believed I understood what the Hill Man wanted. I tossed him the rock. He lay the rock on the paper before smiling at me. Then he pushed himself up and staggered toward me with the rock raised in his hand.

The Hill Man had caught me thinking foolish notions, and if he had been more agile, he would have smashed out my brains. I jumped back, and the rock scraped a swathe of skin off my cheek. The man stumbled to his knees, and I killed him there.

As the Hill Man lay dead at my feet, I said to him, "What was the point of the damn ladle?"

I loped out of town toward the farmers. On the way, I whistled and called out for my horse, but he seemed to have gotten lost or been carried away by little birds. I never did find the brute.

I heard the farmers before I saw them. The mass of villagers hadn't walked even a mile. Screams carried across the open scrub land, and I ran as fast as I dared. If I needed to fight when I got there, I didn't want to be panting and trembling.

By the time I reached the farmers, the screams had settled into shouts and insults. Three gangs of villagers exchanged threats, shoved each other, and hurled dirt clods. Two bodies lay on the ground, one in an impressive pool of blood. Pil and Desh had planted themselves in the middle of all those sweat-nasty idiots, yelling at everyone to shut up and flinching when dirt clods smacked them.

Stan, who was guarding the horses, yelled to me, "They went mad! All this ganking hoo-ha over a sack of water! Or maybe somebody's new dress. It ain't clear. I don't claim to know what crazy people fight about!"

Tira shouted at Yoadie, who was in a different group. I gathered from the howls that the third group had been led by the dead man now sprawled in a small lake of his own blood. The shouting and abuse faded as people spotted me. By the time I reached Pil, the people had fallen to pointing and muttering, like a boiling stew of sweat and superstition.

I said, "Pil, I've come to save you from these raw dogs." I didn't lower my voice when I said it.

Pil nodded at me as she wiped blood off her neck. "Thank you, Bib. Desh is about to ride away and leave me with this mess so he can save more people. Don't you think he's just a damn saint? We have to get these foolish villagers calmed down and organized, and we may have to kill a few, which I thought you might enjoy."

"To hell with it," I said. "I barely survived. The Hill People are tricky and have utensils."

"What?" Pil asked.

"Nothing. Desh, look at how your people behaved, killing one another and making noise." I pointed around us. "I don't think I'd pull a thorn out of my ass for these people."

Desh motioned me to the side. "Are you upset about something?"

I shook my head. "Just complaining. Why are the farmers killing each other?"

"Some want to run, some want to go home, and some want to sit here and cry."

I muttered, "They have to run. They're slow, but if they're moving, we might save a few."

"Bib, would you tell them what they must do?"

"I planned on it," I whispered. "Wait, why do you want me to explain things?" I was acknowledged to be an uninspiring leader.

"They'll hate you and like me better when I take over."

"Well, your logic is pure," I told Desh. Then I turned to the villagers and raised my voice. "Whatever you're fighting about, stop it! Your home is cursed. Demons from the underworld spit blood on

---

it, which is nothing compared to the demons coming from the south. They'll cut you apart like chickens."

The crowd babbled, so I raised my hands to quiet them. "That's bad luck for you, but you have a bit of good luck too. We're here to help you escape the dismemberment and slaughter. We will escort you to the Empire, where these demons can't get to you."

"All the way to the Empire?" Desh murmured.

"Where else?" I whispered. "My aunt Luci's sitting room?"

A tall, young man shouted, "Why would you want to help us?"

I pointed at him. "You don't get to come along."

The young man opened his mouth and closed it twice.

I shouted, "I don't plan to debate this until we have demons crawling up our backsides. Who apart from this idiot wants to stay here and get murdered? Speak up if you do."

I heard some shuffling and murmuring, but nobody answered.

"All right, follow me!" After I led off at a casual walk, I leaned toward Pil and muttered, "In a bit, do you mind telling that tall loudmouth that he can come along if he promises not to be a pain in my ass?"

Pil said, "I don't care if he stays and gets burned alive, because he's not our biggest problem."

I knew just what she was saying. These farmers were traveling only as fast as the oldest, slowest farmer could drag his bones along, and the Hill People could outpace them at an easy trot. "I'll hang back and scout, maybe kill a few who are following us. Pil, do you mind my leaving these folks with you and Desh? He's taking over as leader."

"For a while," Desh said. "There are four more villages between here and the border of the Empire. I plan to warn every one of them before you get there. It won't take me long."

I lowered my eyebrows at Desh. "That's a lot of miles."

Pil murmured, "A magic saddle helps out with that. It makes a horse amazingly fast."

Desh scowled at her.

"Don't make that face!" Pil said. "If I can know, Bib can know."

I considered Desh and his journey for a moment. "How many

people are in all these villages? Five or six hundred? We can't protect that many."

Desh snorted. "We can't protect the eighty we have now. But if I can warn those other villages right away, they really might outrun the Hill People. I'll return before dark."

I stared at the sky. It was midafternoon.

"Magic saddle," Pil whispered. "I wish I had one."

Desh said, "I'll return before dark, I promise. I won't leave quite yet, though."

Pil frowned. "That just leaves Bib, Stan, and me to fight any Hill People who catch us, so we'll probably all be killed. This whole adventure was your idea, Desh, and I was counting on you to fight."

With a straight face, Desh said, "Leave my mother behind to face them. Either they'll stop three days to torture her to death, or they'll cut their throats to get away from her."

Pil grunted. "Bib, take my horse, because if you're scouting, you may need to move fast."

"Thank you," I said. "Desh, before you go . . . that was nice how you made all that stuff-that's-not-blood come out of the ground." I paused, not quite asking the question.

Desh grinned. "How did I do it? I know somebody who can do unbelievable things with water. If we live, I'll tell you about it."

Tira and Yoadie were leading the villagers, each edging and angling to get in front of the other. As I passed the farmers, Desh called out, "I'll be leading you now! Bib will guard the rear, so he'll probably be killed!"

I thought the farmers perked up a little.

As I rode south, I spotted the loud young man who had questioned me. He was skulking and doing a good job of not looking nearly so tall. I shouted, "Hey! You can come with us after all, but you have to be nice. Killing you would be easy. In fact, it would be relaxing—better than a nap."

I knew that was poor leadership on my part, but I didn't care. With luck, the Hill People would come in batches small enough for me to kill.

NINE

The Sandypool villagers started a loud argument before I rode three minutes away from them. They hadn't begun walking for their lives yet, either. I would rather have faced the Hill People than dealt with villager bullshit, but I found it disheartening that the farmers weren't doing a damn thing to save themselves.

I considered abandoning them. I normally held no prejudice against fleeing a bad situation, but I couldn't quite convince myself to run away. I wondered again whether Desh had done something to me.

I galloped Pil's gelding back through the village and on south. A couple of miles farther on, I spotted twenty-three more Hill People running abreast. Or maybe each fighter was hiding ten more behind him single file. It hardly mattered. We couldn't keep twenty-three Hill People from slaughtering every villager. The farmers couldn't be killed any deader by 253.

I didn't have much magical power available, which was a disadvantage. I hated to trade for more by calling on Harik or any of the other smug, pissy gods. In fact, it would be a ridiculous thing to do since they wanted me dead.

To my left, the Void Walker, Gek, stepped out of a hole that appeared in the dirt and then filled in. He gazed up at me, tapping his walking stick against his boot, but somehow I felt as if he was towering high above me. "Sorcerer, it is time to undertake my task. You haven't accomplished anything here, with one exception—your companions will probably die now. If you had withdrawn, they would all have followed you and lived. Fantastic job. Well done."

"I'm not quitting." I looked down to brush dirt off my knee because I had been thinking quite seriously about quitting. I squinted at the Void Walker, but his face was blank except for bright eyes. "I'll decide when to quit." Still no expression. "I'll damn well make sure those ignorant people live. I admit the world won't be much better if they do, but that's my decision." I hitched my sword belt to show I was serious.

"That is inconvenient." Gek limped away a few steps. "I suppose I could assist you."

I held my breath. When a possibly immortal being from another realm offers to help, that's a perilous moment.

"I could transform all the Hill People into . . . something." Gek shrugged.

"What do you mean by 'all the Hill People'?"

"All of the Hill People in the world. Yes, I believe turning each of them into a two-masted ship would be artistically satisfying."

Pil's horse stamped, kicked, and shied away from Gek. I felt the same way.

Gek asked, "Do you propose something different?"

I cleared my throat. "It seems extravagant to kill every one of them."

"I assure you, whether I transform one of them or all, no additional effort will be involved. Come, you're a famous killer within your slice of this realm. I offer an opportunity to kill as if you are fully committed to it." He sounded as if he were offering me a second biscuit.

"Well . . . could you just kill the ones coming to destroy the Empire?"

"Of course. In exchange, you will be my servant for thirteen months."

I snorted. "You mean your slave."

"Slave, servant, the difference is far less noticeable than most pretend." Gek lowered his voice. "Do you accept?"

"Why thirteen months instead of a year?"

Gek frowned. "How disappointing. A year has twelve months, which is a terribly unfortunate number. Do you want to fall into a crevasse or be eaten by crocodiles while in my service? Come, what is your answer? You won't get a better bargain from Harik or any of the other gods."

"Why—"

"Enough! Answer me."

"Understand that I don't mean to disparage a being of your shocking omnipotence," I said. "I just can't abide taking orders, especially from somebody I'm barely acquainted with. So, no."

Gek flashed a smile just long enough for me to be sure it happened. "Very well, but you still owe me a murder. I shall ensure that you are able to deliver it, even if my methods cause you dismay. I predict you will regret not becoming my servant."

The Void Walker scribed a circle on the ground with his stick, and the dirt inside it collapsed as if a cavern were underneath us. He stepped into the hole and climbed down out of sight. When I rode close and looked inside, dirt boiled up to fill the hole. The weeds, bushes, and one horrified lizard returned as if the hole had never appeared.

I galloped toward the villagers and hoped Pil had gotten them moving. It would make no difference at all when the Hill People arrived, but standing around arguing felt unproductive. I let my mind drift as I rode, hoping it would bump into a clever idea that didn't involve calling on that son of a bitch Harik.

When a sorcerer bargains with gods, he had better know what he wants. The gods are pleased to take what the sorcerer holds most precious and give something useless, or even harmful, in return. No idea of fairness exists between gods and men.

Any number of things could save us from the Hill People. In such a complicated world, that had to be true. But I didn't know what those things were, how to ask for them, or what to do with one if the gods were reckless enough to trade it to me.

So, calling on the gods was the stupidest thing I could do.

By the time I neared the villagers, I had not yet thought of any less-stupid things to try. The Hill People would soon be closing with us at their mile-devouring trot. I could probably escape if I wanted, but they wouldn't let Desh's people escape.

So, I did the stupidest thing I could think of. I lifted my spirit out of my body and called, "Mighty Harik, I come to trade!"

Harik, God of Death, he who owned me, did not choose to answer.

I called on Fingit, Smith of the Gods, who didn't mind joking with me on occasion. When that didn't work, I called Gorlana, Goddess of Mercy, who had owned me when I was young. She did not acknowledge me, nor did Chira, Goddess of Forests, who was a bitch but sometimes pretended to be benevolent.

Several of the other gods considered me something to wipe off their sandal, if they thought about me at all. I called them anyway, and each one ignored me. Sakaj, Goddess of the Unknowable, had several reasons to despise me, and she was crazy as hell. She didn't answer me, either.

Of all the gods, Lutigan, God of War, reviled me most. Several times he trapped me in miserable situations likely to cause me harm. Sometimes I only escaped because Harik was grabby about his possessions.

I called out to Lutigan anyway, and I got silence.

The only god I hadn't called was Krak, Father of the Gods. He hated everybody. Sorcerers didn't call Krak because he was touchy, brutal, and for any practical purpose, all-powerful. Unless facing death within seconds, calling Krak was like opening a jar by dropping a granite block on it.

I shuddered and didn't call Krak. At least not yet.

I halted beyond shouting distance of the villagers. Pil was staring at me. I might reconsider Gek's offer to help and become his servant, but the idea sickened me.

Something seized my spirit and dragged it up through my head as if it were made of stretchy resin. Nausea clenched me, but just for a moment. Then I stood in the trading place, where the gods break sorcerers, and sorcerers ask them to do it.

In the trading place, the smell of distant smoke pushed up my nose. I opened my eyes, and morning sunlight revealed the bare patch of brown dirt that I damn well knew not to step off. Ahead of me, a field of charred flower stalks ran downhill to the horizon.

I knew that an unpredictable forest stood behind me and to my right, while the massive, white multilevel gazebo loomed someplace to my left. I didn't dare shift my gaze. I was supposed to be blind and didn't want any gods to notice my gawking at things.

"Your pathetic pleading oozes desperation, Murderer," said Harik. He sounded like a fine orator who could only talk about bookkeeping. "What do you require so urgently? And don't be a slug about it—I'm off to a hunt when I'm done with you."

I turned away from the gazebo, eyes blank. "Hunting fluffy unicorn ponies again?"

"No, leviathan of the Void. Speak! I allow you ten seconds."

"Harik, you hole from which all repugnance flows, I intend to accomplish a magical feat that's never been done. I doubt that you can help me, but my sense of thoroughness demands that I confirm that before I accept my other patron."

Harik paused. I could almost hear curiosity, jealousy, and pettiness fighting inside his head. "No one may trade with you unless they do so through me!"

"I don't need to trade for power outright, Your Magnificence. I need expertise. She told me that—"

"She? Who?" Harik snapped.

I heard Lutigan whisper in a tone that sorcerers normally couldn't hear. "Harik, you dense pile of guts! He's manipulating you!"

"But Sakaj . . ." Harik whispered.

"Ignore her," Lutigan whispered back.

"That flaming slit . . ." Harik whispered.

Lutigan whispered back, "You're whining like a green-assed human child."

"But she's planning something!"

I heard the thump of a hard thing hitting a soft thing. I couldn't believe how well this was going. While they weren't paying attention, I casually turned toward the gods.

Harik and Lutigan were fighting on top of the gazebo. Harik, in his fine black robe, punched and kicked with godlike might. Lutigan, in his red armor made of the hides of the last fourteen monsters he'd slain, dodged every blow and twice whipped in to tap Harik on the forehead. Then Harik clenched his fist. Lutigan squeaked in a non-warlike way and hurtled off the gazebo to crash at the edge of the bare, dead forest.

Harik made a rude gesture and whispered, "You shouldn't wear armor made from dead things! Lutigan, if you do that again, I'll turn your fourteen hundred soldiers into dust!"

"Go ahead!" Lutigan whispered. "I'll chop your five pallid whores into seventy pieces!"

An even, almost distracted voice from far back in the gazebo whispered, "This is as productive as listening to Father recite the history of the last fifty millennia." Fingit stepped out of the shadows and sat in the middle of the second level, a place usually reserved for Krak. Like Harik, his face was so perfectly handsome it was boring, although his hair was red where Harik's was black. He whispered, "Brother, hear the Murderer out, shut him down, and throw him back."

Harik dropped down to the second level and whispered, "Who made you the Father of All Existence? Move over!"

Fingit shifted aside without arguing.

As Lutigan climbed back into the gazebo, I said, "Mighty Harik, you sore on the lip of creation, is everything all right?"

Harik glared at Lutigan as he said, "Murderer, everything is ideal in the Home of the Gods, except the long, wet stain that is yourself. Tell me what you wish to accomplish. If I do not approve, I will forbid it, and defy me at your peril!"

Fingit nodded, but Lutigan sat forward with his hatchet face staring at the floor, elbows on his knees.

I stared at a spot six feet away from Harik's head. "Defy me at your peril? Isn't that a little overdramatic?"

"Speak!"

"I want to travel a long distance in a hurry, like the river spirits do." I knew from experience that spirits could cross a lot of miles in just a few seconds.

All three gods stared at me. Harik said, "Murderer, that may be the most presumptuous thing I've heard in five thousand years."

"I only want to do it once, if that makes it better."

"That does not make it better," Harik said. "Not one bit."

I added, "Does it help that I want to do this with about eighty-five other people? And some horses? And a few goats?"

Fingit started laughing silently.

Lutigan whispered, "I sure as Krak's tongue didn't expect this."

Fingit sat up straight and whispered, "Wait. Harik, you've lost sight of the Murderer a couple of times lately, right? Why does he want to take this trip? It could be an artifact of—"

Harik waved one hand and whispered, "Merely random fluctuation in the Void. A common occurrence. Who cares why he wants to go anywhere?"

Fingit glared and whispered, "Stop and think!"

Harik whispered, "Go off and play with your hammer, little brother."

"You have the intellect of a humping squirrel!" Fingit whispered.

"Shut up, Fingit!" Lutigan whispered. "With you, it's always artifacts, and vectors, and damn flying chariots."

Fingit ground his teeth and started turning red.

I considered the gods' words. Fingit was a precise thinker. To him, a "couple" would mean exactly two. One thing I had done twice lately was talk to Void Walkers. I tucked that notion away for later.

I said, "Mighty Harik, I intend this to be a superb feat that will reflect your glory."

"Bah," Harik said. "You simply do not care to be destroyed by those ferocious short people. You seek my assistance to escape, but I have no interest in that."

"I could sacrifice—"

"Murderer, you could hang yourself from a bell tower and slit open your own belly, and that would not be enough sacrifice to interest me."

"Just be done with him!" Lutigan whispered.

"You'll regret not listening to me . . ." Fingit whispered.

"Both of you, shut up!" Harik whispered. "I wish I could hang you both from a bell tower."

The gods' brotherly antagonism seemed stronger than usual. "What about some sacrifice involving Desh and Pil? I mean the Nub and the Knife?" Desh and Pil belonged to Fingit and Lutigan, just like I belonged to Harik. For the gods, it was like owning a dog that you don't care much about, but you sure as hell don't want anybody else to pet it.

Harik sat up like a deer hound. "What's that? Nub? Knife?" He showed an ugly grin.

I had been right about Harik wanting to hurt his brothers. Well, I had rarely gone wrong by appealing to a god's petty cruelty.

Fingit and Lutigan were whispering so ferociously that their godly spit might have soaked Harik's sleeves.

Harik ignored them and gazed at me. "How would you sacrifice them?"

"How would you like me to?" I asked. "Please make an offer."

Lutigan grabbed Harik's collar and stood. "Stop this, you degenerate fungus!" he whispered.

Harik waved him away. "Krak placed the responsibility in my hands. I say who kills the Murderer and how. Do you want me to call Krak to discuss it?"

Lutigan and Fingit sat down, squirmed, and hit the bench with their fists as they glared.

Harik stepped down to the gazebo's lowest level. "The most expedient approach would be killing them both." He held up a hand before his brothers could object.

Since I was heading down this path in order to save all our lives, murdering Desh and Pil seemed counterproductive. "Mighty Harik, I have seen a pig carved from a block of butter with more subtlety than you. No, I will tell each of them a thundering great lie that will hurt their understanding of the world." I didn't know what lies I could tell, but I trusted myself to come up with the proper lie for any situation.

"You are postponing my hunt for this mild offer?" Harik said. "Very well, kill the Knife and cripple the Nub—and refuse to heal him."

Fingit turned away. The marble bench cracked where Lutigan's hand was crushing it.

I said, "How about this? When we get to the end of this journey, I'll abandon them."

"Hah! They should be pleased to see the back of you. Leaving would be the same as offering them a present. Cripple them both so they cannot walk, and then do not heal them."

"No, you ripe wad out of your mother's armpit. I offer this: the next time we're fighting someone, I'll abandon them."

Harik gazed at the sky. "Unimaginative. Let me take some memories from each of them. I shall choose which ones to remove."

I sure as hell wouldn't do that. Removing a person's memories could change them in unpredictable ways. Desh and Pil had both lost memories in the past. "Take more memories from them? You've already taken some. Taking more doesn't sound too imaginative to me." I sneered. "You might as well give them back memories."

Fingit and Lutigan surged to their feet.

"Stop right now!" Fingit whispered, springing two steps toward Harik.

Lutigan clenched both fists and whispered, "Ask Krak first! Ask him, or I'll kill you every day for a thousand years!"

Their desperation stunned me, and I wasn't even making an offer. I barely stopped myself from asking why they hated the idea so much. But if they despised the prospect, then it had to be good for Pil and Desh.

Harik glanced at his brothers and then gave me a smile so wide I imagined I could see the back of his throat. Maybe this wouldn't be as good for Pil and Desh as I'd thought. Something about it would be bad.

"I accept your offer," Harik said.

"I didn't make an offer!"

"Did the words come out your mouth?"

"Yes . . ."

"That is offer enough for me." Harik flung up a hand. "It is done! Their memories will be restored upon your return. Now, for my end of the trade. If you wish to travel fast and far, there is a path that you must follow. It will be obvious and will accommodate all of these people and horses and goats you must love. It will carry you far in a short time."

"Where does it go?" I barely choked out the question for fear of saying some other reckless thing.

"You didn't specify destination in your request, did you?" Harik grinned.

I sighed again. The path would be useless.

"Cease moping," Harik said. "I cannot abide it."

"You sure do a lot of it then," Fingit whispered.

Harik ignored him. "Murderer, the path will lead in the direction you want to go."

Lutigan whispered, "That's damn accommodating of you."

Harik whispered, "He's a human. The best way to hurt him is to give him what he asks for."

I asked, "How far will it take us?"

"Don't you think you should have already asked these questions?"

I didn't have an answer because he was right. I had gotten too confident. I had believed I could predict what the gods thought and wanted.

Harik said, "On your journey, pay no attention to the weeping sun or the upside-down trees. Or the fish. They cannot hurt you unless you eat one. I should not eat the fish if I were you."

I felt as if I'd been shoved in a barrel and rolled down a hill. I began drifting away toward my body. Harik yanked me back. "Murderer, we are undertaking a new thing, which I consider celebratory, considering the paucity of new things one finds in eternity. Henceforth, each sorcerer shall pay an additional, well-defined fee on top of any trade."

I paused. "You're charging me tax."

"That's a crass way of putting it, but yes. However, you have enormous flexibility in paying," Harik said.

Lutigan and Fingit were sitting again. Both looked shocked.

Harik said, "With each trade, you shall forego one year of your life. Your natural death will be brought forward by one year."

I held still, although it was difficult. "A year . . ."

"Yes, of your life." Harik smiled.

"Damn you. Damn you to a lifetime of apes shrieking and swinging from your testicles! That's insane!"

"I assure you it is not. This is a fine system from which we will all derive superb benefit. I mentioned flexibility. If you do not wish to part with a year of your life, you needn't. Just take ten years from people near you, or rather I will take them. You may select one year each from ten people, ten years from one person, or anything in between so long as it totals ten. Clever, eh? I devised it myself."

"And you're just doing this to me?"

"Oh, no. We are including every sorcerer in the world! Murderer, I know you are a rebellious type, but do not think to refuse me. If you fail to cooperate, I will take twenty years from you and the people nearby—and I will choose who pays and how much. So, how will you be fulfilling your debt today?"

I searched for a clever idea and realized that my only good idea had been not calling the gods. "Take a year from me, Harik, and may your penis be hammered flat in the forge of the gods until the end of time."

"Done!" Harik looked giddy.

Lutigan whispered, "At least there's a chance the Nub and the Knife will kill him for us."

"Wouldn't that be nice?" Harik whispered before saying, "Goodbye, Murderer!" He flung me into my body like a boulder thrown off a cliff. I collapsed to my knees.

When I stood, I saw Pil trotting toward me. I needed to think of some good lies in a hurry.

TEN

The gods had never taken memories away from me. I didn't think so. Actually, I wouldn't have known if they had, not unless somebody told me.

I had seen memories taken from other people. At first, they felt something was missing, but they didn't know what. After Desh traded away his memories of his mother, I saw him poking around and peering under things as if he had lost a spoon. He looked confused, like he might have done some bad thing by mistake.

Desh's confusion passed within a couple of days. I had never heard him mention his mother again until he beheld the vicious old buzzard and her stink of cruelty.

As for regaining memories, only once had I witnessed that. I purchased my daughter's childhood memories back from the gods for her, hoping to make her happier. The first thing she did was hit me, then she cursed me for a while, and then she hit me some more. I guess I failed, because she traded those memories right back to the gods, and I never saw her happy again.

So, I decided not to bring up the subject of memories with Pil lest she start whacking me. As she was running toward me, I called out, "I found a way to escape!"

"What did you do?" she shouted. "You did something to me! What was it?" She balled up her fist but didn't hit me yet.

I opened my mouth to let a lie fall out, but I met her eyes and couldn't say it. She didn't look angry. She stared at me like a child I had adopted and then started beating. "I'm sorry, Pil. To save all our lives, I got some of your memories restored. If we're still alive in an hour, I'll explain more."

"You bastard! This isn't your mind to screw around with!" She stopped for a breath and stared around.

"I'm sorry, Pil, I really am." I reached out to touch her arm, but she flung my hand off.

In a calmer voice, she asked, "You wouldn't hold me down and force yourself on me, would you?"

Mortified, I said, "Of course I wouldn't!"

"Wrong! You just did!"

I didn't know what to say. I hadn't thought of it like that. "You can make me say I'm sorry a thousand times and break my leg besides if you want, but let's get moving before the Hill People overrun us." I ran away from her toward the ragged clumps of villagers who still weren't moving in any direction. Desh was nowhere in view, and Stan was minding the horses as if they were made of gold. He had strapped three Hill People spears to his saddle.

I glanced back and saw that Pil was following me, not holding any kind of weapon that I could see. Of course, her knife was just about invisible.

Charging into the middle of the farmers, I bellowed as I pointed at Pil, "Follow her and run fast if you want to live!" I waved at Pil to join me. She stalked toward me with a glare that could melt two feet of iron.

I turned to Tira and Yoadie. "I'm not exaggerating. Death is a minute behind us, so get people moving."

Tira scowled and started barking at people while shoving the slow ones. Yoadie hurried from one bumbling villager to the next, pointing them in the proper direction.

I gave Pil direct instructions as if I were planning supper. "Take them north, and you'll find a path, probably magical. I don't know what it will look like, but head down it fast!"

She glanced at the empty plains and then at me as if I were dirt. "What will you be doing?"

"I'll slow down the Hill People in case we need more time. That will leave you free to kick these farmers' asses down the path."

She didn't complain that I'd be killed or anything like that. She didn't offer to help me, either. Her jaw moved as if she were chewing nut shells, and her eyes promised to kill me soon. At last, she spun to walk away and shouted over her shoulder, "Bring back my horse!"

That was not forgiveness or even acceptance. But since I had to be alive to bring the horse, I considered it a positive sign.

I trotted through the farmers toward Stan and the horses. The villagers were a blob of whining and indecision, but they had begun following Pil. Yoadie was encouraging them with his boot and the flat of his tarnished sword, and several older men and women pushed their neighbors on.

As I moved through the villagers, most of them dodged out of my way and muttered charms against evil. It didn't take much to terrify them, especially since geysers of blood had driven them from their homes today.

Tira walked straight toward me, glaring and not moving out of my way. As she opened her mouth, I pointed at her and boomed, "My curse is upon her!"

That produced shouts and name-calling that didn't help our overall situation, but it made me smile.

Just as I reached Stan, a horseman appeared in the distance. I drew my sword but re-sheathed it when I recognized Desh approaching with astounding speed. I had feared we'd be gone before he rejoined us.

I jogged toward Desh, and he waved, slowing to meet me. Then his horse veered. Its shoulder bashed into me as I was jumping aside, and I flew before tumbling across the rough grass and bushes.

Shaking my head, I struggled to my hands and knees. Desh, now on foot, kicked me in the ribs and rolled me onto my back. Before I could spin or keep rolling, he dropped a pebble on my belly. That pebble landed like a small boulder, and a moment later, more invisible boulders pressed down on my arms and legs.

I wheezed, "I'm sorry, Desh!"

Desh knelt and punched me in the face, twice.

"Hill People . . . right over there!" I gasped.

He grabbed my hair and bashed my head against the ground.

I began to think this was serious.

Desh smacked my head against the ground again and drew his knife.

I opened my mouth, gurgled, and said, "Desh, wait!"

He hesitated, and I got a clear look at his face. He didn't seem angry, no more than Pil had. Tears covered his cheeks, but he didn't look sad, either. His mouth was pulled wide, his eyes were stretched, and his neck was as tight as a drumhead, as if I were cutting him open and wouldn't stop.

Desh pushed the knife against my throat.

I squeaked, "Talk to Limnad first! Before you kill me!"

Desh dragged the blade across my throat, leaving a shallow cut that didn't tear open anything important. He stood, wiped his knife, and picked up the pebble from my belly. The invisible boulders evaporated in an instant.

I stood and held my throbbing head. "I suppose it helps nothing to say I'm sorry, Desh, but I did it to save all our lives."

Desh walked toward his horse without looking at me.

The villagers had tramped right past us while Desh was pounding the shit out of me. A few of them, despite everything, could still laugh at other people's pain, so I supposed civilization wasn't destroyed yet.

I rubbed my bruised shoulder and wiped the blood off my throat before mounting Pil's horse. Before I could kick the beast into a gallop, Pil shouted from behind me. I almost ignored her, but she yelled again, waving her arms.

The Hill People hadn't yet run out of the village toward us, so I spent fifteen seconds galloping to Pil. She was standing up to her knees in a round pool of clear water.

"I walked into it before I saw it," she said, not looking at me. Yellow, orange, and blue fish as long as my foot circled her and swam between her legs. "I guess this is it!"

"Huh. I guess Harik is sending us through Fish Town, wherever that is." I pointed back toward the village. "Hurry, the Hill People are right over there."

Stan arrived with the horses. "Do we sit in the water? Dive to the bottom? Drown Desh's ma? What?"

Pil raised her voice. "Stop a moment, I'll figure this out! Stan, stay here, I may need you. Bib, you slow them down." She hesitated, still not looking at me. "Give us all the time you can. Now, I need to make sure these fish won't eat us or something worse."

I galloped around the mass of farmers. Desh and Tira had joined Yoadie in thrashing more speed out of the villagers.

Then I saw the Hill People run out of the village toward us, half a mile away. Twenty-three of them approached me at a steady run. I couldn't make out faces yet, but if Semanté wasn't one of them, I'd eat a stump.

I could make them chase me and call a storm to throw lightning at them, but I feared I wouldn't get back to the Fish Town road before it drained away, or the fish drank it, or it did some other inconvenient thing. I dismounted, hoping Pil's horse wouldn't run far but not expecting to be so fortunate.

However, what I had in mind couldn't be accomplished from horseback.

My advantage was that I didn't need to kill these Hill People. If I could keep their attention until the last villagers waded away with their fish escorts, I could jump in and follow them. I doubted that Semanté wanted to chase me down the Mystical Lane to Fish Town anyway. She had empires to shatter.

I didn't need to kill them, but I'd be tickled to kill as many as I could.

Stan was coaxing the horses into the pond, and the villagers were jumping in at a decent rate. I pulled two white bands and called a gale to blow a good quantity of dirt, leaves, and small creatures, both alive and dead, into the Hill Peoples' faces.

While they were blinded, I drew my sword and ran toward them. Such a wind wouldn't stop Hill People fighters, or slow them, or maybe even make them sneeze, and I knew it. While the wall of crap blocked their sight, I flung band after band of power. Soon, I had created seven whirling dust funnels in my enemies' path, each flinging wind and dirt in all directions.

I hoped that this wind and whipping soil was confusing Semanté's fighters all to hell. I let the gale behind me fade a bit and could see the dirt-shrouded outlines of three Hill People scrambling around, probably looking for me and trying not to kill their friends. I marked the locations, raised an even stronger wind at my back, and charged in among them.

Two men stood where I expected, and I cut them both down as I ran past. I didn't bother with thrusts or precision. I slashed with raw brutality without slowing. I sliced the next man's throat as I passed, and I smiled despite the dirt in my teeth. Killing them felt better than a drink, or a solid sleep, or dropping a heavy pack I'd been carrying.

I murdered one woman and wounded another before I reached the other side. I spun up four more dust funnels around the fighters, slammed them with a wind from behind me, and sprinted back in. By the time I had passed through and run clear, I had killed two and wounded two more. I also had a deep scrape on my ribs and a ragged hole all the way through my left arm from a spearhead.

I doubted that Semanté would let me drag my sword through the middle of her formation a third time. Pil's horse hadn't wandered far, so I mounted and galloped toward the Fish Town road, spitting dirt all the way.

Several of the older farmers and a few kids were easing into the water while Pil and Tira shouted at them to hurry. I glanced at the blood oozing out of my arm while I cursed four gods and Semanté's mother.

"Pil! Your horse!" I bellowed and then dismounted. I wasn't close to her, but she waved, so this was close enough for me to argue that I had returned her horse, at least technically.

Then I turned to face fourteen charging Hill People.

Semanté's fighters closed with me, running hard but precisely spaced. Three of them hurled spears. While the weapons were in the air, I pulled three blue bands and rotted the spear shafts just behind the heads. Two spears fell apart and wobbled away. I jumped aside to let the third one thump against the dirt.

The spear throwers were cursing and making thumb gestures at me. I saw Semanté laughing as she ran.

My breath was coming heavier, and the heat was sitting on me like a burning log. For no reason, I wondered whether my sword would grant me strength and speed if I called for it. It would have been thoughtful of Desh to include that power, but all it did was drip a little blood on my boot.

Sighing, I glanced at the pond. Pil, her horse, and the old farmers needed another thirty seconds. I had already used a large part of my remaining magical power, but I spent a little more to pull fourteen green bands and fling them toward the Hill People. I waved my sword in the air and howled like an idiot as I backed away toward the pond.

The fighters charged three steps before half of them fell onto their elbows and knees. The other half strained against the bushes and grass that had grabbed their feet and ankles. Some dropped their weapons to tear at the bushes, while others pointed their spears at me.

If the Hill People expected me to rush over there and fight them, they had a much higher opinion of me than I did. "Enough of this shit!" I croaked at nobody in particular, and I sprinted toward the pond with my lungs and legs wailing.

Still holding my sword, I dove in, stumbled to my feet, and waded after Pil. She looked back at me and bellowed, "Run!" even though it was impossible to run in water. "I don't know how long this—"

I waded face-first into Gek's green silk coat, which was full of Gek.

"You don't care for fish all that much, do you?" Gek asked, stepping back.

I stared at him with my mouth open.

Gek smiled and patted my head. Then he stepped aside and sank as if he had walked into a hole, which I guess he probably had.

The Hill People were still shouting behind me, so I struggled onward. I heard Pil cursing ahead of me. I hoped she was aiming some of those nasty words at the Hill People, but I guessed they might all have been for me.

Then something with teeth clamped onto my leg. I glanced down to defend myself and saw a red fish as long as my arm driving me forward by the knee. A second red fish seized my other leg. I lost my balance and fell backward. The fish dragged me along by the knees as I tried to keep my face above water.

The world became pure dark in an instant, as lightless as a cellar, but I still heard the water and the damn fish were still biting me. The air went from sweltering to chill. The water went from chill to freezing. A moment later, I was sitting on my butt and dripping onto what felt like grass.

I couldn't hear much over the farmers screaming and blubbering, the horses snorting, and the goats bleating. Someplace not far ahead, Pil was yelling for Yoadie.

The sky eased into misty twilight. I waved at Pil. I could see past her to the farmers, but not much beyond that. A massive, wet-looking, black-trunked tree stood not far from me, with a dozen more such trees in sight. The farthest were shady outlines in the dimness. The grass under me was thick and soft, and damned if it didn't look black.

I glanced up to read the sky, and froze. The night was slathered in stars, bright and clustered, and at least half of them shone in various colors. None twinkled. As I watched, some stars crept or even swung across the sky.

The area looked deserted except for us. I sure didn't see any goddamn fish.

"Weldt bite it with all his teeth!" someone shouted behind me.

I jumped up and turned, my sword ready.

Semanté and eleven of her fighters were climbing to their feet ten paces away.

I whispered, "Damn you, Harik. May your teeth shatter and your dick drop off."

Semanté's nose was bleeding as if someone had punched her. She spit blood and gazed around with her spear ready. "Where have you brought us?" she muttered. I supposed she was talking to me, but she didn't spare even a glance my way. It made me feel no more threatening than a goose.

Then Semanté's fighters formed up on each side of her and glared some highly disciplined hatred at me. I felt better.

"I could learn here and do prodigious things," Semanté said, meeting my eyes at last, "but I am already doing a thing. I do not want to neglect the Soulless. You will take us back now."

I paused to consider lies I might tell her.

Semanté raised her spear for an overhand thrust but didn't step toward me. All her fighters matched her move in silent, precise unison. I realized these might be the most dangerous of all her fighting men and women. At least they were the ones I hadn't been able to kill yet.

Semanté grinned for a moment before her eyes went cold. "Take us back now."

ELEVEN

The sorcery masters taught me about the different realms. We devoted a lot of time to the world of man because we lived there. The Gods' Realm demanded a fair bit of attention too, since we dealt with gods who insisted that the name "world of man" must not be capitalized. Who did we think we were to claim capital letters for our lousy little realm?

We didn't study the Void much, because it wasn't a proper realm. It was just a lack of stuff between the true realms. The masters admitted that beings traipsed through the Void like it was a tavern at the highway crossroads. But if we had studied it, the masters couldn't have said much because they didn't know much. That would have been embarrassing.

The masters affirmed that a Void Walker Realm existed. The Void Walkers had to live someplace, so there must be a Void Walker Realm. That was just logic.

And that was about all they could teach us.

Harik had intended to send us to some fish realm, but now I was in a different place, without a fish in sight. Maybe this was the Void Walker realm, but I doubted it. No Void Walkers had shown up to welcome us or destroy us.

Therefore, I felt free to name the place. I called it the Droopy Realm, because everything there seemed gray, black, flaccid, or sad.

In the Droopy Realm, I lowered my sword as Semanté and her eleven squatty heroes stood poised to stick holes in me. They probably wouldn't be happy until they each got in two or three stabs. Semanté had twice commanded me to send them all home where they could indulge in proper mayhem, and I hadn't done it yet. I had not known her long, but she seemed to be a woman who intended to be obeyed.

"Take you back?" I said to her. "Of course, I'll be pleased to take you and your killers home, just as soon as it can be done. You should understand that I personally will not cause any delay in getting you back to your exterminations." I nodded at her and waited.

"Fine," Semanté said. "Do it."

I sighed. "I'm sorry to say it can't be done from right here."

"Why not?" She lowered her spear.

"It's due to the peculiar nature of this place." Semanté opened her mouth, but I cut her off. "It's an entirely different realm from ours, with its own rules. It is a place of strangeness." I pointed down. "Look! By Krak's manly nipples, even the damn grass is black!"

"Ah." Her lips flicked in a brief smile. "Where must I drag you so that what is left of you will return us?"

"Over there." I pointed behind me toward Pil, Desh, and the farmers.

Semanté sighed. "How far?"

"Pretty far. I'll recognize it when I see it."

The Hill Woman snarled.

I had expected my answer to displease her and was considering what half-truth I might tell to blunt her rage. "My mother taught me the way there. I wish she were here because she could take us to the Shredding Place right off. Before you ask, she was still alive and jaunty last time I saw her. She was farming chickens and geese and had sworn to never step off the islands of Ir for the rest of her sweet life. Just married her third husband, and she said to always call it the

Shredding Place because those who pass through unprepared get shredded like bad ham on a holiday."

Semanté shook her head as if trying to fling off spiders. "That was entertaining, but it does not make me want to kill you any less. No more lies."

"My mother always said that lying—"

"Stop!" Semanté yelled, and her fighters all advanced a step toward me. "I do not want to hear about your mother. Your mother sucks octopus arms for money. Tell me how to get home."

"Well . . ." I stared in the direction of the purely hypothetical way home. "I guess I can't know what my mother did when I was in bed asleep. There could have been octopus arms. My people are fishermen, you know. Let's return to the question of getting you back to your proper realm."

Semanté whispered, "If you lie to me again, I will kill you. I can find my own way back. It means nothing to me that you are a sorcerer."

I furrowed my brow for a few seconds. "Well, I'm glad we don't have the question of sorcery standing between us. Prejudice is an ugly thing. Now, here's some truth for you." I turned my head to point toward the farmers, and I found Pil standing fifty feet back with no weapons drawn. Desh stood a few feet behind her, also unarmed. If all this fell to violence, it seemed I was without allies.

I smiled at Semanté. "We intend to travel that direction. The gods brought us here and promised we could find our way back if we don't mind walking."

Semanté leaned on her spear and made a show of examining me from feet to head. "I am not sure you are able to tell the truth. I think you plan to keep us walking and never let us leave."

"I swear this isn't the kind of place I want to stay in."

"It means nothing that you swear."

"Look around." I gazed at the dimness. "Do you see any taverns or public houses?"

She looked at the ground, but not before I saw her smile. "I think that is the first thing you have said that is not a lie." Semanté cleared her throat and gazed at me. My back tingled. I had never seen anybody look more self-assured. She pointed at me. "We will follow you to the place that returns to our world—this Shredding Place. You must give us your weapons."

I pointed back at her and laughed. "I know you have a sense of humor, Semanté, but I didn't expect such hilarity. There may be monsters around here. We need our weapons to protect ourselves."

Semanté's mouth dropped open. "Monsters? If there are monsters, why did you come to this place?"

"We came here to get away from you."

After a moment, Semanté laughed. She bent over and laughed some more. "All right, keep your weapons. I will walk beside you the whole time so I can kill you if you betray us. I am not afraid of you. I have seen you fight."

There was no question of betrayal, since we had no loyalty to one another, but correcting her like an asshole would accomplish nothing. "Sure, I'll teach you the songs of my homeland, in between fighting off the monsters."

Semanté nodded and gave her people a command. I knew it was a command, because she said it with more confidence than I had heard from some kings.

I turned to Pil. She leaned away and didn't look at me, but I went ahead and whispered, "Shit, I may have just made a mistake. She's more dangerous than I thought."

Pil's head whipped around, her eyes wide. "More than you thought? More dangerous? More dangerous how?"

"Shh."

Semanté walked up and planted herself beside me. "Go on. Lead."

"Sure." I flexed my arm as I walked. The spear wound in my bicep was starting to throb, and I would need to deal with it soon.

I pointed at the scattered, complaining, moaning villagers as we approached. "Semanté, I would introduce you to them, but you're so terrifying they might all climb that big tree and throw themselves off. Better to pretend they don't exist."

"I don't care about them now," Semanté said as she examined the disturbing sky.

"You mean you wouldn't have killed them when you reached their home?"

"I would have killed them all. You cannot leave enemies behind, especially when they are soulless and afraid. Those are the most dangerous."

A few of Semanté's fighters had fanned out to the right and a few more to the left. I figured the rest were trailing us. This was probably as close to alone as I would ever get her.

I stopped. "Let's settle this now. You can't kill these miserable, useless people."

Semanté looked at me as if I had said she couldn't walk on the ground. "I will kill them. There is no question. Because of the Soulless Who Shit on the Sea and the Land, these poor people mean nothing."

"By your way of thinking, I also mean nothing," I pointed out.

"That is not true. I need you to take us back."

"I won't be able to take you back if these miserable people get hurt or killed. I'd be sad and unmotivated."

Semanté turned her head away and examined a stretch of black grass for a few seconds while her shoulders moved up and down. She coughed. "That is a lie. I will not waste my time arguing with a liar. This argument is over."

"I don't think it is," I said. "Ask any of my friends here how long I can keep an argument going. If you're walking next to me, we'll be arguing about this all the way home."

Semanté closed her eyes. She might have been counting. When she opened them, she looked calm, maybe even serene. "I will not kill these poor people then. Lead."

I led. I figured we were all safe from Semanté and her fighters until I found the way back to our realm. Then it might be slit throats and impalements all around unless I had a smart idea.

We skirted the farmers, who were shivering and howling like wet dogs. Desh trotted over to get them moving, while Pil walked on the other side of me from Semanté. I put no thought into the path we'd take, other than walking roughly the direction we had been heading when we arrived. If Harik had brought us to the Droopy Realm, then any direction would probably be misleading. If Gek had brought us, I had no reason to think he'd lead us to parties and pretty girls, but at least he'd want to bring me back so I could murder for him.

I decided to walk in an agreeable direction and let Gek make sure it was the right one.

Time was a slippery thing with no sun and a sky like a rag picker's nightmare. I suspect an hour passed while I tried to teach Semanté the songs of Ir. As I sang, she looked at me like I had soiled myself. On the other side of me, Pil grumbled for a while before dropping back a hundred feet.

I was about to give up when Semanté joined me and stumbled through "Liver and Puddles." Her singing voice was poor, about the same as mine. We went through it a few times before I moved on to "Whale Chasing Armpit of a Man," which was both a song and an insult I favored.

When we started "Calli Died at Midnight," one of Semante's fighters joined in, the big-chinned man I had seen during the dust storm. He didn't know any of the words or even speak my language, but at every chorus, he sang along, "Five bells in her window, five rings on her toes!" Once I caught him smiling at Semanté, but he glanced away when he saw me watching.

Six more Hill People joined us on "Mother, Mother, Mother" and "Home with More Fish than You." By then, our voices had gotten too sore to sing.

Semanté said, "I must go to your homeland someday, even though you have no souls."

"That would be interesting."

"I may kill everybody there."

"It's an island far off in the ocean, surrounded by sharks and storms that only Ir-men can survive."

"Of course." Semanté winked at me. "I am sure it is."

The trees had grown closer, now a hundred feet or so apart, with waist-high, gray-leafed bushes scattered between them. I glanced back and saw that the farmers were falling behind, so I slowed down.

"Walk faster!" Semanté snapped. "I own sculptures faster than you!"

I sped up, but not too much. I considered stopping for a loud, pointless argument with somebody to give the villagers a chance to catch us, but it sounded like an ordeal.

A short, bent creature stepped into our path from behind a bush thirty feet away. I drew my sword, and Semanté leveled her spear. It was the first animal or person besides us I had seen in the Droopy Realm.

I squinted at the thing through the thin light. It was man-shaped but too blocky and wide to be a person. Its arms were long and its head as round as a ball. It spoke in a disgruntled whine. "Well, introduce yourselves. You ain't got forever, you know."

Before I could answer, Semanté took one step forward and stood wordless.

"That didn't impress me much," the being wheezed. "I thought Hill People were so terrifying you'd piss yourself. What about you, Ir-man?"

"My name is Bib. Thank you for letting us walk around in your unique home."

The creature shuffled toward us, showing his empty hands. "It ain't my home. I wouldn't wipe my ass with this place."

I said, "I guess we have that in common." Now that I was closer, I saw that the being was naked, with leathery skin and a face as wrinkled as an old apple. It was bent even more than I had thought. I continued, "As the Hill People see it, it would be rude for this woman to introduce herself first."

"She can kiss my butt then. I didn't want to know her name anyhow!"

Semanté rushed forward holding her spear low, as fast as anyone I'd ever seen. She thrust at the creature's chest. He shuffled aside, which hardly seemed like movement at all. Then he was standing there entirely unstabbed, while Semanté had been hurled twenty feet to the side. She rolled twice and came up on her feet.

Semanté shouted a command to her fighters, who were closing

in on the creature. They all stopped, ready to fight and pointing their weapons at the bent-over being.

"Well, that was entertaining," I said. "Better than a juggler. May I ask your name, sir? Or madam?"

"My name's Hurd."

"Hello, Hurd," I said.

"Ain't you gonna say you never heard of me?"

"I wasn't contemplating it."

"Good!" Hurd cackled. "Lots of people say that. If you did, I'd have had to murder you. I've come to these lands for the waters. What about you?"

I scanned the area. Semanté and her people were doing the same. Semanté said, "I have seen no water."

Hurd grinned, and I saw chalk-white teeth. "Bad luck for me then, isn't it?" He pointed at Semanté. "I done introduced myself, so what's your name?"

"Semanté."

Hurd wrinkled his wide nose and wheezed, "Not something I'll think about on my deathbed. I ask it again, why are you people here?"

I said, "First, where is here? I've been calling it the Droopy Realm."

Hurd laughed, making a noise like an ungreased wheel. "That's pretty good. Fits too. Maybe you're the first Ir-man to come here, so you get to name the place. Droopy Realm . . ." He chuckled and then cleared his throat. "You had best answer me this time. Why are you here? And if you answer in a way I don't like, I'll rip apart every last one of you, including the goats."

Pil spoke out, "We want to go to the world of man."

I glanced at her, appalled by her reckless use of the truth.

Hurd sniffed. "Figures. You come all this way and you want to haul yourselves back home right off. The grand scope of existence is wasted on your type. I guess you need a guide."

"No," Semanté said. "Bib knows the way."

"Hold on," I said. "I know a way, but there could be more than one. Some could be better than the one I know. We might consider hiring you as a guide, Hurd."

"World of man?" Hurd said. "I can take you there like you was a clutch of chicks. That's hyperbole. Some of you will probably die, but not all. My fee . . . let me eat all the goats, horses, and babies."

Before Semanté could agree, I shouted, "Just the goats!"

Hurd shrugged. "Goats and horses. And one baby."

"No babies!" Pil yelled.

Hurd pressed a hand to one of his ears. "Why do you all have to shout all the damn time? You'll wake things up."

I said, "You can eat the horses and the goats, but no babies, or any people of any kind."

"Fine. Babies taste like ash anyway. Gather yourselves up and shake a leg. We have a far piece to walk. I'll save my goats and horses for supper."

I turned to look for Desh. He was near the farmers, crouched on his hands and knees with his face close to the ground. As I watched, he pulled up some grass, rolled it in his hand, and sniffed it. Then he sat back and lifted a folded sheet of parchment and a pencil. Before he wrote anything, he glanced up and saw me. He glared for a long moment before standing and walking away.

I said, "Pil, would you please explain matters to Desh?"

Pil sneered.

"Please," I said. "I've said enough things without thinking today."

Pil squinted at me, then jerked. She whispered, "The gods tricked you, didn't they?"

I nodded and whispered, "I'd stab them all in the heart if I could."

"Well . . . that's something. But it doesn't make what you did good!"

"I know it. Now, will you please tell Desh what's happening?"

"You could talk to him yourself, you know."

"Please," I said.

Pil rolled her eyes. "As long as I'm taking the trouble, do you want me to carry notes back and forth so the two of you can gossip about girls?"

I looked down and sighed.

"All right," she said. "I'll indulge you. Next time, you have to grow up, though. If I can talk to you, so can he." Pil took one step toward Desh before turning back to me. "I'm still mad at you. Maybe a little less. I know how the gods can fool you, though." She strode off toward Desh.

Semanté beckoned two of her fighters, and they conversed in whispers.

"Which way?" I asked Hurd. "And I want to see all the droopiest parts on the journey there."

Hurd grasped my good arm with one hand. It felt like my bicep was being mashed between two ships, and I hissed.

Hurd muttered, "You'd better see to that other arm if you don't want it to drop off you at a bad time."

"Soon," I squeaked.

Hurd leaned close and whispered, "Sorcerer, these are the Dark Lands. No good thing has ever happened here."

I stared at him with eyes that I'm sure were damn big.

Hurd snuffled, his nostrils flaring huge. He kept whispering, "So, mind where you put your feet. If you don't get back, I'll have to listen to Gek bitch about it for a thousand years."

TWELVE

Hurd did not want to learn the songs of my homeland, but he seemed pleased to disparage my singing. He complained when I was off-key, but he didn't warn me against making noise the way he had earlier. There was no talk of waking things up.

Maybe criticizing me looked fun. Semanté didn't sing this time. She joined Hurd in throwing venomous jibes that would have discouraged a lesser man than me.

It would have been like a holiday except for all the killers tramping through a mystical land of evil.

After a while, Hurd proclaimed it was time for a nap. He flopped onto the soft grass and closed his eyes. Semanté wheedled him about the delay and insulted him sharply, but Hurd never opened an eye. He slept half an hour, which was plenty of time to heal my arm. In fact, the moment I finished healing, Hurd jumped up and announced it was time to go.

The trees soon petered out and the bushes grew so tall we couldn't see over them. Hurd led us through such a maze of dank shrubbery that we could have turned back toward the place we started. I wouldn't have known it. The sun was missing, the stars made no sense, and my bump of direction had shrunk to nothing.

At one point, Hurd stepped between two bushes and halted. He pointed down and wheezed, "Water. Don't you step in it. In fact, don't go near it."

"Why?" Pil asked.

"I don't have time to explain things to baby sorcerers! If you don't believe me, swim on out there and see what happens!" Hurd shuffled around and stomped away. We followed him through several turns, and I soon became lost again.

The terrain eased uphill and filled up with jagged, black rocks poking through the grass. Hurd made a sound like parchment tearing and spit on a rock. He spit again, and soon I realized he was spitting on every seventh rock.

I cleared my throat. Hurd grumbled, "Don't ask. And you're welcome."

The bushes ended as if some gardener had dug them up. Long-stalked flowers covered the slope ahead of us. They were pale gray instead of black, and they dripped goo that looked like charred honey. Their scent floated over us, so sweet I almost gagged.

"Dang it!" Hurd whined. "This is a fine punch in the nuts!"

Semanté raised her eyebrows, her spear propped over her shoulder. "Have you caused a problem?"

"No!" Hurd snapped. "The problem was there before we came along."

"You are our guide. Fix it," Semanté said.

"It ain't something you mend with a hammer and some snot!" Hurd said. "I'll show you, and then you'll see."

We trudged up through the flowers, which smeared goo on our trouser legs. We topped a small rise. The hilltop ahead of us was split by a wide gorge, and a fine, black bridge stretched across it.

"You see? I bet you see now, don't you?" Hurd squealed, nodding toward the bridge.

Even if Semanté didn't see, I saw. A man-shaped figure in black armor stood in front of the bridge, taller than any person could be. His shoulders were so wide and his waist so small he reminded me of a huge wasp. He held two long, narrow swords, one gold and one white. A massive black sword, two maces, a glowing crossbow, and a spear with a flaming head stood in a rack beside him.

Semanté spit on the grass suspiciously close to Hurd's foot. "Why did you bring us this way? This is not the way guides should behave."

"Last I heard, that fellow was on the other side of the lake!"

I said, "If there's another path around this hill, I would love to see it."

"How long would that take?" Semanté asked.

Hurd sniffed. "Oh . . . six hours or thereabouts."

Semanté stared at the ground for a moment. "No, that will be too much." She glanced at me.

I said, "I knew you were hurrying along, but it sounds like you have an appointment to keep." I nodded toward the being in black armor. "You go on and have fun with him."

She glared at me with her lips pressed tight. "You are also a guide."

"And I'm guiding you to go some other place where you won't get cut in two. I recommend we go around."

She shouted a command to her people, and they all turned toward me.

I smiled. "On the other hand, I am a curious sort. I'll come. After the blood dries, I might write a song about the event."

Or I might push Semanté in front of this ominous creature at an awkward moment.

Semanté, her fighters, and I stalked toward the bridge and halted forty feet from the black guardian.

The guardian's face was so dark I could hardly see his features. He spoke in a voice like a mighty bell. "Do you challenge me?"

"Wait!" I shouted. "I must speak before any challenges are flung around."

The guardian nodded. "Speak then."

"Are you required to wear black? I suppose it's customary, but I suggest that crimson might suit your shading better. You could enjoy some variety as you guard this fine bridge."

The guardian turned and gazed at Semanté again, ignoring me as if I were a weed. "Do you challenge me?"

"Yes." Semanté raised her spear.

"Wait!" the guardian boomed. "Don't you want to know my name?"

"It does not seem important," she answered.

"That's not very nice," he clanged in a sweet bass note. "My name is Bixell, the Dread Hand of the Dark."

Semanté nodded. "Fine."

Bixell lowered his swords. "I swear to Krak and Weldt, I have never been challenged by anyone as rude as you."

Semanté flinched and then lowered her spear.

"I didn't want to say it, but he's right," I added.

The comment about her manners must have wounded her civilized, Hill Person heart. "I am Semanté. If you are a demon, you do not deserve an apology. If you are something else, you may deserve an apology. To be safe, I apologize for being rude. Also, you own lovely weapons."

Bixell gave a sharp nod. "That was honorably done. Do all thirteen of you intend to assault me at the same time?"

"Yes." Semanté raised her spear again.

"That doesn't sound honorable at all."

"I am busy changing the world," Semanté said. "I only have time for a little honor."

Bixell backed up onto the bridge and assumed a fighting stance with the gold sword angled in front and the white one behind it. Then he shook his head and stood straight. "No, I refuse your challenge. I don't like you."

Semanté rubbed the back of her neck. "Well . . . that is good. We will cross the bridge."

Bixell clanked, "No one may cross the bridge unless they defeat me."

"How does that make sense? We will kill you and cross the bridge!" Semanté strode toward the bridge, but ten feet from it, she slammed to a halt as if she had hit a wall.

I laughed at her. I didn't even try to hide it.

"The magic is quite specific," Bixell said. "No one may cross the bridge unless they vanquish me."

"Then fight me!" Semanté shouted. "I must get to the other side of the bridge!"

"No. I don't care a bit your desire to go places. If you're that randy to get over there, go around."

Semanté chewed her lip. "Is there anyone else here you would fight?"

Bixell pointed at me. "I want the coward who thinks he's funny."

"No!" I said, stepping back. "I'm only here to poke fun at all of you. I don't care what's on the other side of your bridge."

"It's beautiful there," Bixell said. "Really. You'd weep. You need not fight me with weapons. I will defeat you with riddles."

"No." I couldn't tell what sort of trap he was setting for me.

"You risk nothing. If you lose, you can walk away unharmed." Bixell sighed. "Don't tell me that you're such a coward you won't help your friends, even though no harm can come to you."

Everybody stared at me. The goats may have stared at me too. I tried to say no, but my moral courage had been crushed to the size of a pea. "All right, sure, I'll riddle with you." I considered proposing something besides riddles, but the situation was too complicated already.

"Good!" Bixell said, pointing me toward a spot facing him. "The first one to make an error loses. Please start by telling me a riddle."

I knew a lot of riddles, but I hadn't learned any new ones lately. Bixell probably knew all the most obscure riddles. I decided to go for something uncomplicated. "The hands sow, the eyes harvest."

After a moment, Bixell said, "Is that all?"

"Uh-huh."

Bixell stared at the sky. "It's terribly short, isn't it?"

I nodded.

"It's a challenge, though . . . never heard it before. What could it be? Can you give me a hint?"

I stared for a moment. "I can't give you a hint!"

Bixell rubbed his jaw. "Well . . . I surrender then! You have vanquished me!"

I squinted at him. "Just like that?"

"Of course! You're a mighty warrior of words. No one could have predicted it."

Semanté stepped between Bixell and me. "Can we cross the bridge now?"

Bixell pointed at me. "That's up to him." He smiled, and I realized his teeth were black. "You are the guardian of the bridge now, Bib. You say who crosses and who does not."

I stared around, locking eyes with Pil for a moment. She was grinning at me, and not too nicely.

Semanté clapped me on the shoulder. "Congratulations."

"I am not the guardian of anything!" I yelled. "I won't do it. You can have your bridge back. I surrender to you."

"You have to challenge me again," Bixell said.

"Fine. I challenge you."

"I don't accept. I hope you like your bridge!" Bixell's laugh sounded like the bells in a church where rich people pray. He loomed over me by three feet. "You may keep all those magic weapons, but they must stay near the bridge."

"Eat a flaming bug, you great bag of ass hair!" I drew my sword and thrust at Bixell's throat, belly, and eyes, just that fast. He slapped each attack away with his hand.

Bixell said, "You had better practice. Some of the beings who arrive at this bridge are powerful, even legendary. I'd start working on that today."

I sheathed my sword. "You cannot force me to stay." I didn't sound as certain about that as I would have liked.

Bixell lifted his chin. "Of course, that is true, I can't force you to assume your duties like an honorable being."

I smiled and said, "Hey, everyone, let's cross the bridge!" I walked around Bixell.

Bixell followed me, bending his head low by my ear. His voiced clanked without pausing for breath, "I can't make you stay, of course, but I can explain, in crisp detail, all of the wonders that a bridge guardian enjoys. Strolling in the gorge, for example—most refreshing to your soul. I can also help you understand every reason why your life will be sad and useless if you are not a bridge guardian. There's a lot to talk about—"

I kicked Bixell in the knee. It felt like I had kicked a fence post. "Mother poke it in the eye!"

"Your kicking could use work too, I must say. Bridge guardians have a surfeit of time to hone their martial skills."

I led the way across the bridge, limping a little. Bixell walked behind, clanking and tinkling in my ear. "Stop that banging!" I snapped. "May your willy be stepped on by the fattest cow in creation!"

"Should have gone around." Hurd snickered from someplace behind me.

I looked around and saw him wink. "You led us right to this ass-damned bridge, didn't you?"

Hurd coughed but didn't say anything.

I waited on the other side of the bridge. "Semanté, this is your fault! I should have killed you during that dust storm!"

"I would have slain you," she said. "I am glad I did not. It would have prevented me from laughing at your discomfort today."

"Goddamn it! I wish I had a drink."

I saw one of Hurd's eyebrows raise.

Turning, I found Pil walking not too far from me. "Pil, would you do something for me, please?"

"Probably not."

I gazed at her, waiting.

She said, "If you want me to call Desh names for stealing your toy boats, forget it."

I shook my head. "If I know poor people, you can count on them to do one thing when rushing away from a deadly catastrophe: bring some beer. Or maybe wine. I'm as thirsty as if I've eaten sand. Could you go back to the farmers and rouse out a few drinks? Enough for three or four healthy men?"

Pil examined my eyes for a moment before she answered. "I'm still mad at you. But certainly, I'll do that."

Bixell said to me, "Your insults are weak. The bridge guardian possesses a fine library, and there is a book filled with ribald language and name-calling."

My patience broke. "Go away! You must want something. What can I give you to leave me alone?"

Crouched behind me, Bixell's clinking voice said, "That is considerate of you. I ask that when you return to the bridge and assume guardianship, please review my entries in *The Chronicles of the Bridge*. Touch up any grammar or ambiguity if you would, please. I confess that I do not possess tremendous writing prowess, and of course I wouldn't want to feel embarrassed later. My portion is only about seven hundred pages. You'll find it in a cave—"

"Quiet! Be quiet!" I shouted.

"Of course." Bixell began murmuring in a voice that tinkled like tiny bells. "You might be concerned about feminine companionship, but have no worry there. Bridge guardians are noble and celebrated figures. You will be pursued, literally, by an embarrassing number of women."

Pil returned with two big leather sacks of beer. I handed one to Hurd as we walked.

Hurd sniffed it, grinned, and then cackled. "Thank you. Not much worth drinking out in these haunted lands." He took three big swallows, and I did the same. I made a point of not offering any to Bixell. In fifteen minutes, our beer sacks were half empty.

"Hurd, what are we really doing here?"

He snorted. "I'm here because Gek said to be here. I don't know why the heck you're here."

I glanced back. "Bixell, is there anything else you'd like us to talk about while you're eavesdropping over my shoulder?"

"I know these things already. Bridge guardians are privy to many secrets, of course, even the secrets of creation."

"Beautiful. Go on, Hurd."

"If you think to get me drunk, well, maybe you will, but you can't make me tell tales." Hurd took another swallow.

"What can you tell me that's not a tale?"

"Hmm. Well, you can't save all these peasants, but that don't matter, not really."

I glared at him. "Why not?"

Hurd lowered his voice. "Some of them's already marked, so it'd be hard to save those at this point."

"Marked by who?" I shifted the beer sack to my other arm. "By Harik? Krak?"

"That would be telling, wouldn't it?" He peered into the sack and then shook it.

"Some other god?"

"Stop talking god shit, damn it! They make me want to smack all those white teeth out of their heads."

At least I had him talking. I said the first thing I could think of. "I'm a sorcerer, so I guess I think about gods a lot. But I don't . . ." I waited for him to fill that silence.

Hurd wheezed, "You don't need to concern yourself with gods much when you're here. They don't know you're here."

"So, this isn't part of the Gods' Realm?"

Hurd lowered his brow and glanced sideways at me. "It's complicated. You wouldn't understand it. Your brain's too small."

Bixell said, "No great intellect is required—"

"Hush! So, the gods don't come here?" I was pushing, but I'd keep on doing it as long as Hurd was talking.

Hurd barked a laugh. "They don't anymore. They don't like to come here." Hurd took three polite swallows.

I matched his swallows. "Why don't they?"

"They just don't."

I let the silence grow.

Bixell said, "Krak's saddle and pony, Hurd! Tell him! He's going to be living here."

Hurd rolled his eyes where Bixell couldn't see, drank again, and sighed. "True, you are bound to know this sometime, so why not jump on it? Two gods died here. Died for good, I mean."

"Fressa and Madimal," I said. Fressa, Goddess of Magic, and Madimal, God of Deep Waters, had been missing. I had already concluded they were dead.

Hurd nodded. "May they suck red-hot nails up their asses for the rest of time."

"Nice insult. So, they died in the Dark Lands." It wasn't a question. I was trying to set the idea in my mind.

Hurd pointed. "Right over yonder, past that valley you can't see for all the dang mist."

This was the most ticklish question of all. "So . . . how did they die?"

"Squished." Hurd belched and took a swallow.

I let that sink in. "Squished?"

"Yes, squished." Bixell nodded.

"How?" I asked.

"Just squished!" Hurd snapped. "The regular way! Now, hush! You're worse than a little dog in love with my shin."

"I'm sorry, Hurd. I didn't mean to push."

"You sure as hell did mean to, and I guess maybe I would too if I was you." Hurd waved away any bad feelings. "One more thing you ought to know, and maybe I shouldn't tell you, but I've been used bad and I'm feeling mean. You know Gek's fancy cane?"

I nodded. "Sweet. Feminine, almost."

Hurd cackled and took another swallow. "Gek got that leg wound here in the Dark Lands, and it ain't never healed. Think about that now. A Void Walker can turn his self into a waterwheel, or a cloud, or a horse apple, or any other thing he can imagine. But Gek has a wound that won't heal, and it don't matter what he turns himself into. Think about that."

"I will. I'm thinking about it right now." I glanced sideways at Hurd. "If that happened to Gek, why did he send me here?"

Hurd shrugged. "I suppose he doesn't like you much."

THIRTEEN

For the next two hours, Bixell paced behind me, his head bent over my shoulder, describing the joys that only a bridge guardian could experience. He spent twenty minutes recounting the history of the bridge itself, the manner of its construction, how he repaired it after a big fight forty-four years ago, the materials he used, and his journal entry describing the event, in which he used 504 words.

I said, "You spend a lot of time looking at that bridge, don't you?"

Bixell quirked his head. "Of course I do. I'm its guardian. Or I was!" He grinned and poked me on the shoulder.

"You don't sound too convincing. Won't you miss it?"

"Of course I will," he clanged as he gave a slow nod. "But I remember my life when there were people I didn't have to kill. Such as yourself! I want to see people like that again."

For a second, I couldn't breathe. Bixell sounded the way I felt sometimes, or close enough for us to be brothers. I muttered, "Don't get your optimism wound up, Bixell. I won't be staying."

Bixell laughed, a clear chiming sound. "Of course you'll want to stay! I just haven't explained it well enough. For example, I am told that your mother is a prevaricating, spiteful waste of the human experience who should be forgotten immediately. Stay. You will never miss her."

"I hardly remember her now. Bixell, why do you say 'of course' so much?"

He blinked. "Do I? I haven't had any friends for long a time to tell me what's wrong with me. Maybe I should get married!"

I grunted and listened to him go on about how magnificent my new job was.

After another half hour, I focused my attention away from Bixell's running commentary, and I leaned toward Pil. "I know you're still mad at me, and I apologize. I truly am sorry and didn't mean to hurt you."

Pil was silent for a while. Then she looked away and said, "The part that's almost the worst, but not quite, is that now I can't know whether somebody's taken my memories, or maybe decided to pour them back into my head. You did it without asking. Am I missing other memories I don't know about?" Pil started to say something else but shook her head instead.

"You can't know that, and none of us can." I tried to sound wise and comforting, unlike the harsh young assholes who trained me. "This is true for every human being, but only sorcerers are privileged to know it's possible. I wish I could make that softer to land on, but I can't."

"I have to reevaluate everything I did while those memories were gone."

I smiled. "No need for that."

She grabbed my shirt and pulled me around to face her. "Yes, I do need it."

Bixell bumped into me when I stopped.

I didn't want to ask her, but I had to. "So, what's the worst part?"

"Oh, the worst? I trusted you, and you did this to me." Pil glared, and I thought she might hit me. Well, I deserved a good whacking if she wanted to give it. She hauled back but ended up just pushing me away. "Part of me wants to hate you, and another part wants to thank you for . . . I don't know what for!"

I didn't tell her that my marriage had been like that about one day in ten.

"You have been keeping some secrets from me," Pil said. "I know I'm keeping secrets from you. I feel the need to throw away all secrets between us and start fresh."

That surprised me. I had expected her to walk away when we got back to our world and forget I ever lived. I nodded. "A fresh start sounds fine." It actually sounded reckless and foolish, but I didn't say that.

Pil said, "I'll go first. I'm under an obligation to betray you when Lutigan tells me to."

I paused. "That's mighty funny," I said without laughing. "I'm under a debt to betray you on Lutigan's command."

Pil stared at me. "I don't think that's funny at all."

"You're right, I just have a perverse sense of humor. What can we do about this? It doesn't sound healthy for either of us."

"Let's cheat," Pil said as she resumed walking. "Not cheat in the technical sense, but . . . let's be smart about it. As soon as I know I'm about to betray you, I'll start talking about pickles or something to warn you."

"I like that. But not pickles. We might really be talking about pickles sometime. Talk about elephants instead, and I'll do the same."

"Good, we should— no, I don't want to overplan it." Pil looked down. "Bib, what if I did things that . . . I would never have done if I had those memories? I can't go back and change that."

If I couldn't apologize to Desh enough times for murdering his father, I probably couldn't apologize enough times for this. "I'll keep what you've said in mind when I talk to Desh."

Pil's voice dropped. "With Desh, it won't be as simple as this."

"More complicated than mutual betrayal and elephants?" I gave her a weak smile.

She didn't smile back. "Bib, don't wait. Talk to him soon. You did this to both of us. Desh and I spent time discussing it and planning how we'd get even."

I shuddered but said, "That seems fair." I watched my boots scuffing the rocks and black grass. "I guess now is the best time to talk to him." I glanced uphill toward Desh and Stan. They were saving the dumb farmers' lives by scolding and shooing them with immense vigor.

Desh's voice came from the side of the line of refugees. I couldn't see him through the dimness and mist, but his voice traveled strong and crisp through the damp air. Ahead of me, Hurd was leading at a modest pace, and Semanté was prodding him to go faster.

I said to Pil, "Maybe I should distract Semanté. I'll bet she's a pain in Hurd's butt. He may get distracted and lead us into a black hell swamp."

Pil stabbed her finger at me. "Go talk to Desh. Sorry, please, awesome sorcerer, whose footprints we aren't fit to lick clean, go talk to Desh." Pil hurried down the hill to catch Hurd and Semanté.

At my ear, Bixell said, "This all seems frustrating enough to cut short your life. As bridge guardian, you will live forever and stay young without even exercising."

Desh saw me coming. He met my eyes, snarled something that looked bad, and stomped off toward the rear of the clumpy line of villagers.

The farmers were trudging and stumbling, strung out over a hundred paces. Even the strong ones were breathing hard and staring at the ground, as if they could make the ordeal go away by ignoring it.

Yoadie led them. I found the pace comfortable, but it must have been hard for such distressed people. He had lost his sword someplace, and now he pushed forward red-faced and shaking, with his fringe of sweaty white hair stuck to his skull. His heart might well burst soon. If it did, his people would leave him behind in the Dark Lands.

I waved at Stan as I passed him, and he waved back with a

glance. An older woman near him had stumbled to her knees and was wailing, "It's not right! We didn't do anything wrong!"

As Stan walked to her, he yelled, "That is exactly correct! You're a smart woman, maybe not as smart as my gamma, but dang smart."

She shied away from Stan when he reached for her, but he lifted her to her feet. As he steadied her, he snarled, "These kinds of unjust doings are twice as wrong in witchy, dead places like this. A blind man could see it. You been treated worse than a gutted frog, so keep going awhile. When I find the ignorant fluff-hammer in charge of this shit, you'll help me kick him in the narbs."

The woman didn't perk up at the notion of narb-kicking, but she did shuffle on down the slope.

"Bib!" Stan called. "Did you leave Pil by herself with all those Hill People and demons?"

"It's all right, Stan," I said without stopping. "They're safe as long as they don't sing. She hates it when people sing."

Stan hesitated, staring into the mist as if he could see the Hill People throwing spears at Pil. "There's a dozen of those rascals, aren't there?"

"Unless she's killed a few already." I shouldn't have poked fun at him. I could see that he was trying to decide whether he was more terrified of the Hill People than he was in love with Pil.

"I suppose I'll check on her then." Stan jogged away down the hill, drawing his sword.

Halfway down the line of farmers, I passed Desh's mother, Tira, yelling at a teenage girl and a man. "Come back here, you floppy whiner, and don't look away from me! Pick up that water! What are you going to do when you get thirsty, drink your own piss?"

The girl, who was stooped and pale, squinted at the water sack by her feet. "It's heavy."

"Water's heavy, moron! You know what else is heavy? Your blood! I bet you think you'll wiggle your ass and cuddle up to some man later to drink his water. You've got another think coming! He'll knock you on the ground, and if he doesn't cut your damn throat, I will, you whimpering twat! Or maybe I'll break your pretty leg and leave you in the dirt to die, since you're too useless to get my knife dirty on! Pick up that water!"

Weeping, the girl lifted the water sack in her arms.

The man with her said, "I'll watch her."

Tira dropped her voice, but I was close enough to hear. "You're worse than she is, you dimwitted goat! The child reflects the father, doesn't she? If you made a creature this useless, you must be twice as useless! Your wife thought so and told everybody about it. Said you're a lazy worker and a lousy lover. I guess your dripping incompetence is why she drowned herself!"

The man was crying now too. "She didn't kill herself."

"The pool is only four feet deep, so unless she broke both her legs, she murdered herself—to get away from the two of you, most likely. So, shut up and walk!" Tira turned away from them and scanned other villagers close to her.

I had to admit that Tira kept people moving, but I hurried on before she decided to brutalize me.

I found Desh encouraging the laggards at the end of the column. He picked them up and shoved them on down the hill, but without Stan's aggrieved encouragement. He shouted commands and threats, but he didn't approach his mother's savagery.

Most of the stragglers were old people and children left behind by their panicky families. I stared around with my mouth open. "Desh!" I called out.

He didn't look at me, but he didn't run either.

I walked toward him. "I didn't know it was so bad back here. Unless our destination is close enough to hit with a rock, half these people will die before we get there."

Desh finally looked up, and I saw his face was deadly still. My hand reached for my sword, but I forced it to stop. In a flat voice, Desh said, "I think you're right. We should tell them to halt." But he made no move to tell even the closest ones to quit walking.

I clapped my hands. "Get the ones back here stopped. I'll take care of the rest."

Running up the line, I yelled at Tira, "We'll rest here for a while. Hurry up and tell the ones in front to stop."

She sneered at me but didn't argue before leaving at an exhausted jog. I couldn't scold her for being slow. I felt wrung out myself.

I considered bellowing at Pil to tell her we were halting. I knew she could hear me from that far away. But I didn't know who else or what else might hear me, investigate, and be displeased by what they found in their lands. Instead, I grabbed the most vigorous young man I could find and ordered him to run forward and give Pil my message.

Then I had no more excuses for not talking to Desh.

I found him standing where I had left him, rubbing his forehead hard. The straggling villagers were trudging away from him.

I said, "I guess these folks will stop when the ones in front of them do. Desh, I'm sorry for what I did to your memories."

Desh shrugged. "It's my fault."

"Well . . . I sure as hell didn't expect to hear you say that."

"I thought the gods would be satisfied that I'll never know happiness, and that would be it. But I suppose they had to do something to make sure of it."

I waited while he looked away from me for a few seconds. I cleared my throat. "I truly am sorry, Desh."

"I'm glad," he said. "You should be sorry. You should suffer." He whipped around to stare at me with his teeth gritted. At least it was a sign he felt something. I had begun to fear I'd caused some disaster in his mind.

"What about this being your fault?"

"I allowed the gods to do it," he said. "You're the tool they used. So, what's fair? Should you shit yourself to death? Should every dog you see try to kill you? And eat you? You could fall in love and have your heart broken once a month for the rest of your life."

"Desh, I had no idea this was so bad."

He nodded. "I know that you're thinking and planning now, Bib. You're figuring out how to kill me before I do any of those things to you."

In fact, that's exactly what I'd begun doing.

"Don't worry, I won't make dogs hate you enough to eat you. I don't think I'll hate you either, or not much. I have other things to think about."

"Damn it to flaming perdition, Desh! What can I do to help you?"

"Nothing. And for the sake of all thirteen gods, don't try to fix it! You've done enough. If I believed in fate, I might think you were fated to do this."

I walked toward Desh until we were at arm's length. "I know that your mother is like a serpent and a wolf and a diseased vulture put together. But how can getting back memories of that bitter, old ass stain cause you so much harm?"

"I'm two people now, or it feels that way. I have mastered sorcery and fear. But I also let that horrible woman crush me like a dry leaf."

I murmured, "It must be hard to negotiate things between the two."

"Not really," Desh said. "There's no need because there can't be any peace. I'm disgusted by the young me. And the young me is furious that I didn't protect him." He shrugged and walked off to join the flopped-down villagers.

I couldn't imagine what Desh had described, but it sounded torturous. He had commanded me to sit on my ass and do nothing to help him, but to hell with that. If we were walking through some damned place called the Dark Lands, then I could find help for Desh.

FOURTEEN

I trudged toward the front of the refugees and felt old.

"Bib! Sorcerer Bib!" Semanté shouted from ahead of me. She emerged from the mist, sprinting up the hill.

"Damn her for being young," I muttered.

"Bib, I did not agree to stop!" she yelled, angling toward me.

Bixell smiled at Semanté. "Bib, know that velocity, motion, remaining at rest, and other such concepts mean little when guarding a bridge. They cannot make you puff and sweat unpleasantly. Your enemies come to you." He pointed at Semanté. "So that you may obliterate them utterly."

Semanté crossed her arms and spoke to Bixell. "You are saying meaningless things. What is the difference between obliterating something utterly and just obliterating it? Can you obliterate someone a little bit? If you just destroy his finger, that is not obliterating him, is it?"

I said, "Bixell, would you like to obliterate Semanté and show her how it's done?"

"If I do, will you assume your duties at the bridge?"

"I sure as hell will not."

"Then I will let her live," Bixell said. "Perhaps after you become guardian, she'll want to cross the bridge someday. I suspect you will obliterate her then."

"This is not helpful," Semanté said. Her fighters had fanned out behind her.

I smiled. "Why, this rest break is a surprise gift for you, Semanté. When you end this journey, you'll want to be refreshed for killing us and all the other wretches without souls."

Semanté scanned the villagers as if they were chickens, or turnips. "If your peasants are tired, leave them behind. You should not have brought them."

"Not to be an asshole about it," I said, "but we were already underway when you decided to join our group. I might even call you stowaways or hangers-on. Logically, your voice carries the least weight in our deliberations."

Semanté grinned. "If I kill these poor people, they would not delay us anymore. I do not need them to get us home. I only need you for that, Bib."

"Hold on, we've discussed that already. If you kill even one of my people, I won't open the way to take you back. Unlike you, I have no battles or appointments to attend back there. And if you kill me, you'll be stuck here forever. Or until something kills you."

"We could make you take us back. We could torture you," she said, smiling.

I nodded. "You could try. So that we understand each other, I have been tortured three times in the past, not including various mutilations and dismemberments. I withstood them, and in all cases, I killed my tormentors. So, think hard before you decide to torture me."

Bixell muttered to me, "When lesser beings like this annoy you, as bridge guardian, you can summon the power of the Dark Lands to—"

I spun and slapped my palm over Bixell's mouth.

The bridge guardian stepped back and stiffened, his lips pulled into a line.

Semanté said in a tight voice, "Bib, I will remember that you made us wait."

"You can also remember that I taught you all those foreign songs!" I laughed and began singing a sea shanty I learned when I could hardly walk, but Pil elbowed me in the ribs.

I needed to rest nearly as much as the farmers did. Everybody ate and drank the little bit they had grabbed before running. Some slept, especially the children. Semanté and her killers gathered fifty paces away and practiced spear drills while staring venom at me once in a while.

Bixell began speaking to me, and I tried to cover his mouth again. He was prepared and dodged so fast I couldn't even touch him. I had to pretend to sleep before he'd shut up.

We waited on that black slope for two hours. I tried not to look at the sky since it made me queasy.

Semanté assigned guard duty to half of her fighters while the others rested. The Hill People kept to themselves as they ate a cold meal. I saw two of them pull books from their bags and start reading. In our lands, a soldier would have to spend a year's pay if he wanted to own a book.

Desh, Pil, and Stan took turns standing watch. I didn't volunteer, and they didn't ask why.

When we resumed marching, Pil, Bixell, and I followed close behind Hurd, while Semanté and her ensemble of murderers paced us. Half an hour brought us down to flat land pocked with short, wide gray trees.

"We're not far now," Hurd said. He squeaked and cleared his throat. "Keep a close watch."

"For what?" Pil asked.

"Oh, dangerous things," Hurd said.

Pil snorted. "That figures."

Hurd turned to glare at her. "All right, you asked. First, there's the trees what flings volleys of dead limbs—big ones—at you from most of a mile away. Then there's the bugs that run up your legs and into your asshole and then blow up like horse bladders once they're inside you. Third, there's the little black birds that fly around you in a cloud and lead you off to get eaten alive by their young ones. Do you want some more? I can go on most of the day."

Pil grinned. "No, that paints a picture."

I asked, "Why haven't we seen any of these horrors yet?"

"Ain't you satisfied with a peaceful little hike?" Hurd snapped. "Do you want me to invite a few over? Maybe some of them bugs?"

"Do you mean they'll come if you invite them?" Pil asked. "I guess you must be keeping them away from us then, which makes me look at you in a whole new way, Hurd."

"Shut up! Damn you ungrateful sorcerers! I hope you all choke every time you tell a lie."

I said, "I'm sorry, Hurd, we didn't mean to be rude. At least I didn't."

Hurd rushed on and didn't bother to answer.

We crossed some uneven ground, although it was still grassy. A while later, Hurd glanced back and squawked at us, "Watch your dang feet!"

I examined the grass ahead and saw big clumps of scattered weeds. Each was as big around as a person's head and would come up to a man's knee.

Pil tapped my shoulder and said, "I'll hurry back and warn the others about these weeds that, I don't know, launch out of the ground and blind you."

My head had been turned toward her, so I failed to see the thing I tripped over. I did succeed in pitching forward onto my hands and knees and almost smacking my face against the grassy ground.

Pil laughed. Hurd looked back and laughed. The Hill People laughed, and they pointed too.

"What the hell did I trip over?" I crawled back to the spot and found something sharp sticking four inches out of the ground.

Hurd rushed back to me. "Leave it alone!"

"Leave what alone?" I asked, as if I hadn't found anything at all. At the same time, I probed the earth around it.

"Whatever thing you stumbled over that's probably cursed!" Hurd yelled like a breathy trumpet. When he arrived, he scrutinized the object. "Don't know what it is, but it's cursed for sure. Leave it."

I was already digging into the earth around the object, which was some kind of metal shaft with a point.

"Stop it!" Hurd shouted and kicked my leg.

I sat back. "Hurd, are you sure it's cursed?"

"Yes!" He drew a whistling breath. "Almost for sure. Better to be safe!"

I wiggled the thing, and it seemed loose.

Hurd leaned down and whispered to me, "Do you remember how I told you that no good thing has ever happened here?"

I left the object alone and stood up, shaking my head. I didn't really need to yank possibly cursed things out of the ground like they were turnips just then. I could wait until I wasn't trapped in some evil realm. "You're the guide, Hurd."

"I am, and you better keep that in mind if you want to live!"

I stepped away from the object.

Pil walked over, bent down, and pulled it right out of the ground.

Hurd took a deep breath but then let it out. "Oh, hell. Guess the damage is done now, ain't it?"

Pil lifted the object so we could examine it. It measured the length of my forearm. The first few inches were sharp and straight, but then it curved almost ninety degrees. Pil mumbled, "What in Lutigan's nasty crop of ear hair is this?"

I asked, "Hurd? Any ideas?"

"Nope. Let's get going. The other world won't wait forever."

Pil turned the thing to examine it from various angles. She shook her head.

Inspiration smacked me. "It's a trident!"

"Nah," Hurd squealed. "Trident's got three pointy ends. You being a sorcerer and everything, I'm surprised you'd make a mistake like that."

"Not a whole one, just one side of the trident. One of the three tines." I took it from Pil and held it up, using my arm to show the weapon's shaft and middle tine. "See?"

"It's a 'dent!" Pil laughed. "One 'dent."

Hurd grunted. "Throw it away. Leave it. Throw it away and then leave it."

Pil grasped the object and closed her eyes. "It's magical. I don't know how much, or what it does, or much of anything, but I'm going to find out!" She smiled at Hurd and me.

"You ain't gonna leave it, are you?" Hurd held his head with both hands. "Fine, get your flesh sucked off your bones by some curse. I don't care at all. Come on."

I might have warned Pil not to take the 'dent with her. It seemed like a bad idea on just about every score. But she was a sorcerer in her own right and didn't need my opinions on anything if she didn't ask.

About two hours later, Hurd held up a hand and stopped. "It's past those trees up ahead."

"And what exactly is past those trees?" I asked. "I want to avoid ambiguity."

"Hmm . . . Hmm . . . It's the . . . well, not exactly a gate, I wouldn't say. It's more of a thin place if you like, or even if you don't. It's the place you'll pass through to get home, or to your world at least."

"Where will we end up?" Pil asked.

"Hell if I know," Hurd said. "Didn't Ge— . . . didn't anybody tell you?"

I said, "Harik told me we'd go far in the direction we wanted to go, so we should be someplace between Desh's village and the Empire."

"That's just lovely," Hurd breathed as he led us forward. "Beautiful as a dang painting."

We walked between the trees and found ourselves on a short rise above a big open area. The mist had been lifting for an hour, so I could see half a mile or more. A huge pond lay to my right, almost a small lake. Not far ahead, I saw a big, irregular depression in the flat ground.

I puzzled over the depression. It resembled a rounded triangle held up by four curved columns. The design wasn't familiar, but it stood out too definite for something natural. Then I considered it upside down and jerked when I saw it was a gargantuan footprint with four clawed toes.

Hurd wheezed, "Interesting day when that print was made. Glad I wasn't here."

From end to end, the footprint measured eight times the length of a horse. That was easy to tell because a black horse stood in the middle of it. The beast was as motionless as if it had been carved there, and it was clad in black armor.

A man-size rider sat the horse. He also wore black, but his only armor was a breastplate and a plain helmet. His face was a shade pinker than snow, and he held a glowing lance in one hand. The hilt of his scabbarded sword glowed too.

I realized that Semanté had walked up behind me because Bixell rushed to say, "As you can see, a large variety of weapons are available to bridge guardians, many of them enchanted."

Bixell talked even faster, but I ignored him and walked down toward the rider. When I was a hundred feet away, he called out in a clear, powerful voice, "This was not something I expected. In fact, it might have been the last thing I expected."

I waved, but the man didn't smile. That seemed ominous. I smiled for both of us. "I agree that it's a hell of a surprise. How have you been, Cael?"

FIFTEEN

Darby the blacksmith taught me the sword. He had once been a weapons master. Then he became a drunkard, and then a blacksmith. By the time I apprenticed with him, he wasn't much of a blacksmith anymore, but he was a magnificent drunkard. Often, we'd leave the forge cold all day while he taught me to fight by bruising and slicing my flesh.

After a year, Darby gave me a rusty, nicked, bent sword. I repaired it and wore it everywhere. I told myself I wasn't looking for a sword fight, because I had no business looking for one. Darby had shown me the vast amount I didn't understand about fighting. But I was young and thought I had to carry it, or else I'd crawl off and die.

That town's young men liked to duel with swords, the kind of duels that ended when somebody got cut once or twice. A year earlier, those fellows had been wrestling in the dirt, not fighting with swords. Just a few years before that, they had been wrestling over toys.

I dueled a lot because I called a lot of people names. I insulted them because they thought they were better than me, and I suspected they were right. I never killed a one of them nor hurt them much, but nobody dueled as often as me. I didn't just love fighting. I yearned for it the way I might for a woman.

Now, in the Dark Lands, I faced Cael, who was a peerless fighter. If I wanted to live, I had better love fighting and killing both. Back when I wore Darby's crappy old sword, I ached to fight, but I remembered not caring a bit about killing. Now the memory shocked me a little, as if I was thinking about somebody else.

I tried to concentrate on nothing but Cael. He had once brought me hundreds of miles to pay his queen a visit, and he'd done it mostly against my wishes. That endeavor ended poorly for almost everybody. My daughter died because I killed her. A monster broke all the queen's bones and then dragged Cael off to another realm. I had figured Cael would die, but he seemed instead to have thrived, or at least lived.

I shook those thoughts out of my head. "I'm pleased that we're meeting again, Cael. I have wanted to point out what a gar-humping mess you made by dragging me back to Bellhalt so Mina could yell at me for no reason. You ought to be ashamed."

Cael smiled now. "You authored every tragic event, Bib, every hurt and indignity. The guilt is all yours."

"Guilt? What exactly did I do to create all that hell on earth?"

Cael leaned forward in the saddle. "I don't know precisely what you did, but you did it, and you can't talk your way out of it."

"I guess you're right then. I can't talk my way out of a bunch of bullshit." I grasped my sword but didn't draw it. I hoped I wouldn't need to, since I had never seen a more perfect warrior than Cael. Now he had magic weapons, and maybe magic armor, and a magic dancing horse for all I knew.

My legs were still tired. It was no time to see how much fiercer he had become.

"Will it help if I say I'm sorry?" I winced and added, "I mean, if I apologize sincerely? Fighting won't call anybody back from death."

Cael's face sagged. In that moment, he looked twenty years older. "That's true. I have tried. You've probably tried as well. We have that in common. And I'm sorry about your daughter."

I held up both hands. "Let's have peace then, although it's probably not the custom in these lands. When did either of us give a damn about custom?"

Cael gazed up at the wild sky, his face still slack. "That mess up in the heavens stares at me every minute, but it hasn't made me insane. I'm proud of that."

"Well . . . that's good. I'm proud of you too." At that point, I couldn't guess whether he'd charge me, throw his boots at me, or lie down and cry.

"Where are you going, Bib?"

"Home!" I said it as if I expected him to carry me there on his back.

"You can't come through here." He glared at me. "Find another way."

My stomach flopped. "Is there another way that's not too far off?"

Searching my face, he said, "I don't know of one, but I don't know everything."

"Cael, this is clearly a hard life. Why don't you come back with us? Bring your horse. I bet he'd love a green field."

The man shook his head.

I sighed and walked back up the rise to meet Pil and Desh. "I'd rather not fight him."

"Lutigan would rather not fight him!" Pil said. "Look at him! How do you know each other?"

Semanté broke in: "I see it is a hard story to tell and probably sad. We have no time for that. Go kill him now."

I grinned. "I'm not the one with a squad of murderers just waiting for my word to attack. I'm also not the one with a fire in her underclothes to get back to the war."

Semanté hesitated.

"Hurd, is there any other way through?" I asked.

Hurd shook his wrinkly head. "If there was, I'd be hurrying that direction right this minute. I wouldn't be waiting for you, neither."

"Wait!" Semanté said. "Wait for a second. Hurd, do you also know how to open the way back from this spot?"

Hurd's black eyes opened wide. He wheezed no in the least convincing way imaginable.

Semanté smiled at me. "Bib, if you kill the guardian, we will all pass through. If he kills you, then you will be dead. I will win either way because I have Hurd and do not need you." She pointed at Cael. "Go fight him."

"Bib," Pil said. "Let's stay in the Dark Lands for a while. Let the Hill People take their chances with Cael."

It sounded fine. Cael might kill quite a few of the Hill People. He looked capable of it. Pil, Desh, and I might kill the rest. Then I could bicker and whine and wear Cael down until he let us go home without a fight. It shouldn't take more than a month to argue the stubborn bastard into it.

I looked back toward the villagers who were flopped down under the trees we had passed. "Staying may not be smart. I bet there's nothing here that's fit to eat or drink. Those farmers would die of thirst in a few days."

Hurd jumped in: "That ain't true at all. They'll get eaten up by monsters a long time before that."

I raised my eyebrows at Pil. She nodded as she drew her sword.

I said, "Pil, please don't come down there with me."

"What? I am not—do you hear me, *not*—going to let you fight that scary son of a bitch alone! In fact, let's go get Desh."

"No. Your magic sword would be like a blade of grass against Cael."

"Well then, I'll drive an arrow through his darn head! I don't care how magical he is, that will kill him." She began stringing her bow.

"All right. And Desh can bounce rocks off his face."

Half an hour later, Desh and Pil stood on the rise with their sling and bow ready. I drew my sword and strolled toward Cael as if I'd been resting for a week. I stopped a good distance from him and called out, "Cael, how did you get here? I last saw you being dragged into another realm. If you'd like to tell your story, I'll listen to it."

"I was sold, but that isn't important. My story is the least important thing about these lands. Bib, if you turn around and go back, I won't have to kill you."

I shook my head. "Go ahead and let us pass through, Cael. How could that hurt anything?"

Cael smiled. "Bib, when you ask questions like that, it is time to beware." He kicked his horse and charged. He and his mount moved so easily that I misjudged their speed. I had to spin and throw myself onto the ground to avoid becoming a favor on his lance.

By the time I hopped to my feet, Cael was wheeling his horse to charge again. Now he was close to the rise, so Pil and Desh fired. The arrow bounced off Cael's breastplate. Desh's sling stone clanged against Cael's helmet.

Cael seemed not to notice, except for one thing. He steadied his horse, shifted his lance to the other hand, and hurled a knife an impossible distance, over a hundred feet, where it plunged into Pil's belly. She folded and collapsed. Desh knelt over her.

I imagined I could hear Pil gasping, although I was too far for that. Cael's face looked almost bored. I pointed my sword at him as his horse charged again. When he reached me this time, I jumped aside and turned, chopping his glowing lance in two. Cael let the lance fall and rode on for fifty paces, where he dismounted and drew his sword.

Cael sprinted toward me, but I closed with him at a careful trot. He jumped at me, cut at my leg, thrust at my groin, and cut at my other leg—quick attacks but powerful enough to shake me when I blocked. I remembered once telling somebody that fighting Cael must be the stupidest thing a person could do.

When Cael thrust at my face, I riposted toward his throat. We thrust and blocked back and forth for ten seconds and disengaged for a moment. He said, "Surrender now. There's no dishonor in it. I promise that you and all your friends will be treated with respect and given shelter and a crown of rubies, and you're not going to attack me during this speech, are you?"

I shook my head. "You shouldn't have mentioned dishonor, son. Your voice tightened and gave you away."

Cael lunged and almost killed me right then, but I parried and left a shallow cut on his sword hand. It didn't slow him at all that I could see.

During the next thirty seconds, twice he came within an inch of skewering me. I almost struck his head, leaving the tip of his nose split and dripping blood. For the next twenty seconds, I hung on as he thrust, faked, and dodged, not bothering with blocks.

We engaged in three more passes, and my muscles were telling me about their fatigue. I pushed harder. Every one of our attacks would have killed or crippled if it landed, and each was barely blocked or dodged. I pinked his arms twice, and he punctured my thigh, so shallow I was hardly aware of it.

My arms and legs were aware of getting wearier, though. Cael looked as calm as if he were hammering nails. That filled me with an urgent desire to end this fight soon.

I had resisted two urges to make crazy and inspired attacks. Both could have defeated Cael, or possibly killed me, or both. When the next urge came, I didn't hold back. Instead of blocking a thrust at my chest, I twisted, lunged so hard that I came up on one foot, and drove my blade deep into Cael's right shoulder. He gave a short scream.

I didn't cheer and applaud, because blood was gushing from the left side of my neck. Cael's blade should have been nowhere close to my neck, but it had been. I fell onto my back, dropping my sword so I could reach across and clap my sword hand against the wound. He must have missed the artery, or I would have already passed out and soon after bled to death. As it was, I felt light-headed and might have only seconds left.

With my left hand, I started pulling a green band to stop the bleeding.

Cael appeared over me, panting, with his sword in his off hand. He muttered, "Sorry, Bib, I have to make sure." He edged toward me, cautious even though I was unarmed.

I let the healing magical power drain away as I closed my eyes and reached for my sword with my left hand. I knew exactly where he and the sword were without looking. As Cael stepped in, I sat up, twisted, and thrust my sword at the same time.

My attack would have killed most men. Against Cael, it would be like poking him with a stick, and I knew it. But it was the only move I had left.

Cael blocked me, and his sword shattered against mine. A shard of his blade slammed into my cheek as my sword pushed through his breastplate between his shoulder and his heart.

Cael's eyes and mouth popped open. He dropped to his knees, swayed, and then smiled at me before falling over sideways. I didn't pay close attention to all of that because I was pulling another green band. Then my stomach clenched, and I turned my head to vomit on the black grass as the shakes hit me.

I managed to keep the power from slipping away, and I stopped the vein in my neck from bleeding. I didn't heal the wound further, though. Instead, I kept my hand over it and wriggled toward Cael, who was only a few feet away. He was still breathing.

Desh ran up, skidding on his knees. "Lie still! Krak, there's blood everywhere!"

"Take off his breastplate!"

"Bib, no, lie back down."

I was fumbling at the buckles of Cael's armor, but my fingers were slipping in the blood. "Just help!"

When Desh pulled the breastplate off to one side, I pulled a green band and slapped my free left hand on the wound. It was bad, and I healed him just enough to keep him alive while a rod of pain grew in my upper chest.

Desh said, "Let me see yours. No, I don't even want to touch that. I might make your head fall off. I don't know about your face, though." He didn't sound confident.

"To hell with my face."

"Bib, I can see some of your skull."

"Huh. Cael nearly killed me twice, I guess."

"Can you walk?"

"Maybe."

"I can't move Pil down here, so you'll have to go to her," he said.

My stomach twisted. "How bad is she?"

Desh helped me stand. "Bad. We should move, not gossip."

On the rise, we found Pil lying on her back with Stan holding her hand. Stan gazed up at me, his shoulders tense. "Damn, you look like something we'd give to the dogs back home." He glanced at Pil. "She couldn't be too bad, right? I mean, you've stuck hands and legs and everything back on folks. This just tickled her guts a bit."

I nodded but didn't answer him as Desh helped me kneel beside Pil. I looked around. "Where is everybody?"

"Hurd just sent the Hill People through and then wandered away," Desh said.

"Already?"

Pil yelled, "Yes, already, it took ten seconds! Forget them, they're gone! I'm still here, barely . . ." She bit back a scream and tried to roll onto her side. Stan mumbled something to her that I didn't hear.

Desh and Stan pressed her flat. Still holding my neck, I pulled two bands and explored the wound. I didn't see how a thrown knife had done such damage. As I had with Cael, I healed enough so that she was out of danger, and the pain in my belly grew as I did it.

While I was working, Desh said, "Semanté wanted to kill you while you were down, but Hurd convinced her to either leave right away or grow old in the Dark Lands."

"That's nice of squishy old button-face," I muttered.

After I finished with Pil, I lay flat on the grass and examined Cael's knife, which was now in Desh's belt. "Do you think that's enchanted? It tore up her insides like they were stale bread."

Desh weighed the knife in his hand. It was long and curved with a black blade and an onyx pommel. "It's designed for throwing, that's a certainty. I'd say it's magical in some way." He shoved it back into his belt.

"Don't you think that should belong to Pil?"

"Oh. I guess it should. If she wants it."

"When—" I turned my head and vomited. It lasted for twenty

seconds. The pain from healing Pil's guts had been growing, and my stomach was already queasy.

"Bib! Bib!" Desh was slapping my shoulder. "You're bleeding!"

I looked left and saw that blood must be pouring from my neck again, although Desh was trying to keep his hand over it. "Shit!" I lay back on the grass and breathed deep. This would be the worst possible time to pass out.

SIXTEEN

I burned yet more magical power to stop my bleeding, then I healed my neck properly. Falling to sleep on the black grass, even if it was nasty and evil, sounded attractive, but I rolled back over to Pil and finished putting her insides back together too.

I had spent a shocking amount of power in the past two days, and I hated to waste more of it on my face. But Desh convinced me that the wound was horrible enough to threaten my life, and after I explored it, I had to agree.

Once I healed my face, I had used up so much power I began to feel depressed. I had a less than comfortable amount remaining. Only the gods could sell me more, and I couldn't see why they would bother.

I pondered the situation for half a minute. Then I told Desh, "Come with me to see Cael."

"To hell with him!" Desh said. "He'll just stand up and kill us."

"Don't assume that. He may only kill me. In a fair world, he would've already done it. Come on."

On the way down the rise, Desh asked, "What is wrong with you? Have you been possessed by some good spirit?"

That struck me as an odd thing to say, so I ignored it. Cael's only dangerous wound was where I pierced his chest with my sword. I healed him into better shape, though nowhere close to full health.

"Cael, you can finish healing the regular way."

Sitting inside the vast footprint with his back leaning against the side, Cael tried to laugh without breathing. "You're a whirling donkey's penis for cheating with magic to . . ." He fell asleep before he finished.

Pain now bounced around in my belly, stabbed my neck, and slammed something flat against my cheek. Hurd came back to confirm that the Hill People were all gone.

I gazed toward the gate's thin spot. From that angle, it looked as if the earth was a bit transparent in that space, and I could see down into it. But whenever I stood on top of the gate, the ground looked solid.

Bixell sat alone beside the gate with his head on his knees. "Hurd, has he been there since the fight ended?"

"He has," Hurd said. "He saw the fight and decided you weren't going to replace him. That seems to have mashed all the vinegar out of him. I reckon he doesn't relish guarding that bridge for another hundred years."

The villagers had straggled in to join us at the edge of the rise. Most of them sat in clumps, probably families. I didn't mind them resting. I myself wished for a few hours to recover before we passed through the thin place. I was sitting on the grass half-asleep when Desh appeared over me with bared teeth and hard eyes.

"Whatever it was, Desh, I didn't mean it."

"It's not funny. Some of the villagers killed themselves." His face was pale, and he sucked a deep breath.

"Does anybody know why?"

"Yoadie thinks so. I'd better let him tell you. Come on."

I said, "They're your people, Desh. You should handle this."

He paused. "They feel like I'm too close to the problem."

"They must be desperate if they're asking me for any help. I'm the demon baby-killer from hell." I crawled to my feet and followed Desh to Yoadie, who stood at the edge of the villagers' hasty camp. He swayed as if he might die on his feet.

Yoadie didn't meet my eyes. "I'd better show you," he muttered.

"Better tell me! Better show me!" I snapped. "Are you going to make me smell the problem next?"

At the middle of the camp, the bodies of the man and girl that Tira had abused earlier were laid out in a clear spot, uncovered. I doubted anybody could spare a cloth to cover them. Each of them had a bloody chest wound.

Yoadie stared at the bodies. "Tira saw you near them earlier and says you threatened them—said they'd be left here forever."

I snorted. "That's crap! Tira said all that."

"Other people saw you there," Yoadie added.

"Did you hear me? Tira was there too! Didn't these unnamed other people see her?"

Two older men had joined us. I gazed around and saw a dozen men and women with enough energy to stand. At least there didn't seem to be any loose stones on the ground.

"They saw her thereabout." One of the old men glared at me. "But she's a woman of our village, and you're known to be a demon. Or at least an evil magician. Evil, no matter what else you are."

It felt like he'd hit me with a board, and I didn't know what to say. I was a sorcerer, and ignorant people might call me a magician. I had accepted being terrible and wicked, even cruel when I considered the question. But I had always scoffed at the idea I was evil.

Maybe when you kill a certain number of people, that makes you evil. Hell, maybe that number of people is one. But I was foolish to think that way and an idiot for paying attention to these dirty-faced farmers. It wasn't like me at all.

Tira had stomped up, swinging her stick. "Look! You see him, right now he's doing it. He's cursing everybody with his evil eye and snaky fingers! Kill that steaming crap pile from hell, or he'll put a charm on us. He'll make us murder the people we love, just like Les! Then we'll have to kill ourselves too!"

Desh said, "Whatever happened here, Bib didn't do it. We're trying to save your lives."

One of the older men said, "There! Desh is denying his own mother. That's bad luck and wickedness right there."

I sighed. "Desh, I'm about to kill your mom unless you say not to."

Tira backed away.

Desh said, "Fine. No . . . don't!"

"Which is it?"

Desh hesitated. He literally swayed back and forth. "Don't kill her. Maybe she doesn't mean to be like this."

"Kill him now!" Tira screamed. "He'll cut off your nuts and tear out your throat, and then he'll spit on your children's dead faces!" She pointed at the girl lying on the grass.

I stepped up and punched Tira in the face, and this time I hit her hard. If I didn't break her nose, it was only because Krak showed up and gave it divine protection. I glared around. "I'm trying to save your damn lives, so don't make me kill you while I'm doing it!"

Tira had staggered backward and was holding her nose while blood flowed down her hands and wrists. She shook her head and kept shaking it, probably trying to get her vision to return.

Desh and I strode back down the rise. He said, "They're ignorant, superstitious, cruel, and greedy, but don't hold that against them. Almost every person in the world is like that, including you and me sometimes. They can surprise you with their kindness too."

"Desh, I'll try not to abandon them. That will be easier if I don't have to see them or talk to them, or even think about them too much. Wait, why did you take me up there among them?"

He didn't hesitate. "I thought you'd want to hear what they were saying about you."

I nodded, but he sounded mighty prepared to give that answer. I didn't like to think Desh had brought me up there to get kicked to death, but I couldn't dismiss the notion.

When I got back to the thin place, Cael was sitting up and I knelt beside him. "You'll heal. You're tougher than the palm of my grandma's hand."

He raised an eyebrow. "Bib, I apologize for accusing you of

139

cheating. There's no such thing as cheating in combat. But . . . to be so lucky, the gods must love you a great deal."

I didn't just laugh. Despite all the pain, I roared until I wept, fell to my knees, pounded the grass, and couldn't breathe.

Cael watched all that. "I guess there's tension between you and the gods after all."

I wiped my eyes. "Cael, I'm damn glad I didn't let you die. I needed that laugh. I never liked you much in our realm, but you've suffered enough here to be tolerable company."

"Go home."

"People keep telling me that," I said. "Once again, I invite you to come along. I bet you could use a grassy field more than your horse could."

Cael turned away and ignored me.

Pil must have been watching us, because when I stood, she stepped in and grabbed my arm. She led me a good distance away from everybody else and faced me, staring.

I said, "Like I told Desh, whatever it is, I didn't mean it."

She didn't grin even a bit. "Bib, when I was wounded—heck, dying—did you stop to help Cael before you came to help me?"

I had hoped I wouldn't need to explain that to her, but Desh must have told her. "That's true."

"Even though I might have died because you stopped to help him? A man who almost killed you? And might try to do it again?"

It sounded outrageous the way she said it, but it had seemed necessary. I feared this was another one of those times it was impossible to apologize. "You're right, Pil, about all of it. I don't guess it matters if I say it, but I'm sorry." I didn't think she would stab me, but if she was holding her sharp knife, I couldn't have seen it.

We held our places, almost trembling with tension. Then she jumped forward with her arms wide and grabbed me in an overwhelming hug. I staggered back a step. "Pil, do you have a disease that makes you lose your mind?"

"No, do you? I hope not," she mumbled with her cheek pressed against my chest.

"You have to explain why you're thrilled about my almost letting you die."

She took a deep breath. "Cael would have died for certain if you helped me, but you saved him even though he almost killed you, and I think that's the first time I've ever known you to be merciful for no reason. And those times you were merciful for a reason, it wasn't really mercy, was it?"

I patted Pil on the back a couple of times and eased her back to arm's length.

She kept talking. "I thought I might have to kill you sometime, which I would do, but it would be awful. I might never get over it, so I've been terrified that you'd go too far, and I'd have to kill you."

"Really? I'm not so easy to kill."

She looked up at me with one eyebrow raised. "When we were fighting Parth, which one of us got the other one impaled?"

"That's a point to consider."

Pil jumped in again. "I've been hopeful, because ever since we started this journey, you've seemed a little, I don't know, less blood-thirsty—not a lot, but I could tell."

"It doesn't seem that way to me." A sudden thought made my eyes widen. "Pil, do you realize that a couple of days ago you wanted to leave all these poor peasants to die?"

"No, I didn't! Wait. Did I? It sounds wrong, but now that you're reminding me, I do remember it." Her eyes widened, and she slapped my face hard enough for my teeth to shake. "You forced those memories back on me! Damn you!"

I nodded. "I fear that recovering them has changed your opinions on certain things." I would like to have known what memories she had recovered, but it would be rude to push her. "Since you've also seen my behavior change for no reason, I have to wonder whether some divine being has been tinkering with my memories."

Pil's face changed to a look of such sympathy I felt ashamed I had ever meddled with her mind, even by accident.

Without considering it much, I said, "Pil, am I an evil person?"

"Yes." She looked at my face. "Oh . . . I mean not to me. And

I'm sure some other people don't think that, like Desh, and probably Stan, so no, not entirely evil."

"So, you thought you might have to kill me because I was doing things that weren't entirely evil?"

Pil stared at me for a few seconds and looked at the black grass. Then she rushed up and hugged me again, harder than the first time.

As Pil, Stan, and Desh guided the farmers down to the thin place, I said to Hurd, "I'm glad you're here to help us. No matter what I told the Hill People, I know less about this place than I do about whales in the sea."

"Figured as much," Hurd wheezed. "I'll do it for you, even if you didn't bother to ask me politely."

"Are you coming with us?" Desh asked. "You'd be the most interesting person in any bar you walked into."

"Thank you for asking, but I need to tidy up the mess we left around here."

We all stared at Hurd for a few seconds.

Finally, Pil asked, "Are you the Lord of the Dark Lands, or something like that?"

Hurd squeaked and kept squeaking, laughing until it got awkward. "Lord of the Dark Lands? That's a good one!" He laughed some more.

I said, "I may never see you again, but if I do, then I owe you a favor."

"I'll remember that, sorcerer." Hurd leaned toward me and whispered, "Be suspicious of everybody."

"Really?" I whispered. "That's your big message at a time like this?"

Hurd pursed his lips. "Even of me."

I rolled my eyes.

Hurd glared at me. "Fine, just fine!" He whispered, "Gek . . . he's the one in your head."

Every sorcerer had bits of a Void Walker living in his head. Sometimes more than one Void Walker. It's what made a person a sorcerer, although I still didn't understand the details.

DEATH'S COLLECTOR: SWORD HAND

"Gek? Are you sure?"

"Now, why would I say it if I wasn't sure? Do I look like some kind of careless idiot? Is that what you think of me?"

"No, I believe you, Hurd, but it's a shock. Thanks for telling me." I didn't know what to think about that yet, but I planned to work it into my next conversation with Gek.

"Go on then! Goodbye!" Hurd shouted with a smile.

Something whipped me upward, not down as I had expected. The world went from dimness to bright light, as if I had pushed through a heavy curtain.

I was standing in a steep-sided, grassy valley at midday.

Five Hill People were fifty feet away and sprinting toward me.

Three soldiers on horseback charged past me toward the Hill People.

A thin volley of arrows fell on a group of Hill People farther down the way.

Pil appeared beside me, looked left and right, and began stringing her bow.

Even farther down the way, a huge slab of the valley wall slid off like mud and buried several Hill People who had run there to escape the arrows.

The five Hill People near us dragged down the three horsemen just as four more soldiers galloped past me to support their friends.

Stan appeared beside me. He glanced around, drew his sword, and glared at me like I had arranged all this chaos just to inconvenience him.

SEVENTEEN

I have chosen a life of violence, deceit, and sorcery, and I've lived it among brutes, liars, and gods. Whenever I find myself in an awkward, maybe fatal, situation, I assume that I deserve to be there. In fact, I may well have created the situation that's imperiling myself and everybody else in sight.

I had it coming, so I might as well not whine about it.

Because of this, I have been dropped into the middle of a battle more than once. But until I left the Dark Lands, I had never been literally dropped into the middle of an entire war. It was an awkward circumstance, and I intended to escape it by the fastest method possible.

Yet the farmers of Sandypool would be joining me in about three minutes. I doubted that any of them had chosen to be a vicious, lying asshole like me. Even Desh was more of a scholarly, even-handed soul. The villagers had pissed me off and might want to kill me, which didn't incline me to try hard to save their lives. I wouldn't miss them if they died scattered across this gritty, unmemorable battlefield, if that's what the world had planned for them.

But I decided in the middle of the fight to alter that destiny for them if I could. I had worked damned hard and bled substantial amounts to get them this far. That work would've all been pointless if I let them die now. An evil man would let them die, of course. I didn't care much about that, but I found I cared a little.

"Pil!" I shouted. "We need to block off this whole area for the villagers when they come through."

She nodded as if she were already thinking about it. She grabbed Stan's arm and pulled him along, handing him her bow. They ran toward the oncoming horsemen.

I trotted toward the Hill People, my sword drawn. I couldn't create much magic in three minutes. The sky was clear, and the grass was short. There was no loose dirt to blow into the air. Calling enough wasps and flies to make a difference would take a long time. I might never find enough.

I imagined a charging horde of ground hogs, and snorted. That wasn't practical, either.

So, it would be the sword. I felt excited, although that was foolish. I pointed my sword at the Hill People near me and laughed. I hoped they wouldn't be laughing at my arrogance around the campfire tonight.

Three of the fighters sprinted toward me, and I waited, breathing deep. One pointed at me and said something in his language. He and another angled off to go around me. That was strange, but I didn't have time to think about it. The third fighter, a woman, began dodging as she ran toward me.

I relaxed to let my sword push inspiration into me, but it was as quiet as a beaten dog. So, I jumped to attack the woman and crossed weapons with her a few times. I grew anxious that her friends might circle around me to the farmers. A good way to get killed in a fight is to be anxious about something not in the fight, so I shook my head clear.

After blocking one of the woman's thrusts, I sidestepped and swung hard. It was the most foolish kind of attack, but the Hill Woman had to block. My sword cut right through her spear and then through part of her skull.

I spun and chased the other two. They were dragging a soldier out of the saddle and spearing him to death. Beyond them, I saw Pil and Stan stretching a long string. In a literal flash, it became a four-foot-tall wooden fence. I reminded myself to compliment Pil on such handy magic. She must have already prepared it, maybe days or even weeks before.

The two other Hill People turned toward me, but for one it was too late. I sliced the side of his neck and then blocked the other's spear.

The man facing me glanced over my shoulder. I rolled aside to avoid a spear from behind and then thrust into the belly of the man in front of me. Without pausing, I rolled back the way I had come and stabbed the one behind me without looking.

Those were insane maneuvers, and I knew it. They felt relaxed, and I didn't want to argue with the results.

Right around me were three dead and dying Hill People, along with a frisky horse. I mounted the horse.

Over the next couple of minutes, I rode back and forth, keeping two, then three, and then four Hill People busy. Two retreated, so I chased them down and killed one. At last, ten more soldiers galloped past me toward the Hill People, who withdrew.

I turned my horse and saw that some of the farmers stood dazed while others shouted and wept. Desh, Pil, and Stan had gathered them all behind the fence. I rode to join them.

Stan yelled at me, "It's bad enough having Hill People around and waiting to get holes poked in us while we sleep! But now we get flung into a whole bunch, thick as my gamma's beard! What the hell is going on?"

"Do you want me to guess?" I asked.

"Sure, why not?" Stan lowered his voice, but his gesturing hands said more than drums and bugles. "I don't suppose we need any real knowledge, as long as whatever you say sounds good, huh?"

Usually Stan was steady, although aggravating. It was unlike him to pitch such a fit. But he did have a monstrous fear of the Hill People, and we had been right up against them for a couple of days.

I said, "I think we're inside the Empire now, or maybe along the border. It looks like we're also in the path of the Hill People's little adventure. The Imperials and the Hill People are skirmishing, and we plunked down right in the middle of it."

"Oh," Stan said. "It doesn't sound good, but it sounds like the kind of shit that would happen to us."

"Desh, are your people all right?" I asked.

"They will be. We have to take them up this valley, away from the Hill People's advance. I assume the Hill People aren't taking this route just to visit the ocean." He tried to smile but failed like a collapsing bridge.

Pil whispered something to Desh and gripped his arm hard. I assumed he had told her the details of his memory problem, and she must have confided in him.

"Desh," I said, "before we go, I'd like to exile your ma from our retreat."

His eyes widened. "Bib! The Hill People will kill anybody they find."

"That's certainly true," a man shouted from above us. I shaded my eyes to stare up the valley wall and saw five men on horses, all dressed in Imperial colors—the soldiers and the horses both. A fellow on the left who was a few years my junior called down, "I have seen a lot of things, but I've never seen something like that. Who are you?"

"Travelers," I shouted. "I'm Caddell, Master of Goats."

Desh sighed.

The man up on the wall laughed. "I just bet that's true. I'm Ludlow." His smile disappeared, and he leaned forward in the saddle. "I'm about to tell you something, and it may seem like I'm sharing important tactical information with you. I am, but there's a reason."

"All right," I called up to him, certain that I didn't want to know anything about his tactical situation.

"We outnumbered the Hill People by ten to one this morning, and they killed over forty of my men. We killed eleven of them. Well, that's not exactly true. We killed six. You killed the other five."

"Pure luck!" I said. "It'd never happen again in a thousand years."

"I have to believe you." He laughed with such obvious pleasure I almost smiled. "I'd never call a fighting man like you a liar, but maybe you're the luckiest fellow I've ever seen. I just have to buy a man like that a drink." He pointed up the valley. "Meet me where the valley gets shallow, about half a mile." Ludlow smiled again and cantered his horse toward the meeting spot, which also happened to be toward the middle of the Empire.

Before I even clucked at my horse, some god grabbed my spirit and yanked it up through my skull. Usually, I have a second to adjust and be sick. This time, my journey to the trading place happened too fast to feel anything.

It was nighttime in the trading place, with no moon and a scattering of stars that I didn't recognize. I was almost facing the gazebo and saw firelight reflected off the marble, the field of fat, cheery flowers, and my boots.

"Where have you been, Murderer?" Harik boomed. The sound staggered me, but I pretended that I didn't notice.

I made my voice matter-of-fact. "I assume this is a test, Your Magnificence, because a scabby, retching dung-house rat such as yourself, who is also the God of Death, must know everything. Therefore, any knowledge I possess is meaningless to you, and the purpose of your question was to see whether I could tell that I was being tested. And I could, just now, so we must be done."

Somebody out of my view whispered, "Excuse me." I heard footsteps.

Harik whispered, "It was not that amusing! Stop laughing and come back here!"

I waited. Nothing I could think of to say would give me an advantage. There were plenty of things I could say unthinkingly that might hurt me.

After a long pause, Harik said, "You are uncharacteristically quiet, Murderer. Tell me about the past couple of days so I can determine whether your memory is accurate."

"It was a magnificent experience, or I've been told that anyway," I said. "I spent most of it passed out."

"Ah. How do you remember that coming to be?"

"Something about red fish and a drinking contest."

Another voice whispered, "He's lying to you." I recognized the voice as Fingit.

"Of course he's lying to me!" Harik whispered. "He would lie even if the truth would save him from drowning and give him a two-foot-long member!"

"Do you want to tell him that you know he's lying?"

"No!" Harik whispered. "I don't know what he's lying about, and if I don't know that, it will be evident that I don't know everything. Being all-knowing is a considerable advantage in negotiations. I have cultivated that image for centuries."

Fingit whispered, "That's a vain and pointless image, but you're right to let this go. The Murderer probably isn't aware that there are places we can't see. But if you reveal that you really don't know where he was, that will tell him there are places he can hide from us."

Harik waited a few seconds. "That almost sounds smart."

Fingit whispered, "That's because you're not quite clever enough to know what smart sounds like. Just don't give him any power, whatever you do."

"I don't need you to chaperone me when I trade!" Harik whispered.

"Krak thinks you do."

I heard the sound of one god smacking another. Fingit whispered a curse.

I stared straight ahead and didn't move. "I beg your pardon, Mighty Harik, he with the most repugnant bodily fluids in all existence, did you say something?"

"Nothing," Harik said. "Be silent."

Fingit whispered, "If Father had been here, you wouldn't have given the Nub his memories. Now he may be ruined for all time."

"Why do you care? He won't trade with you!"

"The certainty of that does not approach unity," Fingit whispered.

"Why can't you just say that there's a bit of a chance?"

"Moron!" Fingit whispered.

"Hack!"

"Wait, are we done with him? You shouldn't have brought him. This is another thing you didn't think through."

Harik whispered, "Be still! Why do you whine about the Nub? You still might salvage him. Lutigan says the Knife is just fine."

"My theory is—"

"Krak's profound ass! Can't you just stop pretending you're the smartest being in existence?" Harik whispered.

Fingit sniffed. "My theory is that the longer a memory has been missing, the more traumatic its reintegration. The Knife's memories were gone for a few weeks. The Nub's memories were missing for a few years."

"That's stupid."

"Maybe. Theoretically, we could give the Murderer back his memories," Fingit whispered. "If we did, then he might be too broken to unlace his trousers by himself!"

Both of them snickered.

I tried to swallow the idea that a god really had taken memories from me sometime. The concept was too big, and I found myself starting to pant. I forced two deep breaths, but apart from that, I stayed motionless. I didn't even close my eyes or clench my fist in case it should give me away. It was one of my life's greatest acts of will.

"But we should consider it with care," Harik whispered. "If we restore the memories, he might become more dangerous."

"Aw, shit! I'll be glad when all this is over," Fingit whispered.

Harik said out loud, "I am done with you, Murderer."

The god threw me back into my body. It wasn't particularly brutal. I had experienced worse many times.

So, I couldn't blame that for the fact that I fell straight off my horse.

EIGHTEEN

After Stan and Pil were done laughing at me for falling off my horse, I remounted and rode up the valley to meet Ludlow and tell him lies. We had known him only a few minutes, and he wasn't entitled to any information that could hurt us or even embarrass us.

I tried to imagine what memories the gods might have taken from me, but I had no way to even guess. Knowing that they were gone made me feel worn, like some weak place in me was waiting to break. But I knew that such feelings pass once sorcerers become accustomed to a situation like mine.

I could discuss my missing memories with Desh or Pil. They would understand, but I wasn't positive Pil had forgiven me, and I was sure Desh hadn't. I hated to suspect that either of them would make a deal to take my memories. However, only a sorcerer could make such a trade, so I couldn't assume they were innocent.

On the other hand, maybe my memories had been taken to protect me. I couldn't resist thinking back on the most horrible events in my life and wondering whether I had been made to forget something worse.

I concluded that one thing was true without a doubt. Whoever had done this to me was unaware that I had found out about it, and it would be best if they stayed ignorant.

Of course, such speculations would only distract me and make me doubt myself, and neither of those would kill a single Hill Person. Instead of continuing to worry in this idle way, I watched the horsemen waiting for me at the shallow end of the valley. One of them waved, so I assumed he was buying the drinks.

I had met thousands of unexceptional people, and Ludlow looked like another one, except for his butter-blond hair that had been ratted by his helmet. Dirt and a little blood stained his red and gold tunic. He sat his fractious horse as if he'd been nailed there.

I rode closer, and Ludlow smiled like I was a good friend who had just returned from a few minutes spent voiding my bladder. The four soldiers behind him were edging their horses forward, weapons ready, as if I had just returned from the privy carrying a giant ax. Ludlow held up a hand and spoke to them before riding out to meet me. His men stayed behind, armed and grumpy.

Still smiling, Ludlow examined me. "It's damn good to meet you, Caddell." Still on horseback, he sipped from a flask and handed it to me.

I decided to soften him up with a fragment of truth. "My name's Bib, not Caddell. Sorry." I took a swallow of some fine and quite expensive spirits. Ludlow must have been a wealthy man.

Ludlow smiled. "No apology needed. I might have been an enemy. You couldn't tell for sure. It was a perfectly acceptable ruse of warfare." He took the flask back and drank. "Since we're talking about war, we have one, don't we?"

"You have one," I said. "I was on my way to some other place."

"Look, just hear me out," Ludlow said. "The Hill People might catch you no matter what direction you go. So, it would be safer for everybody if you come with us."

"I don't know, General . . ." I raised my eyebrows. Instead of squawking about his proper rank, the man raised his eyebrows back at me with a little smile. I added, "Marshal?"

Ludlow shrugged. "General's good enough." He passed the flask over to me.

"General, I am not by nature an order-taker. Say that I do join up. Then one of your captains would give me a dumb order, and I'd tell him to go to hell, and he'd try to teach me discipline. Then we'd have bodies everyplace. I might be one of them, so it doesn't seem worth it."

He shook his head. "No, that would be awful. That's why you wouldn't be in the chain of command. You'd be my adjutant, with an honorary rank of major. Or brigadier, whatever you want. You could ride around and do anything you think is smart, as long as it hurts them and not us."

Assuming he could trust me or intimidate me, it was a smart offer. He wouldn't be able to control me no matter what my assignment. So, he was offering me freedom, which I already had, and making it sound like a gift. It was also horseshit. Generals are in command and can't help giving commands.

On the other hand, the whole reason for this jaunt was getting farmers to safety in the Empire. Well, Ludlow and his people were the Empire. I could just turn the villagers over and forget them in exchange for giving Ludlow a day or two of help.

While I was thinking, Ludlow patted his horse's neck. "I can see that my offer doesn't interest you much. How about this: you'll have the rank of sorcerer second class."

I stared at him with no expression.

He gestured toward the valley behind me. "I saw ninety people just show up from out of the air. There's a sorcerer around, and I'm betting you're him."

I saw no point in lying about it. "Why second class?"

"Cora is my first-class sorcerer." He pointed at a slight, brunette woman standing a hundred feet away.

If Ludlow had a sorcerer working for him, he was more than rich. He was probably some kind of earl or viscount. Maybe a duke. "That's kind, General, but I don't want to stomp all over another sorcerer's grapes. Maybe my friends and I could be like stray dogs that follow the army and eat scraps, although not literally. We would pitch in on any fighting, of course."

"If those are your conditions—"

"I have one more. I need to consider our virtuous, hardworking villagers. They are compliant to a breathtaking degree and wouldn't cause trouble. I know you wouldn't leave them behind."

"Of course we'll take them with us." Ludlow said it as if I had suggested he might cook and eat them instead. "We can't leave them here to die."

"I was about to say that very thing!"

Ludlow scratched at his hair, which would probably have been longer if it weren't so tangled. "Those peasants will be slow, but we won't be too fast, either. I sent couriers to warn the fortress, and they will need time to call in the troops. We're going to delay the Hill People, not run away from them." He scratched at his hair again. "Lutigan damn this helmet! I saw that three of your friends are fighters, not farmers. Will they all help with the defense?"

"I can't promise it, but I expect they will."

"Good!" He stared down the valley toward the farmers. "We won't be moving fast, but we do need to move. Are your virtuous peasants compliant enough to leave right now?"

"If you can spare some horses, that will help them move faster."

Ludlow looked pained. "With forty men dead? I bet we can find them plenty of horses."

I galloped back down the valley and explained to my friends how I had obligated them to trail behind Ludlow. Stan complained on principle, but soon they all agreed that it was the best thing since we couldn't fly over the Hill People's heads to some nicer place.

Desh explained the bones of the plan to Yoadie, Tira, and the elders. Actually, Desh told them to go with those soldiers and don't be a bother if they wanted to live. Except for Tira, the farmers were so scared and beaten down they had no notion of arguing.

Desh's mother started complaining about the soldiers' foul ancestries and their filthy bodily habits. Desh stomped away with Tira following and shouting abuse. When Tira turned her harangue on Desh, Pil caught up and slapped Tira hard before punching her in the stomach. Then Pil walked away, leaving Desh with the old woman who was bent over dragging for breath.

I considered driving Tira away right then no matter what Desh wanted, but it would involve a lengthy argument with him, and I had other things to do. "Pil," I said, "this fence that you conjured out of a string will bemuse future travelers in this valley. I'm sorry you can't turn it into a string again."

She smiled brighter than I had seen in weeks. "Don't worry about it. You'd be shocked to see what I can do with the other things I have in this pouch, like an acorn, a nail, a skunk's hind tooth, and I'll let you guess the rest."

Five soldiers brought twenty horses down into the valley. Desh and Yoadie got the slower villagers mounted. They had used up most of their food and water, but Ludlow promised they would be fed from his supply wagons. Ludlow also loaned mounts to the four of us.

We decided right away that Pil, Stan, Desh, and I would all be needed in the rear to fight the Hill People. That left Tira helping Yoadie keep the farmers moving, which disgusted me, but I could either let it happen or cut off Tira's head.

I rode up to Tira, taking no pains to steer my mount clear of her.

She jumped away and sneered. "You don't think about other people, do you? Big warrior, big hero—well, you're nothing but a nasty outsider with the brains of a water pail and the morals of a weasel, and deep down you know it." She raised her voice and pointed at me. "We all know it!"

I leaned down toward Desh's mom and kept my voice conversational. "If you talk to anybody the way you talked to those two who killed themselves—hell, if you talk to anybody the way you just talked to me—I will ride back here and stab you in the heart without saying hello, asking why you did it, or telling you to kiss my foot. You'll be dead in ten seconds. Consider this a bolt of lightning always hanging over your head."

As I turned away, Tira shouted, "Wait!" I watched her face fall apart like a bridge made of sand. She whispered up to me, "If you kill me, promise you'll take care of everybody. They can't take care of themselves." She trudged back toward her neighbors with her head down.

If Tira expected me to cry for her, she had a harsh disappointment coming. I turned and cantered my horse away. Soon the villagers began moving up the valley at a reasonable pace, accompanied by three mounted soldiers.

Ludlow commanded about 150 men. Forty of them held their ground in the valley, protecting the farmers from any Hill People who might arrive. The rest he stationed on each side of the valley.

Pil, Desh, Stan, and I rode up to join Ludlow, so I heard him speak to his officers. "We'll use those peasants to set the pace of our retreat. Lippy, take thirty men and stay behind us as reserve. Once we start moving, I plan to retreat all night and well into the morning. I don't want them to catch us in the dark if we can avoid it."

Within ten minutes, the shadows were stretching, and the Hill People hadn't returned. Ludlow detailed three men to pass the orders to move.

Desh raised his head and looked around, as if he had heard thunder. I didn't hear anything, but a couple of seconds later, Limnad raced out of the valley toward us. By the time Ludlow and his men grasped that something extraordinary was happening, she had plucked Desh out of the saddle and set him on his feet. She yelled, "I couldn't find you! Where were you?"

Now all the men sat their stamping horses while shifting, swearing, giving orders, and offering unhelpful observations. Limnad ignored them and didn't wait for Desh to answer before she embraced him.

Three heartbeats later, Limnad pushed Desh away and whispered something.

Desh whispered back.

Limnad howled, "What did you do to your spirit?"

I dismounted and ran toward them.

Desh bit his lip. "I remembered something."

"Well, it changed you! Stop remembering it!" Limnad shouted.

"I don't think I can."

"Your spirit is wrong. It's sick!"

Desh reached for Limnad's hand, but she jerked away.

"Why did you do it?" Limnad asked in a more normal tone.

Desh shook his head. "It was done to me. I didn't ask for it."

Limnad grew still and floated a foot off the ground. In a voice like grinding rocks, she demanded, "Who did it?"

Desh didn't glance at me. "The gods."

Limnad spun twice in the air, screamed, and ripped big chunks of dirt out of the ground when she landed.

I opened my mouth, but Desh shook his head. Since he was the expert on river spirits, I stayed still.

Limnad whipped off her necklace and held it out. "Trade. Tell them to make you right."

Desh took the necklace. "I'll try." A moment later, he was holding the necklace in his other hand without having moved. No time passes in our world when trading with the gods, which can lead to some odd effects when the gods want to be whimsical.

Desh sighed. "They won't do it."

Limnad snatched back her necklace and shouted, "You're too sick to touch! Too sick to look at!" She sprinted away so fast I could hardly follow her with my eyes.

"Desh, I'm sorry," I said.

"Shut up." His shoulders were starting to sag. "I didn't tell her what you did because I want her to still care about you."

"It would be fair if she hated me."

"No. If we need her to help us out of trouble, I won't be able to convince her. She may come if you ask, though."

It was calculating. It was gaining a practical advantage by lying to somebody he loved. It was treating his friend as no more than a tool. It was putting expediency above decency.

It was the most purely sorcerer-like thing I had ever seen Desh do.

Desh dragged himself into the saddle as if he were hauling sacks of potatoes along.

Ludlow rode over to me and asked in a commander's voice, "What was that?"

"Lover's quarrel," I said.

"She is his lover?" Ludlow paused to scrutinize Desh. "Is he a sorcerer too?"

"It does seem that way."

Ludlow glanced at Pil and Stan before he leaned toward me. "Just how many sorcerers do you have in your group?"

"Five," I said.

"There are only four of you."

"As far as you know."

NINETEEN

Ludlow moved his force northeast with the villagers that afternoon, and we trailed behind. Desh volunteered to scout for Ludlow. He was not in any way suited to such work, even if he was a sorcerer. He had stayed apart from the rest of us since Limnad screamed at him and left, so I assumed he wanted time alone.

Pil tried to talk Desh out of it, but he paid no attention. I feared that he distrusted me so much he would react badly no matter how I tried to convince him he was being stupid. Pil offered to scout with him, but he told her to take her offer and do something with it that would embarrass any dockside whore.

A few minutes later, Pil said to me, "I don't know what to do about Desh."

"You mean you're not going to do the whore thing he suggested?"

Her eyebrows flattened. "Is it possible for you to not act like an ass?"

"History says no." I smiled at her as gently as I could. "I have an idea, though. Let's ask Stan to go with him. If Stan is persistent and aggrieved, I bet Desh won't run him off."

Pil shook her head. "That's insane. It tops every insane thing you've ever said."

"To somebody who's been treated like dirt, Stan is the best possible companion. Nobody else commiserates about how badly you've been shit on like Stan."

Pil paused. "I might be sending Stan to die, and he's terrified of the Hill People."

"He makes his own decisions. If he decides to be so in love with you that he follows Desh into peril and ruin, nobody made him say yes."

"Eat a flaming toad, you bastard!" She trotted her mount across the fifty paces to Stan, who was busy riding along and eavesdropping on some soldiers. After a minute, I saw Pil and Stan engaged in a confusion of objects handed back and forth. Then Stan waved at me, pale but steady, and rode off to catch Desh.

When Pil rode up beside me, I asked, "What did you give him? Or what did he give you?" The question ran up to the edge of impoliteness for sorcerers, but I asked anyway.

"Oh, I traded swords with him," she said, staring away at the flat emptiness of the horizon.

"Your sword that's charmed to defend your life?"

"I sure as heck didn't loan him the one that was forged by a god!"

I found that to be interesting information. "Anything else?"

Pil shrugged.

"Where's your necklace?"

"Fine!" She glared at me. "I loaned him that too!"

"And it does . . . ?"

Pil rolled her eyes and looked fifteen years old. "Makes it harder for arrows to hit you!"

I chuckled. "Spears too, I guess. And . . . ?"

"All right, I'll tell you, just stop asking! Gloves that help you catch fish. A belt buckle that makes dogs and wolves like you. That black dagger from the Dark Lands."

"The one Cael almost killed you with?"

"Yes, and don't interrupt. Two magical disguises. Two rings—one to make you cool when it's hot, and one to make you warm when it's cold. A marble that lets you see in the dark for a few minutes. And a blue jay's foot that will scream when strangers come close—it only does that once, though."

My mouth was hanging open. "All that? Krak's dipping nose, really?"

She grinned at me. "Yes, and if you knew what Desh carried on him, you'd be terrified. Really, you'd never go near him again."

"And you gave all that to Stan?"

"Loaned. I don't want to send somebody to their death . . . for any reason." Pil frowned. "Not if I can do something about it."

I didn't remind her how she had recently advocated for the farmers' deaths. She knew it, even if she was ignoring it. When her memories returned, it restored her to a view on death she'd held as a younger person. That would be mighty young, since she had turned seventeen a few months ago.

Pil said, "As long as I'm feeling so ass-blasted generous, take this." She held out two small leather bottles. "Desh gave me four of these, but you can use two to help us all get to safety."

I stopped breathing for a moment. Each bottle contained a square of magical power, which was a significant amount. These bottles would just about triple the power I had available. "Thank you, Pil. That's very kind of you. Are you sure you won't need them?"

Pil snorted and waved me off. "Don't act motherly, it doesn't suit you. I have everything I need."

Ludlow had sent scouts in other directions besides straight behind us. He also sent a man to ride along with Desh. I guess Ludlow didn't intend to get killed for trusting strangers too much. He probably was a fine officer, which was like saying he was the best viper in the nest.

Just before sunset, we dismounted and walked to rest the horses. They had been trotting no faster than the heartiest unmounted farmer anyway, which was not taxing. The ground had turned from broken to gradual rolls, but still it was easier to climb than a pile of dirt built by a little boy.

The moon had fallen low toward the horizon when one of Ludlow's men rode back to us. "A pond is sitting up there, or a watering hole sort of thing, right up there, and them ground splitters is already drinking. We're holding these horses back till all the folks drink, so you keep them reins held tight."

Half an hour later, I spotted the pond, which was forty feet across and looked to be runoff rather than spring-fed. The dirt around it showed me that during the wet months, it more than doubled in size. The horses could smell water, and discipline finally went to hell. Horses and soldiers drank indiscriminately, and water sacks were filled.

I had been examining the terrain, trying to make a decision. A little wash, no more than two feet deep, ran across our path and cut through the pond. After I considered everything, I walked over to Ludlow, guided by the sound of his voice. He was giving orders like a blacksmith swinging a hammer and was not inclined to pay attention to me.

I tried twice to catch his attention but failed. Then I raised my voice. "General, would you like me to smite your enemies with the power of the gods here or someplace else? I think here is a good place."

In the silence, a woman snickered, and it wasn't Pil. I peered by the meager light and saw Ludlow leaning down whispering to his sorcerer, Cora. She whispered back. I silently cursed my poor hearing.

Ludlow said, "Wherever you think is best, Bib. What are you thinking about doing?"

"Better that I don't share that knowledge, General, much better. Trust me."

He cocked his head. "Seems like I don't have much choice."

I laughed to sound more fearless. There was no reason for it, but what the hell. "Go on your way, General. I'll catch up after the massacre."

I suppose Ludlow had nothing to say to that, because he gave a few more orders, mounted, and rode away.

"Pil, this is a job for a single sorcerer."

"Be quiet. I'm not leaving you alone. Don't even argue."

I grinned. "You'll break Stan's heart if he comes back and you're dead."

"You are the very spirit of humor," she said flatly. "What can I do to help?"

We rode three hundred paces back the way we came, which was toward the Hill People. "Do you have anything else that screams at strangers?" I asked.

"No, but I can make something like that in half an hour. I need a bird's foot, though."

"Never mind. Just watch for Hill People. Now that the moon has set, they'll be hard as hell to spot."

I pulled some white bands and whirled them into the sky about two miles uphill. The cost in power was low since I wasn't pulling a monster storm together in a hurry. I let the storm build on its own— the conditions were good. I wanted a big, water-heavy storm that I could keep floating along without dropping its rain.

Two hours later, the storm had gathered to my satisfaction. I had expected the Hill People to arrive soon, but maybe they were occupied with other mischief. I spent a steady trickle of power to keep the storm hovering in place and poised to rain like a waterfall.

Three hours after that, I began to fear I'd have to give up this plan. I had used half a square of magic power already.

"Remind me what we're doing," Pil said. "Oh, that's right. Nothing! You're watching a sky that won't rain, and I'm watching a whole lot of things that aren't Hill People!"

"You can go home," I said. "Oh, that's right, you don't have one!"

Pil grumbled. I must not have been worth wasting a curse on. Then she said, "I see them! And they're close! No, it's not them, it's Desh."

Desh and Stan galloped into view, but Ludlow's scout wasn't

with them. Stan shouted, "The buggers are back there, close enough to fart on!"

I stared, let my focus drift, and saw movement at least a hundred paces away. "Come on!" I kicked my horse into a gallop toward the pond, glancing back. Pil and the others were just behind me.

I pulled another band and twisted it. Water fell from the entire storm, but I kept it to a modest rain.

Withing seconds, a trickle of water ran down the wash. We rode across and halted close enough to see how the water was running.

"What is he doing?" Desh asked Pil.

"I have no idea. Either it'll be magnificent, or we'll all die."

"Leave him behind!" Desh shouted.

Maybe Pil shook her head, or maybe she made a nasty gesture. I wasn't looking at her, but Desh must have understood her intention. He drew his weapon and turned to wait with her for the Hill People.

Stan did the same. "Do you want your sword back?" he asked Pil.

"Not yet, but thank you."

"Everybody be quiet!" I bellowed.

The timing would be tricky. I was calculating the speed and volume of the water, the distance uphill and up to the clouds, and what I knew of the Hill People's pace and tactics.

Sorcerers, even unschooled ones, were all exceptional mathematicians, and I had recently formed a theory about how Void Walkers helped us with that. If Gek really was in my head, he could pay his rent now by solving this mess of calculations.

When the Hill People came close enough to be seen again, I released most of the storm. Uphill from us, water fell like it was poured from a trough. However, on top of us, the rain was no more than pelting.

The silent Hill People rushed toward us. I couldn't tell whether Semanté was with them. Three spears flew at us, but I rotted the shafts so that the heads wobbled aside. At least twenty Hill People waded into the wash, where the water now came up to their knees and slowed them down.

I whipped another band and threw as much water as possible

straight onto the Hill People. They hesitated; maybe they were stunned. Just as the deluge became almost too strong to stand under, the immense mass of water that had been crashing its way downhill arrived. The wash was the lowest spot around, maybe for miles, and every smack of water rushed to it over the hard, packed plains.

The wave smashed everybody in the wash or near it. With luck, it drowned every Hill Person there.

Pil shouted, "I can't believe you did that. How did you make that work? I would have bet my virginity that you couldn't do that!"

I didn't explain that Gek had done all the hard work in my head. Instead, I yelled, "This rain is already lightening up! Let's catch Ludlow while—"

I found myself on the ground underneath my horse, which was neighing and rolling on me. When the beast rolled back the other way, I felt something crack in my hips. I closed my eyes and sucked air for a while.

When I opened my eyes, Pil and Stan were coaxing my horse to roll at least partway up. I could see a spear in the animal's shoulder, and he was more interested in writhing than in cooperating. I helped everybody by groaning and cursing, with a little weeping to spice things up.

Desh grabbed my wrists from over my head, ready to pull me out. He bent over me so that I saw his face upside down, and he said, "I wouldn't usually tell you this kind of thing, but I made a bargain with the gods."

"Wonderful!" I said, my voice sliding higher between pants. "Can you give me the details later?"

"No. I couldn't convince them to make Limnad forgive me now, but I made them promise that she would come back to me someday."

"Oh, Desh, you can't trust them."

"I know that." He said it so softly I could hardly hear him over Stan's cursing. "Do you think I'm an ignorant newcomer? I protected Limnad and myself against treachery."

"You're probably right." Sweat and rainwater were running into my ears. "If anybody can get close to an even deal, I guess it's you."

"You told me that the gods now insist that sorcerers give up years of life when they trade—either one year of their own or ten years from people around them. They still do that."

Despite the shouting and furor, everything seemed to get quiet.

"I gave them ten years of your life, Bib."

TWENTY

I didn't kill Desh right away because a horse was lying on me. Also, my hip was probably broken. Either would have put me at a disadvantage in deadly conflict. Plus, I remembered Pil saying that Desh was a lethal and horrifying figure, unless naked and without magical objects. Even unclothed, he could destroy most men. Desh was no heroic fighter, but he made up for that with tenacity and inventiveness.

So, when Desh told me he had thrown away ten years of my life, I swallowed and nodded. Nothing either of us could say would make things any better or any worse. I would be patient. I was a killer, but I didn't have to be a hasty killer.

If Desh had wanted to murder me, the very best time to do it would have been when I was trapped under a horse. He had passed up that chance, so I figured he wanted me alive to fume and worry every minute about those ten years I would lose.

His foolishness shocked me. I was likely to be killed by something long before the natural span of my life ended—almost certainly more than ten years before. I would never miss those years. So, I dismissed Desh's action from my thoughts, except for one thing.

I had to kill him. Even if I was inclined to let his attack pass, he might decide later that taking ten years from me was inadequate. He could go back to the gods and take another ten. Or kill me outright with one of his mortifying enchanted doodads.

But Pil had talked about Desh as if he were a granite warrior with a ten-foot-long weapon and a six-foot-long spear. I would study him and choose my time. It didn't have to be done today.

Besides, if Semanté hurled a spear through my head, or his, none of this would mean a damn thing.

When the floodwater fell, it seemed that all the Hill People had gone. I doubted that my stunt with water had killed every one of them, but any survivors must have retreated.

The sky was shading to gray in the east by the time I had restored my horse and myself to health. I regretted sacrificing more magical power.

Desh and Stan rode out once more to scout for the enemy, and I was happy to see Desh go. The idea of killing him made me glum.

Pil and I rode hard the other direction to catch Ludlow's force. When we overtook them, Ludlow dropped back to chat.

I said, "We killed a neat parcel of them and delayed the rest. But don't have any picnics yet, since they're likely to regroup and catch us before dark. We ought to prepare another ambush. I'm certain they'll be warier this time."

"I think so too." Ludlow flipped back his hair, which was indeed long once untangled. "There's a little cliff that drops off some miles ahead, just about ten feet high. It runs dozens of miles both ways. We can get there by midafternoon."

This already sounded like an awful idea, but Ludlow and his explanation galloped onward. "We've built a big ramp for horses and wagons, but the Hill People can't know about that."

"Probably," I muttered.

Ludlow ignored that. "We'll keep half our men down under the cliff close to the ramp. When our scouts lead the enemy right to the edge of the cliff, we'll use our superior speed to charge up the ramp and trap them."

I hated to ask. "What about the other half of your men?"

"We'll keep them right up against the cliff face, and they'll trample any Hill People who go over the cliff." He lifted both hands and smiled as if he'd just baked the perfect pie.

It was an awkward plan, but to be honest, it wasn't horrible. It likely would shock and defeat most unmounted troops. However, most troops had not trained in warfare since they could walk.

Ludlow must have interpreted my face correctly. "Things are different now that we're in open terrain instead of that damn valley. That wasn't horse country."

I chewed the inside of my cheek. "How do you feel about grasshoppers? A million grasshoppers would slow them down."

Ludlow sat up straighter and smiled. "No, don't go to the trouble. You did the hard work this morning. Now it's our turn."

"If you do this, you're going to wish that your only problem was a million grasshoppers jumping all over you."

He laughed deep in his belly. Then he galloped away to give orders, and maybe get his hair braided.

Before Pil and I could talk about how much everybody was going to get killed, Cora the sorcerer rode up right between us. She was short, delicate, and about twenty-five years old. Her dark braid fell far down her back, and her small mouth was pressed tight. She asked in a surprisingly loud voice, "I don't suppose you have any questions about the plan, do you?"

"No," Pil said.

"I don't guess so," I added. We didn't need any trouble.

She flipped her braid forward over her shoulder. "Not even any questions about which way to run when everybody starts getting speared to death?"

I glanced at Pil. "Now that you raise the point, is there any chance of influencing the general's tactical thinking?"

Cora squeezed her eyes shut for a moment. "I doubt it."

Pil asked, "So, the battle in the valley didn't make him more thoughtful about this war?"

Cora peered ahead as if she could see Ludlow through all the horsemen. "It's like this. He watched that fight through the eyes of a conqueror. It's all about what he can accomplish. My people were conquered. It's easy for me to see what can be done to us."

"Do we desert? I'd rather not," Pil said. "I promised Desh I wouldn't leave those villagers behind, and I don't want him to laugh at me."

"Why are you helping them?" Cora asked.

"They owe us money and promised to put on a play for us," I said.

She stared at me as if I had snot running down my face.

Pil said, "Don't pay him any mind—he's not good for much until you need somebody killed. Then just throw him like a rotten apple at whoever you want dead." She smiled at me when Cora wasn't looking.

I said, "If we're not going to run away, we'd better do something useful. Cora, I'm Bib. I'm a Caller. This is Pil, who is a Binder."

The woman smiled. "I'm a Bender."

That was some interesting luck. A Bender could reshape things, or masses of things, as long at the things weren't alive. As a Caller, I could change and influence living things and natural forces. Pil and Desh were Binders, who could imbue objects with magical properties.

Some sorcerers hated to deal with other types of sorcerers, which has led to feuds in which sorcerers died, or were maimed, or got buried under collapsed castles. However, I had found that working with sorcerers of different types gives us a lot more options.

Sorcerers came in three more types. Breakers could make things not exist, as long as the things weren't living. Burners could cause things to burst into white-hot flames, again if the things weren't alive. Daughters served the Goddess of the Unknowable and almost always went mad before they turned twenty, but their magic was limited only by their imagination and the amount of power available.

I looked back and forth between Cora and Pil. "I don't guess we can take over the battle?"

"No," Cora said, "that wouldn't sit well with Ludlow."

"So, he'll just lose, and everybody will die," Pil said.

"It doesn't have to be that way." I shrugged. "He may lose the battle, but then we can start another one."

While we sorcerers made plans, Ludlow sent riders to find each pair of scouts and explain the plan. I tried to imagine Desh's face when he heard it.

We all reached the little cliff, and most of the force pushed down the ramp. Horses could walk down it six abreast, so the scene resembled an hourglass as Ludlow's men tried to push through.

The farmers were sent on ahead with a small escort. Ludlow positioned his forces, and we sorcerers rode around examining the battlefield. After our examination, we found Ludlow.

Cora said, "Sir, I'd like permission to stand with Bib and Pil during the battle."

"I don't like that." Ludlow frowned. "I need you here with me. Just in case they hit us with sorcery."

"The three of us can defend you a whole lot better if we're together. And over there." She nodded at a small pile of rocks far outside the battlefield.

Ludlow slapped his leg. "I don't know. I . . . well, I trust you, so I guess I'd better say yes."

"Thank you, sir."

We rode down the ramp and far along the cliff. Then we left our mounts at the bottom and climbed up to hide among the rocks. We watched without saying much until midafternoon. Then it came: a piercing, birdlike shriek from out past the battlefield.

I said, "That was beautiful, Pil. It was well worth scouring the countryside for that dead bird."

Two of Ludlow's scouts were leading the Hill People in. Desh and Stan must have still been out searching for the enemy, or else the enemy had found them first and gotten lucky.

Cora grinned up at the sky. "Look at all those vultures. They must know that a battle will be happening soon."

I grunted. "Don't be funnier than me."

The first flaw in Ludlow's plan soon showed itself. The scouts rode toward the ramp so they could head down it. About thirty Hill People were following them, still distant but visible. When the scouts angled for the ramp, the Hill People did the same.

Ludlow must have seen that as clearly as I did. Trapping the enemy would be impossible if they ran toward the ramp. Defending the ramp was pointless. The Hill People could just climb down the cliff wherever they wanted, or better, they could stand on the top and throw spears until they ran out.

The only two alternatives were retreating or rushing as many horsemen as possible up the ramp before the Hill People arrived. There the soldiers could fight from horseback on open terrain. Maybe Ludlow was right, and it would make a difference.

I knew what I would choose. I believed that retreat was a tactic used far too infrequently.

Ludlow did not choose to retreat, and that didn't surprise me. Also, he was the first one to charge up the ramp, and that didn't surprise me either.

By the time the thirty Hill People reached him, Ludlow had gotten forty horsemen up the ramp and ready to charge. Many of the Hill People carried extra spears on their backs, and about twenty of them threw those spears. Each spear knocked a soldier out of the saddle, and the charge fell apart.

That was the first fifteen seconds of the battle.

Horsemen continued to climb the ramp to reinforce the mangled troops on top. While Ludlow was shouting to rally his stunned men, the Hill People charged the horsemen in pairs. In each pair, one would stop the horse with his spear while the other speared the rider out of the saddle.

I couldn't make out more detail than that, although I did spot somebody who I thought might be Semanté. While I was watching, Ludlow fell out of the saddle.

The thirty Hill People speared about forty more soldiers. One Hill Person was struck down. All told, the Hill People were defeating Ludlow about sixty to one.

That was the next minute of the battle.

Beside me, Cora whispered, "By Weldt and his hideous vows, those people can't be human."

"They're human," I said. "I heard one of them fart after supper once."

Horsemen were still charging up the ramp to join the few who had survived thus far. Then for some reason that only Krak and his mistresses understood, the Hill People retreated away from the ramp, toward me, following the cliff's edge. They were moving to the exact spot where Ludlow had intended to trap and slaughter them.

Soldiers surged up the ramp like an upside-down waterfall of horse flesh. Within a minute, over eighty soldiers pursued the Hill People as they fell back. Some horsemen veered aside to begin encircling the enemy.

Shouts and dust rose from the ramp, and some soldiers on that side wheeled their horses. I stood on top of the rocks to get a better view. Another sizable force of Hill People had attacked from the other side of the ramp, and soldiers over there began falling.

The Hill People who had been retreating toward me now turned and charged the horsemen. Ludlow's men were being crushed between two forces. I didn't doubt that the Hill People would kill every soldier who didn't ride like hell away from them.

"It's time," I said.

Cora bit her lip. "There's too many of them. I don't have enough power."

"Do you want to tell that to Ludlow's ghost?" I asked.

Cora blinked. "All right, let's . . ." Her words fell off into a mumble as she stared across the battlefield for ten seconds. Then at the same moment, every Hill Person fell on the ground.

I heard quite a bit of shouting in the Hill Person language, but I didn't pay much attention. I pulled four yellow bands and whipped them upward.

Buzzards and hawks dove out of the sky and savaged the floundering Hill People. Each Hill Person had at least one. That was the first wave. By the time I was done, every howling, crawling Hill Person was clawed and pecked by at least two ferocious birds, which I had spent the previous hour calling from miles in all directions.

Apparently, nobody was giving orders to the horsemen now. Some raced back to the ramp, and some searched the ground for wounded comrades. A good few dismounted and rushed from one helpless Hill Person to the next, killing them with whatever weapon was handy.

I couldn't keep the hawks and buzzards at this for too long. Their nature did not include attacking humans who were alive. After a minute, they flew off, probably disgruntled by this upheaval in their day.

The soldiers had missed twenty or so of the helpless Hill People. Those survivors finished cutting the boots off their feet before they ran back the way they came. I saw Semanté running with them.

"This will probably be a historic defeat for the Hill People," I said, watching their men flee. "Fifty or sixty go to battle, and only twenty come back."

"Cora made it possible," Pil said. "Cora, I'd buy you dinner if only I had anything better than dirt to eat or drink."

"I've never used that tactic before," Cora said with a big smile for me. "Deform and bend the leather to link their boots together. It was hard to do, but clever."

"Oh, I saw somebody do it once." I brushed dirt off my knee. "We're not done, you know. We can't knock off and get drunk yet."

After a short silence, Cora blurted to Pil, "Is he your father?" She nodded toward me.

Pil's eyes blinked open. "No. By Lutigan's fourteen nipples, no! He's not father material."

I was surprised by how much that hurt. I hadn't thought of my daughters enough lately.

Cora pushed on. "Are you two married then?"

I shook my head.

"Lovers?"

"No," Pil said. "He's as old as the hills."

"I see. No, I don't." Cora's eyes were a grassy green, and now she used them to make me damned uncomfortable. "Bib, do you have a lover?"

I swallowed. "Yes, I do." I didn't say that she had called me some awful names and run away the last time I'd seen her.

Cora cocked her head. "Is she here now?"

I shook my head before I could stop myself.

Cora took half a step toward me and smiled like she had found a perfectly ripe apple.

TWENTY-ONE

Ludlow surprised me by being alive, lying on the battlefield with a clean shoulder wound. I didn't offer to heal it, since I didn't care to waste power on a hurt likely to heal by itself. Also, I hoped the pain would remind him to have more respect for the Hill People.

I did say, "General, I know everybody's weary and sunset is coming, but I think you should collect your wounded and ride on as fast as your horses can bear. You don't want to engage the Hill People in open battle again."

Ludlow sat on the ground with his bad shoulder hunched forward and his jaw tight. He hadn't even bothered to comb out his hair. "You're right. I can see it. You warned me, and you saved us when I was too mule-headed to listen."

"I was happy to do it." I didn't mention how much Cora and Pil had contributed. If Ludlow thought I was his savior, his own personal Light of Krak, he might goddamn listen to me about a thing or two.

Ludlow climbed to his feet and forced himself to stand straight even though it must've hurt. He stretched to his full height, which was considerable, and smiled around at the men he had remaining as if he were confident enough to wrestle bears. But he had the tight, shifting eyes of a guilty man. He was capable and brave, and maybe even well-intentioned, but he was arrogant as hell. I recognized it, because I possessed that failing myself.

I decided to help him manage his guilt about leading a disaster. "General, may I offer an observation?"

"Of course," Ludlow said. "You saved us. I'd be foolish to ignore you."

"You seem to be a fine leader. I believe we would be standing knee-deep in your enemies' corpses right now, except for one mistake. You failed to convince yourself that the Hill People could be that murderous and also that efficient. Lots of generals and kings, too many to count, have made that same mistake, so don't condemn yourself. Unlike most of them, you have made that mistake and lived. Now when you fight the Hill People, you'll have that advantage over them."

Ludlow nodded along with most of my pompous speech, but at the end, he wasn't nodding. He gazed down at me with heavy eyes. I heard his teeth click, even through his closed lips. "Thank you, that was some fine help." He stomped off toward his horse.

"What did you say to him?" Cora had been watching us and now came to stand next to me.

I looked away and mouthed a curse. Earlier I had explained to Cora in clear, small words that although I was flattered, I could not explore any sort of romance. She said she understood. But she looked at me as if all she understood was that I hadn't gotten the right offer yet.

Turning, I frowned like a sour old deckhand. "I told Ludlow he was a fabulous warrior and that the kings of old got kicked in the nuts by the Hill People just as hard as he had. And I told him since he knows now that the Hill People are worse than frozen buckets of hell, he can do better next time."

"Bib, you didn't say that, did you?"

"Well, I didn't say it gentle like I just did to you, but about the same."

After a few seconds, she said, "Find Pil and leave. Go right now."

I didn't take that too seriously. "Is he that touchy?"

"He's a damn peer of the Empire! Viscount Haalrade. He is not at all . . . well, I won't say it, but he's not. Just hop on your pony and flee!"

"I figured him for a velvet-wearing type." I glanced at Ludlow in his ripped, bloodstained uniform.

"Yes, and you banged up his pride! It's the worst thing you can do to those people."

I shook my head. "Arrogant and also prideful? Is he slothful too? Given to avarice? How many flaws does the boy have?"

"Stop it!" Then Cora whispered, "No more flaws than the rest. None of them are plums floating in honey."

"No, I can't leave until I see those farmers are safe."

"Weldt and Effla, why?" Cora examined my face.

"It's a story so boring you'd fling yourself under a herd of cattle."

Cora frowned and leaned in closer. "I don't want you to leave, but those peasants are as safe right now as they ever will be. Ludlow won't let them get hurt out here. His pride couldn't stand it."

I leaned away from her just a fraction. "He wouldn't, eh? He's quite a gentleman. Nice to orphans too, I bet. No, I'm staying. Pil makes up her own mind, of course, but I imagine she'll stay too." I paused. I didn't want to encourage Cora, but she didn't sound happy working for Ludlow. I had learned that nothing good happens when a sorcerer is miserable. "When we finally leave, you can come with us if you want. Purely as an ally!"

"Bib," Cora breathed, "I can't go anywhere. I'm Ludlow's slave."

I knew that the Empire sometimes took slaves when they went conquering. I had even heard about sorcerers being enslaved. But standing arm's length from the actual slavery jarred me. For a moment, my stomach hurt. "We'll haul you to the next kingdom over. You won't be a slave there."

Cora's head whipped around as if I had just yelled that we were cutting up the Empress and feeding her to pigs.

I chuckled. "I'll keep it a secret until we leave, don't worry."

"Don't talk about it anymore!" Cora marched away as stiff as dry leather.

Once we were riding again, I explained to Pil my conversation with Cora.

Pil looked at me with no expression. "So, you spoke diplomatically to our ally, the most powerful man within a hundred miles of here, and now he hates us, maybe enough to have us killed."

I nodded.

She took the reins in her teeth and applauded.

Instead of cursing, I shrugged. She was right, and I deserved to hear it, even if her mute sarcasm could cut a brick into quarters.

Pil said, "Maybe we should leave."

"No, I don't feel right about it."

"Fine, I've come to trust your feelings about things, except for women," she said. "Are you going to allow Cora to romance you? I think you should. I like Ella, but you'd be happier with Cora."

I rode without speaking for a couple of minutes, and Pil didn't push me. I thought about the house in Ir where Ella and I had lived, and our flight east with my daughter and Cael, who was a jovial son of a bitch back then.

"Pil, I am a mature fellow, in case you weren't aware. I had a life before I ran into you, but of course it was awful and far less interesting. I learned an odd thing back then, and learning it was costly, but I will give it to you for free."

Pil was fighting a grin. "Thank you. Should I write this down?"

I snorted. "I've never seen you write down a damn thing, and you don't seem to forget anything you see or hear. Pil, happiness can be mortally unsatisfying."

"What?"

"Happiness can be a fine thing, but it may not be the best thing."

Pil said, "Now you're just saying words and hoping they make sense."

"Do they?"

Pil paused. "Perhaps a little."

I nodded. "Now, if you can live your life in a way that proves me wrong, do it."

"Hah! I knew you were just letting words fall out of your face!"

"Of course I was." I, too, had ignored old farts like me when I was seventeen. I had learned to mistrust happiness, but maybe Pil wouldn't need to.

The uneven plains had become a sheet of gentle, tree-pocked hills covered in knee-high grass. We rode across them first by moonlight and then by starlight. Breaks were few.

Even taking breaks, our horsemen would outpace the unmounted Hill People. In theory, we could ride all the way to the capital and remain ahead of our enemy the whole time. In reality, unless the villagers rested, they would move slower and slower every hour.

In the early morning, Cora dropped back during a break to talk to us. "I asked Ludlow to meet with us all, but he said no. So, now I have to carry messages back and forth." She hissed loudly enough to startle her horse.

"All right," I said. "What does he want, where are we going, and how far away is it?"

Cora said, "At this rate, we'll reach the river fort some time tonight. We can't keep going this fast unless we want our trail marked with the bodies of dead peasants."

"That's nice. Does Ludlow have a plan or any ideas?" Pil asked.

"The peasants need to rest. Two hours is all he believes we can afford. What do you think?"

"That sounds right," I said, while Pil nodded.

"He's going to split his force in two. One part will stay behind to delay the Hill People. The others will move up, rest the villagers, and push on to the river with them."

"The delaying force will be wiped out," I said.

"Uh-huh." Cora nodded. "That's why Ludlow will be staying with them."

Pil said, "I'm sure the man has many, many bad qualities, but I guess cowardice isn't one of them."

"Ludlow wants to ask whether you can hold off the Hill People a bit. He's not asking you to help him survive, just do all you can to delay the enemy."

Pil looked at me past Cora. "I bet the three of us can think of something useful, maybe not decisive, but helpful."

"Um . . ." Cora was staring down. "I won't be with you. Ludlow is sending me on ahead."

"Did you piss him off too?" I asked.

Pil said, "I hope you didn't put yourself in a bad spot because of us."

"No, it's not that. Ludlow says it's immoral to order a slave to die."

"Not that I want any of us killed, but couldn't you volunteer to stay?" I asked.

Cora shook her head. "I asked, but he wouldn't listen to it."

I slapped my leg. "To hell with him! He's a bastard one minute and a fine old fellow the next!"

Pil asked, "Bib, how do you want to approach this?"

"Let's each consider it until sunrise. Then we'll see who has the most creative way to get us killed." I winked, although she couldn't see it in the dark.

The call came back to mount up. Cora said, "We'll talk again before the force separates."

Pil said, "Bib. Are you going to let her ride away without kissing her?"

Cora's head came up.

I waved toward Cora. "That was a misstatement. It was a poor joke."

"No, it wasn't," Pil said.

"Pil!" Cora snapped. "That not nice at all. We're not toys for you to play with."

Pil leaned away. "I wasn't playing. I was trying to help and maybe I was enjoying it too much—well, I probably was, but mainly

I was giving Bib a little push, which I think he needs. And I think that my opinion is pretty dang good on this matter."

I knew only one thing at that point. I was sure as hell not going to say anything.

Cora said, "Bib can push himself on his own without your help if he wants to, or not if he doesn't want to. I made it clear what I thought. The only opinion that matters now is his." She kicked her horse but then walked it back around to us. "Although I do appreciate your being on my side, Pil."

After Cora rode ahead, I saw that Pil was watching me.

"Don't say anything," I grunted. "I have to figure out how to kill a whole bunch of people."

I examined the sky, which was cloudless, and the ground, which was covered with tall, feathery grass. Nothing jumped up and said it was an instrument of murder.

I pulled a couple of white bands and let them wander in a circle rippling out from us. The power cost was low since I could take plenty of time and not push. I gained a nice sense of what was living in a great expanse of the plains around me.

After two hours, I ran across something, grinned, and noted it. Twenty minutes later, I found something else not much farther away. I laughed.

When I had been laughing for several seconds, Pil peered at me.

She asked, "Are you all right? Has sorcery driven you mad?"

I kept laughing. Soon the horsemen around us were staring. Pil shifted in the saddle and grasped the handle of her knife.

My laughter began wheezing its way out. I wiped my eyes.

"What was that?" Pil asked. "And don't do it again."

"An amusing mental image." I giggled. "Really not that funny. You know how rare it is in sorcery for the pieces you need to line up just the right way at the right time?" I cleared my throat. "I think today is one of those times."

TWENTY-TWO

Ludlow stayed behind with fifty of his men to face the Hill People. The rest of his force escorted the farmers toward the river. I figured the villagers would cross the Gallant Bridge some time after dark and then be safe behind the Empire's river fortress.

General Ludlow, or Viscount Haalrade, or Bumpy the Gravedigger, or whatever other titles the courageous bastard went by, had decided that his men would fight unmounted. I didn't know whether his soldiers were better warriors afoot than mounted, but against the Hill People, there was little chance they would be worse.

Desh and Stan had not returned, but some of the other scouts had. Ludlow ordered them to search out the tallest hill in this part of the plains. They picked out a graceful, grass-covered mound just forty feet high and a whole quarter mile across. Ludlow settled on it to grab the high ground, although this ground wouldn't be high enough to provide much advantage in combat. At least he could see better from up there. He might merely have a better view of his men being slaughtered before he himself died.

Ludlow knew all of that as well as I did. He never showed any concern or pessimism.

The soldiers raised a short earthen mound to fight behind. Some of them had picked up the Hill People's spears and shields after the earlier battle. Now they hefted those weapons and practiced thrusts, likely hoping to find better reach and protection.

Before the farmers departed, Cora came to us and confirmed that Ludlow still wanted us to delay his enemy. He also expected Pil and me to dutifully get massacred along with everybody else. Cora muttered, "You still have time to run away."

Pil dropped her voice and imitated me. "No, I have a friend who may want to write a song about this battle. He'll be sad if I don't bring him details."

Cora narrowed her eyes at Pil. "You sound like Bib. I mean, your voice even sounds like him."

Pil smiled at me, a sweet thing that bunched her cheeks. "Careful, Bib. I can walk around at night pretending to be you and saying nice things to people. Your reputation will be ruined."

I said, "I don't care what people—"

Cora cut me off. "Don't you mind that those Hill People are going to kill you soon?"

"I would rather they didn't," I said, "but don't concern yourself. If things get tight, our religion requires that we run away and let these other fellows die."

Cora nodded and then held out one hand to me. I scrutinized her hand as if it were a big spider. She ignored that and left her hand hanging. I stayed still until the force of expectation demanded that I either hold out my hand too or walk away.

When I reached out, Cora grabbed my hand in both of hers and kissed the back of it. "If you live, I definitely want to have a long talk." Then she hurried back to where her group was mustering for the retreat.

Pil watched Cora as she trotted away. "Bib, I guarantee that she is a difficult person, but not too difficult. She's just the right amount of difficult for you. If we live, you have to talk to her. A nice, long talk."

I shrugged. "No thank you."

"And don't forget to bring her a present or some flowers. It's customary."

I sighed. "It appears Ludlow will make his stand over there. Let's go." Pil and I tramped across a narrow valley and climbed the next hill over from Ludlow, more than half a mile away from him.

It was early afternoon, and we could see most of what Ludlow saw, but we didn't stand between him and the Hill People's approach. When Pil and I took our position, I whipped a band into the sky and collected some clouds, but I let them drift unsettled. Pil sat beside me with her bow ready, fiddling with her arrows. I felt stiff and wandered around the hilltop to stretch.

By midafternoon, no Hill People had come calling, but I felt they would join us soon. I pulled a white band and flung it out across the land. I found the area not much changed from earlier in the day, which satisfied me. I pulled four yellow bands and hurled them past Ludlow's hill toward the horizon.

When late afternoon arrived, the Hill People were still making us wait. At some point, the farmers would be so far ahead that the Hill People could never catch them. I tried to calculate how much time would pass before that point, but I didn't know enough about the land and the distances.

The calculation was irrelevant. Ludlow hadn't begun to fall back or even take a step toward his horses, so the battle hadn't been canceled.

Pil and I spotted the enemy not long before sunset. They were skirting the hilltops and jogging across the slopes so they wouldn't be outlined against the sky. Also, from halfway up the hill, they could charge down into the valley to either attack or escape if necessary. It was the kind of tactical discipline that had led them to victory in every war they had fought for the last four hundred years.

Pil jumped to her feet. "It's time!" She sprinted down the slope toward the Hill People with her bow in hand.

I threw yellow bands, one after another, out past Ludlow's position. When I was satisfied with that, I pulled the clouds tighter together. I was burning power fast again, but if we were going to do this, we had to whip the horses to the bone.

The light was poor, but none of the fighters so far looked like Semanté. While I was examining them, more Hill People appeared. Then some more arrived, and they kept arriving.

Pil stopped three hundred paces away from the closest enemy fighters. Her first arrow slammed into a Hill Man's chest, and he fell. All the Hill People reached behind them and grabbed their shields. So far, I had counted more than sixty fighters loping toward Ludlow, but five of them now broke off toward Pil.

I threw two more yellow bands past Ludlow's hill.

Pil fired again, striking a fighter square on the shield. Flaming blobs burst from her arrow in every direction. She had warned me about the blobs, which were the size of walnuts and sticky.

The Hill People's front rank slowed in an orderly fashion. I could see a few slapping off blobs that had stuck to them, and small fires were kindling the dry grass.

When Pil shot the next arrow, she aimed at a spot in front of the Hill People, starting more little blazes in the grass. They might become big fires under the right conditions. Pil fired arrows as fast as she could, sparing a couple for the fighters headed her way.

I raised a wind and threw it into the Hill People's faces. The fires surged and crept toward them.

The Hill People began a measured retreat. From the next hill, I heard Ludlow's men cheering.

It was time. I drew out a long, rolling peal of thunder. Then I squeezed out a modest, soaking rain. The fires stopped shooting upward and began to calm. I pressed the clouds for more thunder until it was a continuous rumble.

The Hill People seemed to be looking at the fires, examining the clouds, and pointing at me. Pil was racing back up the slope to join me. Ludlow's soldiers were still cheering.

The next thirty seconds saw more thunder, more rain, less fire, less cheering, and more confused Hill People holding their ground. By the time some of the Hill People saw what was coming and shouted an alarm, it was too late.

A panicked herd of plains bulls galloped into view, through the valleys and across the hills like the ocean surging up onto the beach.

They were a struggling mass of twisted horns, shaggy backs, and smashing hooves. They created a rumble that the Hill People might have heard, if it hadn't been for the thunder.

The herd bypassed Ludlow's hill at an angle, pummeling a considerable swath of grassland in front of his position. The plains bulls edged closer to us, but I had worked hard all afternoon to put them on a path that wouldn't smash us.

If the Hill People had been able to burrow or fly, they might have escaped. Most of them ran, although a few stared at the herd without moving until it crushed them. The ones who ran were trampled too, just a few seconds later. I doubted that any would survive.

I estimated the herd to be two thousand head of stringy, gamy meat. As it passed in front of us, I let the rain slack off since the fires had just about died away. Then I tossed out one more yellow band toward the nine lions chasing the herd.

I had convinced the lions that chasing after plains bulls was about the most desirable activity in their existence. That hadn't been difficult, since chasing down tasty creatures was natural for them anyway. As the plains bulls passed us, I let the lions remember that chasing generally led to killing and then eating. Soon the herd's stragglers began having an unpleasant day.

After the herd had passed, I saw that three of the Hill People had somehow survived. Pil sprinted halfway down the hill with her bow, slowed, and watched the Hill People rush away for a moment. Then she put arrows into their backs one after another.

I glanced over at Ludlow and his men, who had earlier been cheering like paid-off sailors. Now they weren't making a sound that I could hear.

When Pil rejoined me atop the hill, I said, "Young woman, we have done our jobs too well."

"It looks as though we did it exactly well enough." She sighed as she unstrung her bow. Killing people made her melancholy.

I said, "You're technically right, but we allowed the soldiers to see that we are a thing apart. Unaccountable and not like normal people."

"They're not dumb. They knew that we're sorcerers."

"They didn't understand it, though. I've seen this happen before." I pointed at Ludlow's hilltop, which was at last showing activity. "Right this minute, those soldiers are more afraid of us than they are of any quantity of Hill People."

"That hardly seems right." Pil frowned over at the soldiers. "I am one hundred percent certain that we saved their lives."

"It doesn't matter a busted button's worth, and you shouldn't expect it to make sense. From now on, our greatest danger will come from our allies."

Pil turned away. I didn't know whether she was sad, pissed off, or just tired of looking at me.

"It's all part of the joy and glory of being a sorcerer," I said. "But as a sorcerer, at least you can fashion a mirror to let you see people naked."

Pil grinned back at me. "You'd just want to borrow it. And I guess I'd let you."

Two horsemen from Ludlow's group started down their hill toward us. I pointed, and Pil turned to watch them.

"You like killing people with a sword." Pil said it as if it were a demonstrated fact, and I suppose it was. She didn't breathe to let me comment. "You like to kill them with a knife, or a bow, or your hands, or your knee, or holding them down—"

"All right, yes! I'd rather kill than eat or sleep. It's my nature, I'm told, and that seems to be true."

Pil turned toward me and blinked a couple of times. "But you don't like killing people with magic."

"That's foolishness! I like to kill with magic. Maybe more than anything!"

"That surprises me down to my toenails." The hoofbeats were nearing. "I know you, and I pay attention."

The soldiers halted twenty feet away, and one announced, "His Lordship wants me to—"

Pil, still looking at me, put up a hand to stop the man.

The soldier stopped talking.

Pil said to me, "I pay attention, and I see that you're like a fire when you kill by hand, all overwhelming and devouring. With magic you kill like a chisel—it's all angles and force. It's clean."

I had crossed my arms and was smirking. "I don't think you've seen enough to have such bold opinions."

Pil shrugged. "Maybe not." She turned to the horsemen for a moment but then ignored them to look right back at me. "Do you get sad after you kill people with magic? Because I know you do after you kill them with a sword."

"Fah! I don't get sad. That's the bloodlust waning."

"Well . . . maybe you're pining for bloodlust, because you look sad to me." She spun back to the horseman and pointed her finger at him. The man froze and went pale. "What does the general want?"

The soldier she wasn't pointing at said, "His Lordship asks you to come talk over plans for the march. He has liquor, if that helps you decide."

Pil lowered her horrifying finger and leaned toward me to whisper, "Do you want to have some more fun with them? Make them ride back to Ludlow facing backward in the saddle?"

"Let's not humiliate them even worse," I whispered. "We'll have more opportunities during our march to the river."

Pil didn't react.

After a few seconds, I whispered, "That was sarcasm. Actually, we've made two enemies here, along with all their friends."

Pil smiled at the soldiers. She was beautiful, and I had seen hard, cruel men soften when she smiled at them. These men didn't care whether she smiled or talked out of her right ear. They sat straight, and one of them trembled a little.

I faced the man who had spoken. "Please thank the general for his kind invitation. Our magical spirits and uncanny inner sight say that the best spot for a meeting is there in the valley between us. We would be honored to meet there."

The horsemen turned and galloped back toward Ludlow.

Pil asked, "Will he agree to meet us down there?"

"I don't care," I said. "I just don't want to meet him in the middle of fifty men who love him and hate us."

We began strolling down toward the valley. Halfway there, I saw two horsemen trotting downhill from the soldiers' position.

"The one on the left is Ludlow," I said.

Two more soldiers on horseback followed Ludlow and his man. Four more followed them, and four after that, until Ludlow was being escorted by twenty of his fifty men.

I crossed my arms. "It seems careless of him to leave any soldiers behind at all."

Pil nodded. "It seems that way, but the rest can join us in the valley in thirty seconds, maybe less." She yawned. "I didn't bring enough drinks to entertain them all."

"All right, Pil, I give up!" I snapped. "Today you are more sarcastic and flippant than me. You are the victor."

Pil shaded her eyes to scan the valley. "Thank you, but that doesn't matter. We have a decision to make, don't we?"

I nodded. "We can walk down there to ask for horses and maybe get killed. Or we can ignore Ludlow and walk all the way to the river trying to stay ahead of the Hill People."

Pil said, "Well, my boots are pinching a little after all . . ."

"Stop it. This might be the last important decision we ever make."

Pil chuckled. "All right, let's get some horses. We can stay ahead of the Hill People, be in the company of Imperial soldiers to ease our way into the Empire, and make sure the villagers are all right."

I added, "And if we have to kill twenty soldiers instead, that's what we'll do."

Pil poked me on the shoulder. "And the most important reason of all is Cora. She's waiting for you to come for her."

"Harik's flapping nuts! Leave that alone!"

We walked down toward those waiting, armed men who hated us.

TWENTY-THREE

Pil and I paused before we walked onto the valley floor. Ludlow was waiting out there for us to come and wheedle him out of some horses. I doubt that was his plan, but once mounted, we could keep distant from him as we all fled toward the river.

Yesterday, before Ludlow had come to consider me a mouthy, murdering ingrate, he had told me about the Empire's fortifications at the Fargold River. No one had ever breached them, and he predicted that the Hill People would smash against the fortress like an egg against a wall.

I almost called him an overoptimistic ass, but that seemed gruff. Instead, I asked, "Why is it named Fargold?"

Ludlow had smiled. "There are gold mines upriver. And it's far away. Do you see? Far. Gold." He used gestures to clarify his answer, as if I were a child or lived in a tree on a distant island.

I nodded. "I see. I see perfectly."

The man was courageous and loved the Empire, but he didn't understand sarcasm worth a damn.

Now Ludlow waited, standing in the valley with a smile I didn't expect. He and three of his men had dismounted. Two of them held torches since the sun was setting. The rest sat their horses, arrayed on each side of him in two lines that curved toward us.

"Please come drink with me," Ludlow called out, lifting two wooden cups.

He must have expected us to bumble our way up to him like toddlers running to a toy.

Pil whispered, "We can still run away. That will give them the pleasure of chasing us before they kill us."

I sighed and whispered back, "No, let's go meet him. I'll protect us. It's not as if I'm trying to save power. What would I do with power, anyway?" I circled just a fingertip to pull two yellow bands, which I used to get the horses' attention. "If things go to crap, protect me for five seconds."

Pil nodded.

Still smiling, Ludlow gestured toward us with the cups. We walked right up to him, ignoring his soldiers. The cups were half full of something that smelled like a burned-down house.

"To victory!" Ludlow said, draining his cup in two swallows.

I matched him, and I saw Pil doing the same.

The drink tasted like the chimney in that burned-down house. It was merely nasty, though, not poisoned. If Ludlow had tried to poison us, he would have gotten a surprise. Pil and I had both used magic to save ourselves from poison before. If he had given me poison, I would have fallen down, convulsed a little, and called on the horses to kick the shit out of every soldier there.

Ludlow said, "I want to thank you two for wiping out those Hill People. I've never seen anything like it. I admit we were a little scared of your work at first, but that was just startlement."

I glanced around. None of the soldiers looked startled. They looked scared.

"The Empire will reward you for what you've done here, and it won't be stingy."

I said, "I don't care about any rewards, General."

"I might," Pil said, wrinkling her forehead.

"And you deserve it." Ludlow reached to the man beside him, who handed over a small pouch. He offered it to Pil.

Before I could say anything, Pil grabbed the pouch and peeked inside. "Thank you, General! This is sweet of you."

I looked Pil up and down. I had never seen her covet wealth before, but I had never seen her around wealth. She rarely had more than enough money to shoe her horse and buy a few drinks. Maybe she was behaving this way to trick Ludlow somehow. If so, she was being too crafty for me to see it.

Pil jingled the pouch at me and smiled. "Bib, I'll buy us new clothes. Your trousers are about to rot off you! And the best horses in the city, once we get to a city, and something to eat besides gritty rabbit and wormy bread!"

If Pil was being subtle, she was doing a magnificent job.

Then I recalled that she and Desh had each been rewarded by the King of Glass a couple of months back, a nice little sack of gold that would last a frugal person for years. Desh had told me that Pil spent all of hers in three days and didn't end up with much that was worth a damn.

I couldn't count on Pil's greed being a ruse.

Ludlow grinned at us. "You deserve that reward. Now I have something serious to talk about—more serious than your butt flashing in the wind, Bib! I want to hire you."

I didn't answer. Pil was busy poking in her pouch with one finger.

Ludlow cleared his throat. "You'll be attached to the Army of the Empire! Before you go asking about orders, you'll have only these three: don't hurt the Empire, do hurt the Empire's enemies, and stay with my force. You don't have to eat or sleep with us but stay close enough for me to send someone to find you."

I glanced at Pil, who had begun paying attention. I said, "That's a hell of an offer, General. We need awhile to think about it. If you loan us some horses, we'll go on and fight the Hill People for the common good, without being attached to your army or anything else."

Ludlow leaned toward us. "You'll be paid, of course. Gold. Treasure!"

Pil grinned. "How long would this be for? When would we be free to leave?"

"Wait," I whispered to Pil.

"You'll be done as soon as we beat the Hill People," Ludlow said.

"Shit, they may never stop coming!" I said.

Pil bit her lip.

"How about this?" Ludlow said. "You can go either when the Hill People are defeated or after six months, whichever comes first."

I jumped in. "Now we have even more to think about. As I said, we can help you unofficially in the meantime if we have horses."

"I'm afraid we're in a crisis," Ludlow said. "We can only spare horses for people in the army. Or with it."

That was disappointing. Without horses, we would be no faster than the Hill People. Maybe not as fast.

Pil took a step toward Ludlow. "Let's talk more about the treasure. How much is there?"

"How much can you carry away?"

Pil held her breath for a few seconds. "Bib, I'm going to do this."

"For gold? That's crazy."

"Not just gold—treasure!" Pil clenched both hands as if she were already lifting a chest full of coins and jewelry.

I whispered, "You haven't even bargained him down!"

Pil whispered back, "We don't have time! Hill People could catch up while I'm still talking!"

Pil was right about that, and I felt certain that Semanté's fighters could outrun me. She would take home my ears as trophies, at least symbolically. I suspected she was too well-mannered to actually hack the ears off my corpse.

We needed horses, and only Ludlow had them. It seemed I would soon join the Imperial Army, at least for a day or two. I wouldn't feel bad about deserting a mile down the trail if it suited me. But for now, if Ludlow wanted me, he would have to pay. I nodded at Pil. "All right."

I wouldn't say Pil squealed, because sorcerers don't do that. She cleared her throat in a high-pitched, excited way.

I said, "I will agree, but I don't want treasure, General. I want something else."

"If I'm able to give it to you, I'll think hard about doing it," Ludlow said.

"Without it, I won't come along. I want you to set Cora free. Today. Make her a free person."

Ludlow wasn't smiling anymore. "I can't do that. I'm offering you a reasonable reward, not enough treasure to sink a boat."

I said, "I understand that you can't do it for six months of my service. How much longer than six months do I have to work until I earn enough to free her? A month more?"

"That's a ridiculous thing to say." Ludlow's face was getting red.

"Bib . . ." Pil murmured. Her face was getting red too.

"Two months?"

"No!" Ludlow shouted. "It's not half enough."

"Stop me when I get to the right number. Three? Four?"

Ludlow slapped his leg. "You're acting crazy. Stop this behavior and take your treasure!"

The men around us were muttering and shifting, and I could feel how uneasy the horses were. I thought about just stealing two mounts and riding off, but Ludlow might punish the villagers or Cora for what we had done.

I said in a calm voice, "You told me two wasn't half enough. How much is half enough? Six? Will you set Cora free right now if I serve with your army for a whole year?"

Ludlow hesitated.

"You know that most sorcerers die young." I explained it using hand gestures. "Cora might be killed before the month is out. But I'm like an old horseshoe. I'll last forever."

"All right," Ludlow grated. "If you serve a year, I'll set her free."

"You'll free her today."

"No, that's too much. She goes free when you've served half your term."

I raised my voice. "Six months? Your hat must be on too tight. Free her today."

"Forget it," Ludlow said.

Pil cleared her throat but didn't sound excited now. "You can take my treasure back. Use it to pay for Bib's other six months." She sighed.

Ludlow squinted at Pil. "What?"

Pil held up a hand as if she were teaching Ludlow to count. "My reward is worth six months of service. You said as much. Bib offered to serve for a year to free Cora. So, you keep my treasure, and Bib serves only six months." She pointed at herself. "Serve six months or until the Hill People are defeated. No treasure." She pointed at me. "Same thing for Bib, but . . ." She pointed past Ludlow toward the river. "Cora goes free today."

"No, there's something wrong with that," Ludlow said. "The numbers are wrong."

"That's the deal," Pil said. "Take it if you want. If not, we won't save you from the Hill People next time." She grabbed my arm, and we walked away from Ludlow.

"All right! I agree!" Ludlow rubbed his chin. "Are you satisfied? Young woman, has anybody ever told you that you're the biggest pain in the ass they've ever met?"

"Yes," Pil said.

"All the other sorcerers say so," I added.

Soon, Pil and I mounted our borrowed horses and followed Ludlow's men northwest. Heavy clouds had blown in, so we rode in smothering darkness. Ludlow traveled at a snapping pace regardless.

I had no trouble following Ludlow in the dark, nor did Pil. She had become a much more confident rider in the months I had known her. Early on, she had asked me to teach her the sword. I suggested she first improve her horsemanship. I had found that fighting is often less useful than riding away fast.

In the early hours of morning, as I was leading my horse to rest her, I jumped when somebody spoke just beside me. The deep, leathery voice said, "You have almost offended me. You refuse to serve me, but now you enter service with that pompous hunk of insipid flesh."

I took a breath and said, "Hello, Gek. You don't sound too offended."

Something landed on my shoulder. I peeked far enough around to see it was a small bird.

"It pleases me to make you another offer," Gek the Bird said. "Become my servant for thirteen months, and I will destroy the short individuals chasing you, as well as these horse riders who are aggravating you."

Pil probably couldn't see Gek in the darkness since the Void Walker was on the other side of me from her. Also, Bird-Gek was whispering. I lowered my voice to a whisper in case Pil was might hear. "That's a ringing whipsaw of an offer, Gek, just charming. But that won't stop the war or save the people I'm helping. More people will come along to fight, and more people will get caught in it and die."

Gek said, "These things happen over and over, no matter what you do. It seems to me you are upsetting yourself over trivialities."

"I can only deal with the part of life that's in front of me."

Gek was silent for a few seconds. "These small people—I will turn each of them into a wagon loaded with petrified bull members. And the horse-riding people—I will turn each of them into a pot of jam."

I took a deep breath and prepared to speak carefully. "Are you referring to all of the Hill People and all of the Empire dwellers across the entire world?"

"Yes."

That had to be millions of people. "I believe you already suggested something like that, and I said no."

"Ah, but this time I will take the sad, destitute people you've been helping and give them all that land. They will be the most glorious kings and queens in the world."

"But with no subjects." I winced after I said it. This was no time for quick, thoughtless comments.

Gek sounded disinterested, as if he were admiring the scenery. "If I had just been made into the most glorious king in the world, I don't believe I would complain about having no subjects."

"I refuse your offer," I said, "and I wouldn't care to hear any more like it."

The bird shrugged its wings. "You still owe me a single killing. You should move with a greater sense of urgency on that. Travel east."

I shrugged. "If I travel east, the Hill People will punch me full of holes."

"Then I'll destroy them all."

"No! I don't want to hear any more 'destroy them all' crap! Besides, you gave me permission to help these peasants, and I don't know that they're done needing help."

"You were to stand ready to abandon that task," Gek said, as if reminding me to take my cloak with me in a rainstorm.

I said, "How about this? The fastest way east from here is by sea. I'll gallop up to Regensmeet and find a fast ship headed east."

"And you will board that ship."

"I will."

"And stay aboard until it arrives at its destination," Gek insisted.

"Yes, that too."

"If you don't—"

I cut in, "I know! Everybody I ever loved, including me, will get turned into a bat's nether parts, or something worse."

Gek said, "You have entered an agreement with that moist parcel of perfidy on a horse. What will you do about him?"

I chuckled. "I'll sneak out while he's admiring his hair in the mirror. He won't know I'm gone until he needs some sorcery done."

Pil asked, "Why are you laughing?"

"I'm imagining Ludlow's face when he finds out we've deserted."

Pil giggled. "You know we'll have to take Cora with us because Ludlow will enslave her again. He'll assume the deal is off."

"Shit, I guess we will." The bird on my shoulder flew away.

"I'll start looking for flowers," Pil said. "When Cora finds out what you did for her, you won't be able to pry her out of your arms with an iron bar."

TWENTY-FOUR

This would be my third visit to the Empire. On my first visit, I landed at the grimy docks of Regensmeet, the capital. My crewmates had snatched me ten days earlier behind a tavern in a different port and forced me to join them. They had found themselves to be short a crewman due to an unhappy instance of adultery and bludgeoning. I was twenty-one years old and hadn't yet gotten the knack of telling people to go to hell and then sending them there if necessary.

I escaped by rotting the forestay until it snapped. Then I leaped to the dock while everybody else watched the foremast sway like a stalk of grass.

Ready to explore the greatest city in the world, I sprinted around a sailmaker's hut, where four men knocked me down. They threw a sack over me and carried my screaming ass off to their ship to be their crewmate for a while.

That was my first visit to the Empire.

Four years later, a comrade and I acquired far more wealth than we had the sense to possess. We had not stolen it, exactly. We had gone to chastise some rough characters who had done ill to a wealthy man, and chastisement became a ferocious bloodletting.

They could have avoided it by not behaving like such moist, sucking armpits with knives.

My friend and I hadn't expected to find two bags of silver coins under a chair, but it would have been foolish to leave them for the dogs. We rode to the Empire, which wasn't far, and once again I visited Regensmeet. I assumed that anything in the world worth spending money on would exist there.

The streets of the capital astounded me. They were wide, well paved, and clean. We searched through them for an hour until we found a street that was crooked, dark, and nasty. That is where we went.

Four days later, we stumped out with a crop of bruises, stomachs full of bile, four broken toes, and not one coin. Most of our knives, pouches, and buckles were missing too.

The sorcery masters had taught me that four is one of the most ill-favored of all numbers. Those four days proved they were right. We couldn't find our horses and walked out of the city like fleas jumping off the noblest dog in the world.

As I rode toward my third visit to the Empire, Pil and I followed Ludlow's men most of the night. After Gek abandoned my shoulder, I engaged in speculative and unproductive thinking about him. At sunrise, the sky behind us lightened to the color of a pearl. I heard shouting from ahead, and I galloped around the mass of soldiers to investigate.

We had reached the river, where a horse had run over the bank and thrown its rider into the water. The soldier yelled curses at the beast while struggling against the current. Ludlow and some soldiers chased the man along the riverbank while passing ropes forward until Ludlow grabbed a rope's end and dove in. He snagged the soldier, who had stopped shouting, probably because he swallowed a lot of the river.

Ludlow and two men dragged the gurgling soldier out of the water. I looked around at Ludlow's men, the survivors of his failed, deadly expedition in which many of their friends had died. Their bright eyes were looking at him as if he were made of gold and rubies.

As Ludlow led us north along the riverbank, the creeping sun threw our shadows far out onto the river. The Fargold wasn't a swift river, but it was wide, more than a hundred paces across.

There might once have been a river spirit in the Fargold, but there wouldn't be now. Spirits couldn't stand places where men built stone against stone in straight lines, and a stone wall ran along the river's far bank. Short towers poked up over the wall occasionally.

I spotted the bridge before midmorning. For some reason, I hadn't imagined what a subtle bit of engineering it would be. The stone and wooden bridge rested on pillars set into the riverbed, and it spanned the wide river in a shallow arc. I was no architect, but I wondered whether such a span could be possible without magic.

Most of Ludlow's force crossed before Pil and me. When I topped the bridge's arc, I got a fine view of the defenses. A tall wooden gate at the end of the bridge was poised to close off traffic. The gate was set into the stone wall along the riverbank.

A broad expanse of pounded dust lay beyond the gate. Hundreds of men could be packed into it, which would be unfortunate for them. They would be enveloped by the gray, towering fortress that stood in a half-circle around them.

The fortress was a brutal stone monument to the art of taking lives. The face and its battlements showed hundreds of openings for shooting, throwing, dropping, or pouring destruction on the people outside. A more formidable gate had been built in the center of the fortress wall, allowing friendly types, or the bodies of defeated enemies, to pass through.

Anyone crossing the bridge would face the wooden gate. If they broke through the gate, they would walk into a tremendous, squat box of death. The Empire had made it plain that they didn't want anybody coming this way without permission.

We didn't observe Ludlow's arrival, but we saw the results. Men and horsemen hurried around like wicked boys running from their mothers. We found Cora standing beside the bridge gate. She didn't look thrilled beyond her most cherished dreams, so Ludlow must not have freed her yet.

One of Ludlow's officers turned toward us. "Your people are

beyond the fortress." He pointed at the maw-like gate in the main wall, which stood open.

I nodded but turned to Cora instead of going on. "Have Desh and Stan gotten here?"

"No, I haven't seen them or heard a word about them." She reached toward me but just patted my horse's neck.

I glared back over the bridge. "Krak smash it with fire, where are they?"

Pil said, "I can't think of anybody more capable than Desh. And Stan . . . well, he's with Desh. They should be here soon."

"Cora!" Ludlow bellowed from the middle of the deadly courtyard. "It's time!"

Cora swallowed. "You two watch me do this. It's hard, but I'll teach you later."

"Do what? What's hard?" Pil asked.

Cora pushed both palms toward the bridge. It seemed an odd motion. New sorcerers might use both hands for magic, but an experienced sorcerer almost never would.

The bridge gave an enormous, grinding screech. Then the far end lifted and began bending upward. The bridge didn't break, and nothing fell off—it just bent until the farthest hundred feet of it angled up away from us. When it stopped, the far end of the bridge hung thirty feet above the ground.

"How the hell will Desh and Stan get past that?" I shouted, then glared at Cora.

Cora, sweating and pale, leaned against my horse. "I don't know. But any sorcerer—you, Pil, or anybody who knows the technique—can bend it that way or restore it. Some mighty Binder enchanted it centuries ago. I think I'm going to sit down for a minute." She stumbled before walking away.

I hesitated.

"I'll follow her," Pil said, clucking at her horse.

I trotted my horse on through the big gate. A sizable town of wooden buildings lay beyond it. The main road was crowded, and I heard shouts, bangs, and clangs. I asked a young woman about the strange new peasants. She scrutinized me for a few seconds and then jerked her head toward some buildings that stood behind the fortress's back wall.

The first building was full of farming tools and seed, but no Sandypool farmers. The second was disappointing too. At last, I walked past all the buildings and found the refugees beside an open field. A long, complex riverside dock also lay past them, with a dozen wide, tightly rigged boats tied up.

It seemed that most of the villagers had survived. Maybe even all of them, but I didn't count heads. They had clumped themselves in small groups around lean-to shelters built against the fortress's back wall. The Imperial garrison must have given them lumber, blankets, and firewood, as well as food and water.

I found Yoadie lying on a blanket with two women sitting beside him. He was pale and breathing, and his eyes were open, but he didn't answer when I spoke to him.

One of the women said in a dull voice, "He'll be gone soon. He killed himself getting us here. He wore himself out."

"I imagine that's so," I said. "Maybe your people will have a drink and remember him once in a while."

She shrugged.

I considered trying to heal old Yoadie, but he had used himself up. I could heal a bad heart for a while, but vitality gradually wanes, and there was nothing I could do about that. If it were otherwise, sorcerers would heal themselves into living forever.

As I walked down the line of shelters, everybody looked weary. Some slept in such awkward positions they might have fallen down from exhaustion.

"Is that cowardly squeaker too petrified to come talk to me?" Tira stomped toward me as if she could crush my head with every step. "He was always worthless, but he wasn't scared and disrespectful until he met you!"

"I feared you would be too contrary to die on the way here," I said. "It would have simplified things. If existence cared at all about justice, you would be over there struggling for life instead of Yoadie."

"That old idiot can eat his own toenails in hell. I dragged my people here in spite of him and their own stupidity and their soft little puppy dog hearts. So, where is Desh, damn you?"

I gazed back to the east. "I don't know, maybe dead."

"What?" Tira's mouth sagged, and she paled.

"Or maybe not," I said. "We got separated. He may ride around that corner any minute. If Desh says he'll do something, I'd never bet against it."

Tira sneered. "No wonder he's a laggard. You're packing his head full of that bullshit, and he must think he can skip and dawdle wherever he goes. 'Do something,' you say. If he tried to do anything but eat and whine, his dick would fall off and he'd be nothing but an ugly woman!" She drew a breath but let it escape instead of yelling. She mumbled, "You don't really think he's dead, do you?"

"Maybe."

Tira swallowed.

"Why are you such a mean and crusty old bitch? I know why I'm mean, but what about you?"

Her face began getting red as she shouted, "Who are you to talk to me like that, you fancy, liquor-drinking, demon-screwing baby murderer?"

"Well, I'm guilty of three out of four," I said.

A small crowd of villagers had collected around us.

Tira roared and swung her walking stick at me. I leaned out of the way.

I said, "I plan to remove you from this village like I'd pull out a poisoned thorn. You have fifteen seconds to gather up your garbage before we go."

"You'll be gathering up your brains in a minute!" Tira swung, and I dodged again.

"You're not helping yourself," I said.

The people around us were muttering. They didn't sound happy. Certainly not as happy as they would sound once Tira was out of their lives.

Tira tried to kick me, but I pushed her to the ground, saying, "I suppose you already have everything you'll need to survive on an island out in the Bending Sea then. You'll have to be nicer to the birds than you've been to your neighbors. Otherwise, they'll peck you to death."

I didn't intend to take her to an island, not in the Bending Sea or anyplace else, but I had no fine ideas about where she should go. For now, I'd just tie her up and get her away from these farmers until I thought of something better.

Tira moaned, "All right, stop hitting me! I'll leave."

She sat up, sniffed, and then swung at my shin. I had been waiting for it and stepped back out of the way. I had to admire her persistence. Maybe that was where Desh got his.

Tira growled, "I'm not turning my people over to you, maggot."

"Your people will do fine without you or me," I said. "It's time to go now. May every child you ever hurt kick you in the crotch with an iron boot, and when they're done, start all over again."

A voice from behind me called out, "Hey! What are you doing? Stop that!"

I turned and found a young Imperial soldier striding toward us. From his snotty tone, I assumed he was an officer.

"I am in the process of stopping this right now, Captain. Give me a minute, and it'll be stopped for all time."

Tira scrambled to her feet. I stepped back so I could see both her and the soldier.

Maybe the boy really was a captain. He didn't correct me about his rank. He squared off with me and clenched a fist. "Stand back from that woman. I need her."

"Do you want to hurt a wild pig's feelings until it jumps off a cliff?"

"What? No! Who are you?"

I took a bold stance and boomed, "I am Bib, the oldest and wisest living sorcerer! I have walked the lands of man and god. I bargain with Death. I slay with magic, and steel, and my own hands. I am cursed to kill, and I have murdered more than a thousand men, women, and children." I was glad Pil wasn't there to raise an eyebrow and laugh at my exaggerations. I crossed my arms. "So then. What do you really want?"

The officer examined me from boots to hat brim. "Sorcerer? Sure you are."

I muttered, "Shit, I should have said I was a banker."

"Stop mistreating this woman," the boy said. "She's important."

I stepped back. "All right. Before I turn you into a lizard and carry her off to oblivion, I've got to know. Why is she important?"

"She's the only one who can get these people to obey and to get off their asses. I need her for the voyage."

I raised my eyebrows.

The boy looked at me as if the word *ignorant* was painted on my forehead. "We're sailing downriver with them this afternoon! How much farther do you expect them to walk? Look at them!"

I considered that. Before I was done, somebody shouted, "Bib!"

A second soldier was shouting and waving at me from up beside the buildings. "Are you the sorcerer Bib?"

I waved back at him.

"The viscount wants to see you as soon as possible!"

I waved again. "Well, hell."

The boy's eyes were the size of wagon wheels.

I said, "Captain, it looks like I won't be making your brain explode out through your ass today after all." I grabbed his shoulder and squeezed, although he tried to jerk away. "Son, you're very brave. And stupid. You'll go far." I glanced at Tira. "I'll be back to collect you soon."

The second soldier led me through a brass-bound door set into the back of the fortress. I followed him up stairways and down corridors until we reached the battlements.

Ludlow called me over to one end of the fortress so that I could look almost straight down into the river. Cora and Pil stood on either side of him, and he pointed across the river. "It's a Hill Person."

I focused on the tiny figure across the way and then examined the area. "It's more than that. The one you see is Semanté. There are a bunch more we can't see. I know they exist because she's too smart to come here alone."

Ludlow leaned toward Semanté, as if that would make her easier to see. Then he waved at her.

Semanté walked away.

Ludlow said, "Now we know where the Hill People are."

I nodded slowly.

"Good," Ludlow said. "Go kill them."

"Right," I said. "Do you want me to hurt their feelings first? Bring them up here to apologize?"

"Only if it won't slow things down. I mainly want them dead. I hired you to kill my enemies." Ludlow pointed toward the spot where Semanté had stood. "There they are."

I chuckled until I realized Ludlow wasn't smiling. He wore a hard face, the kind noblemen used to send poor men off to die.

Pil glanced at me from behind Ludlow's back and mouthed, "We're stupid."

TWENTY-FIVE

From the top of Ludlow's fortress, I blinked at the spot across the river where I figured a lot of Hill People would be standing soon. "General, you said we had only three orders."

"I know what I said."

I grimaced at the man. "I feel the need to review. We should hurt them, not hurt you, and stay close by in case you want to discuss philosophy or something."

"That's right! Good!" Ludlow said as if I were a puppy that learned not to mess on the floor. "Not the philosophy part, though. I want you nearby so I can tell you when it's time to hurt them. And it's time, right now."

Pil smiled her sweetest smile at Ludlow. "It's more complicated than flapping my hand and watching them fall over."

"Is it?" Ludlow didn't sound impressed or even that interested in the details. "Well, you're mighty sorcerers. If you couldn't solve complicated problems, you'd be mighty stable hands. So, summon your thunder and fire. Conjure terrible animals. Turn the Hill People into ground squirrels. That's why I'm paying you."

I opened my mouth to argue, but I saw it would be like stopping the river by peeing against the current. Instead, I said, "We haven't been paid yet, General. No payment, no ground squirrels."

Ludlow hesitated before glancing at Cora, who had been standing away from the parapet, watching us.

Pil said, "I see that our pay has escaped your attention in all the excitement, sir, and of course a proud man like you wouldn't hold back, hoping we'd die before you paid us."

Ludlow glared at her before he turned to Cora. "You're free."

Cora looked back and forth between Pil, Ludlow, and me, squinting as if Ludlow had spoken in the language of lobsters. "I don't understand."

Pil took Cora by the arm. "You're a free person now, dear, not a slave, and you don't have to lick anybody's boots until they shine anymore. You decide what you want to do."

"How?" Cora's face was as blank as if she'd been clubbed.

Pil patted Cora's hand. "We promised Ludlow we'd fight in his war, which we would have done anyway, so it wasn't an enormous sacrifice, if he would set you free. Right away."

"Why would he do that?"

I said, "I have theories, but they wouldn't sound likely unless we were drinking."

Cora collapsed to sit on the stone floor and would have fallen hard if Pil hadn't eased her down.

Ludlow smiled at Cora. "Congratulations! I hope that you keep on working for me. Of course, I'll pay you."

Cora stared up at Pil. "Why did you do this?"

I caught Pil's eye and gave her a little head shake.

Pil said, "Bib couldn't stand to see you suffer."

I hung my head.

Pil grinned. "Bib is rude and profane, and he's even cruel and murderous, but he believes in love more than anybody I've ever met."

I scowled. "Bullshit!"

"Shut up, you don't know a darn thing about it." Still grinning, Pil said, "That doesn't mean he wants to marry you, Cora, or even make sweaty snuggles. He's just a . . . well, we can talk about it later if we're alive."

I shook my head at Pil. "You've gone as mad as a fish in a water wheel."

Ludlow said, "If you're finished talking about love, and suffering, and mad fish, would you go kill my enemies, please?"

"Come on, Cora." Pil helped the young woman stand. "Let's go kill a lot of people. It's the only thing Bib likes better than love."

"Goddamn it, stop that!" I snapped.

I led the way back into the fortress and down the closest stairway with Cora and Pil behind me. I said, "I lack the power required for a prolonged battle, or even a short battle. Any lives I take will be with the sword. Ladies, this seems like a wonderful time to desert."

"What about Desh's people?" Pil asked.

"Ludlow's men are loading them aboard a ship this afternoon and taking them farther into the Empire. They should be safe, or at least a hell of a lot safer than they'd be with us."

Pil said, "Hm. There are two more things we should stay for."

I nodded. "Desh and Stan. I don't want to leave without them, either."

Behind me, I heard Cora choke and start sobbing. I turned and found her leaning against the wall of the stairwell with one hand on her face.

I held back a couple of curses.

Pil held Cora and told her it was all right, which was a strange thing to say when we might well be dead in a few hours.

Cora stood up straight and wiped her face. "I'm sorry, that was weakness we can't afford right now. It's just that I've been a slave since I could walk, and I thought I'd die that way. It's a shock."

I said, "You'll feel a lot better after we desert and engage in some other criminal behavior. You don't even have to kill anybody."

"But first, we wait for Desh and Stan," Pil said.

I added, "It wouldn't hurt to see the villagers safely aboard their ships. I need to deal with Desh's mother anyway."

"All right," Pil said. "No splitting up. We stay together."

A minute later, at an intersection, Cora said, "Wait."

"Did you forget something?" I asked. "Do you have a pet bird?"

"No, let's go the other way."

"This way is close to the dock." My bump of direction was emphatic about that.

"It's not the fastest way, though. Trust me, I've been here dozens of times." Cora took the lead.

Pil whispered by my shoulder, "If she leads us into an ambush, it's your fault. You wanted to free her. I wanted treasure."

Cora opened a door that led out to the fortress gateway, and she smiled back at us. "See? Don't doubt a woman on her own ground."

Before I could turn toward the back of the fortress, I heard shouting from the wooden bridge gate. Two soldiers ran toward us from it. About twenty ran toward the gate to reinforce it. Soldiers on the wall pointed and jabbered.

Pil looked at me. "Let's check—it may be Stan and Desh."

We shoved our way onto the platform that let us see over the wall, and I forgot all about looking for Stan and Desh. Even though the far end of the bridge hung high above the ground, Hill People were climbing up onto it. Eight of them had already formed up on the bridge.

If Ludlow didn't stop the Hill People from climbing onto the bridge, Semanté could get a lot of her force up before she attacked. I didn't know how big her whole force was, either. The biggest group I had seen was sixty, but she might have twice that now, or a hundred, or a thousand.

Maybe the fortress could stop two hundred Hill People. Based on my intimate knowledge gained by fighting them recently, I wasn't certain.

"We have to stop them now!" a short, brown-haired soldier at the gate yelled.

An older man beside him shook his head and muttered something.

The short soldier shouted, "Open the gate!"

The older man yelled, "I'm your commander, and it stays closed!"

The short soldier shoved his commander to the ground and

shouted, "Bite your grandma's dick!" He pounded on the gate, and men opened it.

I was breathing deep and could taste the Hill People's lives, as smooth and rich as cream. The urge to kill them clamped onto me with uncommon force.

The short soldier led thirty men onto the bridge at a run, calling for the gate to be closed behind them. I charged out too, craving lives and ignoring Pil as she screamed my name from behind me.

Twelve Hill People had formed up in two ranks by the time we neared them. I ran beside the short soldier at the head of his men. A Hill Woman on the right side grew an arrow in her chest and dropped straight down.

Just before I reached the Hill People fighters, all the spears in the front rank bent in the middle at a ninety-degree angle. I thrust into a stunned fighter's chest, shoved the woman on my other side off-balance, and charged on to fence with two on the back rank. The Empire soldiers bellowed and cried out. The Hill People fought without making a sound.

I took a shallow cut on my cheek before I managed to disable one of the rear fighters with a low slice to the belly, and he screamed. I disengaged and snatched a glance around me.

The Hill People with bent spears were all down, and a second Hill Woman had died from an arrow. That left three Hill People standing. All the soldiers but four were dead or dying. Pil and Cora had run past me to the end of the bridge. Pil was firing arrows downward. Cora was kneeling and sawing at a rope.

That glance almost killed me. A Hill Man's spear scraped my neck but not deep enough to catch anything vital. I feinted a retreat and stabbed the man in the chest when he moved to catch me.

A Hill Man climbed up over the edge, and Cora scrambled back to kick at him. He fended her off and then ignored both her and Pil as he ran to join his two friends. I caught him partway there and cut the back of his calf. Even crippled, he made a thrust that I almost couldn't block, but that threw him off-balance, and I shoved him over the side of the bridge.

All the soldiers were lying on the bridge, either motionless or writhing. The two Hill Men still living turned toward me. Then, an intense heat erupted from behind me, and I stumbled forward. The Hill Men staggered too.

I felt dread even before I heard the screams. There was a Burner someplace near, a sorcerer who could make objects erupt in consuming flames. A Burner couldn't set living things alight, but a favored tactic was making a person's clothes combust. Either Cora or Pil was possibly about to die.

If I didn't get my clothes off fast, I might be next.

My stomach clenched as the smell of burning flesh reached me, and the panicked shouts flew through my skull like an arrow. I feinted left, just enough to draw the Hill Men's weapons out of line. I sliced one's throat. As the other thrust, I parried and stabbed him in the heart.

Dropping my sword, I turned while unbuckling my belt. Cora was already halfway out of her clothes. Pil lay by the edge rocking from side to side, yelling and flailing. Flames stood on her flesh. I stripped off my shirt, trousers, and boots in a few seconds and tossed them in a pile. I panicked as I remembered my hat and yanked it off. It exploded in midair, along with the rest of my clothes.

Grabbing my sword off the ground, I ran back to Pil, who was now moaning. Cora and I helped Pil roll to smother the flames, burning our hands as we did it.

Three out of the four ropes that the Hill People had been climbing were already cut. Cora headed that way, reaching for a knife on the ground.

"Don't touch it!" I yelled. "The Burner could melt your hand off with it." I felt the ground near Pil and found the sharp knife she had enchanted. It was enchanted like my sword so was likely to survive a Burner's attack. Using Pil's knife, I sliced through the fourth rope as if it were cheese.

It would be better to tend Pil where she was, but the Burner might destroy us. "Cora, carry my sword and grab anything of Pil's that didn't burn up. Then follow me!"

Pil screamed as I lifted her, but she felt as light as a corn husk doll. I turned away from the Hill People and sprinted back across the bridge to the wooden gate, where we should be too far for the Burner to see or sense us.

When I arrived, heaving for air, the damn soldiers refused to open the gate for us.

I laid Pil flat as Cora arrived and dropped my sword from her burned hands. I glanced over and saw her panting and staring at her reddening but otherwise whole hands. I began pulling bands and sheets to heal some of Pil's horrible wounds. I worked fast and was as sloppy as hell, but I pulled her back from the edge of dying, and I eased a lot of her pain.

Of course, some of that pain set into my flesh to join the pain growing in my burned hands. I was able to add groaning to my sweating. The soldiers finally opened the gate and helped us walk into that empty field of dirt. They sat us on stacked bags of grain and tried to throw blankets over us until Cora stopped them.

Both Pil and I wavered in and out of wakefulness. She wanted to cling on to my hand, which hurt like a nettle on the tongue. It must have hurt her too, because she whimpered and dropped my hand right away, only to grab it again a minute later. One time in the past, she had grown relentlessly attached to touching me after I healed her, and I hoped to hell this wasn't the same inconvenient thing.

At some point, Ludlow arrived, said some things, and smiled. His aide brought us clothes and ordered servants to take us to beds. Pil didn't struggle when they pulled her away, which encouraged me.

I didn't sleep, but I gradually felt less pain. After a few hours, I healed my hands before leaving my room. I found Pil sitting in the hallway, panting. She was far from being fully healed.

"Is it horrible?" she asked. "Am I the ugliest woman alive?"

Of course, all her hair and eyebrows and eyelashes had burned away, which never looks good. But the scars were awful. I had healed her flesh but had no time to heal the brutal scars all over her body, including her face. It might be devastating for a woman who had been so striking.

I said, "You're as beautiful as the first time I saw you. Maybe more, and anybody who says different will get stabbed in the eye."

Pil smiled. "Sure. If you say it, it can't be a lie. By the way, your beard is gone. Looks like shit."

We walked outside to find it was early afternoon. Semanté hadn't assaulted the bridge again, and the question of what she'd do next was driving some robust wagering.

Cora found us and said, "Your people have boarded and have sailed downriver. Actually, they rowed, but they should be able to sail soon."

"Damn it and four times damn it to hell," I said. "I never took Desh's mother away. I can't help it now, though. Well, sit down." I healed Cora's hands, and she just about cried when she thanked me.

After some skulking discussion, Pil and I decided to steal some horses and ride up the river searching for Desh and Stan. Cora wanted to stay in case they reached the fortress somehow, but I feared that Semanté might overrun this place soon. Also, I didn't trust Ludlow not to enslave her again.

We dragged our brutalized selves outside the fortress, and we sat down so I could heal Pil some more. I couldn't afford to use all my remaining power, so I did only what was necessary. She was out of pain and could move without restraint. I still didn't heal her scars, although I promised I would someday.

I was the first one to spot Desh and Stan. They were on our side of the bridge, riding hard toward us from upriver. I waved, and they angled to reach us. Desh had lost his hat and had taken a broad scrape across half his face. Stan's left arm was bound to his body, and the crown of his purple hat had been crushed.

"We found the knobby buggers," Stan said, coughing. "I swear, I could soak in a trough of beer for a week." He saw Pil and froze.

I said, "No. We found them. They're right across the river looking for a way over."

Desh shook his head. "They should ask their friends for advice. I mean the friends who have already crossed the river and are running toward us right now. How many Hill People are you facing here?"

Pil said, "We don't exactly know how many are here. We've seen as many as fifty altogether."

"Or sixty," I added.

Still looking at Pil, Stan said, "Sixty? That's nice. We got hundreds following us."

Nobody said anything for a few seconds.

"How many?" I asked.

Desh said, "I estimate three hundred. They'll probably be here by sunset."

Cora said, "Is this the right time for some criminal behavior? Should we desert now?"

"No better time is coming," Stan said. "I won't even slow down for a drink, not if they hold it out as I ride past." He glanced away from Pil, looked right back at her, and sighed.

A screeching clamor echoed from the river.

"Dragon?" Desh almost smiled.

Cora sprinted toward the riverbank without saying anything.

I watched Cora run and felt hollow. "Desh, I'll laugh about your dragon joke later. Right now, Semanté is pulling open the front door. Come on." The screeching stretched on as Pil and I hurried to catch Cora. Desh and Stan, being mounted, caught up with her in a few seconds.

When I reached the wall at the riverbank, Cora had already climbed up to look over it. She yelled, "They can't do that. They aren't supposed to know anything about how to bend the bridge. They can't know!"

The far end of the bridge was lowering. Soon every Hill Person across the river would be able to stroll right onto the bridge and assault the fortress whenever they pleased.

TWENTY-SIX

S orcerers sometimes fight over questionable knowledge and petty prerogatives, just the way bears fight over territory. While I favor cooperating with other sorcerers, I admit to thrashing or murdering a few who wouldn't shut the hell up about the brilliance of their techniques and the subtlety of their understanding.

I doubt anybody missed them, men and women who managed to be cocky and boring at the same time. Sorcerers are hard to stand and harder to care about, and I am not complaining. I just observe that sorcery is a solitary pursuit. Two Burners can't burn the same thing twice. If another sorcerer and I both call rain, that doesn't put twice as much water in the sky.

When Cora saw that the Hill People's sorcerer was straightening the bridge so they could cross it, she reached out with sorcery to make damn sure the bridge stayed bent. None of us could help her. She struggled by herself against the other sorcerer, who was alone in the fight too. The grinding and screeching noises swelled, and the bridge stopped straightening.

The bridge held position. I don't know how the other sorcerer was handling things, but Cora turned pink, then red, and then she began streaming sweat. Her arms and legs started trembling, but she stared at the bridge almost without blinking. She held the bridge in place that way for three minutes before the air burst out of her and she dropped to her knees, panting. Pil grabbed her before she fell off the platform.

The bridge resumed straightening itself.

"You do it!" Cora gasped as she grabbed my wrist.

"No, Bib!" Desh said. "Save your power. I may get my arm cut off and need you to fix it." He gripped the top of the wall and stared at the bridge. For ten seconds, the bridge continued to drop. "What the crap am I supposed to do?"

"Grab it and lift!" Cora said.

Desh rolled his eyes. "Oh, well, it's all clear now. Grab what?"

"I can't explain it!" Cora beat the wall with the heel of her fist.

"Try!" Desh said.

Cora snapped, "Just feel around for it, you damn idiot! How long have you been a sorcerer, anyway?"

Desh flinched. He hadn't become a sorcerer until he was past twenty, which put him years behind most practitioners. He hadn't been formally trained, either. I had suspected he was sensitive about it, and this proved it to me.

On the other hand, Desh had spent years living with an unworldly creature. He probably saw magic from a perspective no one else could match. I hoped he didn't get distracted now by the fact that Limnad had fallen out of love with him.

Desh glared at the bridge as it dropped straighter. Then he said, "Oh! That's simple. I was trying too hard."

The screeching and grinding crested, and the bridge stopped again. It hung in place as sweat ran down Desh's face. Then it began bending upward, farther out of the Hill People's reach. It moved gradually, almost too slow to track for a few seconds. Then it sped up as if a giant had come along and plucked at the bridge with his finger. It stopped about where it had been before this sorcerous ass-whipping began.

Desh breathed deep a few times. "I don't know how to gauge the strength of that other sorcerer, so I'll say he's stout. I don't want to do that again."

"What do we do now?" Pil said. "I mean, something besides fighting. I don't want to spend the afternoon battling Hill People from two sides."

"What happened?" Stan asked, staring at Pil.

Pil paused, saw the shock on Stan's face, and turned away.

Desh said, "She's been burned, don't you see that? Probably doing something a lot braver than falling off her horse and breaking her arm."

Stan didn't even glance at Desh. "But . . . how?"

"I could tell you," I said, "but you might rather I wait a few minutes for the Hill People to arrive so I can tell them too, and you don't have to hear me repeat myself."

Stan touched his own face. "Does it hurt?" He shook his head at me. "Bib, why didn't you heal her? You healed your goddamn bit-off tongue."

Pil hadn't turned back around to face us. Cora put her arm around Pil and snarled at Stan, "You're a rude man, cruel and rude!"

"Does anybody want to do something with regard to the hundreds of Hill People hurrying toward us?" I asked.

I didn't get an answer. Instead, Desh said, "Stan, be honest about this. Were you only in love with Pil because she was beautiful?"

Stan turned a deep apple red and stared at his feet.

Pil finally turned and put her hand on Stan's broken arm. "It's all right. Even though you thought you loved me, I knew you didn't, so this doesn't hurt my feelings. Don't feel bad."

Stan produced something between a sigh and a moan. "Hell, now I feel like twice as big a pile of shit." He trudged away from us, far enough that we couldn't easily hear him curse or cry.

"Are we done with all this bullshit about hurt feelings?" I asked.

Somebody grabbed my spirit and drew it upward through my skull with a nice, even strain. I felt like a fish pulled from the river.

Harik normally yanked me around like a toy on a string, so I assumed he wasn't calling for me.

Usually when I arrive at the trading place, I take a few moments to assess the conditions. Was it sunny, or raining? What time of day was it? Was there lava falling from the sky? Such observations had never given me a bargaining advantage, but they gave me the sense I was in a real place instead of some illusion the gods conjured up.

This time, I didn't pay attention to the weather, light, smells, or any regular thing. Five feet away from me stood Semanté, jerking her head a bit like a bird that's flown into a wall. That told me she couldn't see or hear anything. I didn't move or look straight at her, which required a lot of eye-straining effort.

"Murderer, we haven't brought you here for trading." Although I wasn't facing him, I recognized the disdainful, lazy voice of Weldt, the God of Commerce. I had dealt with him a few times and had done nothing to make him love me or even tolerate me. He was saying, "I want to properly introduce you to another sorcerer, the Cricket."

"That's gentlemanly of you, Mighty Weldt, but you caught me unprepared. I'm dusty and bloodstained from murdering a great load of Hill People. They aren't nearly so impressive as I once believed. I don't think they're too bright, either."

Beside me, Semanté hissed, although I doubted she was aware of it. I began to make some random turns, some of them jerking and some gradual, that would put the gazebo in my view.

"Murderer!" Harik yelled. "Stop engaging in unruliness when talking to another god!"

"I don't mean to embarrass you in front of guests, Your Magnificence. It's just that you never take me anyplace, so I haven't had a chance to learn manners."

Weldt whispered, "Krak's parts! I hope we needn't endure much of this. I would rather listen to my wife sing."

"This should require but a few moments," Harik whispered. "Think of the glory that will rain upon you when you return to Father victorious."

"I hope so. Krak has treated me like the runt pig these past few hundred years."

Harik whispered, "Mere breaths from now, you shall suffer such unfairness no more."

Weldt paused before whispering, "Are you writing another play?"

"Yes," Harik whispered defensively.

"Void suck out your heart! Stop talking like that. It's annoying," Weldt whispered. Then he spoke out, "Murderer, meet the Cricket. Cricket, Murderer. Say hello."

Semanté spoke right up as if she expected that. I guessed she was cooperating with the gods in whatever back-alley roll they had planned for me. "Bib, I told you to go home. Now look what has happened."

"Semanté, back home, my wife is planning a big party with all her relatives. Getting stabbed in the heart sounds like more fun. So, you're the Burner, huh?"

"Yes," she said. "I kept it a secret from you. I almost killed you. You are a lucky, lucky person. A lucky bastard, as you might say."

"I'm a fine dancer too." I could almost see the gods in the gazebo, but I had lost sight of Semanté. "Well, Your Magnificences, the Cricket and I have met. We have said hello, and we have implied threats and accusations. Farewell, you greasy piles of the vilest bear flop ever known to god or man. I feel certain you can verify that you are indeed the vilest."

I dropped toward my body, but Harik yanked me back. "We must attend to one more item."

I could see them now, both sitting on the lowest level of the gazebo. I realized that the Gods' Realm was enjoying a perfect day, with a skin-tingling breeze and the sun pressing warmth into me. I could smell pine and roses.

Weldt leaned against a column. "We thought you might want to support the Cricket in her upcoming trade. So often sorcerers must struggle through demanding bargains alone."

"I do not agree to support her," I said. "Unless that involves hurling her off a cliff with sharp rocks and venomous serpents at the bottom."

"You can just watch then," Harik said.

Weldt cleared his throat. "Cricket, I offer seven squares of power. What is your offer in return?"

Seven was an astonishing number of squares to receive in a single trade. Semanté would have to put something profound on the table. I resisted the urge to look at her.

I heard the smile in Semanté's voice. "I offer my request that you return Bib's memories to him."

"Hold on!" I shouted. "I'm not even sure I want those memories!" I realized that was the point when I saw the smiles on Weldt's and Harik's faces. "Wait! Is that even allowed? How can she make a bargain over *my* memories?"

Harik shrugged. "You did it with the Nub and the Knife."

I couldn't say much to that.

Weldt clapped his hands. "Done!"

Silence sucked up the next couple of seconds. I said, "What happens now?"

"What happens? You have made hundreds of bargains!" Harik snorted. "What do you mean by asking what happens now?"

"When the Cricket returns, she'll have the agreed-upon power," Weldt said. "When you return, you will have the agreed-upon memories."

Smiling, Harik stepped out of the gazebo toward us. "There is one more thing that must happen. Cricket? Now you must pay your fee. How do you wish to do it?"

I knew it was coming, but the words still shocked me.

Semanté said, "I will pay with ten years of the Murderer's life."

"Very well," Harik said. "I feel that this was extremely productive, don't you?"

Weldt laughed behind his hand.

"I have one question," I said.

"What are you willing to pay for the answer?" Harik asked.

"Not a damn thing. The memories I'm about to get back . . . who made the bargain that took them away?"

"Oh, I'll tell you that for free," Harik said. "You did it yourself. You asked us to take those memories away from you."

Harik launched me back into my body so hard I collapsed. I had been standing on the platform watching Desh fight to bend the bridge. I slipped and fell nine feet from the platform onto the ground.

Then I remembered.

TWENTY-SEVEN

After Darby the Blacksmith drowned in a gutter, I decided to leave my home islands for the mainland. I had no reasons or plans. It just sounded like something a twenty-year-old sorcerer should do.

The *Gard* was the biggest ship I had ever seen, a true giant. It carried eight crew and crammed twenty-four passengers on deck for a four-day voyage. A crewman whispered to me that the ship's name was really *Guard*, but the captain couldn't spell.

I should have known something bad would happen. Four, eight, and twenty-four are some of the unluckiest numbers.

On the second day, we were becalmed. The wind died, the current ceased, and the ship floated in place, slowly spinning on the unmoving water. It was unusual, but not unknown. The ship stocked plenty of food and water, so we weren't too concerned.

At sunset that day, a crewman went mad and killed the captain. Really, he tore the captain apart. Afterward, the murderer didn't remember a thing about it. He was put in irons anyway.

The next sunset, a passenger went crazy and ripped apart the crewman who was in irons. That killer didn't remember murdering anybody, either.

I asked Gorlana, the Goddess of Mercy, what in the goat-groping hell was happening. She told me that a vengeful spirit hated everybody on the ship. She was vague about the reasons. She was clear about the fact that she would not help me.

Sunset became a horrible time. The spirit would possess somebody, who would then rush to gruesomely kill a person. The victim was whoever the spirit had possessed the day before. The killers never remembered a single damn thing about their killings.

At the next sunset, it would start all over.

It took us a couple of days to figure out what was happening and a couple more to see that a person's face changed the moment the spirit possessed them. At sunset the next day, a bunch of us grabbed the possessed person, who threw us all the hell over the place. Then she went right on and committed her gruesome murder.

At the next sunset, I saw somebody's face change, drew my sword, and stabbed him in the heart. I guess that was the trick to throwing out a vengeful spirit, because the man crumpled dead.

But the following day, the spirit came back to possess a little boy, and I killed him straightaway. Killing possessed people became my job. I had the skill and wouldn't hesitate. A woman told me that no person could be as cold and practical as me. I killed her three days later.

I murdered twenty men, three women, and five children. I didn't save anybody except myself. Maybe Gorlana helped me a little after all.

The wind and current returned and tossed the drifting ship onto the coast of the mainland two weeks later. I walked to the closest inn to rent a room for as long as my money would last, and I hid.

"Bib!" Desh was poking at me as I lay on the ground, curled up on my side.

"I'm all right!" I coughed.

"Sure. It was Harik, right?"

I rolled onto my back and sat up.

Desh drew back when he saw my face. "What happened? What's wrong?"

"Nothing. We need to run before we get overrun." I tried to grin at my rhyming, but my lips didn't seem to work. I attempted to stand up and failed in every possible way, including hitting myself in the face.

"Is he drunk?" Stan pushed his way to look at me over Desh's shoulder. "Hell of a time to be drunk. At least he could've shared."

"Stan, help me get him up." Desh grabbed one of my arms and hauled me upright by himself. "Never mind, Stan. I forgot that he weighs no more than a broom."

I didn't feel drunk, but I had to stare hard at Pil until her face made sense. I had done this same thing to her—sent her taken memories thundering back to warp every damn thing in her head. I felt ashamed to have done it.

Pil squinted at me and rubbed at her eyebrow, which didn't exist anymore. "We can't sit down here and have a leisurely chat about what the hell is wrong with Bib. Let's all get a horse or steal one. Stan, find a horse for Bib. We'll meet at that big pile of lumber."

I appreciated her clear, direct orders but realized I wouldn't be able to follow any of them. "Let go," I said, although I would have fallen right down had she done it.

"Hush." Pil patted my shoulder.

"What's wrong with him?" Cora asked.

"He's just happy to be alive," Pil said. "If you want to say the same, go get a damn horse."

Desh and Pil guided me toward the lumber pile, but I felt steadier within twenty yards and was walking on my own. Desh hurried away to steal horses while Pil gripped my arm and pointed me.

"I'll be fine in a minute," I said. "Put me on a horse, and I'll show you."

Pil leaned in and whispered, "Bib! From how long ago was it? Don't even try to play ignorant with me—you know what I mean."

I blinked a few times and tripped, but Pil held me up. "Twenty years. More."

"Shit!" Pil shouted. Everybody within fifty feet turned to look. She lowered her voice. "Shit! Two months made me resentful. Two years made Desh vengeful. What in the name of Krak's knobs will twenty years do to you?"

"Nothing!" I said, shaking off Pil's hand. "It's a relief! I always wondered how I got from there to here."

"Bib, stop laughing."

"Am I laughing?"

"Yes, you're laughing!"

I thought about it and realized I was laughing and giggling, and I had been since Desh picked me up. I cleared my throat and stood stiff, like I might break if I leaned over. "I'm fine now, it's over. Don't yank on my arm! You're safe. I don't have to kill you, not any of you, so don't worry."

Pil stopped and grabbed my face with both hands. "What would you have done differently if you'd never lost those memories?"

My face flushed and my eyes stretched wide.

"You need to know but can't find out, right? You did this same thing to me, you son of a bitch. Hurts, doesn't it?" Pil pulled me toward the lumber pile. "Don't you kill anybody without asking me first. Hey, can I borrow your sword? And your knife?"

"Sure." I drew my sword and knife to pass them over, but I fumbled them onto the ground. "You take them. I don't need them. I'll never use them again. Am I still laughing?"

"Yes. Bib, get on your horse."

I turned and found a horse three feet away from me. I didn't remember walking up to it. I shrugged and mounted the animal. Pil trotted away carrying my weapons, calling out, "Desh! We have to talk!"

I thought about the last few minutes, and none of it made sense. One of my horse's ears was shorter than the other, and I began tugging it to even them out. After a little while, I realized that didn't make sense either, so I stopped and held still, waiting for something sensible to happen.

Soon, Desh and the others had gathered horses, which made perfect sense considering the Hill People were coming to kill everybody.

"We're running, right?" I asked.

Stan said, "Yeah, we're running, not that it makes any difference to somebody who's lost his damn mind."

"Good." I kicked my horse and galloped down the road, away from the river and toward the center of the Empire. People were yelling behind me, but that didn't mean much. I was twice the horseman any of them were, and they wouldn't catch me if they tried for a year.

That proved to be false, not because any of them caught me, but because I didn't ride for a whole year. After passing through several quiet towns, in the afternoon I stopped at a broad, sluggish stream to water my horse. Within a few minutes, Pil and the others caught up and dismounted.

Desh said, "Bib, please don't ride away from us like that anymore. What if some bandits ambush you? You're unarmed."

"Sure, that makes a lot of sense," I said. "Except for the fact that we're in the Empire, and they must have stamped out all the bandits, right? If not, what the hell do you have an Empire for?"

Cora spoke up: "Why don't you ride beside me? I was born in these lands. I can tell you all the stories and secrets."

"That sounds fine." I thought that I still might not be making sense, so this would be a good time to shut up and listen.

We resumed riding, but at a much less tiring pace.

Beside me, Cora pointed at some low hills. "I was born over there, although I don't remember it. Well, of course I don't remember being born, but I don't remember living there, either."

I had been nodding along and smiling. "I'm in love with a woman who's not a sorcerer."

"Oh."

"She left me because I've come east to assassinate a stranger."

"I know. Pil told me." Cora smiled, all friendly and sympathetic at the same time.

"That brings the total number of women I've made happy to one. No, I guess that would be to none. Hell, I'll be killing them in their sleep next."

Cora didn't answer, and I didn't speak for the next two hours, in case I should say something crazy.

Desh and Pil chose to make camp off the road rather than rest at an inn. We ate plenty of rabbit and ground squirrel. With his sling, Desh was a mighty slayer of tasty animals.

The fire had begun to die, the horses were hobbled, and we were wiping our greasy fingers when I said, "I'm sorry about all the craziness. It doesn't seem like I can stop."

"What's wrong?" Cora asked. Obviously, Desh and Pil hadn't been confiding in her.

"Just remembering a thing or two, I guess."

"You don't have to talk about it," Pil said.

"That's a damn good thing."

She continued, "Desh and I know a little about it, maybe not exactly as much as has happened to you, but some."

"Of course you do. I forced you to know it. I see now that I couldn't have done a worse thing to you if you'd been my enemies. Is there any more rabbit?" I smiled at them both, hoping they'd smile back. They didn't. "Desh, why didn't you kill me instead of taking ten years of my life? Nobody could have stopped you."

Desh rubbed his chin. "Honestly, it seemed like something you would do, and I don't want to be like you."

I laughed. "Me neither."

Desh left me an opening to say more, but I didn't. "Bib, I didn't trade away ten years of your life. I just told you that to drive you . . . to aggravate you."

I blinked a couple of times and realized that was all the reaction I could spare for those ten years. "That's a damn good thing too, Desh. Can I have my sword now?"

"Well, you can see why that would make us uneasy," Pil said.

"I understand completely. Do you think that all of you can keep me from taking it?"

Desh, Pil, and Stan traded looks. Then Desh fetched my sword and knife from his saddle.

I held the sword up in the firelight. "Thank you, Desh. I didn't understand this sword until now."

"What do you mean?"

I grinned at him. "You enchanted it to kill me."

Desh sat forward. "You can goddamn be sure I did not do that."

"Really? Well, maybe I'm wrong. I agree that it would be an unfriendly act. Maybe I should stop trying to talk."

I blinked at the firelight reflecting off the blade. I could feel the others tensing, wondering if I was about to kill them. I figured I could finish them in fifteen seconds if I wanted. I lowered the sword. "You're ready to stop me if I try to kill you, right?"

Pil nodded while the others stared at me. She said, "Don't talk anymore, Bib."

"Pil, you're a good person," I said.

She laughed. "The hell I am!"

I laughed too, and so did everybody else. The tension floated away. "These things are relative. You're good compared to me. Compared to our old friend Parth, you're like a holy woman. Pil, you kill me if I need it. I've killed a lot of people like you, so that would be fair. Maybe it would. Things are a little unclear."

Desh said, "If things are unclear, then all of this may mean nothing. Why don't you sleep and think about it tomorrow?"

I nodded. "Maybe things don't mean anything."

Pil murmured, "That's right."

I pointed at her and burst out, "Yes! That's right! You're a good person and smart too!" I sighed and gazed around. "You really want me to shut up and sleep, don't you?"

"Yes!" Stan shouted. "By Krak's thumb hammer, shut it! I been standing here ready to kick the embers in your face and run."

I lay down and stared at the cloudy sky. When I looked over a bit later, everybody else was sitting far back on the other side of the fire. "It's got to be chilly over there," I said.

Pil walked over to join me. "Bib, put your sword away. You don't need it right now."

I looked at my hand and realized it hurt from squeezing my sword's hilt and holding it across my chest. "What the hell?" I got up and hunted for the scabbard on Desh's saddle, scaring the horses in the process. "This is the kind of thing that happens in dreams."

"Lie back down," Pil said.

"Pil, I don't know how to think about all this."

"Sure, it would be funny if you did. We'll talk about it in the morning." When I didn't move, she cleared her throat and tapped my shoulder.

"I wish this was a dream," I said, lying down, "even though it would be a shitty one."

I didn't sleep much, so I was the first one to see the glow. It was a monstrous, orange light showing against the clouds over a whole slice of the southern sky. "Wake up! The Empire is burning."

We all watched the glow for a minute, as if it would change and do something else.

Cora said, "The Hill People must have worked hard to burn down the stone walls."

"There's plenty to burn inside the fortress," Desh said. "Furniture, interior walls, rugs and tapestries. There were a lot of wooden outbuildings too. I'm surprised the Hill People stopped to burn it all."

I considered that, and my head felt clear. "They didn't stop. They organized a little burning crew and left it behind. The rest are jogging toward us right now." After a pause, I yelled, "We can't lie around sleeping on the goddamn dirt, can we?"

Nobody disagreed. We packed up, saddled our horses, and mounted to ride deeper into the Empire.

By sunup, the road was running along the riverbank, and we were pushing our horses hard. Midmorning, Stan spotted five huge boats sailing down the river. They were just coming into view.

Cora pointed at the lead boat. "Ludlow is on that one. You can tell because of the blue pennant."

Stan spit on the ground. "Damn it! The great, hoiking pile of guts escaped. I wonder how many soldiers he left behind to get massacred?"

I said, "The pretty bastard could have charged out and died heroically, I guess, but that wouldn't have killed many Hill People. By running he'll get to the capital in time to warn everybody."

Pil smiled and slapped my back, I assumed to reward me for not talking crazy.

"Look at the water," Desh said from down by the riverbank.

"I'm sure it's pretty," Pil said.

"No!" Desh barked. "Look in the water!" He waded out into the river.

By the time we had all trotted to the bank, Desh was wrestling with something hung in the reeds. Stan splashed out and helped him pull a body up onto the grass.

"It's Yoadie." Desh's shoulders fell.

"He was near dead when I saw him last," I said. "And you can't bury somebody on a boat. Tossing his body into the river wasn't dignified, but it was practical."

Stan said, "Yeah, pretty flippin' practical." He had pulled aside Yoadie's shirt to show a wound over his heart.

"What?" Pil squeaked, which she almost never did. "Why kill him if he was almost dead?"

Desh pulled Yoadie's shirt closed and began laying his body out straight.

Pil said, "None of this makes sense. If they wanted him dead, they just had to wait." She turned to Cora.

Cora said, "I'm surprised. This is exceptionally brutal. It's an economically shortsighted practice too."

"What does that mean?" Pil's eyebrows pulled together. "It sounds like you know a lot that we don't."

Cora sighed. "What did you think would happen when your villagers reached the capital? The Empire would take away someone's land and give it to them? Some artisan would be forced to take them as a partner? Marriages would be arranged?"

Desh stared at the ground. "I didn't think that far. I just assumed the Empire was safe."

"It is!" Cora said. "It's safe for citizens and for visitors. It's even safe for slaves, which is what they'll be."

I stared at Cora, blinking, until Stan yelled from downstream, "Found another one!"

It was one of the oldest women in the village, stabbed in the chest like Yoadie. We explored the bank for a quarter mile each way and found five more old men and women, all murdered.

"They couldn't have sold these elders for two bits and a blind dog, could they?" I asked.

Cora shook her head. "No, the captain would take a loss and might have to give away the slave—"

"They're not slaves!" Desh shouted, and Cora backed away. After a few seconds, Desh walked off in the other direction.

Ever since we found Yoadie, other people had sounded muffled to me, not worth listening to. I perked up when Pil, who was crying now, said, "I don't understand this. I mean, I don't understand how this can happen—any of it."

Stan sneered. "The vile turd grabs up these people, stabs the ones he don't want, and plops 'em over the side. Then he sails on in to sell the rest at a sweet little profit. Happens all the time in the Empire. Or I heard it done. We was fools for riding one inch into the damn Empire—"

A boom and a tearing crack sounded from the riverbank, and water birds flew in all directions. A tall, stout willow tree had split down the middle from crown to ground. Desh stood pointing at it with something small in his hand. While we watched, half the tree creaked and fell away into the water.

I ignored Desh's devastating magic and said, "You don't understand it, Pil? I understand it perfectly. Some people have to die so you kill them fast. You put them over the side so everybody can pretend it didn't happen. You keep killing them until you're done. It makes sense."

Pil looked like she might kick me.

I added, "We gave them to these bastards. Now we have to get them back."

Pil grinned and hugged me. Desh smiled for the first time in days. Stan and Cora both looked sour, but neither objected.

I gazed around. "I don't think I'm talking crazy. Of course I'm not the best judge. If we should run away instead, speak up."

TWENTY-EIGHT

A brief but fierce argument about whether I was talking craziness followed. Desh and Pil prevailed, and we continued riding deeper into the Empire on what most of us considered a rescue mission. Stan proclaimed it was riding straight into Harik's greasy maw. Cora didn't say much but looked worried.

Whenever we reached a town or an army post, we stopped long enough to tell somebody they had best flee if they wanted to live. I doubt that a single soul believed us. As Cora had said, the Empire was safe. Nobody could imagine invaders burning their crops and homes before murdering their families. We might as well have said the Empress was coming to take them away on a flying cow.

We were traveling up an important road in the Empire, the Wise and Benevolent Emperor Justice VII Highway, known by most as The Wise. It took a curving path from the frontier all the way to the capital.

We began this little jaunt at the Fargold River in the province of Chalkfell. We rode across its hills into Melmarch, which had taller hills and more towns. Capswatter province came next, where the hills sprouted grand, looming trees and it rained most of the time.

Two wide rivers and some big streams marked out entry into the province of Bitterfeld, an ironic name if ever one existed. It was flat, soft, and blanketed in healthy crops. The weather was warm but pleasant, and the people were mean as hell.

We had not yet even entered the Empire by some people's reckoning. We had only passed through provinces that the Empire had conquered in the past hundred years. They technically stood equal to any other, but citizens of the old provinces tended to sneer when mentioning them.

We rode hard for four days to cross those outer provinces. Then we reached Silvercutt, the first true Imperial city with a theater, plumbing, a prison, and a garrison of two thousand soldiers who also ignored our warning about the invasion.

In Silvercutt, we luxuriated by washing ourselves and sleeping in beds.

Desh had questioned Cora several times about whether Ludlow would reach the capital ahead of us. She finally told him she couldn't predict the wind, sandbars, or mutinies, but her best guess was, "He probably wouldn't," and Desh should shut up about it.

Our horses were worn down from the hard travel. Desh traded our mounts for rested ones in Silvercutt, and he did the same every other day for the rest of the journey. He poured silver coins from a pouch as if they were pebbles, and for all I knew, they had been pebbles that morning.

Desh rarely had to spend much, since Cora handled the trading. Crusty horse traders laughed at little Cora. Minutes later, she walked away with horses and had paid almost nothing. The traders looked as if they had been smacked on the forehead with a mallet.

During the journey, I slept no more than a couple of hours at a stretch. Sometimes I pretended to sleep because I thought people were giving me unsettling looks. In Silvercutt, I woke before midnight and stomped to the inn's common room, estimating how drunk I could get in four hours. Also, less sleep meant fewer dreams.

I had already journeyed three ales toward oblivion when Cora walked in, sat across from me, and stared. I held out my mug. She shook her head and ordered her own.

Then she said, "What the hell is going on?"

I leaned back. "The best way to hurt them is to give them what they ask for."

"I don't know whether that's a fanciful evasion, or an answer so honest I can't understand it."

I shrugged. "Drink. Maybe it will help you."

"You should have slept longer. I intended to take advantage of you, but you were gone."

That was too complicated to think about, so I drank instead.

Cora frowned. "What happened to you? Desh and Pil are keeping it secret, as if they were bankers with gold."

"I got what I asked for. Don't go around asking for things."

Cora drank and set down her mug. "Do you want me to leave you alone?"

"You will if you're smart, but I've come to believe intelligence doesn't mean shit. Drink." I winked at her and then wondered why. "I won't murder you, if that's what you're thinking."

She nodded and leaned forward.

I added, "Of course, it's well known that I'm a liar."

Cora grinned. "You may be the most honest person around. I can tell the truth by believing the opposite of what you say." Before I opened my mouth, she blurted, "So, I have guessed that you wish you hadn't asked the gods for something. What was it?"

I waved. "That doesn't matter."

"Which means it's extremely important."

I shouted, "It's doesn't matter!"

The other three people in the room stared.

"And it's a rude question," I added.

Cora tapped the table. "So, you did ask them for something. What was it?"

"I should turn you into a hay bale for asking these questions."

Cora put both hands on the table. "Tell me what you asked for."

"Turning you into a hay bale could take a hundred years. I'll slit your throat and bury you now, and someday you'll become soil, and that soil will grow hay. Some sweaty fellow will come along and bale you."

"That's fine, they can feed me to horses. I love horses!" Cora leaned forward and yelled, "What did you ask the gods for?"

I reached across and snatched her mug. "If you keep on about that, I won't give this back."

"Well, that's the end." She pointed around the room. "There's no way I can get another drink in here. I have to give up."

I couldn't stop myself. I poured her drink onto the floor and slid the mug back to her.

She nodded as if she had expected me to do that, and as if she could explain why it made sense. She asked, "If whatever you asked for doesn't matter, then what does?"

"I'm in love with somebody else, so stay in your own bed." I smiled as if I had vanquished ten men in combat.

She didn't change expression. "Fine. I don't lust for you after all. Bib, tell me what matters."

I stared into her eyes. "I have wanted to kill you ever since I met you. Almost ever since." I laid my knife on the table.

Cora glanced at the knife. She might have paled. It was hard to tell in the firelight. "Well . . . did the gods agree to give you what you asked for?"

I looked around the room and ignored her.

Cora slammed her mug on the table. "Did they?"

That startled me. "They sure as hell did. But that doesn't matter, and the thing after that didn't, either." I knocked my chair against the wall when I stood up, and I walked fast back to my room. Five minutes later, I realized I had left my knife on the table, but when I went back, it was gone.

The next morning, when dawn had grown just light enough to saddle our horses, Cora tossed my knife to me as she walked past. "You left this last night."

Desh and Pil glanced at each other.

Stan hooted once. "Damn and horse piss, Bib, that was slow but soon enough, I guess. I figured maybe you got stabbed in the willy or something."

For the next few days, I felt better—maybe harsh and scattered, but not crazy. I kept ignoring anything I didn't want to acknowledge, as if that were the prerogative of madmen. Nobody objected, so I employed the tactic with gratifying success.

Over the next five days, we crossed three big provinces. Some town or city was almost always close enough for us to see the fire smoke. All of us had grown weary and suffered small hurts from travel, and I had to admit that I was the least hearty. We could almost always find an inn nearby for a few hours of sleep, and that sustained me.

Midsummer had arrived, but it rained more days than not. We rode from sunrise to after dark, pushing the horses all we dared. Nobody caught up with us carrying news of the Hill People's invasion, so if anybody was bringing the alarm, we must have outpaced them.

Somewhere along there, our highway, The Wise, became a wide, smooth-cobbled road. Inside my head, I rejoiced, since until then the road had become wetter and stickier by the day.

On the sixth afternoon out of Silvercutt, I saw the Mountains of Regensmeet when a haze of rain lifted. The capital occupied a big corridor in those mountains. We had traveled more than seven hundred miles since we fled the fortress.

Pil said, "I'm afraid I don't have any really good ideas on what to do now, or any ideas at all. Cora, you lived here. How do we get in? What should we expect? Where do they keep the slaves? If I'm forgetting something, pretend I asked and give me an answer."

Desh said, "I don't think we can answer everything yet. How do we get in, and what should we expect? That should get us far enough to regroup and come up with a plan that's not so hasty and jammed together."

Cora took a deep breath and then laid it out as if she were teaching it to children. "Unless we're on a ship in the ocean or want to climb straight up a mountain, the only way in is the main gate. We'll have to explain ourselves and maybe show a pass to get inside. We can do as we wish within the city, as long as we don't break any laws, offend anyone important, or make the guards angry."

Desh glanced at me and whispered to Pil, "I wish Bib wasn't crazy. He could help us plan."

I don't think he expected me to hear him, but I said, "Cora, what kind of people do the guards see a lot?"

"Modest traders. Soldiers, of course. Anybody looking for ways to enjoy themselves to death."

"What do these traders look like?"

"They're usually families, poor but not starving, hauling in goods they grew or made. Whatever the city needs."

I nodded. "The passes you mentioned—what are they?"

"It is a disk made of clay, like a coin, with the city seal imprinted on it. About this big." Cora made a "C" with her fingers to show the size.

I stared at my feet, holding back a brief urge to yank off my boots and throw them at Stan. Would that be crazy, or a service to mankind? I pointed at Desh. "Create five magical disguises. Pil, you and Cora make five of those city passes. Then find somebody who'll take our horses in trade for a wagonload of chickens, or blankets, or goat bladders, along with a mule or two."

Everybody stared at me.

"Go!" I yelled.

"What are you going to do?" Pil asked.

"I'm doing it. Scat!"

Desh came back an hour later. The others returned soon after. They found me scratching hash marks beside the road with a stick. I was making marks on both sides of the road, dodging back and forth among the passing horses and wains.

"What are you doing?" Cora asked me. She grabbed my sleeve, but I shook her off.

"Did you finish your tasks?"

They had. Desh held a small leather bottle full of magical power out to me.

I grinned. "Hell, I knew you were a brave man. Aren't you afraid I'll use this power to make a bull stomp on you?"

He said, "I'll give this to you, but you have to do one thing for me. Heal Pil's scars."

"You sentimental so-and-so!"

"She's conspicuous with those scars, and we may need to disappear inside the city."

I nodded. "Practical and cold. I was like that once. You ought to give me lessons. Don't forget to stab five children in the heart."

Desh stepped back and lowered his hand. "Maybe I shouldn't give you this."

"Toss it here and don't act like an asshole! You may need me to save your life with this power."

Cora and I took Pil well off the road, and I spent half an hour healing the burn scars all over her body. Since the scars were not painful anymore, I didn't suffer from healing them. The best part for me was that I had used only a small portion of the power Desh had given me.

The city of Regensmeet lay in a pocket of hilly land between the coast and a small, sharp range of mountains. The only approach by land brought the visitor, or enemy, through a gap between two mountains. Six hundred years earlier, a regiment of sorcerers went mad or died to demolish the smallest mountain in the range. The city was built where it had been.

The looming walls of the Fortress Before Regensmeet blocked the approach and protected the city. Every thirty or forty years, some conqueror decided he was clever enough to take Regensmeet. Every one of them broke his armies against it, and not many survived.

The three-mile-long harbor offered a more promising point of attack, but the Empire mounted a standing navy four times the size of all the other navies in the world combined. Landing troops was near impossible, and nobody could lay siege to the city as long as the navy kept the sea lanes open.

It was said that any military commander who knew anything at all would rather slam his privates in a door than attack Regensmeet.

Even though I liked my plan, I admitted to myself some worry about getting into the city. The guards scrutinized our passes, poked around in our melons, and kept a few melons for themselves. They never asked us anything. The physician looked us over and decided that Stan might have the rime pox and would have to be quarantined, but Desh's liberal use of silver coins saved him.

Desh craned his neck to see down the street. "Cora, where's this market? We'll go there like good traders, blend in, and then quietly hunt for Mother and the rest."

"Wait," Pil said. "The Hill people could be just a couple of days behind us or even less. We should warn people that they're coming."

"Pitch that idea in the damn pisser." Stan pointed back toward the gates. "We told everybody from barons to idiots about it on the way here, and not a damn one of them as much as looked up from fumbling with his trousers!"

"We can't just do nothing." Pil looked around and met Cora's eyes. "You live here. How do we get them to believe us?"

Cora shook her head and shrugged. "I don't know. Not a single person would listen to me about this sort of thing. Everyone I might know still thinks I'm a slave."

Pil stuck out her jaw. "I'm not going to skip off to the market and let the Hill People attack a city that's unprepared."

Stan said, "You saw the walls, a thousand foot high and boiling oil piped to every window, I expect. Hill People can't defeat this place, even were they to come with twenty-foot spears and riding on bears."

Pil stared at Stan. "Really?"

He looked at his feet. "Probably, I guess."

"Pil, who will you go talk to?" Desh asked. "If the Hill People will be here that soon, what person can we tell who could do anything in time?"

Cora said, "The Empress could make things happen. But anybody she would listen to won't let us even get near them."

I can't say that I thought it through, but I wasn't shy about shouting it. "I'll go talk to the Empress."

"Bib, don't do that. It's unwise," Desh said.

"Desh, how many kings have you tricked into talking to you? Or forced? Probably not more than two or three. When you can say four, then I'll listen to your advice on the matter. Cora, where does she live?"

Cora didn't answer me, but she glanced at a terrace full of white buildings high above us.

I strode that direction like the tallest horse in the herd. The streets were just as wide as I remembered, but not quite as clean. I ignored my friends' calls from behind me.

Pil caught up and said, "Let's get a drink."

"No."

"I bet we can find a dice game."

I shook my head.

"There has to be a hundred brothels here. I'll pay." Her voice was calm, but when I glanced at her, she was sweating.

"After I talk to the Empress." I had no plan for what I might do after I made the Empress listen to me. I didn't know what I'd say, but I trusted I'd think of something. Part of me suspected this was foolish, but it felt right.

Pill ran up to walk beside me, then cleared her throat. "All right, if you're going, then I'll go with you. But don't do anything crazy." She blushed. "I mean, don't kill anybody unless you have to." After five more steps, she yelled, "And don't kill the Empress!"

We reached the foot of the stairway that led to the royal terrace. With sober efficiency, two guards asked our business.

"I'm headed to talk to the Empress," I said.

"Is she expecting you?" the jowly one asked.

"Yes."

After a moment of silence, we all laughed.

The other guard, young and bucktoothed, said, "You can't just talk to her when you want, you know. You'd be surprised how many folks think they can."

I laughed again. "I can't believe they're that stupid! But she's definitely expecting me."

"Bib . . ." Pil murmured.

Jowly pointed past me. "Bugger off, you stinking old turd! Go on! Run!"

"Bib, let's go!" Pil said.

I smashed Jowly in the face with his own spear shaft. He staggered while Bucktooth brought his spear around too slowly. I kicked his knee and threw him onto the pavement. I slammed Jowly against the stone wall, not hard enough to kill him, and I dropped him on the third step.

I trotted up the stairs between them. "I'll tell the Empress that you're fine guards. I'd hire you."

"Bib!" Pil called out.

I didn't need to answer, because I heard her following me.

TWENTY-NINE

I had climbed the first two hundred steps when part of me started wondering whether killing a bunch of guards so that I could force the Empress to listen to me was a good idea. Pil had been begging me to quit the whole way up, which had softened my confidence. I paused and squinted at the next step. I was damn tired of climbing them.

"Good! Good!" Pil yelped. "Come back down with me!" She dragged at my arm.

"That's my sword arm. Do you want to get me killed? Then what will happen to you?" I pulled her hand away.

"More guards are coming down."

I nodded. "You're right, this is a dangerous spot. We'd better keep going." I climbed on toward the heart of the best defended city in the world.

Pil shouted my name, Krak's name, and two intimate parts of Lutigan's body. Two guards were rushing down the steps toward us. I cut one's wrist and then sliced the other's thigh just a smidge away from his crotch. They both staggered aside, and I climbed past them, huffing and sweating.

Pil tackled me from behind. "Stop this, you hardheaded old son of a bitch! This is madness! At least make a plan!"

I turned and nodded. "A plan." I pulled two white bands to explore whatever was at the top of this stairway, which I could swear was getting longer and also steeper. I patted Pil's arm. "When we convince the Empress of the danger, she'll protect us."

Pil growled, "I don't care about the Empire!"

"Me neither, but every plank-jawed guard in the city is charging this direction, which makes it easier for Desh and the others to find our farmers before they get sold." I paused. "Shit, I did have a plan! That's surprising." I took a deep breath, which settled my mind.

Pil grabbed my wrist with both hands. "That's a fine plan, a real whizzer, but there are a million guards between us and the Empress!"

"Oh, you're worried about killing people?" I pulled my hand back to wipe the sweat off my cheeks.

Pil touched my face. "Bib, I can see that you really don't want to do this. So, wait."

"What for? Do you want to ask the captain of the guard what he thinks we should do?"

She reached into a pouch and handed me a pebble. "I made this for you. It's the only one. Hold it under your tongue and don't lose it, and for the sake of every god's toes, don't swallow it!"

I popped the pebble under my tongue and instantly lost twenty years' worth of hard living and bad decisions. I raced up the steps with a young man's vitality, an old man's experience, and a sword that wanted to kill everything I saw.

Twelve more guards met me on the way up the staircase. I left most of them dead behind me, a couple wounded on the steps, and one flying over the rail toward the street nearly two hundred feet below. Pil followed, ready to thrash any that I might miss as I climbed past.

At the top, I fought my way high enough to confirm what magic had told me about the situation. I saw a square, granite-paved plaza that measured at least four hundred feet on a side. "Shit!" I parried before thrusting into a guard's shoulder.

Pil climbed up high enough to see. "There must be a hundred guards there. More." She edged back down two steps as I killed the next guard with a quick thrust to the throat.

"I guess there are," I said. "But that's not the problem. The real problem is knowing which building she's in. There are three palaces up here." Blocking a guard's attack, I shoved him off-balance. "I wonder which one has the nicest privies?"

Guards were racing our way with fierce expressions, coming from their posts around the plaza. Pil took a deep breath. "If we're not going to retreat, let's die like sorcerers."

I laughed as I blocked a swing. "You give up too easy." As I fought, I pulled a dozen green bands, one after another. I tossed them across the plaza, making a corridor between us and the biggest palace. I squeezed them, but nothing happened. The guards kept coming.

"What are you doing? Stand aside!" Pil shouted. She climbed up, but I waved her back.

"I learned this from my little girl!" I pulled another twelve bands and sent them whirling after the first dozen. Then I opened my left fist as wide as my fingers would stretch.

The six guards in front of me hesitated. Then one staggered back, and a moment later, the rest either bent over or dropped to their knees. The two in front of me didn't resist as I knocked them on their asses. I yelled over my shoulder, "Watch where you step!"

The guards in front of me were now groaning. Some were vomiting, and some had dropped their weapons. Beyond them, thirty more guards were kneeling and even rolling on the pavement throughout the wide path I had created. It led to the most magnificent palace, which took up a whole side of the plaza. I figured the ruler of the world's greatest empire wouldn't want to share her shit with anybody else.

I sprinted through the corridor, dodging agonized guards. Other men closed to cut me off, but they faltered when they entered the path I had created. By the time I passed them, they were groaning, puking, and evacuating themselves too.

The palace's main door had the Empress's name and title carved above it, which I thought was damned hospitable. Some fast-thinking guard had barred the main door, which was a true iron-bound, mahogany work of art. I placed my hand against the door, sent a blue band through it, and rotted the thick, wooden bar on the other side.

Pil pushed open the door, and I killed the four guards behind it. She slammed the door shut, and I warped it in the doorframe. They would have to chop it apart to get through unless I made it true again. The palace would have other entrances, but I was counting on getting to the Empress fast.

I didn't imagine that the Empress would be perched on some throne waiting for us to show up. Hell, she might still be in bed. I took a chance and pulled a band to search for dogs. Every king I had ever known loved powerful, loyal dogs. Maybe they thought their subjects would see those dogs and want to be like them. I found four massive, slobbery beasts, and we jogged toward that room.

The dogs weren't far, but we met three more guards on the way. I pushed onward fast, wounding each one enough to disable him. Leaving them alive was like a file against my skin, but I couldn't spare the time to kill them. Anyway, they were just doing their duty.

Less than two minutes after we entered the palace, I dragged open an oaken door and glanced through it. "I'll be damned. It *is* a throne room. Harik disembowel me with a shovel." A young woman who I assumed to be the Empress sat on a comfortable-looking chair that might be called a throne. Her glare dominated the room so that the two advisors beside her, men in their prime, looked no more imposing than sheep.

I stepped into the throne room, killed one guard, and wounded another while making the dogs chase ten more men around, pouncing and licking. The dogs also galumphed and slobbered among a few cowering people dressed in awfully nice clothes.

Pil slammed the door, and I warped it shut.

The Empress watched all of this from her throne without shifting or commenting. She had a delicate face and a wolf's eyes, and of course her hair was blond. I was no expert on fashion, but her blue silk gown was likely the most expensive garment I had ever seen, considering that a thousand gemstones or more were sewn into it.

A jeweled golden goblet sat on a finely carved wooden table to her right. As she regarded me, she reached to a small table on her left and drank from a shabby tin cup.

I sheathed my sword and walked to the middle of the room.

The Empress leaned back and snapped, "Stop all this! All of you! Stop it right now!"

I let the dogs rest but kept their attention. The ten guards blocked me from the throne, and the fancy people fell back to one of the corners.

The Empress continued, "You haven't attempted to kill me right here on my father's chair, so you must want something. Gold? I have plenty. Favors? Maybe, but you don't look deserving. My hand in marriage? I do like an older man, but you stink. I can smell you from here. And you killed my men, which doesn't put you in a good light."

I took a breath and then couldn't think of anything to say. My mind became a wall of mute ignorance.

After a few seconds, the Empress pointed at me. "Speak! I prefer not to command you as if you were a dog, but you dragged yourself and my men through a lot of trouble to get here. You should try to be more interesting." Somebody started pounding at the door with hammers and maybe axes too. "Also, you should speak quickly."

Pil stepped up beside me. "Your Majesty, I am Pil, and this is Bib. Please excuse him, because he's brave and has good intentions, but he has been . . . wounded in his spirit during the trip here. I can speak for both of us."

The Empress regarded Pil without much interest, as if she were the fourth best pair of shoes in her wardrobe.

Pil continued: "We just arrived from the frontier and are probably the first ones to bring this news. The Hill People have mounted an invasion—a huge invasion—and they are coming this way, and nothing will stop them since they've already burned your fortress at the Fargold River. They intend to cause great harm to your people."

The Empress almost smiled. "Not regular old harm? Great harm? Would you not consider it great harm to kill a regiment of my men, as you just have?"

Pil nodded. "I agree that we have been . . . inconsiderate, Your Majesty. But the Hill People plan to kill you and every one of your subjects, and that's great harm in my way of thinking."

"Why should I buy what you're selling, Pil? Those are strange names. Bib? Pil? I guess you're both sorcerers. A lot of sorcerers have peculiarly short names. You did train my dogs as if by magic. In fact, you trained them better than I ever could."

Pil said, "You don't have to believe only us. We were helping Ludlow, and he'll tell you the same when he gets here, but every minute could make a difference. You should start preparing now for war, Your Majesty. If Ludlow agrees with me, and I think he will, you'll already be a step ahead in your preparations, but if he doesn't agree, then your soldiers can go right back home. After all, soldiers prepare for nothing all the time and call it drilling. It's their way of life."

"That's very fine logic, Pil," the Empress said. "You should be a mathematician. What is the cube root of negative two hundred and forty-five?"

"That's -6.25733," Pil said without blinking.

"Exactly?"

"Yes, Your Majesty, to the final decimal."

The Empress dug around in the drawer of a table beside her. "I have the answer right here, already worked out. If you lied to me, I'll have you beaten to death. But you can save yourself by telling me the truth now. Is your answer really correct?"

Pil paused and then stood taller. "I stand by my answer, Your Majesty, but you already know I'm right, because you said you know sorcerers, and I am one. Therefore, you're not testing me—you're just making us wait. You are delaying, Your Majesty. We can hear the men breaking down the door, so that's not what you're waiting for. You expect someone to come through that door behind you."

The Empress flashed the tiniest glance toward the concealed door to her right. I had noticed it when we walked in, and I guess

Pil had too. I had halfway expected we'd be chasing the Empress through it.

Pil always talked fast, and that sometimes made her sound baffled or flighty, which she wasn't. But, as she set the Empress straight, Pil poured hard words onto the monarch, as if she were spilling a load of bricks. I felt proud of her, even if she had made our torture and death quite a bit likelier.

A smile grew on the Empress's face. "Nonsense, Pil. Certainly your news is helpful. But I do not reward traitors."

Everybody fell quiet for a moment. Even the men chopping at the door paused. In that silence, the pebble that Pil had given me slipped out from under my tongue and popped out of my mouth. It clattered against the marble floor and bounced halfway to the throne, then rolled toward the Empress's right foot. I hadn't done it on purpose, and in fact it surprised me all to hell, although it shouldn't have. Pil must not have put enough power into the pebble for it to last long, and when its time was done, it fell out.

Now my knees shook as the vigor I had gained from the pebble disappeared in an instant. I felt every one of those four hundred steps I had climbed.

Everybody stared at me. I still couldn't think of a word to say, so I bowed toward the throne like some dimwit festival juggler.

Ludlow whipped open the door in the back wall and strode into the room with all the gusto of a dueling master. A silver circlet held his hair back. A line of soldiers followed him. As he walked, he said, "I guess the traitors have shown up begging like dogs, Your Imperial Majesty. They swore to serve us and then ran away at the first little bit—" He jerked to a stop and pointed at us. "Who the hell are they? Your Imperial Majesty?"

Pil and I were still wearing the magical disguises Desh had made. We looked like a couple of farmers who came to the city to sell melons.

The Empress leaned forward on her throne. "They said they are Pil and Bib. Those are the traitors, correct?"

Over the past months, whenever I had given strangers a false name, Pil had sighed and mocked me. If she had followed my example now and told the Empress we were the fur-trapping brother and sister, Rondo and Ann, we might have walked out of the palace with just a warning and some mean looks. At least we'd have been a step closer to it.

"Is this some kind of trick?" Ludlow asked us. "Is it magic? If it is, stop it right now, because we'll figure it out."

Pil flinched. After a moment, she spoke out: "It's not a trick, my lord. We're simple traders, traveling these lands on our sturdy elephant, dealing honestly with everybody."

Pil had said *elephant*. Lutigan must have obliged her to betray me at this moment.

I raised my hand and turned away from her, and it's a good thing I did. Pil whipped around and drove her glass-sharp knife straight toward my crotch. My arm didn't do a single useful thing, but twisting my body threw off Pil's aim. The knife plunged into my thigh an inch from my groin. The blade was so sharp it didn't hurt for the first couple of seconds.

My vision was swallowed by what seemed to be a cloud of ash. By the sudden shouting from all directions, I assumed everybody else had the same problem. I grabbed Pil's knife hand by the wrist as she kicked my legs out from under me. That didn't help as much as I'd hoped, since she had switched the knife to her other hand and rammed it toward my chest. I threw my arm out to block. I avoided a pierced heart but gained a shoulder wound and a badly sliced elbow.

Pil sobbed. "I'm sorry!" She wrapped something around my wrist. "New disguise!"

She slashed at my throat. That would have killed me, but I blocked with my forearm, which was sliced to the bone. I blocked her next swing better, but it made a deep cut above my left eye.

"Either kill me or leave!" Pil yelled.

I didn't even consider killing her. I pushed Pil off me with a sad, puny shove, and I'm sure she let me do it.

From that point, I didn't think much. I did things out of reflexes I earned by being alive a long time. Scrambling to my feet, I limped toward the warped wooden door through the ash cloud, which Pil must have caused. I knew my way out of the palace from the door. The door Ludlow had come out of still stood open, but I didn't know anything about it and ignored it.

None of my wounds would kill me soon, so I used the disguise to take on the likeness of a guard I had killed at the stairs. Then I unwarped the door. Five guards shoved open what was left of it as they ran inside. When they had passed, I limped into the hallway.

I didn't try to be sneaky or hide from anybody. Instead, I limped along, shouting, "They're killing everybody back there! Guts all over the walls! Save the Empress!" Blood was pouring down my face like a waterfall from my head wound. I must have looked like a gory nightmare, because nobody stopped me.

I could hear men outside the palace, chopping and pounding at that magnificent main door. I took a few seconds to unwarp it, and then I scooted back as at least a dozen guards slammed through like a wave. While they sprinted past, I kept yelling about the bloodbath and massacre.

Just outside the main door, a squat man with thick arms stopped me by slapping a hand on my chest. "Report!"

Nothing I could say would help the situation, so I fell on the paving stones and closed my eyes.

"Krak damn it to every hell and your mother's twat besides!" the man shouted. He stomped away. I didn't hear him tell anybody to watch me, so I stood up and staggered away from the palace.

My body was telling me that I might be falling down shortly. Bloody sweat was running off my chin. My breath was quick and shallow. I kept trying to wipe the blood out of my left eye, but I still couldn't see with it. I would never be able to limp across the plaza to the stairs. Even if I reached them, the only way I'd get down four hundred steps would be to throw myself over the rail.

I turned right and pretended I knew exactly where I was limping to. Although I was disguised as a guard, I hadn't seen many guards sitting on the ground performing sorcery. I needed a quieter place to heal.

I reached the corner of the palace in a couple of minutes. Panting, I dragged myself down a wide, elegant road to a less busy side street. I was moving slower and slower, scanning for some quiet place to hide.

Swaying, I swung around the corner and bumped into a woman. I squinted hard because she looked like Ella, but she had left me before this damned trip started. I was hallucinating.

The woman said, "Your wounds are shocking, young man. Here, lean on me! I hardly understand how you remain upright." She shouted, "This guard has been gravely wounded! Help! Does anyone know him? Please help us!" She examined my shoulder wound but didn't touch it as she declared, "Some insane person attempted to assassinate the Empress. If you helped destroy or capture him, that was a terribly brave thing to do."

I tried to tell her that I was the insane person, but I only croaked. The world was moving in unpleasant ways. I realized I should say to hell with it and start healing myself. But I saw that she was a tall young woman with tightly pulled blonde hair. She wore a sympathetic expression on a face suited to firmness. I had bounced off her, and she was solidly strong but not hard. On the wild chance that this *was* Ella, I had to talk to her. I recalled that her father lived here in the city. In fact, this was the first place I should have looked for her.

When I spoke, I sounded like a sick cow and was just as understandable. I settled on the next most logical way to communicate, which was flopping my arm over her in a jumbled hug. She pushed me away and held me against the wall, but I had already smeared blood down her blue dress.

"Stop that!" Maybe-Ella shouted. "That is inappropriate. Just ask my father." She snorted. I could count on one hand the times I had heard Ella snort. She manhandled me like I was a sack of turnips and eased me to sit on the pavement with my back against a wall. "It has been a terrible day for you, hasn't it, young man? Look, someone is coming!"

I squinted at Maybe-Ella and tried again to wipe the blood out of my eye. She knelt and cradled my head in her arms. "Help is coming. You are forbidden to die. Do you understand me?"

A few seconds later, she called out, "Sergeant, is this one of your men?"

A deep, gravelly voice said, "Rod? I thought you were dead. Wait, I saw your body! What in the rabbit-shucking hell is this?"

Maybe-Ella stiffened and pulled away. I saw her draw a long knife from her belt.

THIRTY

Magic is how a sorcerer overcomes the impossible. It's also how he obliterates himself by doing stupid things. It doesn't even have to be a bold stroke such as incineration by lightning. I once saw a sorcerer disintegrate the wall of a building, which slid sideways and knocked over some beer barrels, which rolled down and crushed the sorcerer like he was hard candy.

The disguise Pil gave me had covered my escape from the palace and down a couple of lovely roads. Without doubt, it saved my life. Now the disguise made me look like a man I had killed, which was sort of like getting crushed by beer barrels. In this case, a burly sergeant with a white beard would be pleased to do the crushing.

The sergeant grabbed my hair and jerked my head back. He snarled into my face with his unclean teeth and breath like the place where bad chickens go to die. "Who are you, pissant? Why do you look like Rod? Did you kill him?" He shook my head, and my jaw flopped around. That kept me from telling him that his sister said hello and that she wished he'd come see my baby when it showed up in the spring.

The woman who might be Ella said, "Sergeant, he is gravely

hurt. Allow me to help you carry him back to the palace." She sure as hell sounded like Ella.

"In a cow's ass with that!" He glanced at Maybe-Ella and lowered his voice. "My lady. He may die on the way, and I want him to talk before he kicks it."

I already felt bad, but when the sergeant mashed his thumb into the hole in my shoulder, I understood that I had been whining about nothing. I couldn't remember my other cuts and punctures, nor the blood oozing out of them. I also discovered I could still yell loud enough to make people flinch. He likely didn't intend to, but the sergeant encouraged me to take a more aggressive interest in things.

I gasped, "Ella! It's me, Bib."

"What did he say?" the sergeant grunted, leaning down.

The woman shook her head. "Who is Ella?"

I had planned to pull my knife and cut the cloth disguise off my left wrist so Ella could recognize me. I reconsidered that plan in less than a second. My hand must have twitched toward my knife, though.

"Beware!" Not-Ella yelled. "He has a knife!"

The sergeant jerked back, maybe to kick me or at least spit on me, but I grabbed his collar. He shouted, "Get off!" as he straightened, lifting me like a trout that was pulled from the river, just high enough to stab him in the groin.

He screamed, and so did Not-Ella. I pulled myself higher as the sergeant pounded his fist against my wounded shoulder.

I screamed. There was a lot of screaming.

I finished climbing the sergeant and stabbed him in the neck. He flailed, fell, and knocked me down again. When I looked around, Not-Ella was running down the street shouting for help.

This street corner was nearly as bad a place to hide as the Empress's bed. I climbed back up and stumbled away from Not-Ella, ducking into the first opening off the street. It turned out to be a large, expensive-looking garden.

A speared moose couldn't have left a bigger blood trail than me. A tall, thick boxwood hedge stood close to the garden gate, so I pulled a green band. I encouraged the branches to remember how soft and limber they once had been. Then I walked into the middle of the broad hedge, turned, and staggered along inside it all the way down its length. I allowed the branches to get tough again behind me.

Anybody hunting for me would find a blood trail that ended right at an impassable hedge. Despite the situation, I had to smile at that.

I set about healing myself while I waited for the people chasing me. I had too little power left for comfort, so I reserved just a sliver for emergencies. Assuming I would need to fight soon, I healed the wound near my groin as well as my cut-up sword arm. I dealt with the shoulder and everything else just well enough to close the wounds and prevent festering. At the end, I had healed myself enough to be active, if I didn't do something crazy like jump, run, or fight somebody over age fourteen.

My pursuers caught up while I was healing. Not-Ella was with them, and they all sounded unhappy when they reached the hedge where my blood trail ended. The guards flung around quite a bit of blame, even accusing Not-Ella of witchcraft, until their sergeant whacked a couple of them to bring back order, or as much order as they ever had.

Then they began shoving weapons in and out of the hedge. I doubt they expected to find me in there, but it probably made them feel less frustrated. They got tired of stabbing the hedge before they reached me. After some more bitching and recriminations, they left.

I waited a bit to make sure they didn't return and catch me.

Before long, I heard footsteps entering the garden and then stopping where my blood trail stopped. The footsteps trotted to the end of the hedge and around to the spot where I would have emerged, if I had walked all the way through.

"Bib? Are you still in there?" Cora called softly.

For a moment, I wondered whether she was helping the guards. Had she been working for Ludlow this whole time? Why would she be tiptoeing around near the palace?

"Desh sent me to find you and Pil," she said, as if she'd been reading my thoughts. "He wants me to bring you back."

I didn't answer. Instead, I listened for the guards scuffing along in their boots trying to be sneaky.

Cora cleared her throat. "Actually, Desh said, 'Go get the idiot if he hasn't killed himself, or Pil, or half the people in the palace,' and he wasn't smiling when he said it."

I stepped out of the hedge. "I'm still alive. I can't vouch for Pil. She was probably captured. I tried to kill everybody in the palace, but those stairs wore me out. Cora, it still seems unlikely that you just stumbled onto the garden I was hiding in."

"Not if I saw an enormous furor at the palace where the only guards not shouting were the dead ones," she said. "I said to myself, 'That's the kind of place Bib will be.' I looked for somebody who seemed to be out of place, like a blood-slick guard limping all the way down the front of the palace, looking innocent, until he disappeared around a corner."

"You're right, I could have tried harder to blend in." I frowned and then cut the disguise off my wrist.

"I followed but didn't find you," Cora said. "I found an absolute river of blood running here, though. Now, is that enough explanation? Can I come over there without you killing me?" Cora raised her eyebrows until I nodded.

Cora trotted to meet me, and she clucked over my wounds. "You need some less bloody clothes. Even then I don't know how we'll smuggle you off the terrace and to the other side of the city. Desh found his people over there. Maybe Pil escaped just as you did." Cora hesitated. "It would be hard to smuggle both of you across."

I stared at her. "Unless Pil's dead, we'll be taking her back with us."

Cora's eyes widened for a second. "All right, I'm not in a place to argue with you. Take off those rags—it looks as if someone used you to gut a pig." She turned and walked deeper into the garden.

I had just finished pulling off my clothes when Cora came back with a bucket and a burlap sack. She pointed at the bucket. "Wash yourself. Put these on." She pulled some simple, worn, and not-too-clean clothing out of the sack. Then she dumped my bloody clothes into the empty sack and hid it inside the hedge. I was still struggling into my clothes.

When I was done dressing, Cora led me across the garden, bright with summer flowers. We left through another gate onto a different side street. She murmured to me as we walked, "I haven't heard any gossip about any woman captured in the palace today. I haven't heard much of anything today, though."

"Who would know for sure?" I asked. "Can we talk to them? Where are they?"

Cora stared at the pavement as we walked. "I could go back and wander around to catch gossip. Slaves aren't supposed to idle in the plaza, though."

"You're not a slave anymore!"

"Most of the people here don't know that."

"I see. Well, it's risky, and you don't know Pil that well, not well enough to die for her. I'll do it." I turned toward the palace.

Cora pulled me back by the arm and grinned. "That's mighty gallant, but I'll go. You're as subtle as a coach and six horses. Now, you stroll up and down along these three blocks until I get back. It shouldn't be more than an hour." At the next intersection, Cora squeezed my arm and turned toward the palace.

I watched her until she had gone. Then I started planning how to rescue Pil, find Desh and the others, free the villagers, and escape the city, all while avoiding the invasion. I accepted that my plan might lack a few details since I had almost no reliable knowledge to work with.

Half an hour of strolling and planning produced the disconnected pieces of four different plans. I fished in my pouch for a few coins and scanned the street for someplace I could buy hard liquor. Drinking would make everything better.

THIRTY-ONE

I spotted a wine shop down the street. It wasn't strictly one of the streets Cora had asked me to stay on. But if I stepped in and bought a couple of bottles for me and one for her, she couldn't object to that.

Before I could slosh alcohol all over a desperate situation, somebody dragged my spirit up through my head. A moment later, they released me, and I fell back into my body. A few seconds after that, I was pulled, released, and dropped again. I pictured Harik grabbing at me like a boy with greasy fingers trying to snatch a marble. On the third attempt, he succeeded and yanked me into the trading place.

I arrived in warm but faded sunlight. A little breeze pushed brown smoke across the whole area, and just about everything that could burn was on fire. The brown dirt under my feet and the big white gazebo were exceptions. The gods didn't seem bothered by the smoke as they sat on their marble benches. Krak commanded the very center, while Harik, Lutigan, Fingit, and Weldt sat on benches behind their father.

Krak was whispering in a voice not meant for sorcerers to hear: ". . . fumbling little squats shouldn't be allowed to piss without supervision! You've made an ox's rectum out of the whole business. Close your mouths and listen—especially you, Fingit! Don't even scratch your asses. Try to learn something if you're capable of it."

Krak's boys clamped their jaws and sat up straight.

I was standing where I could see the gods, which was fortunate. I glanced to both sides as far as I could without moving my head. Somebody stood to my right, and another person was on my left, but both were too far back for me to make out any details.

Krak spoke out with the power of a hundred drums. "Now that the Murderer has arrived, finally . . ." He glowered at Harik. "We'll get this damned business cut tight and locked away. Cricket, I believe you want the gates to be left ajar as if the city were a bar waiting for sailors to come ashore. Do I understand that properly?"

Off to my left, Semanté said, "Yes, Father Krak, to let the Hill People into the city."

"Wonderful. What do you offer to pay?"

"I will torture the Empress for a long time until she is dead. I expect it to take weeks before she dies. Maybe more."

"Bah!" Krak bellowed. "Do you consider me a fool? You intend to do that anyway. I suspect it will be the very first thing you do. Offer something else!" After a pause, Krak shouted, "Murderer, if you say anything without being asked, I will see that you are eaten by pigs and that the pigs are eaten by your worst enemies!"

I had been about to make a sarcastic and unhelpful suggestion, but I held my breath instead.

Semanté said, "I will find two children of my enemy and raise them as my children. What about that?"

Krak yawned with a magnificence suitable for the Father of the Gods. "These days every conqueror adopts his enemy's children. The next time, meet one who doesn't want to do that, and I'll give him a magic sword and a talking horse. Do you have anything to offer that I won't find tiresome enough to kill a creep of tortoises?"

Fingit chuckled while his brothers grinned.

Through gritted teeth, Semanté said, "I will betray my lieutenants. I will kill each of them at the moment he has served me best."

Krak sighed. "I should have stayed in bed. Be quiet now, Cricket. I need to talk to someone with a little more reckless courage." Glancing at his sons, he whispered, "And stupidity."

The Father of the Gods examined me as if I were something on his dinner plate. "Murderer!" he announced.

"Father Krak!" I tried to stop the next words, but they sprang out of my mouth. "It's a beautiful day to be alive, isn't it?"

"How do you know that's true?" Krak squinted one eye at me. "We may send you back to be trampled by a thousand herbivores. Yes, I saw you do that. What do you want from me?"

"You brought me here. I don't care to have a single damn thing from you, Father Krak. Send me back home, even if you plan to crush me."

"Hah!" Krak grinned. "Murderer, stand right there. We'll see whether you still feel that way in thirty seconds. Knife!"

"Yes, Father Krak?" Pil answered from my right.

"You're being tortured right this moment. These Imperial types are arrogant and disgusting, but they can torture like nobody's business, right?"

"I've suffered worse, and the palace is pretty."

Krak laughed. "That is a lie. You've endured less than a minute of torture and already you're weeping."

I heard Pil smile when she said, "Please forgive me if I don't apologize, since I'm about to die."

Lutigan whispered, "We won't really let her die, will we, Father?"

Harik leaned forward. "Why not? If I lose the Murderer, why shouldn't everybody else lose something too?"

"Shut up!" Krak whispered over his shoulder, spit flying. He pointed around as he whispered, "I'll kill her, and her, and him, and anybody else I see fit to kill. If you talk again, I may start with you, God of Death!"

Krak then roared, "You probably don't want to suffer and die, do you, Knife? Don't bother to answer—people never want to suffer and die. It's universal, like wanting warm socks when it's cold." Krak chuckled, and his sons glanced at him before grinning. "Now,

Murderer, don't you want power with which to save the Knife? After all, you lured her into this colossal misadventure. It's your damn fault!"

"It's my fault, I admit it," I said. "But she did try to kill me, and she might try again. I guess I'll say no to the power and let her die."

"And don't let Krak convince you otherwise," Pil muttered from beside me.

"Quiet!" Krak bellowed, and all us sorcerers staggered back. I staggered extra far so that I ended up a little behind Pil and Semanté. Now I could see both of them and also the gods.

Weldt drew a breath and began jiggling his foot.

Krak hung his head, sighed, and whispered, "Very well, Weldt. I will allow you ten words, but that's only because you're married to Effla and I feel a bit sorry for you. Ten words!"

Weldt tapped all his fingers on his legs, as if his thighs were a keyboard. He whispered, "Let's just destroy him." He pointed at me. "We're making it too complicated." He paused and whispered, "Right?" as he punched Fingit on the side of the head with divine might. Fingit fell over sideways and tumbled off the bench.

Krak hissed. Weldt scooted back to his place and sat up straight.

Fingit climbed back onto the bench and whispered, "Father, I'd like to get ten words too. And a club."

Krak waved his hand without looking back.

Fingit stood and whispered, "Whoever kills the Murderer will regret it. It was . . ." He took a breath. "It was written in the fabric of the Void. I saw it, you should believe it, and why risk it when somebody else can kill him for us?"

Weldt and Harik jumped up, whispering filth and venom at Fingit. Krak raised a hand, and all the gods sat.

My mind flopped around trying to understand what Fingit said. Something was written about me in the Void? That had to have been a lie. I doubted that my own mother ever wrote a word about me. Besides, the Void was, by definition, an absence of anything, so writing in it would be a nice trick. And I knew Fingit to be almost as big a liar as me.

"Father?" Harik whispered. "What is your wisdom on this?"

Krak rubbed his majestic beard. "It's not a momentous decision, of course. I wouldn't even care except for the war. My earlier decision . . ." He waited until Weldt was squirming on the bench. "My earlier decision stands."

Weldt's face twitched and he turned pink, but otherwise he didn't say or do anything.

Krak continued in a whisper, "My reasoning remains the same. Fingit is fairly bright, while Weldt is as thick as an elephant. Now that we've resolved all this shit . . . once again . . . pay attention."

I considered my situation. If the gods really didn't plan to kill me themselves, that was one less worry for me, right? But in that case, every person I saw might be somebody sent by the gods to destroy me. I wasn't sure I had ended up much better off.

Krak spoke up, "Knife! What do you want?"

Pil answered, "Three squares and the use of one hand."

"Betray the Murderer at a time I choose," Krak said.

Pil didn't answer.

Krak shouted, "Very well, you sit and think about it for a minute. Murderer, attend me. Would you care to reconsider abandoning the Knife to be brutalized and slain? I'll bargain with you for the power to save her. Here's what I want you to give me in return, and you should damn well offer it if you want to make me happy."

I didn't answer right away. In fact, I wasn't paying close attention. I was puzzling over what war Krak might be talking about. Ever since I could listen to the gods again, I wished they would explain themselves more fully.

"Murderer, you will leave the gates of that city open to let in the Cricket and her army. In exchange, you will get two squares of power."

I sure as hell didn't want to open the city gates for Semanté. I might as well hand torches and knives to her people as they walked past me, the better to kill babies. "Sad to say, I can't accept, Father Krak."

"Three squares," Krak said.

"I can't do it."

Harik whispered, "How much should we offer the little smudge? He seems resistant."

Krak whispered, "Oh, no more than five."

I tried not to smile. Krak sure hadn't intended to give that away. I wouldn't drop the city into Semanté's hands, not for any amount of power. A mighty sorcerer would take the power and say to hell with the babies, but I wasn't all that mighty and never had been. At least I could aggravate gods mightily if I wanted to feel better about myself.

I said, "Just to feel out the possibilities, Father Krak, and this is by no means an offer, not at all, but how does ten squares sound? If I do something just as ignorant and horrible as leaving open the gate?"

Krak said quietly, "Ten? You truly are insane. Perhaps four. Possibly four, and your only offer can be leaving the gate open."

"Like I said, I'm just exploring for now," I said. "Maybe nine squares."

"Father!" Fingit whispered.

Krak whispered, "Oh, who gives a shit about haggling with this weasel? We can make it up someplace." He shouted at me, "Five, and no more!"

"I see. In a hypothetical way, seven sounds like a proper amount."

Krak thundered, "Hypothetical? I will mash you out of existence with my little toe, you arrogant nit!"

I stayed quiet.

After a few seconds, Krak said in a casual voice, "Fine, six."

"Wait!" Pil yelled. "I'll leave the—"

I shouted, "Stop! Shut the hell up right now, Pil! If you've got some deep-down itch to trade, offer something else. You don't want the nightmares from knowing you helped kill a city full of people."

"You don't either, you dumbass. You didn't even know you were crying on the stairs up to the palace, so I won't let you do it!"

Semanté, who had been silent all this time, said, "If it helps, you can both open the gates. That would be acceptable to me."

"Pil, I was never going to agree to this gate bullshit! I was just screwing with Krak!"

The words just came out. I could only have stopped them if I'd torn out my tongue. Everything grew silent in the trading place, and maybe in the entire Home of the Gods. The breeze died, and the smoke floated straight up. I swear the sun stopped moving.

Krak stood, growing four feet taller in two seconds. He stepped forward onto the patch of dirt, grabbed me around the waist with one hand, and hauled me up to eye level. He gazed into me with unknown millennia of craft and malevolence behind his eyes.

I squeaked but managed not to squeeze shut my eyelids.

Three words, crushing and profound, rolled out of Krak's mouth. "Screwing? Were you?" Then he shook me as if he were a nasty child and I was a puppy he didn't like.

I thought I might die of fright right there. He wouldn't even have had to bother crushing me. I concentrated on staring at his left ear, and maybe that's the only way I survived.

Even if Krak's eyeballs didn't kill me, they should have driven me as mad as a bug in a skillet. They should have hurled me into insanity and never let me come back. Instead, I watched one hair on Krak's left earlobe and tried not to think about how this would end, or whether it would ever end.

At last, Krak stopped shaking me and regarded me with a malignant smile.

I managed to force out some mangled words. "I apologize, Father Krak. I meant I was screwing around for you. For your amusement."

"Indeed?"

"Oh, yes."

"I see." Krak gave me one more shake.

I had never realized how enormous his teeth were, the size of my hand. How the hell big had he grown?

Krak set me down and whispered as he walked back to his seat, "I needed that. Now, boys, watch me really slap them around."

Krak pointed at Pil. "Knife, you offer to leave open the gate doors for the Cricket. I will accept part—and I emphasize *part*—of your offer. I will provide the three squares and restore the use of one finger."

Pil shot back, "Four fingers."

"No, I think one finger is enough," Krak said.

I yelled, "Pil, don't say yes! I'll come get you!"

"You stay away from here!" she said. "Father Krak . . . I'm going to be very foolish. I do not accept."

"Oh?" Krak said. "That's unfortunately sentimental of you. The people of that city wouldn't die for you, so why sacrifice yourself for them? Throw yourself away if you want then. In a few years, no one will remember you. You'll definitely be forgotten in a century."

Krak turned to Semanté. "Cricket! I decree that the gates be left open, even if the Knife and the Murderer are too shy for the job. And if I decree it, you can be certain it will happen. But in exchange, you shall relinquish all credit for this war of yours."

"I . . . I cannot do that, Father Krak."

"Sure, you can," Krak said. "Impress your people's leaders by doing something else. Build a canal or something. That kind of thing's not as dreary as you'd expect, but it doesn't really matter what you do. They've hardly noticed that you've been away conquering things anyway."

I didn't understand what that meant.

"They will notice me soon," Semanté said. "Once I have destroyed the Soulless. I do not need the help of those constipated old women and men."

Krak rumbled, "Cricket, you are doing this for the glory of your people. Isn't that what you told me? Did you lie to me like a selfish little girl?" Krak dropped his voice so low my bones quivered. "I foretell that your army will destroy itself if you assault the wall of that city unaided. And when I say, 'foretell,' I mean there is not a fragment of doubt about it, because I am the damn Father of the Gods!"

"I . . . will not." Semanté said the words as if they were stone blocks she was dragging uphill. "I will never let others take the credit."

I yelled, "Wait! Make one thing clear for me, Semanté. Do you mean that this isn't the entire Hill People army attacking us?"

"Of course it is not," Semanté said. "That is an odd idea. These are simply the few who volunteered to come with me."

"The few?"

"The few thousand."

I paused, trying to imagine what the full might of the Hill People must be like. "So, this Hill People conquest business is nothing but you stealing your daddy's hunting horse to prove you're a better hunter than him?"

After a few seconds, Semanté said, "What conquest?"

"The one where you're killing thousands and thousands of people," I said. "Do you have a lot of different conquests in progress? Are they hard to remember?"

"We do not have any. We make war. We do not conquer."

"Oh, well, let's put that on the damn tombstones of the people you killed," I snapped. "Killed in a war, not a conquest, and don't mix those two up, you miserable mourners!"

Fingit whispered, "Should we stop them?"

"Not yet," Krak whispered. "I'm enjoying the ignorant look on the Murderer's face."

Semanté said, "The Hill People make war to protect you. We are destroying a sick, cruel kingdom that will bring its sickness and cruelty to your home in twenty years, or fifty, or one hundred. After we destroy it, we will go home. We will not plunder or steal land. Hill People are giving up their lives today to protect you and the others who cannot protect themselves."

"Bull. Shit."

"I am not making shit," Semanté said.

I snapped, "Do you have to kill everybody, down to the children and infants? Is that necessary?"

"It is sad, but it must be done. We have learned that if you do not kill everyone, it is the same as spanking the kingdom's behind and going home."

"I will never believe that!"

"What you believe does not matter. The Hill People have done this for centuries, so a smart person will trust us more than—"

I yelled, "What about credit? If you're so noble and as pure as cream, what's this crap about you taking credit?"

"Well . . ." Semanté said in a tiny voice. "I am . . . not a perfect person."

Lutigan whispered, "Father, that was fine work, I can see how confused he is." Lutigan was staring at me. The shit-sucking, thimble-dick God of War was right. I was confused.

Fingit licked his lips. "Father, if I may review, you have set three traps to kill the Murderer, and of course you did it masterfully."

"Pull your nose out and get to the point," Krak whispered.

"Having accomplished all that, it seems you can declare success and relax. No one could criticize."

"Of course they can't criticize!" Krak stood. "No. I don't just want him dead. I want him beaten, shamed, and destroyed."

"Oh," Fingit whispered. He glanced at his brothers, whose faces held nothing but sublime ignorance. "Then I guess I'm wrong."

"Murderer," Krak said, "I regret that I cannot trade with you for those six squares. Not unless you are open to a different bargain. I offer you knowledge in exchange for them."

If I said yes, Krak would tell me something I would certainly not want to know. "Yes," I said, without hesitating. My gut said this was the thing I was here for. My gut also wondered whether Gek was in my head making me feel that way.

"Yes? Just that fast?" Krak asked.

"I'm ready." In fact, if I had to wait any longer, I'd howl and bite the dirt.

Krak whispered over his shoulder, "It's too easy when they've gone mad."

He smiled at me and said, "You are a stubborn strip of hard leather, aren't you, Murderer? I'll make it simple because you're no smarter than a baboon. You didn't want to know you were a child killer, so you begged us to make you forget. But that knowledge is hard to stamp out."

I said, "That's wonderful, Father Krak. I guess we're done then?

How about those squares?" Beneath my arrogance, I was confused and scared too.

Krak rolled on. "If you have an overwhelming need to kill, then you aren't really guilty of murder, are you? So, you forced yourself to have that need. Then you killed more people than you would have imagined. Some of them ought to have lived."

I shook my head. "I don't remember any of this shit."

"How many people have you killed?"

I swallowed. "One thousand one hundred and four."

Krak showed his teeth. "How many could you have spared?"

I mumbled, "I don't know."

"Charming," Krak said. "That is the sort of amusement that makes eternity less tedious." He sat down in the middle of the gazebo, his butt on the place of power. "I understand that's a lot to think about, Murderer. Try not to let it distract you from anything important." Any jackal would admire his smile. "Now, how will you pay your fee? A year of your life? Or ten years from people nearby?"

I hesitated, trying to grasp what Krak had told me.

Krak said, "Murderer, I suppose you will take years from the Cricket?"

I took a breath and tried to focus. "Oh, no. Not Ludlow, either. Taking life from somebody you're going to kill soon would be a waste." I wavered and then asked myself whether this was what Krak meant by letting myself get distracted. "Pil, who's torturing you?"

"Two men—an old, chatty one and a young, mean one."

"That's good. Father Krak, take ten years from the old, chatty man torturing Pil."

"Fine. I'm done with all of you then." Krak slammed me back into my body. I fell and scraped my chin on the pavement.

Two women were muttering and pointing at me. I struggled to my hands and knees, crushed by the knowledge Krak had given me.

Then I shook my head and bounced to my feet, laughing.

Krak was lying to me, of course. Lying about the doomed ship *Gard*, about my whiny struggles over killing, and about my creating some fake desire to kill. The Father of the Gods wanted me dead, so I should assume anything he told me was bullshit.

I shook Krak's crazy ideas out of my head. Well, Fingit had mentioned that Krak was setting three traps to kill me. Maybe I should believe that.

I stopped worrying about traps and lies. Instead, I embraced a grease-hot desire to murder whoever was torturing Pil. I trotted toward the palace, since that's where Pil had told me she was.

Cora would just have to come find me.

THIRTY-TWO

I had looked like just another melon farmer when Pil and I created hell in the Empress's throne room. Now my disguise was cut away, so I ran toward the palace looking like regular old Bib. Nobody there knew me except Ludlow. It was almost as good as having a second disguise, although if I had my preference, I'd have chosen something other than a gardener with canvas clothes, drippy hair, and a magnificent sword.

That stopped me. I couldn't pretend to be a dopey servant while I carried a sword that screamed death. I sure as hell wouldn't prop it under some window and hope nobody stole it. If I had another disguise, I could make the sword look like a stick, or even a broom. But each disguise could only be used.

I bent down, adjusting my boot while I considered the problem.

"Bib!" Cora called, not quite running to catch me. "Why did you leave? I told you not to leave. You don't know this city! You might have stumbled into a guard post."

"Do you want to shout my name again? You weren't facing the palace the first time."

Cora blushed.

I waved that away. "You know this city well, don't you?"

"I know every bit of it!"

I had been pushing away a stupid idea. Now that Cora was here, it still wasn't a good idea, but it wasn't entirely stupid anymore. "You must know where Brak Fourstairs lives."

"Do you mean the Earl of Fourstairs?" Cora asked.

"Ah. Of course." I felt a little aggravated with Ella. We'd been in love, so why would she bother to tell me that she was an earl's daughter, with a gold chamber pot and her own baby unicorn when she was a girl?

Cora was still talking. "He keeps a house in the city, but his lands are three days away. Less if you steal a horse."

"Cora, please go to his house and ask whether his daughter, Ella, is there." I gestured around. "She may not be. Hell, she probably isn't. But if she is, find her, give her this sword, and say I need her to meet me. Bring her right back here."

I offered Cora the sword, and she took it with a sigh. "This is the woman you're in love with, I suppose. I'm sorry, but don't hope for too much. Nobody spends the summer in the capital unless if they have a choice." She walked away with strides as long as her short legs could manage.

I trotted toward the palace, just another servant doing what he was told. On the way, I stole a small wine cask from a wagon nobody was watching. I hadn't healed as much as I thought from Pil almost murdering me, and after a few more minutes of walking slower and slower toward the palace, I reached the scarred and chopped-up main door.

"Bringing wine for the dinner tonight," I said, smiling at the big, mouthy guard.

"Go around back. And what dinner are you talking about?" He slapped the barrel.

I shrugged. "I don't know. Rich people have got to eat, I guess. You know, I saw another cask sitting where this one came from. I could bring it to a friendly guard if I wanted."

In an instant, Hodge the guard became my best friend. But before I could start sweetly interrogating him, his three unimaginative fellow guards began yammering about duty and punishment until he scowled at me again. "There were a hundred men killed here today, and somebody near assassinated Her Majesty, so everybody's walking around too scared to blink." He glanced at his friends and sighed. "Get out of here, dog dick."

I smiled and walked around to the back of the palace, where I found the stupidest-looking, most preoccupied person there. "Hodge sent me around from the front with this." I jiggled the cask.

The young, stringy, stretch-faced woman glanced at me, jerked her head toward the doorway, and went back to digging through a box of vegetables.

I just about skipped inside where I was stopped by a guard the size of a mule. He scowled down at me from under a crooked brow and grunted, "Where're you taking it?"

"They told me the cellar." I hoped that was someplace close to the dungeon.

He pursed his lips and rumbled, "Go on." He stood aside for me to pass.

I headed down the hall at a trot since every minute I took getting there was another minute of torture for Pil. I passed five more guards standing in the hallway and then realized that Mule was following me. The Empress must not have liked strange servants and tradesmen wandering around the palace unescorted.

When I hesitated at an intersection, Mule pointed to the right. "That way." I hustled down the hallway, and Mule said, "You don't have a hat."

"Is that a problem?"

"You ought to have a hat. It's summertime, so you ought to protect your head."

"Well, thank you for that."

"Before you leave, you should sit under the awning out back for a while." Mule pointed. "Turn left here and down those stairs."

"Thanks for that too. My name is Don. I'm embarrassed to admit it, but I'm scared of pain and screaming." I tried to sound meek. "So, we're not going anywhere close to the dungeon or torturing, are we?"

Mule chuckled. "Lots of people don't like it. Don't worry, we've got no dungeon."

"No wonder the Empress is called the wisest woman in the world! But there's not any torture happening around here today, is there?"

"Open that door up there. Don't worry about screaming—you won't hear any of it from this far down." He patted my shoulder like a big brother.

So, Pil would be on an upper floor. I had been pushing down the urge to kill Mule, but it seemed I'd be leaving his body on the cellar floor after all. I shoved open the door and found two inconvenient witnesses rearranging things in the long, low room.

I stopped three steps inside and turned to Mule. "Do you know where they might want this heavy thing stored?" As he scanned the cellar with me, I set down the cask with a sigh and rolled it toward the closest witness. Everybody but me watched it roll. I darted around Mule and back out of the cellar, slamming the door. I spun a blue band and warped it shut before anyone pulled at the door.

My breath stopped when I realized I had lost the chance to kill those three men. Even worse, I had wasted power to do it.

I hurried up the stairs, wondering whether I could rely on finding Pil by her screaming. She had told Krak she planned to break free, and I didn't doubt her. But escaping torture was different from escaping the whole damn palace.

Maybe Pil would wait to escape until I arrived, if she believed I was coming for her. She might not. After all, she had tried to kill me and had done a fair job, so she might wonder whether I meant her well.

I climbed the steps fast but unhappily, the way I believed the palace servants might. At each landing, I paused to listen. On the third floor, I heard somebody shriek. I had heard Pil scream often enough to recognize her. That fact made me doubt for a moment the wisdom of how she and I lived our lives.

The door stood open, so I leaned to get a look inside. It wasn't a huge room, maybe thirty feet by twenty. Pil lay in her shift on a bare wooden platform that was splashed with blood. A man in gory working clothes stood beside her holding a smoking iron, and I smelled burning flesh. An older man lay on the floor near the wall. I saw two guards in corners of the room, but there might have been more I couldn't see.

I didn't spot Ludlow, the Empress, or anybody else with clean fingernails.

The man with the hot iron threw something on the floor, and it looked like an arm. He sneered, "Bitch of sorceress! I'll make you a runny, boiling mess for what you did to Cark. I can cut your favorite things off you and not be done for a week."

I craned my head from the hallway. Pil's left arm had been cut away above the elbow. Something like a bright, metal cone covered her right hand, probably to prevent her from using magic.

Rescue could be ticklish. I might be able to kill an unknown number of armed men with just my knife. I also might be able to reach Pil by doing cartwheels and then killing everybody when they stopped to applaud.

Pil was swinging her head from side to side and moaning, tied down with ropes around both ankles and her remaining arm. She stopped moaning when she saw me past her torturer, and she met my eyes while nodding.

Pil pulled the rope around her wrist tight so that the rope lay under the heel of her hand and the bottom of the metal cone covering it. She dragged the metal cone's edge across the rope, and it parted as if the cone's edge was sharper than a razor. Clearly Pil had been busy enchanting it.

By the time Pil finished with the rope, I was running into the room. A guard waiting inside the door hadn't moved yet and probably didn't understand that Pil was about to escape. I broke his knee and shoved him to the floor so he could see the rest of the story play out in a leisurely fashion. I did grab his sword, though.

The old torturer lay dead against the wall. I ran toward the other one and screamed to get his attention. When he looked at me, Pil sat up behind him, reached across herself, and slammed the point of the cone against the side of his head. His skull collapsed as if she had hit him with a ten-pound hammer.

Spinning, I stabbed the most alert guard in the neck. He dropped his sword and grabbed at me, asking me to save him as he fell. The last guard was lean and hard-faced. He fenced with me, showing some real skill. We engaged three times before I gave his thigh a deep cut and knocked him onto the floor.

"You're a real swordsman," I told him. "Don't let this event make you doubt it." When I turned back to Pil, she had cut the rest of the ropes and was sitting on the edge of the table, her head down.

"Can you stand up?" I asked. "Because we need to get out of this room right the hell now. I'll tell you later how happy I am to see you in not too many pieces."

"I can stand. I can't promise anything else." She slid off the platform to her feet and swayed, but she stood.

"Where's Ludlow?" I asked. "Nobody but him knows what we really look like."

"I don't know. Watch out!"

I ducked and turned. The real swordsman had thrown a knife at me. He might have killed me if I hadn't ducked, because he aimed well. That was evident from the knife handle sticking out of Pil's remaining arm.

For an instant, I considered berating the man for squandering my mercy, which was a rare enough thing. Instead, I thrust my blade through his right eye, and he quivered before going slack.

When I reached for the stump of Pil's severed arm, she shook me off. "No time. Besides, they stopped the bleeding with that iron." She shuddered.

"All right." I pulled the knife out of Pil's arm with a smooth, quick motion, and she yelped. I asked, "What do you think? Can you walk?"

She panted. "Faster than you, old man. This doesn't hurt as much as being burned alive. Wait! I can't leave without Krak's sword! He'll crush me from the feet up!"

I wanted to tell her she was full of crap, but I couldn't. I once carried that stupid sword for Krak, and I knew what losing it meant. I scanned the torture chamber for a chest or cabinet.

"There it is!" Pil said, pointing with her chin toward a rack of torture implements. The Blade of Obdurate Mercy, which was forged by a god and allowed men to see as a god sees, hung between a pair of tongs and a bloody saw. Pil's other enchanted sword hung at the end of the rack.

Pil had no free hands. I stole the old, dead torturer's belt and cinched it around her. Then I shoved both of her swords under the belt. "I'm sorry we can't find your knife," I said.

Pil shrugged, and I helped her into the hallway.

A couple of guards had heard the noise, and they met us on the way down the stairs. Pil hung back, leaning against the wall. I opened one's throat with a neat, economical slice, then thrust past him into his friend's heart. I tried to ease them down quietly, failed, and set off the screams of some finely dressed women at the next landing. They shrieked while running straight at us. I managed to avoid killing them, but I did defeat three more guards on the way to the back door, killing two as they lay helpless.

I was prepared to fight any number of guards at the back entrance, but I found only one. He looked astonished as he died, as if it was unfair of me to kill him while I was escaping from the palace rather than trying to sneak in.

We cut across the palace gardens as fast as Pil could manage with my help. A few minutes later, we reached the least conspicuous street I could find, which was wider and nicer than any street in almost any city in the world.

Pil leaned against a house wall, bloody and panting.

I said, "We need to find someplace that's less exposed. Maybe in the Empress's bathtub."

"Let me catch my breath." Pil panted, her head hanging.

"After that, I have a rendezvous," I said.

Pil stared at me, her mouth open.

"It's a complicated situation—too involved to explain on the run," I said. I helped Pil down the street, not making eye contact with anybody.

"Go ahead," she said. "It will distract me from all this fun."

"Well, I think Ella may be here, and I sent Cora to fetch her, and we're meeting two blocks over there."

"That's fine." Pil gasped. "Just stick me in a hollow log someplace to wait for you."

I didn't find a hollow log, but I found something just as good. Half a block later, I spotted a tall, drooping tree behind a white stone wall. Some of the branches swept out over the street. We ducked in through the next opening, which was a gate into another garden.

"Why are there so damn many gardens in this place?" I growled, helping Pil stumble toward the tree. "Did they pass a law? Is there a contest?" I rounded a big bush with white flowers and spotted a squatty gardener just after he spotted me. He was already running, so I let go of Pil and chased him. By the time he had been tripped, kicked in the butt, and punched twice, he seemed pleased to surrender rather than die.

I shoved the young man back toward Pil, who was leaning against the tree trunk. He had lost his hat and now pushed back his brown hair over and over.

I glared at the man, and I hoped he thought I was fiercer than an ogre. "If you stay still and be quiet, you'll have a good story to tell for the rest of your life. If you don't"—I pulled out my knife —"I'll leave you lying on the ground in a pile of your own guts. Now nod. I don't care if you understand me—just nod because it makes me happy."

He nodded and sat where I pointed.

Pil leaned toward me, laying her bloody cheek against my chest. "Thank you for coming, Bib. I didn't deserve it."

"That's crap. You'd do the same for me. You'd try to kill me first, of course." I pushed her to stand up straight before I probed her knife wound.

She winced and then sighed. "I'm sorry. I'll never try to kill you again."

"Shit, you can't know what you'll do."

"Let's promise not to kill each other."

I peered at her face. It was pale, and her legs were shaking. "Fine, I promise. You need to sit down."

"Will we stay here for a bit?" Her eyes closed.

"A little while."

She nodded and held up her right hand, which was still bound by the cone-shaped steel device. "Please take this off. I don't care where we go or what we do as long as you get it off me." Then she slid down the tree trunk and passed out when she sat on the ground.

Unconscious Pil didn't get to appreciate the glory of my next magical feat. Several green bands convinced the tree's branches to droop closer to the ground, even all the way to the dirt, and they wove themselves into a cunning screen.

"It won't keep out bears, but the bears won't see us," I muttered.

I used magic to get the cone off Pil's hand. Underneath it, her fingers had been crushed and twisted until they no longer looked like part of a human being. Only one finger looked as if she might have been able to wiggle it. I supposed that was how she had enchanted that damn cone into such a weapon.

I worked fast to heal her fingers. Then I turned to the knife wound, which wasn't too bad, and I examined her stump, which was a ragged monstrosity. I didn't make her whole, but she wasn't about to die.

While I was finishing with Pil's stump, she sat straighter, awake again. "That feels better. Thank you."

"Buy me a drink some time. Or curry my horse. I don't have a horse anymore, so I'd choose that one. Now, you stay here and make sure Flappy the Gardener doesn't run and give us away. You have my permission to disembowel him if you have to, or if you think it would be fun."

Pil glanced at the terrified gardener with sympathy.

I slipped out from behind the branches and left the garden. Then I ran toward the spot where I would meet Ella, sure that I was too late. Then she'd be pissed off and never want to see me again. I ran faster.

I stopped running when I saw Cora strolling by herself holding my sword. I had warned myself not to hope that Ella would be here.

When I didn't see her, I realized how fully I had ignored that warning.

Cora held my sword out to me. "I'm sorry, but she wasn't there. Did you find Pil? How is she?"

"I found her. They cut her up like a pie, but she's better now and waiting for us."

We walked fast back to the garden. Pil was sitting in front of the gardener holding her enchanted knife.

I stared at the knife for a few seconds. I muttered, "My mother damn it to my daddy's ass. You were wearing your shift and nothing else. Where'd you hide that thing? Sorry, do you feel like telling me how you held on to your magical, Bib-slicing knife?"

Pil shook her head, still pale. "It's a deep mystery. Your head would explode."

I said, "Well, let me work on your fighting arm some more, Pil. I want to make sure that when you stab somebody, they stay dead forever. Cora, here's my knife. Watch our good friend the gardener. Has he told you his name, Pil?"

"He has not."

"He will if we stay. He'll fall in love with you and tell you his name, not realizing that you will listen to it with great repugnance."

"Bib!" Pil said.

I chuckled, still healing her arm. "He can stand a little teasing. He hasn't peed on himself yet, so I'd say he's moderately brave."

"Bib!" Pil snapped, pointing.

I turned, and my sword was halfway drawn before I recognized Ella through the screen of branches. She was creeping along the garden path near us, scanning the shrubs and flowers.

"Bib!" Ella called out softly. "I can hear you, but I cannot find you."

I pushed straight through the branches, tangling up my head and my sword. I tripped over the scabbard and fell onto the dirt in front of her.

THIRTY-THREE

I lay on the dirt in front of the woman I loved, my cheek scraped, and grunting like the very spirit of romance. For a moment, I feared that would piss her off somehow. With a loose smile, she grabbed my elbows, pulled to help me stand, and merely squeaked when I grabbed her tight to proceed with the kissing.

That continued for a while. At some point, I heard Pil say, "Cora, that is the competition."

"Well, shit," Cora said.

I turned my head toward Cora. "You said Ella wasn't in the city!"

Cora, who was already a small person, shrank even smaller. "You told me to ask if she was here. When I got there, I asked, 'Is Ella here?' They said no."

"You what?" Pil breathed. "All right, that isn't funny."

Ella crossed her arms. "When I came home, the doorman informed me that a young woman with a beautiful sword almost taller than herself had inquired after me not a minute before. When he said I was away, she swaggered—that was his word—away down the street eastward."

Cora stepped back and wiped her palms on her trousers.

Ella gazed at Cora with blue eyes in grim slits and went on: "It seemed odd, especially so because he described the sword as beautiful. Thus, I pursued her." Ella turned to me, and her face softened in an instant, smiling again. "Bib, I spotted you a moment before you entered this garden." She looked at Cora again, and her face assumed all the tenderness of a disemboweling tool.

I stalked toward Cora, and she shrank back through the ripped screen of branches. I walked with my feet wide apart so she couldn't link my boots together. I drew my sword, which was a weapon I bet she couldn't bend.

Cora burst out, "Are we going to spend our time killing me when guards might be here in seconds?"

I raised my sword. "If you betrayed us on this, you'll betray us on anything."

"Bib, wait," Ella said. "You and I have found one another as if it were fated, and this young woman played a part."

"She tried to screw up the whole thing!" I glared at Cora.

"True, and that is a part, is it not? Should we mark our reunion with vengeance and killing? No. We should come together in forgiveness."

I stared at her. "This is not at all like you, darling. I didn't expect you to murder her, but . . . while I love you forever, I have to point out that mercy and forgiveness are not ideals you have embraced. What happened?"

Ella's face went blank. "I killed my son."

The pain on her face punched me. As a governess, Ella had raised and loved a boy as her own, but later she killed him to save me.

She said, "Who can do something worse than that? I have no business withholding mercy from anyone." She examined Cora from face to feet. "Of course, I'm not perfect. Sometimes I slip."

Cora held as still as a cornered bunny.

Pil spoke up: "That's sweet and fine then. I know I can do with an afternoon free of any more killings. I'm sure that Cora agrees."

"I do," Cora said in a tiny voice. "I'll be good." Tears started trickling down her face.

I said, "Young woman, I guess you don't yet know how to behave like a free person. You'd better find out fast. I'm sure as hell not bringing you with us."

"Bib, if we leave her here, she'll betray us," Pil said.

I threw up one hand. "Oh, sure, why not, let's bring her along! She's a sorcerer, so at least she can fight."

Ella's eyebrows raised at that, but she embraced me and whispered, "I shouldn't have left you."

I whispered, "Goddamn right you shouldn't have, although I admit I could have made staying more attractive."

"I won't leave you again." She stepped back and glanced around. "Let us go away from here and make our plans. I presume you have not come to sample the diversions of the capital."

Pil smiled. "That's right. We need to move before somebody stumbles over us here, and all of our sacrifice . . ." Pil held up her stump and pointed at it. "Is for nothing."

Cora said, "I can tell you that Desh and the others are—"

"Stop!" Ella and I barked at the same time.

"On the commercial terrace near the slave warehouse," she finished.

We all stared at Cora.

"They are!" she said. "I'm the only one who knows, so you can either believe me and succeed, or disregard me and probably die. I wouldn't lie to you now. I know you'll kill me for it."

Ella whispered, "No. You're not the only one who knows now."

I drew my sword and said, "I'm sorry, son." The young gardener wasn't a child, but he looked like one to me when I thrust my sword into his heart. I didn't hunger for this killing. I felt like a thief.

Pil stared at the dying young man with huge eyes in her white face. Ella looked away.

Cora clenched her fists and gasped for breath. "Why did you do that? You didn't have to do that!"

Cleaning my sword, I said, "Yes, I did have to do it. You told him where we were going and why. We couldn't take him with us and we couldn't leave him here. Even if we tied him up, he'd be found and would tell everything he knew."

Pil shook her head. "It's awful. Mathematical."

"It had to be done if we want to live," Ella said.

"Bib," Pil said quietly, "I think I liked you better when you thought you absolutely had to kill somebody, or else your penis would fall off."

I sheathed my sword. "Let's go, before a bunch of kids wanders in here and I have to kill them all." I stomped through the garden gate to the street, swallowing hard.

We walked in awkward silence for a short time, but we had to make plans soon. Ella took Cora aside with no sign of displeasure, and they whispered together for a few minutes. Then Ella smiled at me. "We have selected a route. It follows less well-traveled roads almost exclusively, but it is not without risks. We must avoid attention and remain moving. Should we encounter guards in serious numbers, we are unlikely to escape."

The Imperial Terrace was scant compared to the rest of the city, but it still measured just shy of a mile from end to end. We were going to traverse most of it. I stared ahead and nodded. "Right. Walk. Keep walking and don't stop," I said. Except to kill harmless people as soft as doves, I didn't say.

The sun set an hour later while we were shopping for clothes. Ella had brought us into a shop to avoid a guard patrol. She purchased clean, plain clothing for all of us.

I paced while we waited, expecting two dozen guards to charge in through every doorway. I knew I was unnerving the customers, but I couldn't stop.

Finally, Ella told me to go buy a hat and to make it a damn good one. I selected a sleek, forest green cap with a narrow brim. It cost five times what the same hat would cost in less civilized places, but I didn't care since I told the shopkeeper Ella was paying for it.

Pil snorted at my hat. "Your clothes cost three copper bits and your hat two silver nobs? Sure, no guard will look twice at that. Put it back."

I stuck out my jaw. "I'm tired of looking like the inside of a mule's asshole." I was just being contrary because I hated everybody and everything.

Ella had been busy while I was struggling with hat decisions. When we walked out of the shop, she wore a blue silk gown that the Empress wouldn't have been embarrassed to wear in public.

Cora sighed. "That's breathtaking."

"It's a farewell gift from my father," Ella said with a straight face.

"But can you fight while you're wearing it?" I asked.

"Yes. I can even force you to surrender while I'm wearing it."

Cora glanced away, blushing.

Three hours after sunset, we reached the battlements. They spanned half a mile along the top of the fortress that protected the city. A road from the Imperial Terrace to the commercial terrace on the other side of the city ran along the top.

"How do you want to handle the guards?" I asked Ella as we approached the road. "I assume the air will be thick with them."

"Not to the degree one might expect. This spot lies far from the palace and is guarded with less zeal than are the stairway and the ramp. Don't worry, I shall convince them to let us pass."

I trusted Ella more than I trusted anybody else, but I loosened my sword in the scabbard anyway. I shouldn't have worried. Ella smiled at a guard, announced herself, and named us as her servants. The guard looked at her gown and waved us through.

A few minutes later, Ella moved close and said, "Bib. Escort me."

"Are you going someplace I don't know about?"

"You know what I mean. Is this truly a time you wish to be humorous?"

I held out my hand, and she lay hers on it as we walked along.

Ella said, "I must ask why you are here. Did you come here to find me?"

I wanted to lie, but I said, "No, Ella, I didn't know you were here in this city when I came here."

She frowned for several seconds. "Oh . . . well, I don't care. You came here and you did find me. Even though it was accidental, for you that constitutes heroic romance."

"I'd have come if I'd known you were here. Does that help?" An instant later, I cringed. Since I had known that Ella had family here, this was the first place I should have looked for her. I had just said a dumb thing, and I waited for Ella to tell me about it.

She smiled instead. "I know you would have. It helps immeasurably. I wish I had gone with you. One could find more rest and comfort in deadly combat than I have found in my father's house. I did not appreciate you as I should."

"Don't worry, I'll aggravate the hell out of you again soon."

She chuckled. "Yes, you are a true prince of love. Further amatory comments, and I intend there to be many, must wait until we reach a safe place."

Halfway across, we met three more guards. A portly one said, "That girl's arm is missing. Hey, girl, what happened to your arm?"

Ella said, "I have important business, so do not cause me delay."

"Sorry, my lady, but this girl's arm is missing. Captain said to grab on to any girl like that. Hey, girl, what happened to your arm?"

Pil said, "It's right here, sir, but it's too small to see. Just like your dick."

Portly and his friend laughed. "I like that. You're a brave girl. I still have to take you, though."

I stepped in front of Pil.

Ella shouted, "Wait!"

Nobody had drawn a weapon yet, but it would happen any moment.

"Look!" Cora yelled, pointing past the battlements, away from the city. "What's that?"

Portly smirked at Cora. "Sure, I'll run over there and gawk, since this is my first day in service and I'm as stupid as a goose."

The guard was too smart to look, but not me. I stared through the darkness and saw at least a hundred fires more than a mile away. As I watched, more fires flared, tiny at that distance. They were sparking twenty, thirty, or fifty at a time.

I said to Portly, "Have your friend blink two or three times in that direction on your behalf. I dare you."

A few seconds later, the other guard blurted, "Krak's ass! What's that shit there? Shit like that shouldn't be out there on the road to the goddamn city, especially at night."

"What is it, Gavv?" Portly asked without looking away from us.

"I dunno, you bastard! Didn't the words 'What's that shit there?' just fall out of my damn mouth? You think I said that because it would make somebody laugh?"

Portly clenched his teeth, hissed, and actually pulled his hair. "Watch the girl so I can go look."

Over the next twenty seconds, the guards and all the soldiers nearby began shouting, exclaiming, and arguing about the fires. Gavv never even looked at us, so Ella and I grabbed Pil and Cora. We traveled the rest of the road at a snapping pace, but not quite fast enough to draw attention.

A total of seven or eight hundred little blazes had popped up before we left the road. Cora said, "I don't think that's enough Hill People to breach our wall."

Pil and I glanced at each other, and I pointed toward the fires. "I imagine there are two or even three Hill People for every fire. Have they yet done anything so foolish as inviting their enemy to count them?" I shook my head. "There are a lot more than that."

Cora murmured to Pil, "Can we trust him on this? He doesn't sound crazy anymore."

Ella laughed. "He may be outrageous, but he is assuredly not insane."

Pil and Cora held still and didn't comment.

Ella took a step toward them. She was a tall woman and looked down at them. "What do you mean by saying he does not sound crazy anymore?"

"It means nothing, darling," I said. "As you know, I am a genius, which a regular person might mistake for madness."

Cora cleared her throat. "Well, at least we should tell somebody that there are a lot more Hill People than fires."

"Oh, your generals will figure it out on their own." Actually, I had no confidence that Ludlow and his cronies would figure it out until they saw the entire ocean of Hill People at sunrise, but I was done trying to warn him and the Empress about things. "Come on, Cora. Take us to Desh and Stan."

Cora paused. "I know this is blunt and maybe outrageous considering everything that's happened, and I don't want you to kill me, but it's a desperate situation. Bib, why aren't you acting like a madman anymore?"

"My thinking has cleared. I realized I'm not the biggest liar around." I didn't admit that maybe I really was the biggest liar.

Cora cocked her head.

"No, those aren't crazy words." I smiled to show just how crazy they weren't. "Krak has been lying to me about something. Lying, and I just figured it out this morning."

"The gods!" Ella said as if she were talking about diseased maggots. "Would that we could live somewhere that they have never existed. If we must continue speaking of gods, I shall throw myself off the terrace."

"Turn here." Cora pointed down the cross street. "By the way, we're only eight blocks from your villagers now."

"Hell, we don't need Desh!" The words just started coming out of my mouth. "Let's hop over there and set them free!"

"Not yet." Ella looked worried as she held on to my hand.

Pil glanced sideways at Ella. "This is what we meant." She whispered, "Crazy."

"Genius!" I said.

THIRTY-FOUR

We reached Desh just ten minutes after we entered the commercial terrace, daring to walk the same ground as pasty rich men. Desh had been sheltering with Stan in a small, deserted warehouse. They had discovered the villagers in a barracks at the edge of the terrace.

Desh waved us inside. Stan was stretched out snoring in the corner. Ella smiled at them both and said, "Who else is here? The innkeeper from that shabby establishment in Glass?"

"Ella, I'm glad you're here." Desh said. "Will you help me save a village full of people from enslavement?"

"Certainly, but I must don my armor." She grinned and held up a sack, pulling out a blue-black costume more appropriate than her gown for bloodshed and ill behavior. She shrugged. "Sadly, I am weaponless apart from my knife."

"Here." Pil held out her life-defending sword. "You've used it before—a lot better than me, by the way—so take it."

"I had no intention of refusing, Pil. This is very kind, however."

Pil sat on the floor against the wall. "Don't lose it if you can avoid it, but it's not worth anybody's life." She touched the stump of her arm for a moment.

Stan sat up and yawned. "Bib. Are you done drinking tea and eating sweets with the goddamn Empress?" At some point, Stan had decided that addressing me as Lord Bib had become optional. Now he mostly did so when he wanted to be sarcastic.

"We're done," I said. "They'll be writing songs for a hundred years about the women we left behind. I turned their heads with my beauty while Pil robbed them down to their skin."

Stan snorted and farted at the same time, and Desh regarded me with a small frown. "Done making jokes? I can only assume you meant those to be jokes."

"I'd call them lies," I said.

"Fine. My people are being held west of here. There are only a few guards, and you'll do away with those. Then we'll rescue the villagers, sneak them down to the harbor, and take them aboard a couple of ships."

"Or steal two ships. Or three," Pil said. "We'd need at least three big ones to carry eighty people."

Desh frowned but nodded. His grasp of sailing and ships had never been strong.

"Will we descend via the ramp?" Ella asked from behind some crates where she was changing clothes.

"We have to. I don't think we can get my people down the stairway."

Ella had described the ramp to me earlier. The rich traders in goods lived on this fine terrace high above the city, but they weren't satisfied with that. To make their lives even easier, they built a half-mile-long ramp against the mountainside. It curved from the terrace down to the marketplaces in the city.

Desh said, "Since we're here and eager to do some good, here's how this will start. Remember, it has to be done with no noise, or as near as can be." Desh pointed at Ella and me. "You'll kill the outside guards—*quietly*—and pull the bodies out of sight. Then you'll creep—again, *quietly*—inside and kill the two guards there."

Ella held up a hand. "Tell me, Desh, do you wish this done quietly? You may need to clarify that three or four more times for me to be certain."

"Personally, I was thinking I'd scream like a hawk," I said.

"All right." Desh held up a hand. "Maybe I am overexplaining it. Bib, once the guards are dead, you stand back in the shadows to watch the doors. There's a big main doorway and a small side door, but you can see both at the same time. The rest of us will go inside and free the captives."

"And then Fingit will carry us all away in his flippin' magic chariot, pouring booze and handing out oranges," Stan grumbled.

Desh hissed like an overworked fishwife. "I know you don't like it, Stan, but this is the plan. We'll escort the villagers straight to the ramp, walk down into the city, and head to the dockside. There we will commandeer two big ships . . ." He glanced at Pil. "Three ships and force the captains to carry us east."

Cora had stood against the wall so far, not offering any ideas. Now she said, "So, we're going to become pirates, is that it?"

"Looked at from a certain perspective, yes," Desh said. "But we'll pay the captains double what they'd normally make for such a voyage and double what they would have made on a return journey."

"Desh Younger, you're a crunched-up bastard!" Stan said. "This morning you wouldn't let go of a copper bit to buy me a single drink."

A sick feeling had grown in me as I listened to Desh's plan. "Not to be a defeatist, Desh, but one part of your plan seems insanely overoptimistic. All the other parts seem overoptimistic in the regular way, but I'll ignore that for now."

Desh said, "You're talking about sailing past the naval patrols."

"You are surely correct. I mean that."

Desh lowered his voice. "We'll need your help with that, Bib. Once we've cleared the harbor, I want you to call Limnad to aid us."

"She may not attend me, Desh."

"I think she will. She told me dozens of times about the high regard she has for you. It started to make me jealous, to tell the truth. But a river spirit can push currents and wind well enough, maybe better than you'd think. We'll need you to call her. It won't be wrong to do it." His jaw tightened. "I wouldn't let you misuse her."

"All right, I'll call her," I said. "Assuming all these other parts of your plan work."

"Damn it, Bib! Do you have a better plan?"

"I do. Let's bring your people to this warehouse and relax here while you and Pil make disguises. You'll buy us food and plenty to drink while we wait. When you're done, we'll board ships like decent people and sail away, having parties every night."

Desh smiled. "I wish we could do that. I really do. We have to rescue them tonight because they'll be sold tomorrow. Once we free them, guards will search every building on the terrace. Maybe in the city. I've learned that slaves are an important business for the Empire. So, you see, we don't have time for disguises, or drinking, or parties."

"Shit," I said. "I want to tell you right out loud that this is a crazy plan."

"But you'll help us?" Desh asked.

Ella rejoined us, wearing her nice set of clothes, suitable for a young man whose parents wanted him to look good while he ordered other people to do work.

I had an idea, and I stood taller because of how wonderful it was. "Ella, you can buy them all! Everything will be legal, and nobody has to get killed. We'll have parties and drinking after all."

"I cannot, dear. My father has allowed me more than enough credit to purchase a ridiculous dress. My remaining funds might buy five or six slaves, but no more. I am led to understand that quite a lot more people than that require our help."

I scowled. "Fine. In principle, my idea is still the best one, apart from that tiny detail."

"Bib, we need your help." Desh clamped his jaw, and his nostrils flared.

I thought about telling Desh to go sit on a frog. Ella and Pil didn't look worried, so they obviously didn't understand what was going on. Cora looked terrified, which was a mark in her favor. I shouldn't let them try this without me, though. In spite of the plan's many flaws, we might succeed, if a whole lot of things went right.

I sighed. "Desh, what do you plan to do if a patrol spots us, or a guard yells like a bull, or if some of your people can't walk? What do we do if we find a hundred men on guard?"

"We improvise." Desh didn't have enough shame to look away when he said it.

I stared and planned to keep staring until he explained that.

He used both hands to jiggle two of the pouches tied to his belt, and he raised his eyebrows.

Maybe Desh was enough of a mystical terror to mash a hundred guards into butter and cut his toenails at the same time, but I doubted it. I really didn't care half a damn about the peasants. I had agreed to help them, a foolhardy act to be regretted. I could change my mind now if I wanted to tell everybody I loved or cared about to go suck rocks. Letting every farmer die or be enslaved sounded like something an evil person would do, but I doubted it could be that simple.

I shook that thinking out of my head and I admitted I was going. I had known it the moment I walked into this building and had been lying to myself since.

Smiling at Desh, I said, "Of course I'll help you. How could I say no to you? But . . . you have to give me an hour for attending to Pil's arm."

Desh agreed.

An hour later, after Pil's arm had been restored, all five of us stepped into the street. It was still before midnight. We could see well enough as we strode through the streets under moonlight and scattered clouds. Skirting two torchlit, guarded intersections delayed us, but the walk still lasted less than ten minutes.

The building that housed the farmers was a long, high, white-washed wooden structure that had itself once been a warehouse. A wide door for moving goods faced the broad road out front, and a smaller side door stood at the other end. The building backed up against the edge of the terrace.

A guard stood by each door. I nodded at Ella, and she crept

toward the side-door guard before rushing him. He struggled a couple of seconds and then slumped to the ground. While Ella pulled his body away into deeper shadows, I crept along the side of the building and slipped around the front corner. The guard there was looking the other way, so I charged, grabbed him, and stabbed him at the base of the skull. Thirty seconds later, his body lay in the darkness near the first guard.

Ella and I stood next to the side door. At our signal, Desh opened the main door on the other end but didn't show himself. I walked in through the side door, doing my best to sound like a guard coming inside to get a drink or gossip. As the guards inside watched Desh's door foolishness, I grabbed the closest one from behind and killed him while Ella ran past me. The other guard shouted "Wait!" before Ella tackled him. Ten seconds later, she stood up, but he didn't.

The caged villagers babbled and asked loud, useless questions. Some of them cried. Cora and Ella trotted from cage to cage trying to shut them up. Desh and Pil opened locks almost as quickly as they could walk from one door to the next. It was sorcery for sure.

I ran back outside and stood in the shadows watching for guards.

As soon as I got there, I heard Desh's ma bellow as plainly as if she were standing beside me. "Your father was a dawdler too, slow and lazy in every pathetic thing he did. Where have you been? You made me think you were dead! You must have drunk whiskey in every bar and disappointed every whore all the way here! I will not be quiet! Don't grab at me, you useless twit! Nor you neither, you stringy-headed, man-grabbing little bitch!"

This viper of a woman would kill us all. I stalked inside through the main door.

Pil was holding Tira down while Desh tried to shove a nasty rag in her mouth. Pil growled "Be quiet!" loud enough for me to hear it over the struggle.

Tira kicked Desh in the knee and tried to sit up while he cursed. Her eyes rolled white like a terrified horse. She blared, "I'll see you dead in a ditch, girl! And you! Get away from me with that smelly

thing, you useless little boy! Useless all your damned, squirting life."
She was shaking, probably with fear, but she drew a deep breath for
another round of echoing abuse.

I stepped up and thrust my sword into Tira's throat. Her body
clenched, and then she grabbed at her neck, coughing blood and
rolling from side to side. It made things a little challenging when I
stabbed her in the heart a few seconds later.

Desh was sitting on his butt, gaping at his mother as she died.

Pil stared up at me and breathed, "Bib . . ."

"I improvised. Get all these people free and out the side door.
That's the plan." I walked back toward the main door. "I'll see how
many more guards we have to kill."

Glancing out on the street, I spotted two guards coming at a fast
walk. I would have preferred to ambush them when they came
inside, but that would put the fight right next to the farmers. Some
might be killed, or recaptured, or bumble into my way and get me
killed.

Only one of the guards had his weapon ready. I ran at him like a
bear and sliced him across the face. His wise friend dodged and
backed away, shouting for help. I slashed his throat three seconds
too late to prevent the noise, then spun to kill the first man with a
quick thrust.

I muttered, "At least I'm done worrying about when the plan
will fall apart." I moved farther into the street to draw any guards
toward me. Enough of them would overrun me eventually, but I
trusted Ella to tell me when I could retreat. Hell, maybe Desh would
turn all the guards into little elm trees or make them wander off
looking for a bowl of soup.

Two guards came running out of the darkness and slowed when
they saw me. One of them snapped, "Throw down that sword! A
dozen—"

I thrust into his belly with a snap. Ten seconds later, he was
struggling away on his hands and knees, while his friend lay crumpled on top of his spear. I nudged the wounded man on the shoulder. "Crawl on out of here! And don't talk so much next time." He
did start crawling off. If determination counted, he might live.

The next guard came at me alone, a short fellow with long arms. He cursed a river of profanity at me, but he set up a careful defense. None of it mattered, because I killed him with one thrust and stepped back to let him fall.

I began to feel more confident about this enterprise. Then four guards ran into the light and stopped. I saw them eyeing their five comrades on the pavement around me.

"Don't worry," I called out. "Your friends tripped and stabbed each other. I had nothing to do with it."

My taunt didn't make them run away, nor rush me in a reckless clump. They spread out to flank me, methodical and working well together, so I said to hell with it. I lunged to kill one on the end and then crippled the startled man beside him. As he was staggering, I faked a retreat, leaned in toward the last two, and cut them both down with one slash.

That was a crazy thing to have done, of course, but I didn't question the results.

The fight had gone well thus far, so it seemed right that the next two guards almost killed me. One cut my left shoulder and the other pinked me hard on the chin, an inch above my throat. I fenced with them both for a dozen exchanges before I crippled one and killed the other. Blood was running from my shoulder, and more ran down my neck from my chin. It felt like the skin had been torn off the point of my jaw.

Now eleven guards lay dead or wounded around me. I'd have been more impressed by that if I hadn't been breathing hard and bleeding like a crushed tick. I assessed the situation and pronounced it shitty. Some officer was going to look at this slaughter and send fifty men at me in a wave, or fire twenty crossbows.

I retreated without Ella's permission, backing away toward the side door, down the alleyway between the prison building and an identical structure beside it. A glance showed that farmers were still shuffling out through the side door and heading away from me toward the terrace edge.

Three guards arrived at a sprint and followed me into the shadows between the two buildings. They slowed to advance with caution, and so did their two friends who came along thirty seconds later. The narrowness of the alley hindered them, however. I gave all five bad but nonfatal wounds. I reasoned that five agonized men stumbling around in the dimness would hamper the pursuit more than five motionless bodies.

I backed away some more, and Cora showed up at my elbow. "Withdraw now!" she yelled just loud enough for me to hear over the wounded guards.

I followed Cora at a run past the side door to the back corner of the building. When I turned toward the ramp, which was our escape route, she grabbed my arm.

"No! This way!"

"But the ramp's over there." It was a foolish statement since Cora had lived in the city most of her life and knew where everything was.

"Desh said to go this way." She pointed down the long walkway with buildings on the right and the terrace's edge on the left. I could just make out Stan far off in the dimness as he cursed and cajoled the villagers to move along faster than a by-god waddle. Then he disappeared into a mist that was thickening out of nowhere.

A sharp creaking noise came from the direction of the street behind me. I glanced back to see three boards bend down from each of the buildings behind us, partly blocking the alley we had just rushed through.

"There!" Cora shouted. "Now go!"

I sprinted alongside the railing at the terrace edge, chasing Stan. Cora ran just behind me. When I reached the alley between the next two buildings, a guard charged out of it and slammed into me. As I skidded toward the rail, I twisted my body in an awful curve and thrust my sword through the guard's neck, back to front. It was another insane feat of swordsmanship that I was in no way skilled enough to accomplish.

I didn't have time to admire my unearned martial glory because three guards had followed the one who ran into me. I rolled to my feet and blocked two attacks. Cora bent a board from the building so fast that it whacked the third guard on the head, and he dropped as if all his bones had dissolved.

A man lunged at me, and I crippled his wrist. Another swung at Cora. She threw herself to the ground, and I killed him before he brought his sword back in line. Two more guards were coming at us fast, but I was busy. They'd have to wait their turn to kill me.

Cora concentrated hard for a few seconds before shouting, "Damn it!" Whatever magic she had attempted didn't go well.

I grabbed her with my left hand and ignored the pain in my shoulder. "Follow Desh!" I shoved her in Stan's direction. She scrambled away as the two charging guards arrived.

One of them came at me too fast and got thrown over the railing into two hundred feet of not a damn thing. However, he left me with a deep cut across the scalp. I retreated three steps toward Cora before lunging to wound the second man.

More guards were running toward us along the railing, and another eased around the corner from the alley in front of me. A board bent and smacked him on top of the head. He collapsed like an empty sack.

"Damn it, Cora, run!" I shouted.

"I'll run when you do!" she yelled.

One of the guards threw a knife at me, and I knocked it out of the air with my sword. I would have been prouder of that feat if I had also blocked the other two knives that came with it. One of them whirled past my head. The other struck me on the left cheek-bone but hit me handle first. My face blossomed in pain, and I thought I must be blind in that eye. I staggered back but didn't fall.

Cora and I ran away toward Stan as she bent board after board from the walls behind us to create obstacles. That stopped when she flew forward to land flat on the ground. I recognized the sound of a crossbow from close range.

From her groans, I could tell Cora was still alive, but a bolt was buried deep in her back, probably through a lung. She groaned as I grabbed her by the collar to drag her away. My vision was wavering. I had been whacked hard on the face, and blood was running into my eyes from the scalp wound.

I shouted "Desh!" as more guards advanced on us. The crossbow would take forever to reload. I sure hoped they didn't have another one.

It was clear I couldn't outrun the guards while dragging Cora. Hell, I was panting so hard I probably couldn't outrun them if they each had their own woman to drag. I let go of Cora, who was quiet now, and stepped between her and the guards. I almost bellowed at Ella to come save me, but I realized I didn't want her anywhere near this shit.

Three guards edged forward to attack me. I wounded two of them, but the third cut my sword arm deeply and sliced my shin to the bone. Three more rushed up to join the vicious survivor, pushing me back as they tried to surround me. I spun, jumped back, and cut a man across the belly. Two guards grabbed me, but I writhed free. I was dizzy and losing my vision.

I decided that I had to abandon Cora. In fact, I had already been pushed back past her. I retreated at a damn fast hobble, cutting at two pursuers. I sensed a man charging me. I skipped back fast to cut at his legs, but I stumbled backward over the railing into the empty air.

THIRTY-FIVE

Any situation, no matter how grim or painful, can always get worse. I know that sounds pessimistic, but it's not. If the situation can get worse, it can change, and if it can change, then it can also get better. In fact, if the situation is already awful, there's a lot more room for it to improve than to deteriorate.

No matter how much pain life has given me, I've always chosen to live because things might get better tomorrow. There's hope. And even if things don't get better, at least watching the unexpected ways they get worse can be entertaining.

After I fell over the terrace railing, I had time to think, "I'm going to die," along with some words that would give my mother a stroke.

My left arm crashed into something, and I felt sure it had been torn off. So, my second thought was about how much dying hurt.

Other parts of me slammed into things, or bounced off them, but no more of my parts seemed to get ripped away.

When my parts stopped smacking into things, for an instant, I wondered whether I was dead. Because of how much I still hurt, I decided I might not be. I smiled when I imagined how the gods were cursing and ranting about my still being alive.

I had halted lying facedown on a mess of branches with leaves in my mouth and a twig in my ear. I breathed through the pain for a few seconds and confirmed that I wasn't dead, but I bet somebody could be forgiven for looking at me and thinking I was.

I had made a bad job of getting killed. I first assessed my body. My left arm hadn't quite been torn off. I tallied up that arm along with a shattered right forearm, five broken ribs, some bruised insides, a wrenched back, a knee that pointed the wrong way, several sword and spear wounds, and far too many cuts, scrapes, and bruises to count.

Fine, I could deal with all that, but not while dangling like a plum. I couldn't see much. Maybe I was only seven feet off the ground. I spun a white band to examine the situation around me.

I had fallen fifty feet from the terrace right into a titanic oak tree growing in the city below. The tree branches held me more than a hundred feet above the ground. Although the situation was difficult, it was luckier than anything I could remember happening to me, or to anybody else. I had always been a lucky fellow, but not like this. That much luck was suspicious.

Since I couldn't think of anything else productive to do, I pulled a band to stop the blood from running out of my arm wound. It wasn't detailed work, and I could staunch the bleeding without touching the wound. But my forearm on the other side had been smashed to hell. Putting it back together would require touching it to guide the bits of bone back into place. I could try to heal the arm without touching it, but it might be useless, and I'd never be able to climb down that monster tree. Then I'd be up there until the leaves fell, making my corpse a curiosity for the local children.

Too bad neither of my hands could move enough to guide a damn thing. Even if they could, I would probably fall straight to the ground when I rolled onto my back, flopped my arms, and screamed.

A bird landed on a branch near my head, and I recognized it as Gek. He said, "You are upbraiding yourself about not becoming my servant, aren't you? I would never allow one of my servants to dangle this way. It's undignified."

"Hello, Gek," I wheezed. Clearing my throat, I said, "I have at times enjoyed better prospects than I do now, that's true. But servitude . . . it just sounds nasty, like something a drunk physician would do to you."

"Then aren't you going to ask me for assistance? Or request that I make you an offer?"

Although it was dark, I made a show of examining my destroyed forearm. "Not yet. Gek, I am led to understand that you have been in my head all this time."

"It's lucky for you that I am."

"Have you been enjoying your journey inside my skull?"

"I hardly ever pay attention to anything that happens to you," Gek said.

"Why am I so fortunate then?" I asked. "Why does the mighty Beak-Face travel around in me?"

"Once in a while, I find you entertaining. You are like a foul puzzle that drinks too much. Bib, what are the odds that this tree would be right here when you fell?"

"I'm too tired to calculate it."

"They would be quite a lot worse if I were not in your head."

I snorted. "So, you made me fall from that exact spot on the terrace?"

"No, that's silly."

"Well, I don't think you made this tree grow underneath me when I fell."

"Of course not." Bird-Gek shook his head. "But someone had to plant this tree here."

"Bullshit!" I said it with less conviction than I would have liked. "That must have been hundreds of years ago."

"You're right, the whole idea is outrageous. Bib, do you enjoy seeing and hearing the gods? Aren't they amusing?"

That stunned me like a whack on the head. I had never imagined that Gek was the one letting me observe the gods when we traded. "I admit that has been handy. Thank you."

"You're welcome."

"Wait, are you saying that I can see the gods because of something you're doing?"

"I am almost positive I didn't say that." I didn't know whether beaks could smile, but Bird-Gek sounded like he was smiling. "Come serve me now, just for thirteen months. I will save you from this situation."

"Why do you keep hounding me about serving you? Aren't you inside somebody else who's more gullible?"

"Are you jealous?" Bird-Gek asked. "I have interest in others. I won't mourn if you act foolishly and obliterate yourself."

"The answer is still no. I'd rather fall out of a tall tree than serve you."

"At least tell me what you have learned from all this."

I chuckled. "I let people talk me into things, and bridge guardian must be the worst job in existence. Also, Krak is a lying bucket of slop."

"Ah." Bird-Gek twisted his head to stare into my eye. "I haven't found that to be true about Krak. Not at all." Bird-Gek flew away.

I closed my eyes and breathed deep, wincing. "Gek, you chop-chinned, dirt-walking barrel of filth, I would rather die than be your slave."

I pulled a green band with my forefinger and explored the tree, which was healthy and full. So, I reached into the branches around me. They bent and twisted as if turning toward the sun. Small bends multiplied along the length of a branch and became large curves. Within a few minutes, the limbs and branches around me had eased my body down to the branches below. After more time, those branches had carried me down another layer.

It required more than an hour of sweating concentration and a barrelful of magical energy to reach the ground. No citizens seemed to be walking around there in the dark, early morning. If any were, they could tell a nice story about seeing a tree defecate a dead man while they were walking home drunk.

The branches had turned me over onto my back with quivering care. Now I lay on the moist ground and cleared my mind. I decided to heal my right forearm. I did it badly but well enough to heal the left arm to a better state. Then I rebroke the right arm and healed it properly. After that, all the other healing fell into place, although by the end, every bit of me hurt like poison thorns and a broken heart.

Before doing anything else, I limped around under the tree until I found my sword.

Stumping over to a row of houses, I sat on the ground beside one, mostly out of sight. As I closed my eyes to rest and let the pain fade, I accepted that I would be climbing four hundred goddamn steps again.

My mind wandered, but I didn't fall asleep. If Gek thought that Krak was an honest, straightforward fellow, then Void Walkers were stupider than toads. The gods were liars, and Krak was the worst one of all. I thirsted to kill, but I could fight it, and as sure as horses are hairy, I didn't create it.

After a couple of hours, I accepted that I couldn't convince the tree to toss me back up onto that terrace. A good bit of the pain had faded, so I urged my creaking self to stand. I trotted toward those damned-to-Krak's-mighty-loins stairs and started climbing.

The dawn was just beginning to show when I reached the top step, panting and sweating. I had fought only two guards on the way, which puzzled me. At least some more of the pain had drifted away.

I stepped onto the terrace proper, sword drawn and wary of any guards who might recognize me. Instead, I nearly stumbled over a guard's body. Five more dead guards lay scattered around, which explained why the stairs were defended worse than a deserted privy.

The first person I saw was a Hill Man, who thrust his spear at my head. I killed him in three exchanges and managed not to get stabbed myself.

Three more Hill People were in sight, two fighting guards and one chasing a portly, well-dressed man. I gazed around for more of them and stopped, letting my sword's point drop as I looked up.

Hill People were climbing down to the terrace from the mountain. From where I stood, I could see dozens of them descending on ropes. They weren't arriving fast, but they were entering the city in a steady stream. I bet it would surprise the Empress. It sure shocked the hell out of me.

I had assumed that Semanté's assault on the city wall last night had failed, mainly because I hadn't seen Hill People marching through the streets killing everybody. But as a diversion, it had been an astounding success. I doubted that any person in the Empire believed that the Hill People might invade over the mountain. Nobody had ever tried to before.

I knew of only one place to look for Ella, Pil, and the others, so I jogged there to find his secret headquarters, which lay near the middle of the terrace. When I reached the proper street, I scanned both ways and saw no Hill People. I ran down the road to the spot where Desh's warehouse should have been, but it wasn't there. I looked on both sides of the street in both directions, but I couldn't find it.

Doubling back to make sure I had taken the right street, I surprised two Hill People at the corner. I killed them both but got a shallow stab wound in my leg. Now cursing, I ran back down the road, but the headquarters still wasn't there. There wasn't a gap where it had stood, either.

I felt my way from one building to the next without success. Maybe Desh had transported it straight to the docks. If he had, I swore to apologize to him for anything I had ever done to offend him and anything he imagined I might have done. I had only known one other sorcerer who could have managed such a thunderous feat.

A hand reached out from the air and pulled me in through a door. "Stop that," Desh said. "You'll draw attention."

I opened my mouth to congratulate him on his illusion, but he looked so pale and tense I closed it. Before I could think of something useful to say, Ella ran across the room, seized me, and kissed me three times before letting go.

"Gods! What happened to you? Sit down!" Ella stepped back.

To conserve power when healing myself, I had only healed the bruises and cuts to the point of relieving the pain. I must have looked as if I'd been beaten against rocks. I smiled and hugged her.

"This? I got flung right off the terrace. It was horrible. Took me a whole hour to get over it."

Glancing around the building, I saw Stan and Pil with the villagers, who were scattered around on the floor and on crates. "You probably know it already, but the Hill People are in the city; they came down the cliff face. It's a good thing you disguised this place so cleverly, Desh."

"Thanks. It will last about another half hour. Then we're exposed. Where's Cora?"

I had been trying not to think about her. "She's probably dead, although I can't swear to it. They shot her with a crossbow before I fell over the railing. She fought like a lion. I was right to be suspicious of her, of course, but now I feel bad about it." I walked to some old, stacked wooden crates and leaned against them. "Those stairs whipped me like a bad horse, so I'm going to rest over here."

Pil had walked over to join us. "How do we know you didn't kill Cora?"

"Pil!" Ella said.

"How do we know?" Pil repeated, her face hard.

I said slowly, "I can't produce the bolt, or the crossbowman. And my word is worth less than a dog turd. So, I guess you can't know. If you don't trust me on this after I just about died saving you, I guess you'll never trust me on anything."

"Conditions have been fraught here since the escape went badly," Ella said. "Forgive her."

"Shut up!" Pil snarled at Ella. Looking back at me, Pil said, "You killed Desh's mother while she lay on the ground, as helpless as a fish, right in front of him, and you killed his father too."

I glanced at Desh's tight face.

"Bib . . ." Desh said, but he stopped. He glared at me and opened his mouth to talk several times but stopped every time. He reached for a pouch but let his hand fall away. "Nothing I want to say makes sense. I want to thank you and then kill you."

"That's all right. Maybe it doesn't make sense to anybody else, Desh, but it does to me. Now Pil, everything you said is true. Desh's father was a misunderstanding, but his mother was giving us all away."

"Why didn't you hit her on the head then?" Pil started to yell but lowered her voice. "You could have helped us gag her. You could have walked away and trusted us to deal with it!"

"It needed to be done." I said it before I thought it through. Desh turned and walked away to the other side of the room to talk with his people.

Pil bared her teeth. "Don't you mean you needed to do it? That you needed to kill somebody, and you had an excuse to kill her? I realized something today. I've seen you kill quite a lot of people, and do you know what? You didn't have to kill most of them!"

"No, that's not true," I said. "No."

Pil said something else, but I didn't listen.

Tira had to be killed. She would have bellowed and bitched and killed us all, even if she didn't mean to. I couldn't explain that to Pil, though, or to Desh.

Pil went on berating me. I didn't answer back, but disgust and condemnation from Pil hit me like a scourge.

Krak was right. I had given half my life to killing people, and a lot should have lived. I chose to forget the harshest parts of murder, and if I had remembered, I would have been somebody different. Not someone who killed people who didn't deserve it, and not someone who did things that killed people I loved.

But I did choose to forget, and I couldn't bring back a single man I murdered, or any child I killed, or the half of my life that I threw away. No wonder I didn't care to contemplate whether I was an evil man.

I tried to stop thinking about it all, because this sure as hell wasn't the time for contemplation. But I couldn't know all this and do nothing.

The thing I could do was kill. I was a tool for killing. I walked to the door.

Stan watched me. "Hey, has Bib gone crazy again?"

Pil had turned away, worn out from chewing on my ass. She shrugged. "How can you tell?"

I drew my sword and grabbed the door latch.

Pil and Ella both called out for me to stop.

I looked at them over my shoulder. "Kick everybody in the ass and get them moving. I'll lead our Hill friends away from you."

"No!" Ella said. "That truly is the pinnacle of recklessness."

I said, "Darling, it's the farthest thing from it. This is our most logical chance to succeed. I defy anybody to prove me wrong." I knew it was true when I said it. I turned to Pil, my hand out. "Cael's black dagger. Give it to me."

Pil hesitated.

"Give it to him!" Ella snapped. "Or if you do not wish to do so, you may go with him and carry the damn dagger until he needs it." Tears floated in her eyes, but they hadn't started running.

Pil handed over the dagger but looked at the floor instead of me.

I kissed Ella. Then I stepped outside and immediately questioned my logic when I saw how many Hill People were waiting in the street.

THIRTY-SIX

I enjoyed a fine advantage over the Hill People who stood in front of Desh's warehouse. I expected them to be there, although I wouldn't have predicted there'd be four of them. However, they did not expect me to step out of nothingness carrying death in my hand. They didn't expect that at all.

One died without ever seeing me, and the second had only a moment to glance my way before I slashed her throat. A third stood down the street between me and the mountain, so I charged him. He saw my artless assault and set himself to impale me, and it was the right thing according to what he saw. But my sword broke his weapon, cut off his hand, and halfway severed his head. My blade did the hard work, but I helped by never slowing down.

The fourth man was sprinting to catch me. Eventually he would succeed, or else chase me into some of his friends. I slid to a stop, spun, and corkscrewed my body to avoid his thrust. Then I pierced his chest so thoroughly my sword's point reached a foot beyond his back. It was sloppy on my part, and I breathed deep to relax.

Desh would march from the middle of the terrace across to the ramp, which started at the terrace's corner, all the way against the mountain face. I ran three blocks toward the mountain and then turned toward the ramp, disabling three Hill People on the way. I planned to stay between Desh and the mountain, dragging as many Hill People as possible to me.

On the next block, two Hill Women rushed out, their spears pointed at my heart. They probably expected me to wait and let them commit themselves before I attacked. Maybe they thought I would charge. I doubt they expected me to howl and grab my crotch as I danced around. They hesitated, and then I rushed them. I left them both wounded and limping behind me.

I sprinted to the next block to get away from the spot where I had howled like an idiot. Hill People from all around would be closing in on it. Then I turned toward the mountain again.

Grabbing my privates was unlikely to be a successful strategy all morning, so I whipped out two white bands to explore the terrace. The sky was clear and still. It would take me an hour to pull a thunderstorm together, but the terrace lay up on the mountainside, which might be useful. I spun several more white bands and a couple of yellow ones.

At the next intersection, five Hill People came at me from three sides. I dodged two and killed the third, while the fourth stabbed me in the head, leaving a deep, bloody cut from my chin to my ear. I hamstrung the fifth one and ran for ten seconds while I asked my sword if it had any good ideas. I didn't expect an answer, since the sword had never talked before. It didn't speak up with any ideas this time, either.

I swung to assault the three Hill Men chasing me, roaring the way I imagined a dragon might if they still existed. The Hill People didn't seem concerned even for a moment. Two cuts later, I had split two spears and disemboweled a woman. The survivors now seemed concerned. I lunged, slipped, and fell on the ground, scraping the other side of my face. As the two surviving men leaped at me, I grabbed a rock off the street and hurled it into one's mouth. I stabbed the other in the groin two seconds later.

Maybe I should have killed the one I hit with a rock, but I didn't. The idea of killing him made me feel tired, or perhaps running and fighting for eight blocks had made me actually tired. Instead of killing him, I took away his spear and knocked him down before running toward the ramp, which was still five blocks away.

As I ran, I shouted, "Hill People, I'm here! I carry death! Come and let me kill you! Semanté, you translate!" I couldn't imagine that would break the Hill People's spirit or will to fight, but this was likely the last hour of my life. I was entitled to fun.

I sheathed my sword, jumped, and climbed onto the roof of a warehouse. Running at a crouch along the rooftop, I listened to Hill People speak harshly to one another as they arrived and didn't find me.

I crossed the rooftop at an angle to the next street, which was closer to the mountain. The street was empty, so I hopped down. Probably every Hill Person within three blocks was back on the other street bitching at each other about who let me get away. I spun another white band into the sky and ran down this new street toward the ramp.

After the next intersection, I shouted, "Hill People! Where are you? Why don't you want to be killed?" I ran along the edge of the street and considered ducking into the next warehouse, but I didn't know what was in it.

Five steps later, a Hill Woman thrust her spear out through the warehouse door, piercing my side just above the hip. I gasped and then wished I hadn't. The woman recovered, ready to kill me with the next thrust, but I grabbed the spear shaft with my free hand and shoved her backward. Ten seconds later, she lay on the warehouse floor with a sliced neck.

I moved on toward the ramp at a limping jog. The wound in my side wouldn't kill me, but it slowed me down, and speed had been the main thing keeping me alive. Also, I wouldn't be climbing up on any more roofs.

When I was twenty paces from the next intersection, a Hill Man rounded the corner and stopped. Rather than charge him, I shifted my sword over and hurled Cael's black dagger at him. It was an act of trust. I was a respectable knife thrower, but I couldn't hit anything that far off on my best day. The enchantment on Cael's dagger made the difference, and it plunged into the man's chest.

I grabbed the dagger as I jogged past toward the intersection. Now I was panting. Looking around, I saw pursuers behind me, to my left, and to my right, maybe eight in all. I pulled a white band and squeezed as I pushed myself to run. The temperature dropped a few degrees, and a nice, thick mist filled the streets within seconds. I couldn't see past ten feet.

Stepping into the door of another warehouse, I healed my side just enough to stop the bleeding. I heard several Hill People pass, then I doubled back to the intersection and cut over one block closer to the mountainside. I jogged on toward the ramp.

I stopped every couple of hundred feet to listen in the fog. The third time, I heard Hill People shouting a couple of blocks behind me, just about where I expected Desh and his people to pass soon.

"Hill People! I see you out there!" I bellowed. "Come here and let me wave my dick at you before I kill you!" The words didn't matter. My enemies would be drawn to the noise. I ran as hard as I could endure along the edge of the street. Hill People from all over should be closing in on the spot where I had just insulted them.

It was still foggy, so I don't know how many Hill People I stumbled into on the next street. There were at least five and probably more. Maybe they had heard me coming and silently blocked the road until I ran right into them like I was the rawest recruit in the shittiest army in the world.

Some sound or movement warned me. I twisted as a spear gouged some flesh out of my left shoulder. I rolled, and a spear swept over my head close enough for me to feel the air. I came up in a crouch and ran a few steps down the street before crashing into a short person. We tumbled onto the street in different directions.

I crawled twenty feet toward the mountain as quietly as I could manage before standing up. Hill People's footsteps still patted all around me. I crept toward what I thought was the edge of the group, and I was right. A Hill Man saw me there, and that's when the fight really started.

My greatest disadvantage of course was that there was only one of me. That was also my greatest advantage, since I could kill anybody I saw and feel sure they were an enemy. The Hill People had to make certain they weren't killing their sister, or comrade, or maybe Semanté herself.

It was hard to recall details about the fight in all the fog and confusion. I killed or wounded a couple of people as I tried to escape. That didn't work, and for my trouble, I got stabbed in my left shoulder for the third time since I entered the city yesterday.

Pissed off, in pain, and suspecting I wouldn't walk out of the fog alive anyway, I concentrated on killing as many Hill People as possible. It was two minutes of thrusts, counters, dodges, and blood, never knowing when one of them would come out of the fog behind me.

I didn't finish them all, but I killed or wounded several before I slipped away. Slipping away looked a lot like me limping along trailing blood. Apart from several unimportant wounds, I had taken a deep thrust to the thigh that would kill me if I didn't heal it soon. The moment I realized that, I limped right out of the fog. The mountainside stood less than a block away. Hill People were still climbing down on twenty ropes spread from mid-terrace all the way to the ramp, which I figured was a block to my right.

I backed up into the mist and sat against a wall, light-headed. The fog was dispersing, and soon I'd be as conspicuous as a whale on a dinner table. But if I spent time to refresh the fog, I might well bleed to death. Either way, I'd be dead. On the other hand, Desh should be at the ramp soon, and bad visibility would help him more than my sword ever could.

The fog pulled back until I could see the mountain again. Pil rushed around the corner and knelt, not looking at all surprised to see me.

"Where the hell did you come from?" I asked.

"Shut up! Where are you hurt?"

"Right leg."

Pil squinted at it for a moment before pulling off her belt.

I wanted to know how Pil had found me, whether Desh had reached the ramp, and why Ella hadn't come. It was stupid to talk now, though, so I shook my head and pulled another white band. I dragged at it, and mist rose around us.

Pil yanked the tourniquet tight, and I grunted. I lay my head back against the wall for a moment.

Pil slapped my face hard.

"I'm awake!"

"I know, I just wanted to hit you," Pil whispered. "Be quiet, there are Hill People in this city. Do I need to carry you?"

"I haven't finished creating hell out here for Semanté." I pulled a white band and tossed it toward the ramp.

"Hurry up," Pil whispered. "Nobody's going to think you're heroic no matter what you do, so you might as well not die." A few seconds later, she asked, "Are you done? Can you walk?"

"I doubt it."

"That's just like you," she whispered. "All right, heal yourself back onto your feet."

"How did you find me?"

"Don't talk! Heal!" After I laid my hand on my leg, she whispered, "I always know where you are, Bib. You should be more careful about where you leave your hair cuttings."

I nodded but didn't answer.

"Lutigan crush it!" Pil muttered. "How did I get stuck with you?"

"What?" I whispered, not looking up as I worked.

"I must have done something very bad to end up with a friend like you."

"What are you talking about?" I breathed.

"Never mind. If you want to know what I'm talking about, you have to make sure we live."

For two minutes, we stayed quiet and mostly still as I worked on my leg. During that time, we heard someone trot right past us on the other side of the street. At last, Pil helped me stand. I could limp along, woozy but not about to bleed to death. Pil helped me walk through the fog toward the ramp.

"Wait," I whispered.

"What?" Pil sighed as if I were a child who didn't want to go someplace.

"Something useful. Maybe." I pulled a yellow band and threw it.

We limped down the street just fast enough to stay unheard, or at least I hoped so. Frankly, I doubted we were any stealthier than a trotting pig. I whispered to Pil, "It was the pigs, right? The unliving hell pig that nearly killed you at that pissant fair. Is that what you mean about being stuck with me?"

"No," Pil whispered. "Be quiet. You're dragging that foot like it was a box of nails."

I'm certain my response, if I had thought of one, would have been sarcastic enough to cut stone. I never knew because flames exploded some distance down the street, flaring orange through the fog.

I whispered, "I guess Semanté arrived with the early wave."

THIRTY-SEVEN

I feared that Semanté was burning things up right where Desh and his carnival of lost peasants needed to pass. I wouldn't have minded Desh helping Pil and I fight the Hill Woman. But Ella, Stan, and the farmers would arrive with him, and they might all get burned to death.

"We need to stop Semanté now," I said.

Pil didn't answer. When I glanced over, she had already pulled off her clothes, lest Semanté set them alight and kill her. I took that to mean she agreed, so I struggled out of mine too, including boots and smallclothes.

"Krak's 'nads, Bib," Pil breathed as she looked at me.

I understood what she meant. The past day's activities had covered me in scrapes, cuts, and partly healed wounds. "Oh, sure. Forget all the slavery and slaughter. My getting battered a little is the real tragedy here."

I still had over half of the six squares I'd gotten from Krak, but I didn't want to waste any. I chose the most promising opportunity for magic I could find in the area, although it was unlikely to be decisive. I pulled two more yellow bands and sent them up the road along the mountainside.

When we had prepared ourselves, I carried my sword in my right hand and Cael's black dagger in my left. Pil carried her stupid god-named sword in her right hand. She also carried a pouch on a belt around her waist.

"You are liable to be burned in two. Not even I can heal that," I said.

I saw Pil smile for the first time today. "I enchanted this after Semanté turned me into a walking scar. I made it unburnable. I hope."

"I can't judge that. In fact, I'm not too sure how Cael's dagger reacts to fire. The damn thing may blow a giant hole in the city."

"Oh, thank you for warning me about that, Bib. I can see that you're really concerned about me. I'll stay on the other side of the street from you."

Pil walked out of the fog still one hundred feet from Semanté, and I limped out a moment later. Semanté stood just twenty feet from the mountain face, watching a battle underway on the ramp below.

I could see the fighting too since the ramp was half a mile long and shallow. Thirty Hill People had moved one-fourth of the way down it and were advancing against several dozen Imperial soldiers. It was a bad day for the Empire so far. Two dozen soldiers lay on the ramp, and three more fell in the few seconds I was watching. Some more big groups of soldiers were climbing the ramp at a run, however.

None of those fighters was likely to pause and step aside to let the villagers trudge down the ramp. I intended to remind Desh about this flaw in his scheme the next time we planned something, which would likely be never, but even thinking about it was satisfying.

I tossed another yellow band up the road. Then I flung the black dagger at Semanté while she wasn't looking.

Two men near her spotted me throwing. The first swung his spear to deflect the dagger, but he missed. The second jumped in front of Semanté, and the dagger struck him below the throat. He fell backward and knocked Semanté down.

Pil charged the Hill People. I limped forward a few steps and reached a broad space of harsh-smelling wet pavement. It hadn't rained.

I shouted, "Pil! Come back here!"

Pil skidded to a stop and looked at me, her eyebrows raised, but she didn't come back. I could see that she had run past the space of wet pavement.

Semanté was standing up.

"Pil, stay there!" I yelled as I hustled across the wet pavement as fast as my wound would let me.

"Which is it?" Pil called back to me. "Do you want me to sink into the earth next?"

Semanté saw us and smiled. I smiled and waved back at her. Two seconds later, a sheet of withering flame shot up from the wet pavement behind Pil and me. It threw me forward.

I was still on my hands and knees when Pil shouted, "All right! I see now. Let me help you."

"Stay there!" When I reached my feet, I saw that the wall of fire ran behind us from the edge of the terrace on our right to a building on our left. Since Burners couldn't quench fires, Semanté needed a path for escape, so she left both the ramp and the road along the mountainside unblocked.

However, when Desh arrived, he wouldn't be able to cross the fire, not unless he could pour a river out of his hat or pull a blizzard out of his trousers.

"Where do we run if we need to?" Pil shouted, scanning the area. "I don't think we can fight past all those Hill People to get to the road, and the ones on the ramp will kill us. They'll definitely kill you."

"Think creatively!" I yelled while I watched Semanté. "We can run through the wall of flame. Or we could also throw ourselves off the terrace. It's not so bad." Semanté was staring at me, and I believed she was trying to burn my sword, although I couldn't see her fingers move.

Semanté stopped staring at me and switched to Pil. After a few more seconds, Semanté snapped at a man beside her, who flung a spear at me.

I rotted the spear shaft into two pieces that wobbled aside, passing within three feet away of me. There they exploded when Semanté set them alight. It knocked me sideways to the ground, and the left side of my body screamed with shrill, searing pain. I rolled on the ground just in case actual flames were on my body.

I raised my head in time to see Pil leap and roll far away from another spear. Semanté didn't bother setting that one ablaze. She spoke to another of her men while nodding toward me. He threw his spear at me, but I was more prepared this time. If I rotted the spear into pieces, I would only create more missiles for Semanté to burn me with. I rolled aside as fast as I could, screaming all the way. This spear exploded before landing six feet to the side of me, and it scorched my back from head to heels.

"Why aren't we attacking her? Or running away, or surrendering, or doing something?" Pil yelled at me.

"I'm waiting for the sun to get just high enough."

"What?" Pil shaded her eyes and looked up. Semanté saw her and looked up too.

Another man hurled a spear at Pil, but I didn't twist my head to look. Instead of burning the spear, Semanté smiled at me. My sword had flown out of my hand and landed farther away than I could crawl in a few seconds, so I ignored it. Instead, I lifted my right arm and waved at Semanté as I smiled.

Semanté peered at me before whipping her head to look behind her. At the same time, one of her men shouted and pointed up the road. Hill People began scattering.

Thirty pigs waiting to be sold had escaped their pen and were charging toward the ramp. Spurred by vast, unreasoning hunger for the food I had convinced them was here, the pigs tried to smash through and over anything in their path. Since they each weighed four or five hundred pounds, they were almost always successful.

Anything will burn if it gets hot enough. That includes dirt, air, and stone. When Semanté set the pavement afire in a large "V" between her and the oncoming pigs, she must have spent an obscene amount of power. I doubted the flames were all that fierce, and they didn't last long, but the pigs broke around Semanté like fish swimming past a boulder.

It was an elegant feat of sorcery. Semanté pushed power into the fire just long enough to let the pigs pass. That was also long enough for me to crawl to my sword and stand, but I was still too far away to attack her. Wiping soot off her face, Semanté spotted me and grinned.

She was enjoying this. I might have enjoyed it too, if I hadn't been a bare, walking nerve.

I whipped three blue bands into the sky. Seconds later, Hill People above us started screaming, and everybody except me looked up. Several Hill People were climbing down each rope, and I had rotted through the three closest to Semanté.

Nine Hill People plunged with their arms whirling toward the pavement. Some of the people on the ground ran and some froze, but everybody watched the disaster happen. A man slammed onto the road between Semanté and the mountain face. She jumped to her right and then changed her mind, dodging left. A woman crashed into another woman who had run the wrong direction. A third person smacked against the ground a few feet away from Semanté as she dodged back the other way.

Semanté backed away from the mountainside while the men and women fell. It was all an enormous, horrible mess, but it hadn't hurt Semanté, and I hadn't expected it to. Once the last man hit the ground, she turned around to deal with me and dodged just as I put my blade through her chest. She had forced me to miss her heart, but the wound would be fatal unless I saved her with magic.

I withdrew my sword, and Semanté gasped as she dropped to her knees.

I said, "I guess I wasn't as pathetic and slow on my feet as you thought." I had made a good show of crawling like a caterpillar while she was watching, but I rushed her when she turned to dodge plummeting Hill People.

"Don't talk, you idiot!" Pil shouted. "Kill her!"

I stepped back to end it by stabbing Semanté in the heart, but I was dragged to a stop when she lurched forward and grabbed my willy, which, to be fair, was the only thing at her level that could be grabbed. For a soon-to-be-dead woman, she had a robust grip.

Shock and pain halted me, along with the sense that if I backed away, I'd be dragging a sack of potatoes with my dick. I shifted my grip on my sword so I could cut her throat from her arm's length. Then I noticed the fingers on her other hand twitching.

I saw it in an instant. She was about to ignite everything she was wearing in awful, searing flames so I would die with her. It was an act of single-minded malice that I had to admire.

If I tried to pull free, I'd be caught in the fire. I was too close to stab her in the head with my sword. Cutting off her arm would set me free to be immolated a moment later.

I swung my sword, cutting two fingers off her fire-making hand and smashing the rest. Semanté moaned and scowled as she let go of me. I jumped back and slashed her unwounded hand, but I didn't catch every finger. I turned and ran away as fast as a burned and beaten man could run.

Semanté's clothing exploded with shocking heat. The blast threw me to the ground and scorched the rest of my back. Now I was as bald as an eyeball.

I sat up and looked around. Pil stood a good distance away, her arms over her head. A dozen Hill People had retreated up the road, away from Semanté's body and the smashed corpses of their friends. I imagined they were conferring over the military situation and wondering how much worse it could get. Nobody was standing near the ramp.

Semanté's corpse burned like a bonfire, although that couldn't last long.

I crawled to my feet and was swaying more than is proper for someone who is victorious.

"Bib, you're smoking!" Pil shouted. She reached out, hesitated to touch me, and started waving smoke away instead—probably the most useless thing anybody had done all day.

I wanted to lie down so badly that I almost envied Semanté. But things were going well, and I wanted to capitalize on it. I was inspired to convince the pigs that the food had moved to the bottom of the ramp. They rushed down, filling the ramp side to side and squealing all the way. I peered down the ramp and saw pigs charging through Hill People and soldiers who were run down or knocked over the side.

Desh had arrived with the villagers. He and Ella started herding them toward the ramp.

"Pil, where's Stan?" I had a sick feeling. "Is he with Desh?"

"No. It seems that he broke his leg tripping over a curb." Pil grinned. "I intend to remind him about it until the end of time. The villagers are carrying him."

"That's good," I said. "I think I'll take a breath." I sat straight down on the ground, let my head hang forward, and fell asleep.

THIRTY-EIGHT

I couldn't have slept for more than a few minutes when Pil yelled, "Bib! Wake up! We're leaving without you." When I peered at her, she grinned. "Not really, we won't leave you. Sorry I shouted, but I couldn't find a place on you that's not burned or cut up, so I couldn't poke you. I won't carry you, so get up."

"All right." I clambered to my hands and knees before I had to stop.

Pil said, "Wait. Sit down, you look like a pony. Can you heal yourself enough to walk? If you can't, well, I lied. I will carry you, as far as you need to go." She reached out but stopped and said, "Heal yourself so that people can touch you."

I didn't answer any of that. I started pulling bands to heal my worst wounds.

Pil walked back and knelt beside me some time later. "Better?"

"Some. A little sore."

"You mean it feels like you've been whacked with clubs all day." She reached to help me stand, but I waved her away. "I'm sorry, your clothes were burned up. I found this long shirt for you." I shrugged into it with care, since I had plenty of unhealed wounds left.

At the ramp, I saw that Desh had proceeded one-fifth of the way down before he was stopped by sixty soldiers headed up. One of the soldiers was yelling, and Desh was answering in a calm voice.

Pil and I pushed down the ramp. She wove us through the farmers, so I joined Desh and Ella before Desh used a magic doodad to fill sixty men's lungs with rock salt, or something just as horrible.

I smiled at the yelling soldier. "General! Thank you for saving us, General. The Hill People almost killed us."

The wide-eyed man stared at me with his brows pulled together. "What happened to your hair?"

I hadn't expected that to be his first question. "That's how hard we fought when we whipped the Hill People. We fought until our hair fell out, but the dogs are running now!"

Pil stepped up beside me. "He's telling the truth, General. Several of us died. I almost died." She nodded at me. "He's going to die any minute now. Please help us while a few of us are still alive."

Ludlow appeared in the rear and stepped forward, although the tall man stopped four ranks back. "You're a bunch of traitors, and we've got to fight a war up there. Arrest them and push them all back up."

I saw Ludlow and felt a thirst to kill stronger than anything I'd known in months. There was no logic. I just wanted the man dead, and I wanted to be the one to make him that way.

I pushed that feeling down. I couldn't think of a thing that would help us here. We'd die if we fought them, and they'd catch us if we ran. I didn't have time for magic, and my pigs were wandering around in the city pissed off because they couldn't find the wonderful food. Nothing I threatened Ludlow with was the least bit believable.

"Wait!" I yelled. That didn't make the soldiers stop, but when we pointed our swords, they paused to point theirs back at us. I said, "Of course, we'll obey and go back up the ramp." Desh stiffened when I said it. "But let us help these poor people back up there without hurting them. They've suffered so much. You can arrest us when we get up there."

I felt Ella, Desh, and Pil glancing at me, but none of them balked.

Ludlow gazed at the peasants behind me, his iron-hard face softening. "Well . . . since you knocked back the Hill People, we could stand to wait a minute to let the next company reinforce us. Fine, go on and lead them like lambs. But hurry it up!"

I turned to Desh and Pil. "Please lead them. I'll try to think of something to do. I'll make it obvious if I have an idea. You do the same."

"Hurry!" Ludlow bellowed. "Move, don't talk!"

Pil and Desh pushed their way up through the crowd.

I leaned toward Ella. "Please stay with me."

She smiled, turned, and walked backward, pointing her sword at the dozens of soldiers following us.

I shouted at the farmers, "Everybody turn around so we can walk back up. Don't worry, everything will be fine. Desh will show you where to go."

The exhausted, numb, disorganized villagers shuffled to turn and waddle back up the ramp.

"Thank you, General Ludlow!" I called out.

I jerked when I saw Cora standing on the other side of the ramp from Ludlow, over beside the railing. Her face was strained and pale, and she looked down after meeting my eyes. Her shirt was stained with blood. Ludlow must have had a Caller who saved her life.

I waved to show Ludlow that I was forcing the peasants to move faster.

Bird-Gek flew up and landed on my shoulder. "I find you in a predicament, I see."

"That's pretty damn observant," I whispered. "I guess you only need one hand to find your ass."

Bird-Gek's eyes got brighter. "I rarely forget where things are, that's true. Do you wish to say any particular thing to me?"

"Don't shit on my shoulder."

"I wouldn't consider that, even if I disliked you. Anything else?"

"No, my friends and I are all fine," I said. "We're planning a party tonight. We'll be eating little birds and drinking ambrosia."

DEATH'S COLLECTOR: SWORD HAND

"Sadly, I can't attend. I have business in the Void."

"Happily, you're not invited. If this conversation has a point, get to it, you long-winded disappointment to your hyena mother. If you have a mother."

"I do not," Bird-Gek said. "I feel privileged on that score, having observed Desh's mother. Be my servant now. This is not a demand in any way. Consider it a final opportunity."

"No."

"Final, because it is the only way you will ever leave this city. Your bones will remain here until the end of time."

"You can't know that I'll die here," I said. "I admit that you can have an extremely strong intuition, but you can't know."

Bird-Gek's voice grew louder. "Who are you to say what I can and cannot know? I withdraw the opportunity to serve me for thirteen months."

"Good!"

Ella murmured "What did you say?" without looking at me.

"Nothing, just praying."

Bird-Gek said, "You and every person you brought here will die before the sun sets. I can save you all if you serve me for eleven months."

"You withdrew that offer!" I whispered.

"This is a different opportunity." I heard a smile in his voice. "It's for only eleven months."

I didn't answer.

Bird-Gek said, "I find this city harsh, don't you? You may bring along anyone you wish to complete your tasks, as long as they are human. Or even sorcerers."

I glanced at Ella. I didn't care to die now. I had found her. Gek's offer tempted me.

Gek said, "Occasionally, I might give you knowledge, the kind you would truly wish to have. It is a perquisite of being my servant."

Gritting my teeth until they hurt, I whispered, "One month."

"That's not a very intriguing offer. I suggest seven months."

"Three months then," I said.

"As you would predict, I now offer five months."

"I might agree . . . if you will save all of us here and also take us to a place I choose."

Bird-Gek paused. "Bib, I would consider no less. I am not trying to cheat you."

"That means that you're trying to cheat me with every breath!" I whispered.

"You wouldn't say that if you knew me."

There wasn't much point in thinking too hard about it now that I had come this far. "Five months. I agree."

"That gives me prodigious satisfaction! We will accomplish momentous things together. We will shake the foundations of existence. Now, first I will save all of you. I will go explain the safe path to Desh." Bird-Gek flew away.

"Goddamn it!" I said.

"What?" Ella asked. "What is the matter?"

"I'm reckless and stupid."

"We cannot honestly consider that a new issue, can we?"

A few moments later, people began shouting a hundred feet up the ramp. The group stopped while Desh and Pil called out what sounded like orders and threats. The mass of people began moving again.

Soon, I saw the problem. A big hole had appeared in the ramp, wide enough for three people to stand in at once. Desh and Pil were urging the farmers to jump into the hole. Sometimes they threw people in. Every person who went into the hole disappeared.

I stared at Ludlow before I reached the hole. The blood in my veins shrieked to kill him. My brain expressed minor concern that I might not escape afterward.

I muttered, "Ella, I'm about to be stupid." I charged Ludlow, killing two soldiers in front rank. My body was still pained from healing, but my sword seemed to carry me along. I killed one more in the front and wounded two in the second rank, pushing forward. Ella pressed in to cover my flank. Cora caught my eye, smiling with pained happiness.

Ludlow bellowed and turned red, ordering his men to tear me to scraps. A few seconds later, he began promising to do the job himself.

I halted and wounded another man as he swung at me. I glanced and saw Cora reach out one hand to me. She and Ludlow were the same distance from me in different directions.

Cutting toward the railing and the third rank, I killed two men in five seconds. Now most soldiers were pulling as far away from me as space allowed, but few were moving to attack me. I shouted my frustration and turned toward Cora. She smiled and shoved herself toward me between two soldiers, both her hands stretched out.

I reached for her with my free hand, but a man on my other side slashed at it, chopping deeply into my wrist.

I cursed in pain, ready to turn and kill that man, but Cora was being pulled back as soldiers retreated from me. Her face was twisted and strained, but she was still reaching toward me.

Blinking once, I dropped my sword, lunged, and grabbed Cora's hand. I pulled, and she stumbled, but I dragged her back toward the hole in the ramp.

I hadn't thought much about the problem of fighting my way back out with no sword and a useless hand. A soldier appeared right beside me, so I bashed him with my shoulder, dragging Cora along. Another grabbed my shirt, but it was badly made. I ripped right out of it. The man who had chopped my wrist sidestepped and raised his sword to kill me. Before he swung, Ella's blade clanged off his helmet, staggering him.

Ella stepped in and held off the soldiers, backing away while Cora and I ran toward the hole. I was feeling weaker, but when we reached the hole, I pushed Cora in before I fell to my knees. Ella was behind me, still fighting. Just in case she decided to be foolish and sacrifice herself, I grabbed the back of her belt and fell forward into the hole, dragging her along with me.

THIRTY-NINE

W hen I fell into the hole Gek had created, I expected to
land somewhere, maybe on my face since I had fallen
forward into lightless emptiness. I wasn't prepared to
feel dirt under my bare feet as if I had stepped off a garden path.
When I shuffled forward, I banged my knees against some hard-
packed, earthen steps, then I stumbled against them.

"More damn stairs," I muttered.

"I would carry you," Ella said from behind me, "but I doubt
that your vanity could abide it."

I was required to climb only five steps, though. At each one, the
light grew a bit brighter until it was a few shades above nighttime.

"Back in the goddamn Dark Lands. I guess Gek doesn't have a
single imaginative bone in his parrot-faced body."

From behind me, Ella said, "Come, let me see your wrist."

I waved her away with my good hand, which should have had
my sword in it but didn't.

Ella raised her voice. "Sit down at least!"

I trudged away four steps like a pouty teenager and lay down on
my unburned side. The black grass was cool and soothing, so I
cursed it. Then I cursed the Dark Lands, Gek, the gods, and that

idiot Ludlow until I ran out of breath. I panted, "Tell me if something comes to kill us. I want to die sitting up."

Ella had knelt down and was examining my partly severed wrist. She smiled, but her brows were drawn. "Not so bad." She began cutting strips off the hem of her shirt. "Who is Gek?"

"My new boss."

Ella paused. "What?"

"Never mind."

Pil squatted down beside us. "Bib, I'm your friend, so maybe you'll believe me when I say that what you did for Cora was a good thing, a fine thing. I hope you believe me. Now get the hell up."

I lifted my head and squinted at her.

Ella twisted toward Pil with both fists clenched, one of them full of bandages. "He requires rest. Whatever chores you have for him can wait!"

Pil plucked at the grass. "I'd be happy if that were true, and I'd do them myself if I could."

"What must be done?" Ella asked, her jaw tight. "I will do it if you promise to take care of him."

Pil didn't answer her. Instead, she put a hand on my unburned shoulder. "Bib, listen, if you sleep for a day right now, or even a few hours, your wounds will start corrupting. Then they'll be harder to heal, which will eat more power, and at the end, you'll still have almost all the same pain, which means you'll be useless. So, heal yourself now, before you sleep." She paused. "If you say yes, you'll get a surprise."

"We require no surprises from you!" Ella said.

"No, she's right," I said. "Pil, you're thinking like a sorcerer. Go ahead and push me hard. I'll suffer more, but you'll have a stronger ally for it, and you'll have him sooner. Remember, how many friends does a sorcerer have?"

"None," she answered quietly.

"As a rule, yes. It's a good thing I'm an unruly sorcerer. My teachers tried to beat it out of me, but I broke every whiny-ass rule that was ever written down. Help me sit up and have somebody drag Stan over here."

Pil smiled, which cut a couple of years off her age. "Cora?"

Cora stepped up, holding my sword. Her smile was too wide to jump over.

My mouth opened, but I couldn't say anything.

Pil slapped Cora on the shoulder. "We were a month on the trail, and I couldn't get him to shut up. Nicely done."

Cora said, "I bent down and grabbed it while you were pulling me away from them. So . . . surprise!"

"Thank you." I nodded, but that was all. As she handed over the sword, I couldn't decide whether she had done something that would help me or hurt me. Maybe I had dropped it because I should have left it behind.

Ella backed away far enough to see us all. "Very well, if this is what the cabal of sorcerers has decided, if we must ape practicality, I shall point out that we stand upon an island. More precisely, a black island with black trees in the middle of a black lake. Desh says you crossed these lands two weeks ago." She gazed in every direction, including up and down. "What should I know about this place?"

"Don't challenge anybody to anything," I said. "Oh, Cael is here. I hope I don't have to fight him again."

"You fought him and prevailed? I'm astonished. I am even more astonished that you allowed him to live after defeating him. Bib, what has happened to you? Whatever it is, I approve. Indeed, it makes me happy for you. But I mistrust it."

"I don't know that I've changed one bit. Pour a few drinks into me, and you'll see that I'm the same as I ever was. Wise, generous, friendly, and good-looking."

Pil beckoned two village men carrying Stan. He smiled at me, a horrible sight. "Thank you for helping my poor leg, Lord Bib. And may you never get a disease of the dangler for the rest of your life, no matter how much you fly your flag."

I touched his leg to explore the break. "I'm Lord Bib again, eh?"

"You was always Lord Bib, and you will be now, yesterday, and till you're moldering in the dirt. Once in a while, I may forget to say it, if I get distracted or something." He didn't sound at all embarrassed or apologetic.

Once Stan had trotted away, I dealt with my own wounds. They included a hacked-apart wrist, a lot of burns, which hurt like a scorpion in every orifice, punctures, bruises, cuts, and some broken fingers. Then I fell over, throbbed in pain for a few minutes, and finally slept.

Most of the pain had gone by the time I opened my eyes, and Hurd was staring at me from three feet away. "Beauty sleep ain't going to get you home. Looks like it ain't making you beautiful, neither."

"Hello again, Hurd," I said. "I'm happy to find you here. I have no idea where to go or what to do if I get there."

"First off, I found you, not the other way around. Second, put on some blessed clothes! The sight of your bare hide could make a goat puke. And third, did you bring along anything to drink?"

"I apologize. We didn't have time to bring beer or anything else to drink. Some of us didn't even have time to bring clothes. I promise to take extra beer along the next time I come."

Hurd's face drooped as he murmured, "Don't come back here. It's a bad place. Once you're gone, I'll be burning up the grass running out of here."

"Why doesn't Gek come talk to me here?"

"Oh, Gek never comes here." Hurd said it as if that explained everything that could be known on the subject. "Come on, find a pair of trousers and let's get going."

"Wait, how do you know where I want to go?"

"How do you know which end of that sword to poke somebody with?" He might have rolled his black button eyes, but I couldn't be sure.

"I'd feel better if I just told you," I said.

"Stop!" Hurd held up a hand. "I have it clear in my mind right this minute. Don't muddy it all up with words—it'll just confuse everything. Now, clothes!"

I searched among the villagers for five minutes but found nobody with spare clothes, even trousers. Ella went and threatened them about it for a while, but they didn't know her well enough to be afraid of her. Their muttering made it clear that they wouldn't loan me trousers if they had a thousand pairs. Not only was I an evil demon sorcerer, but I was the evil demon sorcerer who murdered Tira as she lay on her back, helpless.

"Your efforts to save them count for nothing," Ella said, breathing hard from shouting at the farmers.

"Ingratitude is in the character of most people," I said. "At least we can be sure they're normal folk and not possessed by spirits."

At last, Desh talked to them. He came back to me with a pair of boots. "This is all I got."

I laughed. "At least they're in good condition."

"They were the best pair in the whole community. They belonged to Yoadie."

"How?" I asked. "I bet the slavers didn't yank off his boots before they heaved him over the side."

"Actually, they did. But Yoadie's sister stole them back and wore them over her own boots. Something this nice is an heirloom, but she said Yoadie would probably do something stupid like give them to you."

I sat down on the grass and pulled one on. "Nice fit. I don't promise to make Yoadie proud, but I'll try not to embarrass him. Hurd, I guess you'll have to be offended by looking at me nude. Do we swim across? I'm dressed for it."

Hurd pointed toward a wide black bridge that I hadn't noticed. It ran from the near shore across the water until it disappeared into the mist.

"Well, that's as ominous as hell," I said.

"Did anybody see that bridge appear?" asked Desh, who had come back from settling some villager's quarrel.

"No," Stan said. "I swear it wasn't there when we was dragged back to this awful place. Then, while I was sitting there crippled in pain but still vigilant for danger, the ass-damned haunted thing was right there when I looked around, stretched out like you see it now. Maybe some kind of turtle-dragon thing floated it up on its back."

"So, it's a magical bridge," Pil said to Hurd. "Will magical things happen to us when we walk across it?"

Hurd's forehead wrinkled even more than usual as he shrugged and walked toward the bridge.

Ella and I led the way with Hurd. Desh and Pil led the farmers, while Stan and Cora walked at the rear. The bridge was dead flat and two hundred paces long. The whole length stood one foot off the water with never a pillar to hold it up.

When we reached the bridge's far end, a clanging voice called out, "Stop!"

I answered, "Bixell?"

The towering, black guardian stepped out to block the bridge. "Oh. It's you."

"Did you switch bridges?"

He stood even taller. "I guard all the bridges in the Dark Lands."

"Bixell, I'm sorry I couldn't take over as guardian, but I was performing an important task."

"Everybody's got an important task. You're not special." He crossed his arms.

"And now I'm serving an important being, so I can't just walk away from that obligation. And you have to admit that while you didn't cheat in our contest, you did strain the rules mighty hard. Right?"

Bixell had uncrossed his arms. Maybe he had enough honor to feel shame, or maybe he worshipped the rules like a bookkeeper. He asked, "You serve an important being?"

"Yes," I said, now uncertain. "I do."

"He sure as heck does!" Hurd added.

"Who?"

"I'm not sure I should tell you."

Bixell rubbed his forehead and then his eyes. "All right. What task are you performing?"

"I don't think it would be proper for me to say." I held my sword ready without pointing it in his direction.

The guardian turned his gaze to Hurd. I couldn't make out

Bixell's expression because his dark face was shadowed inside his helmet. After a long silence, he sighed. "If you had accepted your obligation, this task might be mine. I could be the one serving."

"It's done, Bixell, and I doubt we'd be allowed to switch now."

Bixell didn't comment, but he stepped aside.

As I tramped past him, I nodded. "Thank you, sir. You possess great character."

"Tell him . . . never mind. Tell him I said hello, if it crosses your mind."

When we had all passed the bridge, Ella muttered to Hurd, "Is it like this throughout these Dark Lands? Magic and soaring melodrama?"

"Of course, it's magic and melodrama! What do you think realms are made of? How do you think they get unmade?"

Ella grabbed my hand and squeezed so hard it hurt.

We traveled for a couple of hours, and nothing worth noting happened. Ella remarked that Hurd must have been teasing her with his talk about magic and drama. Hurd then grouched about her snippy comments and banged into her leg twice as we walked, by accident, he said.

After Hurd calmed down, I asked, "Are we going to the place that Cael is guarding? I hope not."

"Krak forfend," Ella grumbled. She and Cael were not on easy terms. In fact, Ella had prickly relations with all my acquaintances.

"No, we're going to a different place," Hurd said.

"And that place is . . .?"

"Right over there." He pointed at a low hill that I likely wouldn't have noticed if he hadn't mentioned it. "There's a cave over there. That's where you'll go."

I jerked my head around toward the flatlands because something out there had glinted. "Hurd, what kinds of things will cause us harm around here? Because one of them may be coming for us. There!" I pointed at the glint of light off in the murk. "Tell me that's just a will-o'-the-wisp or a fancy bug."

Hurd peered toward the glint when it happened again. "It ain't no bug." He glanced left and right. "Since these are the Dark Lands, we'd best assume it's something bad. Let's hurry. And let's do it now."

Although I hadn't seen any actual threat, the back of my neck told me one was out there. The villagers couldn't live through any serious attack. Hell, running to the cave might kill them. Our best chance for the most people to survive would be for me to distract whatever was out there. I decided that in a moment, but it felt right, almost inevitable.

"I'm going to scout whatever that is." I trotted that direction.

Ella, Desh, and Pil all called for me to wait.

I turned back and met their eyes. "You'll either be useless or get me killed."

Nobody answered for a moment. Then Ella said, "That is certainly a presumptuous sentiment."

"Listen, I don't need to kill this thing. I just need to make sure it doesn't kill us. Correct?"

They nodded.

"If I can kill it myself, wonderful. I don't need you. But if you're there, I might get killed helping one of you instead."

Pil started talking, but I cut her off.

"On the other hand, if I can't kill whatever it is by myself, I'll make it chase me. But if you're with me, I might get killed helping you instead of running like hell. So, let's not throw any more time away on this conversation."

I ran toward the glint, which was appearing and disappearing more regularly.

Desh called from behind me, "You can't order us to do things."

I glanced back over my shoulder. "No, but you'll do them if you're smart."

He was catching up with me. "Wait!"

"Damn it, Desh, stay here. You're the only one who can kill something that killed me."

"Yes, your logic is correct. But I want you to take this." He held out a thick silver chain with a sapphire as big as my eyeball.

"What is this?"

"It will help you in combat," he said. "The harder you try to protect yourself, the harder it will try to protect you."

"Thank you, Desh, you're generous to offer me something you enchanted so cleverly."

"I didn't enchant it, and I'd like it back when this is over. Limnad gave it to me."

I nodded at him and jogged away. The glint seemed to have disappeared, so I ran toward where I had last seen it.

The black grass had grown soggier during the past hour. As I loped away from the others, small pools of water splotched the soft ground. I passed a few tall but haggard trees with gray leaves. Even in this dimness, my eyesight was superior and I finally saw what was creating the glint.

A long-armed man wearing armor and tall boots was striding across the sticky ground as if this were his yard back home. The feathers on his hat were pinned there by a brilliant stone, maybe a diamond, which had been reflecting light. I couldn't see his face well, but I knew it bore two scars. His boots were crimson and his armor pink. I couldn't see that, either, but I knew it all to be true because he was Zagurith, the son of Lutigan.

Zagurith and his demigod brothers had once threatened to kill me because I destroyed their pain-in-the-ass sibling, Memweck. I should have been dead seconds after they made that threat, but I struck a roaring great bargain with their father. He had commanded them to let me live. They hadn't looked happy about it then, and I doubted that anything had changed since then that would make them happier.

I crouched, hoping he might not see me. Maybe he would go squash kittens and lambs, or make it rain on the virtuous, or whatever else he had planned for his day. But I could tell after a few seconds that he would pass close to the cave, or maybe he was headed right there.

Standing, I shouted, "Hello, Zagurith! Still doing your father's bidding without any will or thought of your own?"

The demigod turned and raced toward me at a terrifying speed, or at least it terrified me. He stopped one hundred feet from me and stood as if posing for a statue, one hand on the pommel of his sword. "Murderer! Have you always been so scrawny? And poorly endowed? I wonder that some woman hasn't cut your throat as you slept for leaving her monumentally unsatisfied."

I peered hard. "What's wrong with your throat?" It looked as if somebody had cut it with gusto.

"Is this what passes for wit in your realm?" Zagurith smiled an almost perfect smile. Then he whistled so loudly I held my free hand over my ear.

I stood straighter. "Really, have you been wounded in the throat? I am a healer, you know."

"Hah! The only way you'll touch me is when your entrails spill out over my sword hand. Five."

"I'm sorry?"

"Four."

When Zagurith's count reached two, I saw them. Something silver rushed across the marshy land toward us, while something mottled approached from another direction. By the time Zagurith reached zero, he and two other beings had spread themselves out in front of me.

A short, broad figure wearing a green coat and orange trousers had planted himself in the middle. He wore no hat over his yellow, braided hair, and his black shoes shone brighter than Zagurith's hat pin. He was Gondix, the eldest son of Lutigan.

The third being was tall and slender. He wore a shaggy bearskin coat that shone like silver, and the bear's skull served as his hat. He held an eight-foot-long spear in one hand and was pointing it at my face. This brother was Paal.

"So, this is where you've been skulking!" Gondix said. "Father's been agitated about you."

"I'm flattered," I said.

"You should be flattered." Paal rumbled. "And honored."

I smiled. "Please thank your father, the Rabid Chipmunk of War, for me. I'd like to get back to the subject of Zagurith's neck. What the hell's wrong with it?" I didn't really care about his neck, and maybe nothing was wrong with it. But talking about his neck was better than any of the other things that could be happening.

"One of us should go tell Father," Paal said.

Zagurith sneered. "He's not coming here."

"Do we take the Murderer's head home?" Gondix looked at each of his brothers with his eyebrows raised.

Zagurith chewed the inside of his cheek. "I think it's all right if we do it."

Paal lowered his spear. "Our first duty is to report."

I said, "Did Zagurith's throat land on something sharp?"

"Shut up about his damn throat!" Gondix snapped. "I sliced his blasted-to-Krak throat open!"

"We were supposed to stab one another in the heart." Zagurith frowned. "It's the accepted way."

Paal said, "If you two had the courage to hang yourselves, we wouldn't be having this conversation."

I scrutinized the brothers. Gondix had a bloody wound in his chest. Paal's neck was crooked. "I never appreciated before how mighty and indestructible you are."

"Quiet!" Gondix whipped his sword in a circle. "You can't flatter us. We don't care what you think."

"Maybe we can make a bargain," I suggested.

"Hah!" Zagurith said. "We are the sons of Lutigan. We don't bargain. We kill."

"And report," Paal added.

Gondix turned to Paal. "We're going to kill the little turd squirter. You can go report if you want to. But . . . if you stay, you get to kill him."

Paal raised his face to the sky, and his neck produced five awful pops. He winced. "I'll kill him. I don't want to chase him, though. I'm tired of chasing things."

Zagurith pointed one finger and wiggled it. Walls of sticky earth rose high around me, one behind and one on each side. I ended up at the back of a tall, fifty-foot-long mud alley.

Paal strode down the alleyway toward me, light-footed and loose. He advanced behind his spear, which he pointed at my left eye. I moved to meet him with my sword high. When he saw me coming, he half smiled.

Even if I survived Paal's first thrust, it would push me farther out of range. So, I charged him. He sure as hell wouldn't expect that.

Maybe I surprised him, and it slowed his thrust by a fraction. I could tell he wasn't treating me as a serious threat. His guard wasn't perfect, and his footwork was a bit lazy.

Those were my advantages. My main disadvantage was that my sword might just bounce off Paal's semi-divine skin. Not many enchanted weapons could harm a demigod, and there wasn't a practical way to test your weapon before battle.

Also, part of me burned to kill him, but it was a small fire buried deep. I didn't know whether that was an advantage or not.

My body was already moving as I considered those things, and the considerations fell into place in a blink. Paal thrust, and I guided his spear aside with my sword, which wanted things to be really, really dead. Then I lunged and thrust my blade like a flash in and out of his heart.

I didn't assume that would be enough to kill a demigod. Paal's brother, Memweck, had been astoundingly hard to kill. As I recovered, Paal stiffened. I rushed forward two steps and severed his head from his body. All the parts of Paal came to rest on the mud at the same time.

Gondix and Zagurith were staring at me from the mouth of the alley.

I picked up Paal's spear in case it was so powerful they might be afraid of it, and I pushed out my chest. "Gentlemen, the secret of my victory is being relaxed and unconstrained. Paal, poor fellow, was tense and restricted. You should strip off those pretty costumes before you come in here. I'll kill you anyway, but you might not look so pathetic while you're dying."

They intended to destroy me no matter what, so I might as well insult the groping dogs.

Zagurith pointed his finger. I recognized that and ran toward him. Before he got done waggling, I was charging out of the mud alleyway with the walls collapsing behind me.

Neither Zagurith nor his surviving brother looked a bit scared, so I dropped the spear. When Gondix swung, he should have split my head. I blocked, spun, and leaned, which wasn't quite enough. Astoundingly, Gondix's swing was off just a bit so that he sliced away my ear and a bit of my cheek before crushing my left shoulder. Screaming in my contorted position, I saw the opening as if I had planted it there yesterday. I knew it had to be there. Every muscle that could drive my sword arm snapped tight as I bent backward and stabbed Gondix in the heart through his armpit.

As Gondix staggered away, I crouched and rolled, screaming again as my smashed shoulder touched the ground. Zagurith destroyed the air where I had been standing an instant before. I swung one-handed while sitting on my butt, which was the most ridiculous and impossible fighting position I could imagine. But it was the perfect place to be if I wanted to slice through Zagurith's ankle, and that's what I did.

Zagurith fell to a knee as his severed foot rolled out from under him. But now he was ready to kill me in one of the many ways a man on his butt can be killed.

I couldn't possibly be faster than a demigod, and I couldn't see the future. But I saw all the pieces that were coming together, so I was able to move before Zagurith. I did one of the least likely things possible. I spun, twisted, and cut off his other foot.

When Zagurith fell, I thrust my sword through his eye. Then I jumped up and decapitated both Gondix and Zagurith to make sure they were really, really dead.

FORTY

I healed my shoulder before trekking to the cave. Lutigan was such a randy dog he might have a hundred more sons, and ninety-nine of them could show up any moment to avenge their dead brothers. Even with two good shoulders, I couldn't kill them all, although I could put up a fight that wouldn't embarrass Yoadie.

Hurd was alone and waiting for me in the cave. "I wouldn't have believed it. I saw you do it with my own eyes, and I still don't believe it."

I thought he was going to ask me to explain how I killed Lutigan's sons, but he didn't. That relieved me, since I couldn't fully explain it myself.

Hurd clapped once, and I thought he might applaud. "I'm glad that you're not such an idiot as to bring back their swords and such. If you was to take them out of the Dark Lands, the gods would know right away what you done."

"I didn't need to bring them. I carved my name on their foreheads."

Hurd stepped back, his eyes and mouth huge.

"No, I didn't really! I wanted to, but . . ." I shrugged.

"Good! Son, I sent your people through all right. But I can send you someplace else if you want."

I had been pondering that. Ella, Pil, and the others might not prosper in the service of Gek. They might die, and even if they didn't, little good could happen to them if they came along. It would be a foolish step and unlikely to help me succeed or even survive.

Some of them would want to come, of course. Denying them would come easier for everybody if I just went someplace else today. It was the clever thing to do.

But like the dimmest idiot in the stupidest village, I said, "No, send me after them. If I'm going to tell them they can't come along, I'll do it right there where they can hit me."

"Fine. Don't try to hunt me down in this place if you ever come back." Hurd smiled. "I'm going home to play with my grandkids and their kids too. And to drink."

I walked through the wall at the back of the cave. Then I was standing in a field bright with sunshine and blue wildflowers. I didn't remember anything in between.

Somebody yelled, "Krak! Krak's fist, it's cold! Oh, damn it! So cold."

I was naked, and the air felt no more than brisk. But just downhill from me, the farmers who had been born on the searing hot frontier were milling around, arms crossed and cursing the frigid weather. Past them, all down a three-mile-long slope, stood many dozens of farms, fewer dozens of shops, and a vast, spreading castle called the Eastern Gateway.

As I had intended, Hurd sent us to the Denz Lands in the far south of the world. It was a place where people had once abused Ella and me in some harsh ways, but later they celebrated us for weeks. I hoped they remembered the celebrations more than the abuse.

A couple of years ago, the Denz Lands had suffered a widespread and deadly illness before a cure was found. Thousands of their people died, which was a tragedy. Moris, the Denz King, now had farms untended and workshops empty all across his kingdom, and I hoped that would be a happy thing for our farmers who needed someplace to settle.

We sent Stan and some villagers down to the shops for clothes and blankets. Desh provided the silver, and Ella warned Stan not to stop for drinks, gambling, or whores. Then Desh, Ella, Cora, and Pil crowded around me to hear about the monster I had faced.

"Biggest damn bear you ever saw," I said. "Almost tore my arm off." I handed the sapphire necklace back to Desh. "This charm is the only reason I prevailed." That was probably true, and it was the only true thing I told them. They threw skeptical questions at me, told me they knew I was lying, and tried to undercut my logic. Pil even pouted.

I stuck to the bear story, no matter how stupid it sounded. Answering difficult bear questions was far easier than answering difficult demigod questions.

All this fun ended when a patrol of Denz soldiers found us. I played idiot, letting Desh and Ella answer their questions. The troops were unlikely to heed me anyway since I was wearing only boots. The king was not currently visiting the Eastern Gateway, but the local viscount would sure as hell want to question us himself.

Two hours later, I stood, clothed, in front of the viscount. He was a middle-aged, broad-shouldered, broad-bellied man. He was also nearly as pale as snow, like all Denzmen. He questioned us with gusto. During that hour of magic and joy, I daydreamed about working some sorcery that would astound and terrify the man. I lied about everything I was asked, then let Ella and Desh clean up the lies.

None of it seemed important.

At last, the viscount decided not to execute us as spies. Some of his advisors and soldiers knew us from before, and when they vouched for us, he offered decent hospitality. He promised to grant farmland to the Sandypool villagers. When Desh brought them the news, they were still bitching about the cold. They were at it even after Desh promised to pay for whatever they might need to begin their new lives.

The viscount gave us quarters, which I used to bathe and then sleep for most of two days. When I at last got out of bed, a maid brought me enough breakfast for five people. I understood that better when Desh, Pil, Cora, and Ella showed up to confront me over a table full of sausages and barley soup.

Pil and Ella sat next to each other and chatted easily.

I said, "It's nice to see the two of you sharing a table instead of trying to poison each other."

Pil glanced at Ella before she smiled at me. "We've reached an understanding."

I muttered, "I don't see how this could be good."

"Yes, an understanding," Ella said. "Pil has helped me understand that she considers you to be almost as ancient as a thousand-year-old tree stump. You are friendly, comforting, even beloved, but so, so very old."

I thought about smiling but nodded instead before asking the serving maid for more soup.

When most of us had finished eating, Ella said, "Bib, we know that something sorcerous is happening. I am not upset about that, but please do us the courtesy of explaining. I feel we have earned it."

None of the sorcerers at the table looked at me or spoke up to support Ella. Although I would never knock her across the room for asking me insolent questions about sorcery, I'd be within my rights if I did. Maybe the others would disapprove, but they wouldn't interfere.

I leaned away from the table and sighed. "I'll give you ten words. Ask me in ten words, and I'll answer."

Ella turned red, but she didn't throw anything at me. "What happened to you? Who is Gek? Should we worry?"

"Damn. I should have given you three words instead of ten. I'll start with Gek. He's the Void Walker who took over for Dimore. I now owe Gek a killing." I didn't need to talk about being Gek's servant. Technically, she hadn't asked for such details.

"What happened to me?" I pointed at Pil and Desh. "After your memories were restored, you were different, right? That happened to me too. I went back a few more years than you did, but it's the same sort of thing. Lastly, you shouldn't worry about any of this, because when I leave here, I'm leaving alone."

In the silence, Cora burst out, "Thank the gods! I didn't know how to tell you that I'm not coming with you. I don't want to seem ungrateful." She smiled and sighed.

"That satisfies everybody then," I said.

Pil and Ella both started talking, and they didn't sound at all satisfied.

When they had quieted a bit, I said, "This is my decision. I'm sorry."

Ella and Pil glanced at each other. "Certainly." Ella tilted her head. "This is your decision. Of course it is."

Her calmness unsettled me a bit. "Yes, it's my decision!"

"Everybody has the right to make decisions," Pil said lightly. "They make them all the time."

"I mean it!" I snapped. "You're not coming!"

Pil stared at the ceiling, nodding. Ella grinned at me.

"Shit! Damn you, Hurd, you should have made me listen."

Desh had been quiet and mostly still. "I respect you, Bib, but your decision may be . . . a challenging one."

"It may suck," Pil said, pointing at me.

"That's right, it may suck." Desh sighed. "I need to think about this."

I glared around the table.

Cora broke the silence again. "Has anyone heard whether there's a feast tonight? I'd like to attend, but I wish I had something else to wear. Something pretty and without my blood all over it."

Breakfast dissolved into intense deliberations over feasts, gowns, and where to hide weapons in gowns.

After breakfast, I invited Desh to go for a ride. We spent half a day working our way into the foothills, a good long distance from the farms. I dismounted in a nice, even clearing.

As soon as Desh's feet hit the ground, I said, "Limnad, I want you."

The river spirit stepped out from behind a big, standing rock, and she stared at Desh. "Bib, let me help you quickly, and then I will leave. I grieve when I am near him."

Desh asked, "How do you know that you grieve when you're near me? You haven't been near me."

Limnad stopped moving. "I may have seen you as I passed on the way to someplace else. A few times."

I said, "Limnad, Desh is this way because of me. I got some of his memories restored, even though I didn't intend to. I don't know if that makes a difference to you, but this change is not his fault. It's mine."

Limnad's face went blank. She floated off the ground to the height of two men. Then she clenched her fists, and water poured out of them. She gave me one hard look before rushing to swirl around Desh. He held still as she touched his chest.

Her nose wrinkled, but she didn't pull away. "I can't be in love with you. I don't know what I can be."

Desh said, "Limnad, please don't kill him." I hadn't known she was about to move, but he must have.

I found myself lying on my back with Yoadie's boots ripped to pieces. All ten of my toes had been torn off and scattered on the ground like grapes.

Limnad slipped behind the standing rock and was gone.

I restored my toes, and we rode back to the castle without talking.

After I returned from pissing off Limnad, I slipped down to the cellar to steal some wine. On the way in, I met Pil coming out carrying two bottles. She stared at me with raised eyebrows and then offered me a bottle.

I shook my head. "I don't want to take that from Desh."

"How do you know it's for Desh? Maybe I have a rendezvous with a handsome young man who is brave, and kind, and wealthy, and I mean wealthy to an obscene degree, and who loves me and will go where I say, do what I want, and buy me anything I ask for."

"Do you love him?"

"Screw him. And no, not literally, since he doesn't exist." She shifted both bottles to the crook of one arm.

I glanced at her free hand but didn't see a knife. Finally, I said, "Pil, what do you anticipate happening next? Will you try to kill me again? Decide I'm evil, untrustworthy scum? Save my life? Help me kill people? Just ride around with me and give me shit? Life has shown that I can deal with any of those, but I'd like to know what's coming next. It would be comforting."

Even in the torchlight, Pil looked bright red. She said, "I'm under no debt to kill you, and I promise I won't."

"That's true now. Five minutes from now, you may have debts with three gods requiring you to kill me. You can't know."

"By that logic, nobody can know anything," she said.

"That's some damn good logic then. I'm not trying to run you off, but why do you stay around? I expected you to leave five different times in the past two months."

"I want better for you," she said.

"You could buy me a better horse."

Pil grabbed one of the bottles by the neck but didn't swing it. "Stop being an ass for five seconds, all right? My first teacher was a notable man, wise and generous."

"Oh?"

"You're nothing like him. When we met, I saw that you were brave, dashing, and indestructible."

"That sounds unlikely."

"And you were arrogant, and petty, and murderous, and given to anger, and such a liar—"

"There I am." I smiled. "That sounds like me."

Pil grabbed my shirt front with her free hand. "I see better things come from you sometimes, and I want to beat you with a pan when you throw them away!"

I paused for a couple of seconds. "Pil, I understand you. But you need to understand that I may not deserve better. I'm pretty sure I don't."

Pil pulled back her hand and set her jaw. "Bullshit. I don't accept that. You'll have to prove it to me." She stomped past me toward the staircase leading up.

I called after her, "So I guess you're not going to help me carry all this wine I'm stealing."

From the day we had arrived at the Eastern Gateway, Ella had stayed with me in my chambers. After I laid in twenty bottles of wine, Ella and I fortified my rooms. No intruder was allowed unless he brought us food, more wine, or hot water.

We stayed there for ten days. As we chatted on the last day, Ella said, "Big bear, my ass. What did you really kill?"

"Oh, one of the gods' hunters."

"What designates him a hunter? Does he have a bow? Or a hound, perhaps?"

"It's a secret."

"You know that I am discretion in human form. Tell me."

"Yes, I know you are," I said. "It was one of Lutigan's sons."

Ella stared and pulled away so far that she almost fell out of bed. "A demigod? Was he hunting you?"

"No, but he was pleased to have found me. I got lucky."

She took a deep breath. "Bib, tell me how you have changed, and I do not wish to hear any shit about restored memories."

"You don't need details. No, you really don't. I was a cold, calculating son of a bitch before I started hankering for lives. But I decided to lust for killing instead, and a thousand people died."

"Hush. It's not a thousand people."

"No, it's more—most killed in big bunches by magic. Now I'm trying to lose the bloodlust and get back to the cold son of a bitch." I shook my head. "That's a hell of a note, isn't it? What a fine goal."

Ella was quiet for a time. "Bloodlust is horrible, and what you have done with it has been horrible. You will always bear the guilt. But tell me, without all those years of yearning to kill, how would a cold son of a bitch have fared against Lutigan's son?"

"That was insightful," Gek said from behind me.

I rolled over and found regular-size, non-bird-Gek sitting on a stained wooden chair against the wall. Even though he wasn't smiling, his eyes crinkled.

Ella rolled off the other side of the bed and grabbed her sword from where she'd propped it against the bedframe. She faced Gek with her sword pointed toward him and her clothes on the floor.

When Gek didn't move, she said, "You shall depart now in whatever manner you arrived. Otherwise, I shall toss you out the window in pieces."

I sat up and scrambled across the bed toward her. "Ella, don't—"

Her sword instantly became a sizable smoked ham. A hooded blue cloak with a snug, red belt appeared from nowhere to clothe her.

Still sitting, Gek said, "Ella, I really don't want to annihilate you so that no person remembers you existed." He sighed. "But I often do things I don't want to do."

"Don't hurt her!" I snapped. "Tell me what you want. Point me at anybody. I'll kill them deader than that ham."

"No insult?" This time, Gek did smile. "I enjoy a clever insult. I prefer my servants to be disrespectful and surly."

"Bib! What is this?" Ella's voice hit a high note. Her face showed pale within the blue hood.

"Sweetheart, this is Gek, a collection of the most profoundly repugnant ass-drippings in the Void."

Gek grinned.

Then I said, "I'll be serving Gek for a while."

Ella charged Gek, prepared to shatter his skull with a devastating ham attack. She pitched forward and slid across the wooden floor when the cloak pinned her legs tight. When she came to a stop, she roared and flung the ham at Gek. He slid off the chair and stepped right out of the way without seeming to move fast.

"I like her." Gek leaned down toward Ella. "Do you want to go with him?"

Ella didn't hesitate. "Yes!"

"Even if you die?"

Ella hesitated this time. "Yes."

"Leave her the goddamn hell alone!" I yelled. "She's not coming!"

"I certainly am. Where are we going?" Ella asked quietly.

The floor disappeared out from under us. Before I could call Gek a baby-kicking asshole, all three of us stood in a field of tall, maroon grass. I saw a big stand of trees with cobalt leaves a short walk away. The sky was a piercing blue with sweet white clouds, no sun, and a mammoth circle of black emptiness right overhead.

Ella and I wore dark brown shirts and trousers, with our scabbarded swords riding on our hips. Ella's breath caught, but then she smiled. "Although unlike home, I am certain this world possesses charms."

"I think it looks like a dead hog in a puddle of crap," I said.

Gek chuckled. "I made that very observation when I first came here."

"Where's this person I'm supposed to kill? I want to cut off his head and go home."

Gek leaned on his cane. "Soon. Hurd told me about your adventures in the Dark Lands."

I said, "Why don't you go there and look around for yourself?"

Gek's eyes brightened. "I did enjoy the way you dispatched Zagurith."

"Happy to serve since I'm your servant. What should I do next? Let me guess. Kill somebody?"

Gek held up a hand. "Soon. Enjoy the landscape. We may return here, or we may not."

I shook my head. "Damn it and damn it ten times, Gek, you can wave your middle toe and kill every bucktoothed man in the world. You can do that, right?"

"I can."

"What the hell do you need me for?"

Gek pointed at me with his cane. "Bib, can you breathe at the bottom of the ocean?"

"No, but I can drink my way to the bottom of a beer barrel."

"I have no doubt. Let us say that you want to kill someone at the bottom of the ocean. You'd need somebody to do it for you."

"That sounds like a juvenile evasion to me," I said.

"Don't be concerned. We shall embrace the killing soon enough." Gek rubbed his fingers together. I had never noticed how long his fingernails were, almost the length of his fingers. "We just have a few things to do first."

Gek hesitated before stumping away toward the cobalt trees. "Please stay here. Now, I admit that one of your tasks may strike you as overly ambitious, but I assure you that it's possible. I understand the risks entirely. I must convince you of that, however." Although the Void Walker hobbled with his cane, he had already reached the stand of trees and disappeared among the tree trunks.

Ella reached out and touched my arm. "Bib!"

"Hm?"

"I'm afraid! Why am I afraid?"

"It'll be fine." I wanted to run but didn't know why. Telling her that wouldn't help anything, though. I realized I was nodding and wondered how long I had been at it. Probably longer than I'd been struggling not to pee down my leg.

I shook my head and forced my voice to be steady while shouting, "I'm open to discussing plans in a rational way, Gek! Most problems can be knocked on the head with sufficient planning. Come on back here so we can talk!"

Something lifted up from behind the trees. It rose and rose some more, and it kept rising, even though in a sane world that couldn't be happening. A colossal, purplish-black, feathered head appeared first, with a beaked maw and eyes that burned like furnaces. I was too horrified for close observation, but later it was determined that the maw was big enough to eat eight oxen at once.

A monstrous, green, manlike neck and torso followed. It appeared to be covered in scales. Two muscular, sinewed green arms supported enormous hands that could each crush two heavily loaded wagons. The fingers ended in ruinous, black claws longer than a man was tall.

By that point, I could see why Gek had given me new, brown clothes. I was about to void myself of everything I had. I glanced at Ella. She was sitting with her eyes closed on the freakish grass holding her head with both hands.

Broad, leathery, black legs pushed the head and torso up to an impossible height. I couldn't see the thing's feet, or flippers, or whatever it got around on because the trees stood in the way.

If this creature was one hundred paces away, and I believed it was, then it stood one hundred paces tall. Three hundred feet. Of course, the thing was an illusion, or a dream, or my last hallucination before dying. Or maybe I had gone insane again.

The monster spoke in a profound bass carried by the power of its immense lungs. "It's a fine thing to let pretense fall away, Bib the sorcerer, in whose head I reside. I am Gek. I am also known to be Cheg-Cheg."

Was this the being whose heart was the blackest thing in existence? Who destroyed mountains? I wanted to ask that or ask why he was here talking to me. Instead, I gaped and peed a little.

After a pause, the creature leaned toward me and raised its voice. "You know, Cheg-Cheg!"

The blast of his words staggered me.

Leaning farther forward, the monster enunciated, "Cheg. Cheg."

A great sorcerer would have said something fearless and pithy right about then. I couldn't think of anything, so I shook my head. "I'm sorry . . ."

Cheg-Cheg looked at the ground. Towering streams of drool ran from his maw onto the trees, which started dissolving in a cloud of vapor. When he shook his head, immense globs of acid-mucus flew far out to both sides. "What do they teach sorcerers these days?"

"Well, I missed the last six weeks of classes." I felt a little pride that I had almost sounded like a sorcerer for a moment. Then I turned away and vomited. "Excuse me."

Cheg-Cheg spoke as if he were a teacher. "I am Cheg-Cheg, Dark Annihilator of the Void and Vicinity. Does that make sense? I am the most potent of the Void Walkers. I am the thing the gods fear. Do you understand? Nod if you do."

I started nodding again. "I don't know what to say now."

"We will have many opportunities to converse in the days to come. You are my servant for the next four and a half months. That's plenty of time for you to assassinate Krak for me."

ABOUT THE AUTHOR

Bill McCurry blends action, humor, and vivid characters in his dark fantasy novels. They are largely about the ridiculousness of being human, but with swords because swords are cool. Before being published, he wrote three novels that sucked like black holes, and he suggests that anyone who wants to write novels should write and finish some bad novels first. You learn a lot.

Bill was born in Fort Worth, Texas, where the West begins, the stockyards stink, and the old money families run everything. He later moved to Dallas, where Democrats can get elected, Tom Landry is still loved, and the fourth leading cause of death is starvation while sitting on LBJ Freeway.

Although Dallas is a city that smells like credit cards and despair, Bill and his wife still live there with their five cats. He maintains that the maximum number of cats should actually be three, because if you have four, then one of them can always get behind you.

CONNECT WITH THE AUTHOR

Bill-McCurry.com
Facebook.com/Bill.McCurry3
Twitter.com/BillMcCurry
Instagram.com/bfmccurry

Sign Up for Bill's Newsletter!

Keep up to date on new books and on exclusive offers. No spam!

https://bill-mccurry.com/index.php/newslettersignup/

LEAVE A REVIEW

Please leave a review on the platform of your choice!
https://linktr.ee/reviewswordhand

PURCHASE OTHER BOOKS IN THIS SERIES

Book 1 — *Death's Collector*
Book 2 — *Death's Baby Sister*
Book 3 — *Death's Collector: Sorcerers Dark and Light*
Book 4 — *Death's Collector: Void Walker*
Book 5 — *Death's Collector: Sword Hand*

Companion Book — *Wee Piggies of Radiant Might*

Shop at: https://tinyurl.com/billmccurrybooks

PREVIEW OF DEATH'S COLLECTOR: DARK LANDS

CHAPTER ONE

The knobby bastard laughed at me the whole time I was killing him, so I laughed back as if that would hurt his feelings. He giggled and farted divine air before all ten feet of him fell, dragging me down with him. Death didn't mean a damn thing to his kind. By dawn the gods would make him whole again, but not the thirteen guards he had torn up like paper. Those men weren't useful to gods and would stay ripped apart forever.

I stood and yanked my sword from his chest while glancing around the enormous throne room. The other two monstrous imps lay in ponds of blood and body parts, as if they had been fountains of gore rather than the gods' mystical thugs.

The imps had appeared out of nothing and brought four dozen soldiers with them for a jolly assassination, or maybe a kidnapping. Twenty survivors were still carving their way toward the king, who was protected by only ten men. More guards were trickling in like beer from a keg though.

Desh and my three other companions were racing to save King Moris, but Pil slipped and slid on her belly across the bloody floor. She dropped her sword, which clattered away. Nobody bent to help her. I charged toward the soldiers, and I didn't stop to help her, either.

Every soldier was dressed in uniform, but only one hadn't drawn his weapon. I peered at this notable young man, who was tall and slim, and saw him slip something from a white pouch. Two seconds later, every king's guard dropped his weapon with a sound like glass breaking against the stone floor. A few invading soldiers lost their swords too. They cursed and glared at the man with the pouch.

"Sorry!" the man called out. "That one was my fault!"

I saw shards of sword blades strewn across the floor. The man was almost certainly a sorcerer creating hell and destruction using bones, carvings, and wads of unlikely crap he had enchanted. I changed direction toward him.

Some soldier yelled and warned the sorcerer I was coming. He spun to face me, reaching into a yellow cloth pouch. A guard yelled for everybody to fall back and protect the king.

The throne room was a looming stone box big enough to hold a market fair, and I had slain that jovial imp a fair distance from the throne. I was still sprinting toward the sorcerer when he pointed at me and rubbed a dirty-looking rag across his palm. It was hardly a terrifying act.

My feet lost all purchase on the floor, and I sprawled. I didn't slide as far as like Pil had, but when I put a foot down to stand, it slipped right out from under me. The soles of my boots had become as slick as butter.

The sorcerer dropped the rag and smiled, displaying fine teeth, before he reached into a brown leather pouch. I was twenty feet away, but he advanced on me a couple of steps. Maybe his next attack would involve a stick, or a magical biscuit, or a virgin's earlobe, and he had to be closer before he could turn my heart to jelly.

I pushed up to my knees, pulled out my knife, and threw it at the man. It wasn't the most awkward stance for throwing. That would have been lying on my chest facing the other direction. But it was tolerably challenging, so it gratified me to see the knife impale the lanky sorcerer's left forearm as he raised it to protect his throat.

The sorcerer's enchanted doodad flew out of his hand. It looked like a mummified mouse, but I never saw it again to confirm that. The man didn't cry out or even clutch his arm. He reached for a canvas pouch but paused and peered at me when I made a show of fumbling with my sword. I felt that dropping my weapon might be too obvious.

Once I steadied my sword, I rushed toward the sorcerer. I was not rushing too fast since I was walking on my knees, swinging my arms hard like a five-year-old.

The sorcerer made a mistake then. He should have backed away, pulled out another devastating mouse corpse, and tried to destroy me from a distance. Instead, he came at me with his sword.

An old man huffing along on his knees must not have terrified the sorcerer. Killing me by hand would conserve magical energy, which was always desirable. And the man moved with the grace of a trained swordsman. He deserved to be confident.

The sorcerer thrust at my heart, a solid attack that wasn't fancy except for his splendid form. I parried and thrust into his knee. When he yelped and tried to recover, I stabbed him just below the breastbone. He shuddered but didn't fall.

When fighting sorcerers, it is poor practice not to kill them right away in the most thorough manner possible. Even a dying sorcerer can kill or cause immense harm. Hell, even a naked, dying sorcerer is a respectable threat.

Still on my knees, I stretched up and sliced the sorcerer's throat. Blood sprayed from this fellow whose name I had never known.

Some god seized my spirit and stretched it straight up through the top of my head. He or she was bringing me to the place where gods trade with sorcerers, who give up the things they love in exchange for power—which will make them suffer and die young.

As I left my body, I felt Pil grab on. It was a thing that sorcerers could do if they're quick and canny. I wished she hadn't done it. She probably wanted to protect me, but there wasn't a single way she could do that. There were plenty of ways for her to accidentally invite trouble from the gods, though.

I glanced around the trading place as well as I could without moving my head. Heat crushed me and standing under the sun was like being punched. I didn't even pay close attention to the god inhabiting the marble gazebo.

I found myself staring right at the sorcerer I had just killed. He looked fine, not bloody, or even disheveled. He must have called on the gods a bare moment before his death and then convinced them to summon me.

From behind me, Pil said, "Bib, are you alright?" Her voice sounded confident and even a bit offended.

As the gods had designed things, I shouldn't be able to hear Pil unless they wished it—but for some reason that I didn't understand, I could. I preferred that the gods not find that out.

I also preferred they not find out I planned to assassinate their father.

I called out, "Mighty Harik, you have summoned me with your lips, which are drier and more repugnant than lips fashioned from the private areas of many venomous reptiles. In fact, how do you convince your wife to kiss you? The Goddess of Life must be repelled."

Harik stepped out from the gazebo depths and its benches that were suitable for the asses of the gods. His black robe and hair stood out stark against his blandly perfect face. "I am the God of Death, and I am concerned with matters more profound than kissing. I leave that to Effla, Goddess of Love."

Two ragged imps like the ones we had killed in the throne room shuffled out and stood to Harik's left, one step behind him. I had never before seen Harik with imp bodyguards.

Harik continued, "However, that does bring us to your offense, Murderer. It is an offense against Effla."

"I offend a lot of people," I said. "Whatever I did to offend her, I volunteer to do it twice to you."

"You stole Effla's property. You have murdered the Gosling here."

"That's right, you took me away!" the sorcerer said in a high-pitched, almost sweet voice.

"I am sorry about that, Gosling, but you came attacking me, and with imps along to harvest the arms and legs. So, I'm not too sorry."

Gosling snorted. "Of course, you're not. You shouldn't be. We might be enemies today and allies tomorrow. Or we could have been."

I said, "That's mighty damn open-minded of you, Gosling. I like speaking with a man of subtle thought. But let's keep any regrets in the sack for a minute. Harik, why were you screwing around with King Moris? He was an inoffensive old walrus. Why do you care if he even existed, let alone send your toad belly-dragging hooligans after him? Gosling, I don't mean offense by that."

The sorcerer grunted.

Harik paused. "We need not explain ourselves to you, Murderer." Then Harik whispered over his shoulder, "That's especially true with certain actions that are too Void-sucking ignorant to contemplate."

"Hush, Harik." I recognized the Goddess of Love's voice. "Don't distress yourself, dear. You won't be able to enjoy every little bit of the party tonight."

My spine shivered when I heard Effla's voice. In an instant I wanted her so much that every other woman I had known seemed as coarse as a filthy wad of hair stuck to a goat's ass.

Effla whispered, "Besides, better opportunities have popped up." Her voice slowed to a breathy tease. "We could hurt the Murderer a delicious amount. Couldn't we?"

Harik whispered back to Effla, "Hurt him? I would applaud that. But you just attempted to kill him and failed, as I predicted. Do you want to bring the curse on yourself? Must I distract you with well-oiled demigods every hour?"

"It's lovely of you to offer," she whispered. "Watch me, dear brother." Effla slunk out of the shadows, her unblemished mahogany skin as smooth as gossamer and caressed by a silk gown shimmering with every hue of red. Her blonde hair was disarrayed in such an enchanting manner that I wondered whether she had a team of demigods working to keep it that way at all times.

My legs trembled. Before I closed my eyes, I saw two imps follow her and stand to her right.

"Oh, Gosling!" Effla called out. "You have come for your final trade before death. Congratulations, my darling! Let me be clear. You cannot save your own life, no matter what you ask for or receive."

If Gosling couldn't help himself out of this trouble, what did he want? I looked harder at Gosling's face, and he was showing his teeth. He said, "Mighty Effla, I want—"

"Wait!" Pil shouted. "I want to make an offer first!"

I said, "Pil, please don't. It's my problem."

"Your problem is that everything is always your problem, and you won't let anybody else help you with your stupid problems!" Pil took a deep breath. "At your age, you can't keep having all these adventures by yourself. You're going to adventure yourself to death."

Harik frowned at Pil. "Silence! Knife, if you do that again I will hollow you out and float you like a buoy, and Lutigan can be damned if he doesn't like it. If you want to stay, you must be quiet and respectful."

"Fine," Pil muttered, sounding like a teenage girl, which she was.

"Are we done?" Gosling said. "Does anybody want to sing now or talk about life back on the farm? I want one square of power. In exchange, I will use the last decision of my life to hurt the Murderer."

Now it made sense. At the end of his trade, Gosling would be required to give the gods a year of his life, or ten years of other people's lives. In this case, he was going to take ten years of my life. I had already lost ten years in just this way, and I might not have many more to lose.

Effla and Harik were nodding at each other. Effla said, "Done!"

Harik flourished the sleeve of his robe. "Now, for your fee. How do you wish to pay? With your own life, or with the lives of others?"

"Others," Gosling said. "Take all the years from the Murderer."

And there it was. Another ten years had been ripped off the end of my life. It wouldn't age me now, but I'd die twenty years sooner than my allotted lifespan—if I died a natural death. Of course, the chances of that were damn thin.

"To be sure I understand," Harik said, smiling, "you want all thirty years taken from the Murderer? Correct?"

"Yes." Gosling nodded.

"Hold on!" I shouted. "What happened to ten years? The last time I was here, you taxed us ignorant sorcerers ten years of life for each trade. What happened to that, huh?"

"Conditions are always shifting with the whims and eddies of the Void . . ." Effla offered a shrug so languorous I almost fell to my knees. "This is the new arrangement."

"No, wait!" I bellowed. Both gods flinched away from the sound of my voice and then stared at each other. In a calmer tone, I said, "Wait. This means that a total of forty years will be taken away from me. And I'm already over forty, so . . . when you send me back, will I fall over dead?"

"You might," Harik said.

"You're the God of Death!" I shouted. Both gods peered at me, and I lowered my voice. "You're the God of Death. Don't you know?"

Effla whispered, "Is he doing that on purpose? He shouldn't be able to. Is he an oddity, like a three-headed sheep?"

"I don't like it," Harik whispered in a drawl.

"Really?" Effla whispered and then sneered. "I am astounded. You don't like it. One of the deep mysteries of existence has been revealed, for we now understand that Harik doesn't like it. The Murderer is yours, so this is your fault! Assuming this is anything besides a coincidence, and I don't commit to the notion that it is!"

Harik hauled back, and I thought he would hit his sister. Instead, he punched the imp next to her on the side of the head. The hulking creature flew as if hit with a tree trunk, tumbled over a marble bench and plunged to the gazebo's lowest level. It didn't move.

Effla had jumped aside with immense grace. Now she seized a thick, marble bench that must have weighed four hundred pounds.

She hurled it at the imp beside Harik, who made no effort to dodge. The bench slammed into the monster's jaw and kept going, taking the imp's head with it as the body thumped onto the floor.

Effla grabbed another bench and waggled it at Harik like it was a serving platter. She grinned and whispered, "Ah, Bro-bro, you are the most predictable of creatures. But I enjoy anticipating what you will do." She dropped the bench with a slam, and the two embraced. It was a long embrace.

I felt uncomfortable, but I couldn't turn away. I closed my eyes and said, "Harik? Effla? Are you still there? Can I go now?"

"No!" Harik said. "Just wait there."

Effla whispered, "All right, let's run through this. We can't kill him unless we want to be cursed. So, we're not killing him, not at all. He just happens to be among those whose lifespans we have chosen not to know."

Harik nodded. "He and the other twelve. Did I say that I don't like this?"

"Pish, we are not at fault. Even though the fee is thirty years, we can't know with certainty that this will kill him. We're just following the rules we set for everybody. Well, for thirteen people. If he plops down on his bottom dead when he gets back, that's not our fault. No one could reasonably say we killed him, so no curse." Effla smiled, and I closed my eyes again so I wouldn't run over and beg her to make love to me until I died.

Harik whispered, "I do not feel confident about avoiding the curse in this fashion. We cannot fool the laws of existence. Krak's hairy chin, we can't even fool ourselves. Wait—I think the Murderer twitched. Do you suppose he's listening to us?"

Both gods examined me with disturbing intensity.

"Never mind," Effla whispered. "He's too dim to understand anything he hears."

Harik nodded and spoke out, "Diversions of far grander signifi-cance await us, so we—"

Pil burst in, "No! Whatever is going on, just no." She took a deep breath. "Take the thirty years from me. That much time will kill him, but I'm young."

"Hah!" Gosling laughed.

"At least take half the years from me!" Pil lifted her chin.

Harik said, "Knife, that is entirely enough out of you. And you too, Murderer. Goodbye."

I didn't even have time for a ripe insult before he flung me back into the world of man.

I returned to the throne room at the precise moment I left. As Gosling toppled over, I waited to die, breathless and still on my knees. I was so distracted that a boy could have walked up and killed me using nothing but a bent spoon.

But I didn't die.

Still on my knees, I turned toward Pil, who had finished sliding across the floor and then gotten to her feet. She was blinking at me. Her lips were trembling, and I could see the pulse throbbing in her neck.

A soldier who ought to have been attacking the king turned away from the assault for no reason I have ever been able to understand. It put him right behind Pil. I shouted at her, but she just stared at me. I reached for my knife to throw it, but all I had was an empty sheath.

The soldier swung his sword and struck Pil on the back of the neck. She fell straight down with all her limbs slack, settling in an untidy pile. Her blood welled out into the generous bloody pool already spreading across the king's floor.